A Line In The Sand

A Line In The Sand

by

JEFFREY GREEN

CREATIVE ARTS BOOK COMPANY
Berkeley • California

Copyright ©2003 by Jeffrey Green

No part of this book may be reproduced in any manner
without written permission from the publisher,
except in brief quotations used in article reviews.

Although some settings actually exist,
any similarity to persons
living or dead is purely coincidental.

For information contact:
Creative Arts Book Company
833 Bancroft Way
Berkeley, California 94710
1-800-848-7789
Fax: 1-510-848-4844
www.creativeartsbooks.com

ISBN 0-88739-443-4
Library of Congress Catalog Number 2002110714

Printed in the United States of America

I dedicate this book to my mother, who gave me my heart, and to Leslie, who did the impossible and healed it.

FOREWORD

Ironically I read *A Line in The Sand* while at sea on a recent expedition for the Sea Shepherd Conservation Society of which I am the founder and President. Although it is largely a work of fiction I found the environmental issues covered in the novel ranging from international whaling to widespread pollution both comprehensive and factually accurate. I was reminded of Edward Abbey's classic novel *The Monkey Wrench Gang*. Unfortunately the environmental issues facing the planet at the time of that novel's publication have increased at an exponential rate.

I was impressed with the passion and enthusiasm portrayed by the characters depicted in the novel and while the issues covered in the story are serious and should be of great public concern I found the novel to be suspenseful and entertaining.

I believe as I mentioned in an article I had once written titled, "Lights, Camera, Ocean" that the best way to engage the populace and use the power of public opinion is through the media, specifically the entertainment field.

I have always felt that the majority of people are greatly concerned about the environmental issues that are taking place in the world's oceans. The problem is that they have not been adequately informed or have been mislead about the seriousness of the issue. It is this lack of widespread public information delivered on a regular basis that has created an atmosphere of apathy and acceptance.

Knowledge is not power, action is power but to take action one must know that a problem exists and the problem must be presented to the public in a way that they can feel and that they can relate to their own lives. Not an abstract idea like global warming but a tangible everyday need such as clean air and water for their families and a future for their children.

A Line in The Sand clearly illustrates on a widespread scale numerous issues confronting the world today, issues many people mistakenly believe have already been resolved such as the killing of baby seals in northern Canada, international whaling, and the continued ongoing slaughter of dolphins caught in fishing nets. Every year the cumulative amount of oil spilled into the world's oceans, lakes, rivers, and bays dwarfs the Exxon Valdez disaster in scale, yet we hear very little in the media about what amounts to a global crisis. It is only when a supertanker runs aground in a pristine wilderness area or off the coast of a California community that the nightly news shows interest.

I found the novel to be well balanced and it presented not just the problems but some solutions as well. It illustrated projects currently underway by many international corporations and governments to treat the harmful byproducts of their production such as bio-remediation, for treating sewage, the increase in fish farming, and natural ways of dealing with oil spills such as oil eating microbes.

Today more people get their information from *Entertainment Tonight* and *Instyle magazine* than from the nightly news and the line between serious journalism and entertainment becomes increasingly blurry. Celebrities and entertainers are the spokespeople and role models for today's youth and many are assuming a role as leaders in the fight to protect the future of this planet.

It is the groundswell of public opinion that originally halted the slaughter of baby seals, initiated a ban on whaling and created dolphin safe fishing. And I have found that overall, people will fight to protect their most important heritage and their God given rights once important issues and injustices have been brought to light.

Novels such as *A Line in The Sand* continue to shine a spotlight on important issues and by doing so in an entertaining way engage a portion of the populace that otherwise might not have been made aware.

As the character Lionfish in the novel says, "The problems facing the world's inhabitants today are culturally universal. The environmental issues depicted in the novel are not just for the so-called tree huggers and the save the whale people. No matter whether you are an industrialist, an artist, a banker, or a logger, you have to care whether you can trust the water you drink, the food you eat, and the air you breathe."

I found *A Line in The Sand* inspiring and provocative while not being too self righteous or condescending, and while the novel could be viewed as a platform on which to educate, it was also extremely entertaining.

> CAPTAIN PAUL WATSON, Co-founder of Greenpeace and President and founder of the Sea Sheperd Conservation Society

Some of them were angry at the way the earth was abused by the men who learned how to forge her beauty into power, and they struggled to protect her from them only to be confused by the magnitude of her fury in the final hour.

Jackson Browne, "Before the Deluge"

A Line In The Sand

CHAPTER 1

THE MOON WAS FULL TONIGHT, and although it looked quite beautiful as it illuminated the silver clouds that passed in front of it, it did not make for ideal conditions for RedTide's mission. Lionfish, as he was known by Interpol and the American law enforcement agencies that pursued him, was just finishing up his briefing to the small assembled group of eco-terrorists known as RedTide.

His partner and closest friend Stingray was anxious about an article that had appeared this morning in the world's newspapers. It mentioned that a large Japanese conglomerate had enlisted mercenaries to rid itself of what had become a very costly problem for them.

As the leader and founder of what had grown to be an internationally recognized terrorist organization, Lionfish had only one concern, to stop the destruction of the world's ecosystems by whatever means necessary.

His organization had done more in the last five years to bring attention to the numerous problems which plagued the world's oceans than all the other environmental activist groups and their lobbyists combined.

He had learned a long time ago, as a member of a politically correct yet impotent environmental organization, that politics and greed will always win out when the only weapons of the just are benefit concerts and limited funds from sporadic donations. Tonight's mission would once again focus the world's attention on international whaling. Lionfish's famous temper had erupted when he heard the news that Norway and Japan had decided to continue whaling in spite of united world pressure for them not to.

Well, he would show them pressure, and he was not the type who believed in organizing boycotts or embargoes. The only commodities Lionfish knew people couldn't live without were air and water.

"Load the men into the boats and be careful to keep the plastic explosives and the detonators in dry compartments away from the other ammunition," Lionfish instructed his men.

The two Zodiacs were outfitted with M60 machine guns on their starboard sides. Both had been stolen from a Marine Corp base in North Carolina and were purchased illegally by RedTide. RedTide had many friends who were sympathetic to its cause and supported its violent methods. There were two boats, each with ten men aboard. The men were all camouflaged in thick black wet suits and hoods and wore black face makeup as well. Both drivers and gunmen were wearing night vision goggles. Lionfish and Barracuda were the only assigned divers on tonight's expedition, and were the most experienced members of the underwater demolition team.

Next to Stingray, Barracuda was Lionfish's oldest and most trusted friend and was second only to Stingray in rank and status. Stingray never went on missions and was considered the chief technical supervisor for the organization.

He was not in the muscle department of the organization for two reasons. He did not have the temperament or disposition toward violence, and Lionfish wanted to protect him whenever possible. Every member of the team carried a small machine pistol and two men carried sniper rifles equipped with silencers and long range night vision scopes. These had been used for picking off lookouts and sentries posted on the bridges of the ships that RedTide disabled.

The organization also participated in occasional kidnapping and assassination but it primarily focused on the destruction of property. The first kidnapping/assassination had been handled by Lionfish personally when the organization was just getting started. It involved the abduction of an executive from Nexxus oil. The man was kidnapped after the company had accidentally dumped millions of gallons of oil into a bay in Alaska.

The company was supposed to have maintained a fleet of skimming units including a 612- foot containment boom with skimmers and a self-powered floating pump unit. It was designed to be towed by the so-called vessels of opportunity, which were all supposed to be kept nearby for just such an emergency. The company however, had decided to increase its margins and lower its overhead, so the vessels were deployed elsewhere, just before the entire fleet was downsized.

In Prince William Sound, the full weight of the clean up fell on the shoulders of the Coast Guard cutter *Sedge*. Lt. Commander George A. Capacci was quoted as saying, "If we had one of those skimming units operating in the first week we could have collected 600 gallons a minute for days, because the oil was thin and easy to pump. That's 16,000 barrels a day, theoretically, if we had a barge to pump to."

As it was it took two days just to deploy the boom and the oil got thicker and harder to manage. The company compounded their negligence by dragging their feet during the cleanup and by refusing to cooperate with local agencies. Some particularly heartbreaking film from the Alaska spill showed large brown bears, their legs covered in grimy black oil in the Katmai National Park and Preserve. They were dragging their cubs across oil-soaked beaches, urging them toward the shelter of the tree line while killer whales lay dead or dying on the beaches.

The camera also showed some of the 5000 American bald eagles which inhabit the area being lifted into nets, dead from the oil, a total of over 150 in all. The camera panned back and focused on one whale that was desperately trying to push her baby forward to safety through the thick oil. The desperate, baleful, agonizing screams of her calf as it lay dying on the beach could be heard for miles. Seals died by the thousands although an accurate count was difficult since the oil soaked animals sank quickly to the bottom.

Lionfish remembered watching the footage with tears rolling down his face while the rage and anger swelled up inside him. On the nightly news the executive in charge of damage control for Nexxus spoke quite eloquently about how the company had looked into double hulled ships years ago but that the costs were prohibitive and would have meant huge increases in the price of gasoline to the end user. Lionfish knew the true cost to the consumer would have meant a couple of extra pennies per gallon at the pumps.

He also said Nexxus was willing to accept full responsibility for this tragic accident. He assured the public that Nexxus would pay the costs for whatever was necessary to adequately take care of the cleanup. *They would pay all right*, Lionfish thought, if he had anything to say about it.

The Chief Executive Officer of Nexxus Oil, Inc. was captured and held for three months while RedTide continued to issue its demands. The company continued to drag its feet during the cleanup, doing as little as possible until the government began to levy heavy fines. The cleanup itself caused large scale mortality in beach organisms after the hot water washes and because of the flushing away of oil-coated sediments there was ten times the amount of hydrocarbons in the intertidal and subtidal zones than even after the initial spill. The long-term effects of the spill were and still are disastrous. As the spill broke up, it drifted to the Alaska Peninsula and hit four national wildlife refuges, including Chugach National Forest and three other national park areas. Salmon hatcheries at Main Bay, Sawmill Bay, Esther Island, and Cannery Creek were threatened by the spill that came just weeks before the spring bloom of zooplankton upon which salmon fry feed. RedTide sent out investigators posing as reporters and scientists to study the long-term effects of the spill and to interview members of The National Oceanic and Atmospheric Administration (NOAA) and found that many scientists were not permitted to discuss their findings. RedTide's own scientific investigation, headed by Stingray and a small team, had been following the effects since the spill and their findings along with the published findings of NOAA and the department of the interior were disastrous.

Bears, river otters, and foxes that scavenged for oil-coated seabirds suffered greatly in the months to follow. Although death may have come quickly for many birds, for animals such as sea otters, physiological systems were ravaged. The only sea animals that lack blubber, many succumbed after their dense fur became saturated with oil and provided no insulation. Others developed respiratory ailments, possibly because volatile elements of the oil weakened membranes in their lungs. Some suffered liver and kidney damage probably caused by ingesting oil while cleaning their coats. In the effected area more than one thousand otters were known to be killed probably a third of the total. Similar illnesses effected common murres, one of the areas most abundant seabirds as well. Their contoured breast feathers form a watertight seal and the feather shape is maintained by tiny interlocking barbules. The oiled feathers lost their shape and their ability to insulate. The oil also degraded the seabird's red blood cells and caused anemia.

Our great American symbol, the bald eagle, was contaminated after they scavenged oil- soaked prey as well. They carried the contaminated carcasses of seabirds to their nests where they contaminated the eggs of their young. Out of 125 eagle nests surveyed, two-thirds failed last year. And this great spill, although it did capture the public's attention, only focused around the sound and neglected to show the widespread awful reach of the spill.

Kodiak along with Kenai and the Alaska Peninsula received almost no attention in the early days of the spill. Even though a broad patch of sheen, a thin oil coating accompanied by streamers of an oil/water emulsion called mousse drifted down from the sound.

In early May, however, officials of Katmai National Park and Preserve announced that ninety percent, NINETY PERCENT! of Katmais 260-mile coastline had been devastated.

Mark Wright of the United States Park Service said, "We consider this oiling to be the ultimate insult to a National Park. It will be years before we know what damage has been done to the bear and eagle populations and to the shoreline ecosystem. Aren't national parks in Alaska supposed to be protected? We protect our other national parks. Last year I visited Yellowstone and I couldn't even enter the park without leashing my dog. Where is the legislation that mandates adequate protective technologies for ships such as double hulls and where are the requirements for skimmers and barges to be adequately dispersed?

"The profits the oil companies drain from Alaskan soil each year is staggering and man's thirst for oil is unquenchable, driving companies like British Petroleum to drill in some of the world's last untouched wildernesses like King George Island in Antarctica, which has recently come under attack. The government stands by idly while our last great American frontier is exploited and devastated."

The media did little in the way of follow-up in Alaska and, as is typical with an institution more interested in ratings than anything substantive, it moved on to the next headline story, a celebrity murderer and a politician who had been caught with a prostitute.

What happened that day in Alaska was only the tip of the iceberg. There are over twenty-five spills a year in Alaska from grounded vessels to fueling accidents.

David Kennedy of NOAA was quoted as saying, "In addition to Nexxus oil, our laboratory has found that fisheries have been closed for bilge oil, diesel fuel and hydraulic fluid. Although the drama of an oil tanker sinking captures the public's attention and plays well on the evening news, tanker spills contribute only twelve percent of all the oil that enters the oceans annually. More than forty-five percent of the oil comes from marine transportation, and most is from routine operations such as cleaning out tanks and bilge's, municipal outfalls, refineries, and other industrial facilities that release thirty-one percent of the oil. Natural seeps and erosion account for nearly eight percent and another five percent runs off with rainwater from fields and urban areas. Offshore drilling accounts for about one point five percent of our oil pollution."

Only days before Lionfish recounted the story of the kidnapping, Stingray presented him with the most recent findings, now two years later, on the status of the area. The report showed that even after two years since the Nexxus oil spill, sea birds in the Prince William Sound area had still not recovered. Sixty to seventy percent of the breeding colonies of murres were lost. The total mortality rate is estimated at 300,000. Studies show that existing colonies are smaller, breeding is later than normal, and breeding synchrony has been disrupted. These changes caused reproductive failures in 1989 and 1990, a loss of at least 215,000 chicks.

Bald eagles also showed severe reproductive failures in 1989 and 1990, as high as eighty-five percent in some areas. In addition, scientists including Stingray were concerned that sea ducks, pigeon guillemots, and other birds that depend on the intertidal and subtidal zones most affected by the spill for feeding and nesting will be susceptible to continued exposure to petroleum hydrocarbons for several more years.

Lionfish recounted how the final demands from RedTide had been delivered to the ninety story Nexxus building in the middle of the night by three armed men who had commandeered an oil delivery truck earlier that night. The men opened the valves of the truck and unloaded thousands of gallons of oil into the fountain that circled the Nexxus building like a moat on New York's 6th Avenue.

When the fountain was completely filled, the men set the fountain ablaze and left a note in a metal cylinder just outside the front doors. The smoke could be seen as far away as Oceanside, Long Island and the bottom three floors of the building were scorched black by the surrounding fires that climbed as high as the fifth floor.

The photo on the cover of every newspaper in America showed the building with the Nexxus flag burning on its pole in the foreground. The response was immediate and overwhelming. Every law enforcement agency in the country immediately received funding to set up a special RedTide task force, while all other environmental protection groups quickly issued statements disassociating themselves from the group.

A $500,000 reward was issued for the leader known only as Lionfish. After another month with little or no response to RedTide's demands, Mark P. Cooper III was found dead on the steps of the EPA building in Washington, D.C. He had been drowned in Nexxus brand 10WD40 oil and was lying beside a plastic bag containing four empty quarts.

So began the fugitive career of the most feared and hated environmental protection group in the world. RedTide received a negative backlash from the public and the press and Lionfish was at first disappointed that no one seemed to understand that they were fighting a war and that war involved casualties and collateral damage.

"RedTide wasn't doing this for the people anyway," Lionfish reasoned. "We are trying to save the oceans and the seas from the people. How many millions of warm-blooded innocent creatures have been slaughtered in the name of greed, or have been killed just for sport. If you were with your family at the Monterey Bay Aquarium and some maniac was breaking the necks of sea otters; you would rush up to him and stop him. Even if it required violence on your part you would do what you thought was right. Right outside the walls of the aquarium, pollution and urchin fishermen are killing the very same animals that they see competing with them for sea urchins, threatening their livelihood. The same people who are charmed by these animals at the aquarium read about it and do nothing."

In spite of being portrayed by the corporate-controlled media as bloodthirsty, senseless killers, RedTide's numbers began to swell. This took place through underground recruitment and attrition by members of more laid back organizations that were frustrated by a lack of action, despite the pretty words and the benefit concerts starring U2 and Neil Young.

Tonight we will once again defend those who cannot defend themselves, Lionfish thought. "Barracuda, you take the lead boat out and I will follow up behind."

The seas were rolling gently with two to three foot swells but no whitecaps. *I love the ocean at night when the moon is full*, Lionfish thought. "The color is a dark almost navy blue and as the waves roll by the tops look shiny black and soft as velvet."

There was a stiff breeze in his face and he could taste salt water on his lips. Once while night diving in the Cayman Islands, the moon was so bright he shut off his lights and dove for almost an hour by moonlight. The rays of the moon were breaking through the surface like sunlight and the reef looked almost iridescent. It was quiet with only the sound of his bubbles and the water was eighty-five degrees and clear as gin. It was one of the most serene and peaceful moments Lionfish could remember. There was a time long ago when diving was almost a religion for Lionfish and he tried to convert as many of his friends and family as possible. *Those days are gone forever*, Lionfish thought.

Lionfish could see through the night vision glasses that their target was less than three miles away and he instructed the pilot to slow down. Something didn't look right about the position of the ship and Lionfish got an instinctively uneasy feeling in the pit of his stomach. He signaled to Barracuda in the lead ship to stop while his boat came about and pulled up alongside.

"What's up? Everything looks okay to me," Barracuda said as Lionfish motioned for him to stand by his side.

"I don't know exactly, but something just doesn't feel right about the way that boat is positioned. The screws are turning and her anchor is up but she's standing still almost in neutral," Lionfish said. "I don't see any lights on topside either, and that in and of itself is unusual."

"Come on Lionfish. I think you're just rattled about the report in the paper today about bounty hunters for hire. The ship is probably getting ready to move. Lots of ships travel at night, and the lights are probably out because of the moon; there's no need for them. We have a lot of time invested in this operation, not to mention the cost of shipping everything 4000 miles to this location. That boat is sitting low in the water because it is already half full of slaughtered whales. You can smell it from here."

"You've known me over ten years and you know my instincts are seldom wrong," Lionfish said. "I don't get spooked easily and I have almost twenty years of military training and experience to back up my hunches. I'm telling you, something is not right."

"Mako," Lionfish called to the sniper nearest to him, a tall Samoan ex-Navy SEAL who had joined the group two years earlier. "Hand me that rifle." The scope on the rifle had a greater distance for viewing and Lionfish wanted to be prepared in case he saw a threat he needed to remove.

As Mako leaned over to hand Lionfish the rifle the top of his head blew apart, spewing brain matter all over Lionfish's chest as he collapsed at his feet.

At the same time floodlights came on above deck and four Zodiac boats filled with armed men pulled out at high speed from the bow of the ship. Lionfish could see that the men in the boats were carrying short-range weapons that could not reach them yet.

The shot that killed Mako had to have come from a sniper on deck he thought. "Get this boat moving!" Lionfish shouted. "I've got to take out that sniper. If we can keep those boats out of range we can pick them off with the sniper rifles while we escape."

"Manta!" Lionfish yelled to the sniper on the other boat. "Aim for the drivers."

Lionfish raised his rifle and quickly scanned the deck. He could not find the sniper until he heard the report and saw the flash from the top of the bridge, but at that point it was too late to save Manta, the only other qualified sniper they had left besides Lionfish himself.

There was a loud tearing noise as the impact of the sniper's round hit Manta in the chest spinning him around and throwing him backward into the water, along with his rifle.

Their sniper was well trained, Lionfish thought. *He was going for our snipers first and then probably he would shoot the drivers.* He had to stop him, now!

He scanned the top of the bridge and looked for the next possible place a sniper would have repositioned himself. *This guy was a pro,* Lionfish reasoned, *and would have moved after his last shot gave away his location.* Lionfish finally located him and centered the cross hairs in his chest. He fired just as his boat hit a wave and his shot went wide and high.

His opponent in this deadly game had the advantage of a steady platform, and Lionfish knew that he would be the next target. He quickly dove to the right as the shot that was intended for him tore into the arm of the man behind him.

"Someone get a tourniquet on his arm!" Lionfish shouted. "You two men manning the M60s, I want you to fire continuously at those oncoming boats to give me time to eliminate that sniper."

Lionfish quickly located his target running in the direction he had anticipated. He fired two rapid shots in quick succession and through the night scope on his rifle he saw a green colored mist appear where his target's head had been.

"Now haul ass and get us out of here," he shouted.

Lionfish looked behind and spotted Barracuda's boat but he could not see his old friend. The enemy boats had closed with Barracuda's boat earlier and Lionfish had listened attentively to the heated fire fight just minutes before. It appeared as though Barracuda had eliminated one of the boats, leaving only three to contend with.

Lionfish's chest tightened and he feared the worst for one of his closest friends and most trusted allies. Lionfish sighted his rifle on the driver in the lead boat but the distance was over 300 yards and his boat was rocking like a mechanical bull. Instead, he aimed for the rubber shell of the Zodiac and fired three rounds. There was an explosive release of high-pressure air and the boat began to slow down immediately.

Two more boats to go, he thought.

In all the years since RedTide had begun, this was the first armed conflict in which they had been caught off-guard. Everything had always been planned meticulously and the leaders had maintained the utmost secrecy until the final stages.

Could there be a leak? Lionfish wondered. *Impossible.* RedTide's screening and recruitment process was comprehensive and they had numerous contacts and informants in every law enforcement agency in the world. "Then how did they know exactly where we would be and when?" he asked himself. *Ambush*, Lionfish thought to himself.

Just then Barracuda's boat pulled alongside and Lionfish could see that he had a serious chest wound. He was laying in the bottom of the boat, making a deep gurgling noise and was bleeding from his mouth. He had lost a lot of blood and would never make it back to port alive. "Quickly, hand me that box of explosives and be careful," Lionfish called out.

There were two more boats trailing behind them about seventy-five yards away and they were firing like mad in their direction. They were in range, but the turbulence and serpentine driving of RedTide's seasoned pilots made it impossible for them to be effective until they got closer. Lionfish set the timers on six high explosive charges for thirty seconds each and gave three to Eagle Ray, one of his lieutenants on the other boat.

"Pull away from me and drop these into the water every five seconds as soon as one of the boats breaks off and follows in your wake," Lionfish directed. "NOW," he said as the other boat pulled away hard. Just as he suspected, one of the enemy boats followed. When they were lined up with the enemy only 100 feet behind them, Lionfish dropped the bombs in the wake behind his boat. He spaced them about five seconds apart.

The first bomb exploded seconds too soon missing the boat entirely but threw up a tremendous wake in its path. Just as the bow lifted over the wave the boat rose high in the air. It was pointing straight up as the second bomb detonated directly under the inverted stern by the engine and exploded the rear end. As all the air in the Zodiac rushed out, the explosion projected the boat like a missile twenty feet into the air.

Those who survived the explosion floated in the water, some with horrible wounds and missing limbs. Lionfish looked out in time to see that all three of Eagle Ray's bombs had missed but that they had gotten in close and had literally shredded the enemy boat and its crew with the awesome power of their M60 machine gun.

Lionfish's boat pulled up to the wounded men in the water. Some were screaming in pain while others screamed for mercy. Lionfish's mind flashed through images of his own dead and wounded, including Barracuda his long time friend.

He grabbed the controls of the M60 away from Yellowtail and he strafed the men in the water.

"Let that be an example of RedTide's mercy," he whispered.

As they began their journey back to port and planned their escape, Lionfish couldn't help but think about the poetic justice of the dead men he left behind being consumed by the very sea that they had helped to destroy.

CHAPTER 2

It was the coldest day in forty years the voice on the car radio announced through the static. It was twenty-six degrees with the wind chill and I was feeling every degree. I looked at the photo ID of the taxi driver stuck to the dashboard of the 1990 Town Car I was driving in.

"Excuse me Sami," I said. "Do you think you could pick up the pace a little. I've got fifteen minutes to catch my shuttle back to West Palm."

I learned in a recent sales training course that people are more responsive and are much less defensive when you address them by their first name. Ever since the class, I had been trying the technique out on everyone from waiters to prospective customers with mixed reviews.

Sami just grunted and began speaking in tongues as he pulled in behind an enormous Cadillac, the car of choice for the elders of South Florida. At the moment it appeared to be driven by a gnome. When we finally passed the car I could see that it was a Florida octogenarian peering over the top of the wheel.

My head was pounding as we pulled up to the curb with only about ten minutes left to make my connection. Murphy's Law of business travel was in full effect. The line at the ticket counter was a mile long and so I decided to try out a "travel trick" my regional sales manager had told me about.

I went to the first class line where there were only about two people waiting. When I got to the counter my mood was as foul as it had ever been but I was soon to learn that the woman behind the counter was in an even worse mood. She asked me if I was an Elite Club member or if I was a first class passenger.

The trick, as it was explained to me, is to ask about available room in first class hoping that it is full. Step two is to inquire about the price of the upgrade and then balk at the price, deciding after all to just remain in coach. By this time you have already bypassed the long line for coach and they will almost always check you through to coach without a hitch.

"Works every time," I could hear Al Chadwick saying in that incredibly confident and often arrogant way he has.

"I'm sorry but if you're not flying first class and are not an Elite member then you will have to get back in line with everyone else." She said it with a look in her eye and a tone in her voice that instantly elevated my blood pressure to dangerous levels.

"I'm sorry, Helen," I said, spying her name tag, "but I can't afford to spend $600 to upgrade. I didn't think it would cost that much and I only have seven minutes left to catch my flight."

I was grinding my teeth and my hands began to shake. I could feel myself losing control again and I was afraid that soon I would be beyond all rational thought or action. Helen looked at me with what could only be interpreted as pure contempt and told me to get back in line or I would definitely miss my flight.

"Whatever happened to customer service?" I shouted. "No frills is one thing but this is fucking ridiculous! When are you people going to stop sticking it to the business traveler? We support the airlines, not the tourist who wants to fly to Florida once a year and pay $100 for what used to be a privilege."

I was yelling so violently that spit was flying from my mouth and I could see that the people in line were beginning to become nervous and agitated.

"All your fucking penalties and restrictions. It cost me $1,800 to fly to New York last week for what should have been a $200 ticket all because I didn't book thirty days in advance, even though the flight was empty."

I reached down and felt for the stainless steel 9MM Beretta I kept in the waistband of my pants. I was going to put it in a locker on the way to the gate before I passed through the security scanners. The ringing in my ears began as a gentle humming like the sound of an air conditioning unit, and built in intensity until it became an agonizing, high pitched whine that could drive me to the brink of madness.

A young marine in his pretty dress blues took a step toward me and warned me to "chill out" and get back in line.

I simultaneously pulled my weapon from my waistband as I turned and screamed at the top of my lungs that he should mind his own fucking business. The young marine reminded me of a time in my life that embodied senseless suffering and structured and organized degradation. His timing was unfortunate.

I fired two high velocity Black Talon hollow points in rapid succession. They blasted through the chest of the teenage leatherneck whose heroic death should have taken place on some battlefield in a faraway place where he had no business being.

Instead he chose to bleed out on the carpet of the Tampa International Airport. I then turned my attention to Helen. By now people were running and screaming in all directions and their voices were blending into one long continuous cry for help. Out of the corner of my eye I could see that several armed security guards and two policemen were quickly approaching. They were only ten or twenty yards away and already had their weapons drawn. They were ordering me to drop my weapon and I knew I would only have one chance to erase the catalyst for today's events.

I fired a shot point blank into Helen's face, eliminating any chance she ever had of improving her attitude and becoming Employee of the Month.

In slow motion out of the corner of my eye, I could see the officers fire their weapons in my direction. In slow motion I could see the lead projectiles spinning in mid air on a direct path for my upper body but for some reason I could not move. I turned my head just in time to see Helen's face explode and vaporize into a swirling mist of monochromatic shades of red.

The red cloud that had once been Helen spread out in all directions and showered me in a torrent of red blood cells. I was completely enveloped in a pink mist. I blinked to clear the blood from my eyes and the world looked pink as if I were seeing it through rose colored glasses, a thought which made me laugh incongruously. I blinked again and I awoke beside my mother's hospital bed where I had been sleeping for the past three days.

It was late, and the only sound in the room was the labored breathing of my mother, wheezing through the plastic sheeting of her oxygen tent. My heart was racing and blood was pounding in my ears. God almighty, what a horrible dream. The stress these past few weeks had been unbearable. Three nights ago my oldest sister Jacqueline and I had an enormous fight which almost led to blows right here in my mother's room.

If Conor, my brother-in-law had not stepped in between us to protect Jackie I'm sure my sister and I would have killed each other. It started innocently enough with my sister asking me to spend more time with our mother, and deteriorated quickly to the point where she was accusing me of caring more about my work than I did about our mother.

"Jake," she said, "you always do what's best for you, and to hell with anyone else."

This accusation of being egocentric and self-involved coming from my sister was ridiculous. She was the youngest lawyer ever to make partner at Stone, May, Landau and Haig; one of New York's most prestigious law firms. My perfect sister who skipped two grades to graduate high school at sixteen and went on to be valedictorian at NYU before she finished in the top five percent of her class at Columbia Law School.

Jackie also happens to be beautiful, and she can cook like a gourmet chef. Except for Conor's continued love and support, Jacqueline had also done it all on her own. A self-made woman you might say. Our father had walked out on us when we were very young and my mother went back to work to support us as a cosmetician at a small neighborhood salon.

My sister had always worked, even when she was a teenager, and she always had a fierce desire to be a success even as a little girl. She unfortunately grew up bitter and angry over our father's betrayal of our family, and is defensive and guarded about her feelings. She is one of the most feared partners at her firm, and has a reputation for being ruthless in business.

It was rumored that she had once overheard an intern with a promising future at the firm gossiping about the possible reasons for her promotion to partner. She had torn him to pieces so viciously in front of a group of his coworkers and then in front of one of the senior partners behind closed doors that she had reduced him to tears.

He was terminated two days later. My sister to her credit is also one of those rare women who manages to have it all. She is raising an adorable little girl named Erin while putting in her eighty hour weeks. She does this, of course, with the help of her husband Conor.

Jacqueline and Conor met in high school when she was only fifteen and have been together almost twenty-five years. Conor was seventeen and a junior in high school. He was tall and handsome and was the captain of the wrestling team. They fell in love at first sight and were inseparable. Conor took a lot of abuse and ribbing from his friends about dating a Jewish girl in what was a predominantly Irish Catholic neighborhood. There were even a few remarks written in his high school yearbook about his Jewish girlfriend.

In my eyes, I always saw them as opposites and wondered what kept them together. Conor has a sweet, patient, gentle disposition, while Jacqueline is a shark who will rip out your throat if she doesn't get her way or if she is losing an argument to you. My sister and I have almost come to blows over a game of Trivial Pursuit, since we are equally competitive and are even worse winners than we are losers.

Conor is a painter who makes a modest living doing freelance illustrations for books and album covers. He works out of the house and during the day is the primary caretaker for my niece. He is a loving devoted father and is one of the most beloved members of my family. I, on the other hand, have always been somewhat of a disappointment to my family, especially my sister, who in light of my mother's illness has become the self-appointed matriarch of the Stein clan.

I was always the gifted, talented underachiever who always gave up, walked away, or took the easy way out. I have been hearing it all of my life from every teacher on every report card I had ever gotten. "Jacob is very bright and would do very well if only he would apply himself." I always received an F for bad conduct.

My mom would cry whenever I would bring home a string of Fs and she would say "A 137 IQ and you get Fs. Jacob, you're one of the most talented children I know. When are you going to apply yourself? Look at your older sister. She works after school everyday and does her homework all night long. I don't even think she sleeps. I try to tell her to slow down. I tell her that she's a young woman and she should have some fun. I beg her to go shopping with her mother. She has no friends except for Conor and all she does is talk about the future while she races through the present. I have one child who does too much and one who does nothing but daydream and get into trouble."

Trouble I did get into, and lots of it. I hung around with a bad crowd and smoked pot day and night. I was arrested four times for shoplifting and once for vandalizing property. I was always angry with my mother for dating lots of different men and for parading them around the neighborhood in front of my friends. She dated young men, fat men, and even a black man once. I can tell you although I'm no racist it was tough living in white middle class Long Island in the seventies. That one date supplied the neighborhood kids with lots of ammunition to increase their assault on me.

She was always crying and she was always afraid and she tried to teach her children to be afraid. I had no respect for what I perceived were her pathetic displays of weakness and her total lack of self control. Growing up, I had worshipped my mother and could even have been described as "a momma's boy." I thought she was so beautiful and she was always so warm and affectionate with us.

This was in direct contrast to my father who was cruel to his children and was colder than a block of marble. The only time my father ever spoke to us was to belittle us or to verbally abuse us. He was hardest of all on my mother who fought an ongoing battle to protect her children from him. She would have to beg for money to buy us some nice clothing or to take us on a trip. My father would come home from work and without saying a word would go upstairs and close the door to his bedroom and we would not see him again until morning.

When my father took off for good, it was the happiest day of my life. I felt the way the French people must have felt when the allies rolled into Paris and they were finally liberated from the Germans. I thought everyone would share in my joy, and was stunned by the way in which his departure had affected not only my mother but my sister as well, who for some unknown reason worshipped our father.

I can only guess that she more closely identified with his intellect and his no nonsense humorless style. He was a very intelligent man. My mother and my sister are so different in so many ways. My mother is flamboyant and loves to go to parties. She loves fashion and could shop all day long. She has hundreds of friends and never loses touch with any of them. My sister is a loner who has no interest in wearing makeup or trying on clothes. I doubt that she has ever even seen the inside of a *Vogue* or an *Elle* magazine although she does dress sophisticatedly if not ultra-conservative for work.

It is only in the last few years that I have begun to see the more important similarities between my sister and my mother. It is as if since the birth of my niece that I am finally able see my mother in my sister's eyes as she looks at her daughter. The loving way my sister has with her daughter and the way she held her when she was a baby. The love and the pride with which she speaks about Erin to other people. I can now see in the midst of the agonizing torture and the degradation of the lung cancer that killed my mother her strength and the courage and the love with which she raised us. I now see clearly for the first time that my mother was a hero. That she was a strong survivor who taught her children to be strong and to survive.

How could I have been so blind for so long? My mother gave us all a gift, which I am only now, when it is too late, beginning to appreciate. She gave us a passion and a love of life and an ability to feel so much.

Whenever I listen to a favorite old song or see a work of art and am able to appreciate it I will think of my mother. When I am in my favorite place, fifty feet below water diving on a coral reef and I am enraptured by the beauty of what surrounds me, I will think of my mother. When I am falling in love and when I am holding my children in my arms I will think of my mother and I will whisper "thank you."

CHAPTER 3

I AWOKE AT THREE A.M. from the strangest dream. I was ice diving through tunnels and tubes of varying shades of blue and turquoise but the water was warm and I wasn't wearing the dry suit one would normally require for such a dive.

I was trying to find my way out through an endless maze of interconnecting tunnels, all no wider than a midsize car. The ice had the ancient glacial coloring of light blue and above me I could hear the loud cracking and roaring of what sounded like ice calving away on the surface.

I looked down at my pressure gauge and it told me quite alarmingly that I only had 200 pounds of air left in my tank. I began to panic when I heard what sounded like a high-pitched whining all around me. As I got closer, it increased in intensity and I was able to recognize what it was I was hearing. I had heard the sound once before while on a diving trip in the Turks and Caicos islands. It was the sound of dolphins singing underwater from a great distance. That sound had teased us all week long during our trip with the promise of glimpsing a dolphin up close underwater, but we never actually saw them.

Now the sound seemed to be leading me to safety and I followed it to a vertical tunnel above me in the ice. The tunnel was actually a vertical tube in the perfect shape of a cylinder 300-400 feet high. It seemed to be bored into the ice from above and I could see sunlight at the surface. *Could I possibly be that deep*, I wondered. *Could I really be that far down beneath 400 feet of solid ice.*

I checked my depth gauge and it confirmed that indeed I was 420 feet below the surface. I had never been deeper than 130 feet before, the maximum allowable depth for a recreational diver, and knew that I would not be able to ascend slowly enough to avoid getting the bends with only 200 pounds of air.

I was also not feeling the effects of the depth or suffering from nitrogen narcosis; an ailment brought on by a build-up of nitrogen in the body due to exposure at depths exceeding 100 feet. The symptoms are similar to a disorienting drug-induced high that in some cases can be extremely dangerous, "the rapture of the deep." I started to ascend as slowly as my air supply would allow and the cries of the dolphins got louder and louder.

More available light was filling the shaft and creating beautiful prisms of color. I checked my depth gauge and air pressure gauge and they read 210 feet and 150 pounds of air respectively. I would never make it.

About one hundred feet from the surface, the sound of the dolphins had become a tortured scream pulling me upward. I swallowed my last breath of air and kicked for the surface as hard as I could and blew the air out slowly so I wouldn't burst a lung. I reached over to the purge valve on my buoyancy compensation vest and sucked a breath of air from my jacket.

I could see the surface; it was maybe ten feet above me. Suddenly, the water began to turn red and the color spread out around and below me. It was as if someone had poured hundreds of gallons of red dye into the water. As I broke the surface, I realized that the bodies of hundreds of dead or dying bottlenose dolphins surrounded me and I began to scream as loudly as I could.

That's when I awoke bathed in sweat and feeling completely wrung out. I remembered I was in North Shore Hospital, recovering from a bout of Malaria I had contracted on a recent trip to Cozumel, Mexico.

My fever had broken and I was lying on a refrigerated mattress. No doubt my dream was brought on by a television special I had seen on CNN last night about an incident involving the terrorist group RedTide.

The news report included some photographs that were captured by a *National Geographic* crew on the scene. The report said that six men, all dressed in black paramilitary uniforms and wearing full face black masks, had appeared at a small Japanese fishing village called Futo, a man-made harbor town nestled against the mountains of Japan's Izu Peninsula.

The men suddenly appeared at the annual roundup and slaughter of dolphins in Futo's harbor. The news report included an explanation of the inhumane fishing practice and also included some extremely graphic and disturbing footage of the slaughter of over a thousand dolphins that were herded and trapped in Futo's harbor two years ago.

Just like in my dream, the water ran red with blood. It seems that this year RedTide turned all the dolphins loose and burned twelve fishing boats in the harbor, the entire fleet, of the community.

The reaction from the Japanese government was very strong, and denounced the action as cold-blooded terrorism of the worst kind. The Japanese media explained that the fisherman in the village would now have no means of visible support and would likely starve. It also tried to explain that this traditional hunting of dolphins is no different than fishing, even though dolphins are in fact mammals and not fish.

The reaction in the States to RedTide's raid was extremely positive among the public and the leaders of RedTide known only as Lionfish and Stingray were being romanticized in the tabloid press. Some went so far as to liken them to the Butch Cassidy and the Sundance Kid of the sea.

The news program ended by announcing that Stingray would be appearing on *Larry King Live* later in the year. I wondered how he planned on showing up without being immediately arrested by the FBI. The network would have to make some guarantees about his safety and security.

I pressed the call button beside my bed and called out for my nurse. Beth, my nurse for the 11 P.M. to 7 A.M. shift walked in and said, "Ah, so you've decided to rejoin us, Jake. Now get back in that bed before you fall down and hurt yourself."

Beth was a beautiful woman, but was tough as nails and was definitely not your stereotypical nurse with the heart of gold. Most of the time, she seemed to be pissed off about something and she complained non-stop about her working conditions while she treated me.

I tried flirting with her earlier in the week and used some of my most persuasive sales techniques and charms to seduce her. Maybe the fact that I was delirious with fever and had not properly bathed in a week was working against me. Man oh man, I had been out of the field for weeks now and was desperately close to losing my hold on the lead for Salesman of the Year with only two months left and the holidays almost upon us.

After returning from the company meeting for sales award winners in Cozumel, I had decided to take a month off to visit with my mom in New York. I was feeling so good about the news that her lung cancer was in remission, and I was so high from my trip when I returned that I was even more devastated when my sister called me with the news that the cancer had spread to my mother's brain.

What an emotional roller coaster the Stein family had been on these last six months. I felt guilty about returning to Boca Raton where I have lived for the past two years, but I needed to take that vacation in Mexico. I also had to get back to Florida to catch up on business in my territory.

I asked Beth for the phone since I needed to check my voice mail, and call my mom at home to see how she was recovering from her latest transfusion.

She had moved home from the hospital where I had spent my last three days with her sleeping in a chair before she was released and my fever spiked. She went home and I moved up one floor to a room of my own. She was now receiving hospice care around the clock at home while my sister and I were taking shifts as our schedules allowed.

When I had mentioned the idea of taking a leave of absence at work, my manager Al Chadwick at first pretended to be sympathetic. Then he launched into a story about how proud my mom would be if she knew I was Salesman of the Year for 1995.

Al is the best salesman I know, but he is also the slimiest, most self-serving and manipulative scumbag I have ever met. Everyone at LifeForce Technology respected his ability to overcome an objection and to close a deal, but no one respected his leadership.

He was the kind of manager who discouraged any type of opposing viewpoint and was critical in front of others. He believed in management strictly by intimidation and had the highest turnover rate of any manager in the country. To his credit, he was also an extremely energetic and creative problem solver with tremendous sales instincts and perception. His region was consistently the most productive.

His favorite saying plastered in giant letters behind his desk, was

"Those who say it can't be done should get out of the way of those who are doing it."

Al and I had a love/hate relationship. He had a great sense of humor but could be cruel and abusive when his mood changed, which it did at least five times daily. In many ways he reminded me of my father and he liked to see himself as a mentor or father figure. Sales was the perfect vocation for me and I was a natural at it. Al would always say that the rest of the sales force had to work five times as hard as me just to keep up, and that was probably true.

I never had a great work ethic. When I was selling in New York I always enjoyed goofing around during work hours with my friends down at the Hard Rock Cafe for a three-hour lunch, or on a sunny spring day riding around on the Circle Line tour drinking beer and eating hot dogs. Then, come crunch time at the end of the month, I would bear down and would magically produce the orders I needed to pull ahead.

It drove my sales managers insane because they knew what I was capable of producing if only I increased my effort. This arrangement worked just fine for me. I still made over $80,000 last year and never worked more than a thirty hour week. My big shot sister makes less than $120,000 and still owes more than $100,000 in student loans.

Although she claims being a lawyer is a more prestigious and highly respected profession it just seems like a lot more work for the same money. As for being respected, I've heard many more lawyer jokes told than jokes about salesmen.

We fight constantly about which is more of a low-life profession, being a salesman or being a lawyer. It's a very loving and supportive relationship. For a while I had a routine where I would sell for one year with a company until I got burned out or bored. I would save all my money while I lived at home with my mother until I had saved enough money to take off and travel. I would travel for three to six months at a time, then when the money ran out I would come home and start all over again.

I've sold everything from copiers to elevators and have always been number one in whatever company I was working for. I've left behind a string of brokenhearted sales managers who had all desperately tried to convince me what a bright future I could have if only I would stay and work my way up to management. Blood sucking maggots, every one of them.

When push came to shove, and their loyalty was put to the test they invariably revealed themselves to be using me with no more concern for my well being than the homeless they stepped over every day on their way to work. Quota and the bottom line were all any sales manager cared about. The minute the numbers fell off or your sales dropped, they dropped you.

Well that's okay, I won't get too self righteous or indignant. I'm using them and their company's products to achieve my own ends as well. Truth be told I am not the least bit concerned about what happens to them or their companies when I'm gone.

I guess you could call salespeople greedy, opportunistic, and manipulative, most people do. It's the nature of a business where you spend all your time trying to get people to do what you want.

The next day I was leaving the hospital and I was planning on taking my mom for a drive up to Bear Mountain to see the the fall colors, if she was feeling up to it. When Jackie was here to visit two nights before, she told me it was supposedly prime time in the upstate region of New York and that the colors of the leaves were at their peak of beauty.

Fall was always my mother's favorite time of year. When we were children we would go apple picking and visit some local pumpkin patches. We would always stop for lunch and sip hot apple cider with lots of cinnamon or mulling spices. I would crawl into my mother's lap and she would kiss me and scratch my back with her long nails.

Jackie had taken care of all the arrangements and she had even rented a wheelchair although we both agreed my mother would never use it. We both promised Conor that we would call a cease-fire for the day and that there would be no arguing between us. After a week in this hellhole I was looking forward to the cool crisp air of autumn and to being with my mother again for what I hoped and prayed would not be the last time.

CHAPTER 4

BLOWFISH WAS EASING HIS WAY OVER QUIETLY TO THE WORK SHED where Lionfish was working on his hobby, manufacturing custom-made stained glass lamps. They all had underwater scenes of coral reefs and kelp forests. They sold for up to $5000 in private galleries under an assumed name.

Lionfish is a very unusual man, Blowfish thought. Blowfish had seen him literally tear a man apart with his bare hands and now he was in his workshop listening to tapes of Bob Dylan while he created a thing of rare beauty. Lionfish explained, when asked, that doing stained glass helped him to relax and that he did some of his best thinking and planning when he was alone with his art. Then he would make some highbrow comment about the duality of man.

The only duality Blowfish recognized in his own life was that he liked to fight almost as much as he liked to fuck. No one would ever mistake him for an intellectual. Lionfish had just had a heated disagreement with Stingray about his scheduled appearance on the *Larry King Live* show in three months. Even though it was to be held from a prearranged, mutually agreed upon secret location, Lionfish was worried. For three years Blowfish had been a part of Lionfish's "Marine Iguanas," named for the monitor lizard that lives in the Galapagos Islands and is a carnivore that can eat animals as large as goats.

The Iguanas were the elite Praetorian Guard of RedTide, and Lionfish's personal security force. In those three years, Blowfish had never seen the two men argue, especially in front of the men. They were as close as brothers and Stingray, was the only person Lionfish was known to confide in. Like most of the members of the Marine Iguanas, Blowfish was an ex-Navy SEAL with insurgence experience and a background in special operations.

Many SEALs had joined up with RedTide after the Gulf War. Many were outraged by the mass destruction of the environment they had witnessed at the hands of the Iraqi madman and some had assisted with the cleanup of the oil that was intentionally spilled into the Persian Gulf. Others had joined after fellow SEALs had gotten sick from the severe biohazards their own government had exposed them to during the war, outraged at the lack of responsibility or recognition on the part of the government and the Veteran's Administration to help returning soldiers afflicted with illnesses.

RedTide also paid extremely well for the services that only these ex-SEALs could provide. Blowfish had once believed in the cause but had never been as zealous as the rest of the team. He was well paid and that was his main concern. RedTide seemed to have limitless funds, and since the group did not collect much in the way of donations, where the money came from was always a topic of much discussion and speculation among the men. As Blowfish entered the shed, Bob Dylan's "It Takes A Lot to Laugh; It Takes a Train to Cry" was blasting through the overhead speakers. As he stepped farther into the room he began to feel a little anxious.

Blowfish was over 6'5" tall and weighed nearly 220 pounds, all of which was thick, well-conditioned muscle. Lionfish was the only man he had ever met that he could remember feeling physically intimidated by.

He had seen Lionfish move at a speed and strike with a destructive power he had never seen before, and his temper was legendary among the elite guard. He looked over at Lionfish by his workbench. Lionfish never once looked his way as he entered the workshop. Lionfish didn't seem to notice him, and from long experience, Blowfish knew he could not give him the chance. Lionfish was holding up a long dark green piece of glass to the lighted window in front of his worktable, examining it for just the right place to make his next cut. As Blowfish came up behind him, he slipped a ten-inch double-edged Marine combat knife into his hand, sliding his fingers through the brass knuckles that were a part of the weapon.

He knew he would have to strike fast while the element of surprise was still on his side. He was sweating heavily and could feel his heart racing as the blood pounded in his temples. Dylan was wailing away on the harmonica covering the sound of his footsteps as Blowfish rushed forward and swung the weapon in a downward arc on a path for Lionfish's back.

At that instant a cloud passed in front of the sun and the translucent glass in Lionfish's hands became dark and reflective. Lionfish caught the reflected image of Blowfish rushing toward him in the dark green of the glass. In a spilt second as the blade swung down Lionfish ducked out of the way. He simultaneously kicked backward with the full weight of his body.

The knife sliced easily through his thick faded denim shirt and the fabric immediately turned crimson from the deep gash the blade had opened up in Lionfish's shoulder. The kick had landed on Blowfish's chest, and he was thrown backward where he toppled over a small stool.

Lionfish spun around to confront his attacker as Blowfish quickly got to his feet. Blowfish was breathing hard; this was not what he had counted on.

He rushed at Lionfish as Lionfish spun and threw a backward roundhouse kick. The air rasped and blood flew in an arc from his shoulder as the kick snapped across the jaw of his assailant. Blowfish was down, but he was a strong, hardened combat veteran and Lionfish knew he would not stay down. Blowfish charged for the last time as Lionfish grabbed a long heavy dagger-like piece of glass from his table and hurled it at the oncoming target. The glass lodged in Blowfish's upper bicep. Blowfish pulled it out, spraying dark arterial blood across the room as Lionfish snapped two quick sidekicks into his face.

He was unconscious before his enormous body crashed to the ground. Lionfish knew he would have to act quickly if he were to stop the bleeding and keep him alive. It was crucial that he not die before he told all he knew about who had turned him and how much they already knew about RedTide's operation.

Regardless, Lionfish knew they would have to break down the compound tonight and move to their permanent headquarters. Lionfish quickly grabbed the soldering iron he used to weld the pieces of his lamp together and while applying pressure to stop the bleeding, he shoved it deep into the wound on Blowfish's arm.

Even though he was unconscious, Blowfish's eyes opened wide and he let out a blood curdling scream that could be heard over the entire compound. He passed out again from a combination of pain and shock. Within seconds six members of Lionfish's personal guard including Stingray rushed into the room with weapons locked and loaded.

Two days later they were in their new location on a small hilly island off the coast of Central America. Blowfish had regained enough strength to withstand the interrogation, although he was to wish moments later that he had bled out on the floor of that cabin.

Three men carried Blowfish to the makeshift lab where Stingray was conducting marine biology experiments. His current project was to study the venom of several marine invertebrates, including the deadly Australian box jellyfish. The box jellyfish or chironex fleckeri, also known as a marine stinger or sea wasp, is the most venomous creature on earth and prolonged exposure to tentacles of over ten feet in length can bring excruciating painful death in under four minutes to an adult human.

The box jellyfish can grow to over fifteen feet in length and has enough venom to kill sixty men. Its sting is burning hot and has been described by victims as similar to being burned by scalding or boiling water. The venom effects breathing, and is absorbed into the circulatory and lymphatic systems. It slows the heart and can often stop it completely. The tiny stinging darts of the jellyfish called nematocysts are cocked and fired upon contact with its victim, releasing two types of toxins as they puncture the skin.

Stingray had showed Lionfish photographs of survivors in the marine biology books they had to haul from location to location, along with all the other exotic and costly equipment he collected. The victims' bodies were covered with horrible red and pink lesions. The scarring was permanent and grotesque.

"Haul Judas over to the tank and throw him in," Lionfish shouted at the men guarding Blowfish.

The men began to drag him in the direction of the clear 5,000-gallon Lucite tank. Inside one could see a dozen juvenile box jellyfish with tentacles no longer than five to six feet in length. It would take the repeated stinging of more than six or seven for a prolonged period of time to kill a man as large as Blowfish, if at all. But after ten minutes he would be begging Lionfish to blow his brains out.

Lionfish walked up to Blowfish and put his face inches from his own.

"I'm going to give you a chance to save yourself a lot of needless suffering," he said. "I'm going to make this very easy for you. I'll ask you direct questions and you answer them. No conversation necessary," Lionfish said.

"Fuck you, Lionfish," Blowfish answered. "I'm as good as dead anyway and you know it. I've worked along side you for three years now and I know the way you operate. The only way I'm leaving this place is in pieces."

"You're right, you are as good as dead," Lionfish answered. "You were dead the minute you made the fateful decision to turn your back on our cause and to whore yourself out to our enemies. But I've decided to be a sport and to give you a gift you don't deserve. I'm going to allow you the right to decide how you die. It can be quickly with a shred of dignity or it can be the slow miserable death of a coward and a traitor.

"Get that harness and block and tackle over here and tie his feet and hands together after you remove all his clothes," Lionfish shouted to the men in the corner.

When Blowfish was all prepared Lionfish had him lifted into the air and wheeled over to the tank where he was suspended three feet above the water. Lionfish had an electric winch set up so he could quickly lower and raise Blowfish from the water. To his credit, Blowfish showed tremendous restraint and discipline in controlling any outward signs of fear. But in a few minutes that would all change and he would be reduced to a blubbering idiot begging for mercy. Lionfish sent all the men outside except Stingray who's expertise was required.

He knew the other men would hear Blowfish's screams but he wanted to spare them having to witness the gruesome task that leadership had thrust upon him. Lionfish pressed the red button on the hand control and lowered Blowfish into the tank. For several minutes the jellyfish seemed to ignore him and then they began to attack. One jellyfish wrapped itself around Blowfish's upper thigh and another wrapped around his neck and jaw.

When they released their stinging darts Blowfish screamed and almost exploded from the water. He began to thrash violently from side to side churning the water in an attempt to shake them loose. His screams began to escalate until they were a shrill, high-pitched whining and he began to cry for mercy.

Lionfish pressed the black button on the control and raised Blowfish from the water. He had to take this slow or he would kill him before he asked his first question.

"How does that feel big guy? I wonder if it hurts as much as the forty plus stitches you put in my back," he called out to Blowfish who was sobbing like a baby.

Long red welts were forming on Blowfish's neck and arms and around his upper thighs. One of his testicles was bloated and purple where one of the jellyfish had stung him. His throat was swelling shut and he was wheezing horribly.

"Fuck you," Blowfish screamed through tears and rage.

Lionfish walked away a couple of feet and asked, "Who paid you to kill me and how much do they know about our operation?" No answer.

"Who sent you?" Lionfish screamed at the top of his lungs, his famous temper starting to surface. No answer.

Blowfish had regained a little composure and had summoned a reservoir of courage in order to make one last determined stand. He looked in Lionfish's direction and spit.

"Drop him again, only up to his knees this time," Lionfish said softly to Stingray as he handed him the controls and circled around the tank.

The jellyfish were all congregated around the center of the tank and seemed to be waiting although Lionfish knew that was impossible. The box jellyfish is mostly water and has no real brain. When Blowfish's legs were in up to the knees they all seemed to attack at once and all twelve were swarming around his calves and knees. The screaming almost reached inhuman proportions and Stingray ran from the shed in disgust leaving Lionfish all alone in the room with the assassin.

"Help me. For God's sake, help me. Get me out of here. I'll tell you anything," Blowfish screamed. His calves were enormously swollen and blood and sticky yellow liquid was oozing from hundreds of puncture wounds.

"For the last time who sent you?" Lionfish yelled. "This is the last time I will ask you, then I'll drop you and I will leave you to die. It could take hours."

Lionfish knew he had gone too far too fast and would only get to ask this one all-important question before Blowfish went into shock. The rest of the answers would have to wait until he met the man in question himself. Blowfish took a long deep breath slowly through his constricted windpipe and with enormous effort shouted, "Yamaguchi!!! Yamaguchi, m-m-m-million dollar contract."

In the blink of an eye Lionfish pulled his 9mm SIG from his shoulder holster and mercifully double-tapped Blowfish in the forehead.

CHAPTER 5

AKIRO YAMAGUCHI ROSE SLOWLY from behind his antique eighteenth century, American cherry wood desk and walked over to the window of his office on the fortieth floor of the building which bore his name. He had been thinking about his son and the memory of how he had died filled him with deep pain and regret.

Nobuaki was Yamaguchi's only son and Akiro had insisted that he work his way up through the company from its lowliest positions. He sent Nobuaki off to work in several of his factories and planned to send him off to sea to work hauling fish on one of his commercial factory fishing vessels. His plan was for his son to start at the bottom. Nobuaki would work in positions of manual labor for three months at a time at different sites for a period of three years at most of Yamaguchi's small independent subsidiaries so that he could learn the business. This way Yamaguchi reasoned he could appreciate the hard work that went into building his father's empire. Before he could ever hope to achieve a position of authority or ownership of the huge Japanese conglomerate that Yamaguchi had built with his own hands from the ashes of postwar Japan, Nobuaki would have to walk a distance, albeit a short one, in his father's shoes.

The corporation had many satellite subsidiaries and manufactured everything from laptop computers to fertilizer. Yamaguchi also maintained the largest cargo fleet in the Pacific and also maintained one of the largest fleets of factory fishing vessels in the world.

It was on the night shift at one of Yamaguchi's chemical plants, which manufactured synthetic industrial chemicals used in making paint and electrical transformers, that his only son and heir was senselessly murdered.

The renegade organization RedTide had been issuing warnings for months to Yamaguchi through his senior advisors to stop the poisoning of the local waters in and around the Yokagawa chemical plant that his company was a majority owner in. They had mailed literally tons of scientific data indicating through extensive research and testing that the dolphin and general marine population in the area was being poisoned. PCBs or Polychlorinated Biphenyls were being dumped into the water from his factory and animals were suffering from lesions and rampant disease in connection to the chemicals his company was producing.

Most of the letters came to him after the company's security bureau and Yokagawa's attorneys had reviewed them. Very little discussion had taken place between Yamaguchi himself and the day-to-day staff and management at Yokagawa in regards to what was at the time considered a trivial annoyance.

Yamaguchi ran a multi-billion dollar corporation with hundreds of subsidiary companies that manufactured thousands of individual products and was advised not to concern himself with so trivial an affair.

His son was on his three-year rotation through an assortment of Yamaguchi's individual companies and Yamaguchi had lost touch with him over the last six months of his life. This was another painful regret that he could not make peace with.

He had no idea that he was working that fateful night and tried to tell himself that it would not have mattered in regards to what had transpired. That evening around 12:00 A.M. RedTide tied up most of the staff including his son in a basement sub level and set explosives in carefully selected locations designed to cripple the factory. RedTide was careful in the placement of the explosive charges. They did not want to cause a fire or a chemical leak that might endanger the population in the area. It was explained to Yamaguchi by the head of security, just prior to his termination that it was a carefully planned invasion carried out by a professional crew.

Unfortunately, due to the stress of the explosions on several key manifolds a small leak did occur and the deadly fumes which leaked into the basement killed his son and thirteen other employees that were bound and gagged there.

They became violently ill and suffocated slowly on the noxious fumes that burned their eyes and seared their lungs. Yamaguchi's son had strangled to death on his own vomit and his face was bloated and purple. Yamaguchi collapsed to one knee and wept for the first time in over forty years when he went to view the body of his son at the facility.

He had been so hard on the boy when they had last spoken, demanding that he give honor to the family name and that he do his duty as described to him by his father. His son had not uttered one word of defiance about having to use his Ivy League education to net fish. His last words to his father as he turned to begin his years of manual labor were that he would make him proud and that he would earn his respect.

As Akiro Yamaguchi stared off into the distance he swore again the same words that he had sworn to his son that night at Yokagawa as he held his lifeless hand and remembered him as a little boy. He promised his son that one day he himself would kill the man that had taken him away and that he would not rest until his son was avenged.

He turned from the window to welcome Mr. MacGregor, the man he had hired to find and kill his son's murderers into the room. His sadness was instantly replaced by a much more comfortable and familiar feeling, intense anger. Yamaguchi had been excruciatingly patient these last two years while lead after lead went nowhere.

RedTide's security and anonymity were still well protected and despite enormous expenditures and bribes totaling millions of dollars no progress had been made. That was until recently when Tom Lowell, AKA Blowfish, one of Lionfish's trusted insiders signed on to deliver Lionfish into his hands. Now he was missing.

He had not reported in on the satellite telephone that MacGregor had issued to him in almost a week. After the failed ambush attempt he had helped to arrange weeks earlier in The North Sea he was supposed to have killed Lionfish and made his escape.

That was over six days ago. Yesterday he was supposed to have met with MacGregor in the Cayman Islands to collect his million-dollar bounty. Yamaguchi had already deposited the funds there in a secured numbered account and MacGregor would turn over the account numbers and codes when Lowell presented evidence that Lionfish was dead.

After the ambush went awry, killing his brothers in arms, Lowell had a change of heart and decided for his own protection not to give away the location of RedTide's headquarters. He was adamant about betraying only Lionfish and in protecting his fellow soldiers.

That really didn't matter to Yamaguchi as long as Lionfish was eliminated. "Cut off the head and the body would surely die" he had read somewhere, maybe in Sun Tzsu's "The Art of War," one of his favorite books. They were now back where they had started two years ago, with no leads and little hope.

Their inside man at the FBI had so far collected over two hundred thousand dollars and had delivered nothing. MacGregor kept insisting that you had to cover all the bases in regards to networking for information and that it was impossible to tell where or when something might break. How Yamaguchi dreamed of one day facing the man known as Lionfish and killing him personally, after he exterminated his men one by one in front of him.

His hatred was a tangible thing with a life of its own and increased daily in intensity. Since his sons death, he had increased illegal whaling in his fishing fleets and was disguising the whale meat or Kujira his company sold at Tsukiji, the great Tokyo fish market as dolphin and other products in order to avoid the world wide ban on whaling that now existed.

This was becoming increasingly difficult since the International Whaling Commission had been doing random DNA testing on meat sold in the market. He would hurt his enemies any way possible and destroy what they cherished most. He took comfort in the deep feelings of malice, which he rationalized as retribution.

"Well, Mr. MacGregor, what do you suspect has happened to our man Lowell?" Yamaguchi asked.

"My best guess is that he's dead and that his body has been well disposed of."

"I don't pay you fifty thousand dollars a week to make guesses," Yamaguchi responded angrily. "I waited over six months for you to organize this attack and now when I was so close to punishing the man who stole my son's life, you make guesses. What do we do now?" Yamaguchi asked in a more relaxed tone.

"Yamaguchi San, MacGregor replied, "I know you aren't going to like this but we have to wait for another major break. I know how frustrating this is but we are dealing with one of the most secured organizations I have encountered in over twenty years in the intelligence business, and so far they have not made any mistakes."

"Blowfish was the first major break we've had in over two years. There are over 100 local and international law enforcement groups on RedTide's trail and Lionfish has managed to elude them all. We suspect that he may at one time have been a member of the armed forces or some military intelligence organization."

"He is well funded and he most certainly has informants and friends in the right places.

"We can't trace his origin and we haven't been able to follow the money trail.

"Be patient a little while longer and I promise something will turn up soon," MacGregor said, while he secretly hoped that what he said was true. Yamaguchi was a good man and he treated MacGregor and his men with respect and dignity. He also paid top dollar and MacGregor had a reputation to protect. MacGregor was regarded as the top man in his field, with experience in the United States Army's Special Forces and the CIA.

He was a determined man and he didn't like to lose. Lionfish and the rest of RedTide's comic book heroes had been avoiding every trap MacGregor had set for them these past two years and he was not a man who particularly enjoyed or handled humiliation well.

He was also not a man who made excuses or tolerated them from others. Something had to happen soon. Lowell, or Blowfish as he was called inside RedTide's organization, had given them little information that they could now use. Lowell did mention, however, that the one Achilles heel that Lionfish seemed to have was his strong protective feelings toward his friend and partner, the man known as Stingray. Surprisingly, Stingray had arrogantly scheduled an appearance on CNN's *Larry King Live* show sometime in the next few months.

How could MacGregor find out where they would broadcast from and could this possibly be the opportunity he had been waiting for?

"Yamaguchi San, I assure you we will increase our efforts tenfold, and we will recruit more informants from the FBI and Interpol and from the media."

Especially CNN, MacGregor thought to himself.

"I won't let you down. You have my word," MacGregor said as he bowed and left the room. Yamaguchi went back to his desk and lowered himself into his highback leather chair. He reached out to pick up the antique silver frame that held a photograph of his late son. He stared at the photo of his son graduating from Yale university in the United States and with tears in his eyes he promised his son for the last time that he would not let him down.

CHAPTER 6

I AWOKE THIS MORNING feeling much stronger than I had the past few days. The Primaquine and Chloraquine seemed to be doing their jobs in eliminating the Malaria parasites that had built their dream home in my liver. What a horrible picture that made for, tiny little microscopic organisms feasting on my organs while they raised a family.

The doctors said that there was almost no chance of a recurrence according to the lab report information about the type of strain I had become infected with. That was good news. I didn't relish the idea of a life filled with recurring 105 degree fevers. Jacqueline was going to pick me up this morning around 10:00 A.M. and then we were going to pick up our mom for our trip upstate.

The weather outside looked beautiful through the window of my room and I was hoping it wasn't too cold. I had a dream last night that I was visiting with my mother in prison, more specifically death row, where she was spending her last few days before her scheduled execution by lethal injection. She was crying as I held her and I was pleading with the governor to issue a stay of execution or a pardon. I told him that she was dying of cancer and that she only had a few months left to live anyway. There really was no point in executing her and furthermore it would be more humane to let her out so she could spend the last few days of her life enjoying her freedom.

I remembered feeling so frustrated and so utterly helpless as I pleaded with this man who so obviously felt nothing for my mother's suffering. I have been having alot of dreams lately, some more disturbing than others. I can't remember the last time that I woke up not feeling desperately unhappy.

Two weeks ago while I was driving back to my mother's apartment from a friend's house in Manhattan, I called her to see if she wanted me to pick up anything for her to eat. She had almost no appetite left due to the chemotherapy and she had wasted away to skin and bones. It broke my heart every time I looked at her and remembered how beautiful she had once been, not so long ago and how proud she was of her thick curly hair and her high cheekbones.

Now her face was swollen from the steroids she was taking and she was forced to wear a ridiculous looking wig in order to cover her head, which was completely bald. She had not really eaten anything in a week and I was excited when she said yes to having me pick up some pasta for her.

My excitement quickly disappeared when she told me that she wanted rigatoni a-la vodka from Don Giovanni's in little Italy. I had crossed over the Triborough Bridge from uptown Manhattan fifteen minutes earlier and was now well into Queens on the Grand Central Parkway.

I told her I would stop at La Viola's in Fresh Meadows instead. The food is just as good and it was on my way. Her reply was that if it was too much trouble I shouldn't bother and that she only had a craving for Don Giovanni's sauce and she didn't want anything else.

This response was mixed with a combination of sarcasm and good old fashioned Jewish guilt which is an art form in the Stein family. We are quite expert at pushing each others buttons and in striking a nerve. My mother was definitely feeling better that day.

This was a very familiar pattern between me and my mother who I always perceived as being extremely dramatic and overly emotional and I fell into my role with ease. I play the part of the bratty, selfish, insensitive son.

I told my mother in no uncertain terms that I was not turning around and going all the way back to the city and furthermore that she was being ridiculous. I was actually starting to become angry with her. I told her that if she were really hungry that she should eat the pasta from La Viola and that she should also appreciate the fact that I was still doing her a favor.

Just before she angrily hung up on me she told me that I was an inconsiderate selfish child and that I shouldn't come into her room and bother her when I got home. For an instant I felt guilty and I considered turning around but it was too late in the play for that.

I had already switched into angry, stubborn mode and there was no turning back. I began pounding the steering wheel and the dashboard and was screaming at the top of my lungs from frustration when I looked to my right and saw a car full of teenagers laughing at me. I thought about picking up a bowl of pasta for my mom at La Viola anyway but I knew she would die of starvation before she would eat it. She would make me suffer for awhile and then eventually she would forgive me. My sister always says that she can't believe how much crap my mother has taken from me over the years and she constantly reminds me of what a lousy son I am. I of course feel frustrated and misunderstood because I'm the one who called my mother in the first place to ask if I could pick her up some dinner and now despite my good intentions I end up being the bad guy anyway.

Although my mother has a temper and can be incredibly stubborn she loves her children unconditionally. She called me every day that I was in the hospital and Jackie had to nearly tie her down to keep her from visiting.

My mother had mentioned on the phone the other day that she wanted to sit with me and my sister individually during our day's outing and talk privately about some things she had been remembering about our lives. I think that this was going to be the first step to her saying good-bye to us and I hoped that I would have the strength to listen to what she had to say without letting her see in my eyes or my face how painful this encounter was going to be for me.

I hoped that today I could stop being mad at her just long enough to tell her how much I loved her and how much I appreciated her. I still couldn't think in terms of saying or thinking that I would miss her for that would mean accepting the inevitable and I still couldn't deal with that reality, either in my heart or in my mind. The conversation that I knew my mother wanted to have with me today was one that I had been desperately trying to avoid and I knew in this brief moment of clarity which felt like a slap in the face that the time was quickly approaching for us to say our good-byes.

Jackie arrived at about 10:15 A.M. with a wonderful surprise in her hands, a homemade chocolate mousse pie. It is my personal favorite, next to her apple pie with the handmade crust. I always say that if I were

Conor I would probably weigh 300 pounds from all of my sister's cooking. She has no equal in the kitchen in my eyes. My father liked to consider himself a gourmet chef, although most of his cooking was inedible.

He did however bake wonderful breads and one of the few pleasant memories I have of him is being downstairs at the little nook in the kitchen and watching him teach Jackie to bake. The smell of the honey wheat bread and his specialty sourdough bread would permeate the entire house and we would all crowd around the kitchen table and eat it right out of the oven with lots of fresh melted butter. I remember watching my sister all covered in flour laughing and giggling at our father's obnoxious sense of humor. How she had loved him I thought, and how he had broken her heart.

My sister looked upset about something and I took this window of opportunity, a moment of possible vulnerability to engage her in conversation. She was chewing the inside of her cheek, a nervous habit that we all had in my family and her face was all contorted from what I knew from experience was an attempt to reach an existing cut or a piece of hanging skin.

Sometimes after a family fight we would all sit quietly in our neutral corners chewing away, from the onset of tension in the room. To an outside observer it would look like the mental ward at Bellevue, I suddenly thought to myself and I laughed out loud.

"What's so funny?" Jackie asked.

"Nothing I just had a funny thought. I think I'm just a little stir crazy from a week of being inside. What's bothering you beside the usual? Is Mom all right? Are we still going?"

Jacqueline turned to face me and her eyes were red and puffy. One tear ran down her cheek from her right eye. I could see she was fighting to stay in control when she said. "No Jacob, Mom is not all right. She's dying and that's what I wanted to talk to you about.

"Conor and I were talking on the way up here about what to do in regards to the arrangements."

"What arrangements?" I asked.

"What do you mean, what arrangements?" she responded in anger.

"Are you that fucking stupid or are you just going to pretend to ignore the horrible responsibilities we are all going to have to deal with? Are you planning on slipping away to Florida, leaving me and my husband to take care of everything?" Jacqueline screamed at me.

"I'm sorry Jackie," I said. "I admit I've been stalling for as long as I could but I don't really feel like having this conversation today. I also don't appreciate your negative attitude. The doctor said that the lung cancer had shrank to half its size and that there was a possibility that with radiation the tumors in Mom's brain could shrink to the point where they might be operable using pinpoint laser surgery or the gamma knife at Loma Linda.

"Can't this conversation wait till tomorrow. I was hoping we could just have a pleasant day in the country with each other and we both agreed that for Mom's sake we wouldn't fight. There's plenty of time to talk about this," I said.

"That's a typical response, Jake. It's unpleasant for you. Lets not interfere with Jake's plans or ruin his day. Mom's not here now and she can't get upset by this conversation.

"I don't like it any more than you do but the fact of the matter is that you're going back to Florida soon and time is quickly running out. Mom can hardly breathe without that oxygen concentrator and she's starting to forget things. She never eats, and when she does she can't hold it down for more than a few minutes.

"Who do you think holds her head and wipes her mouth and cleans her up? It certainly isn't you. She is starting to become incontinent and two days ago I had to help her put on a fucking diaper. How do you think that made me feel, Jake? Ten minutes earlier I had just finished diapering my daughter."

Conor to both our surprise actually chuckled at that remark until Jackie shot him a look that would frighten Satan himself.

"You come to her house for a few weeks near the end. We've been here dealing with this everyday and I haven't told you the half of it."

My sister continued unabated and every time she would describe the pain and indignity my mother had suffered the last few months it was like a blow to my midsection. I could feel my breathing become more rapid and a pain was beginning to rise in the pit of my stomach. My face became flushed and I could feel myself gradually losing control of my emotions. Suddenly the wall which I had been constructing over these last several months to protect myself started to deteriorate and I could feel the tears running down my face. The pain was expanding from the core of my body, searing and excruciating.

For the first time whatever instincts of psychological self preservation I was using or whatever defense mechanisms like denial that I had built around myself about the circumstances of our mother's illness had disappeared and the thought of actually losing her at this moment was agonizing beyond description.

I had never felt such a deep and penetrating pain in my life and I screamed as my crying deteriorated into a long anguished wail which I think shocked both my sister and Conor with its sudden unbridled ferocity.

Both of them broke into tears and we sat on my bed and held each other tight while my sister rubbed my hair and kissed me. It was the closest I had felt to her in a very long time and suddenly I felt a great relief at the release of so much pent up emotion. This was the first time I had allowed myself to cry since I had first heard the news of our mother's cancer.

On the drive over to our mother's house, we stopped at the grocery store to pick up some halvah, a dessert which is made from sesame seeds and is a personal favorite of our mother's. It was a beautiful autumn day and my first steps outside into the fresh cool air were joyous. The sky was cobalt blue and filled with large white and gray clouds The air temperature was approximately 62 degrees and I was looking forward to seeing my mother for the first time in a week.

Our mother's hospice worker, Clarice let us into the apartment and Mom was sitting up on the couch waiting for us. She was wearing beige, loose fitting corduroy pants with a beautiful cable knit sweater and dark alligator shoes.

Our mother was one of the best dressed women I knew and had very sophisticated taste. Growing up we always found it amusing how her large group of friends would imitate her changing fashions. She would always manage to outdo her wealthiest friends with only one tenth of their financial resources. She had become an expert at finding discount designer outlets and was unmatched at the art of accessorizing.

She worked at a prestigious hair salon on Long Island called Optimus and had recently become a full partner in the makeup and spa center. Her customers worshipped her and the owner, Ralph Cozzolino, was savvy enough in business to protect his client base from following her to her own establishment.

I got my natural talent for selling from my mother who could charm anyone out of anything. My sales manager always reminded us that people buy from people they like and one of his favorite expressions is "People don't care how much you know. They want to know how much you care." My mother had a gift for telling people just what they wanted to hear and in a way that made them believe it. I walked over to the couch and gave our mother a kiss on the cheek.

"Hi, Mom. I missed you this week. How do you feel today?"

"Never mind me, how are you? I've been worried sick. Your sister bullied me into staying home and not visiting you. I feel terrible. Malaria, of all things, she said in mock wonder with a trace of sarcasm. "You're very international and exotic, Jakey."

"I feel good, Mom. Just a little weaker than usual, but I'll be fine. How are you? Your color looks good."

"I feel pretty good today, Jake, although I'm a little pissed off. Your Great Aunt Esther was here this morning and I asked her to pick up a couple of pillows for me on the way over. She actually had the chutzpah to collect the exact amount from me including the tax. She asked me to get out of bed to give her $15.49 cents, can you believe the gall? Then when she was leaving she stole the appetizing dish your sister brought the other morning, right out of the fridge.

"She said she was visiting her children this afternoon and wanted to bring them a little lox. She took everything, the sable, the whitefish, over $100 worth of appetizing. She doesn't visit me for over two months and then she robs me.

"I called her at your cousin Joseph's house, "The Bigshot Gynecologist" and we had a big fight. I told her that after I'm dead if she rushes over and gets here before the coroner arrives she can probably make off with my jewelry.

"She burst into tears and hung up on me and now I'm feeling guilty about it. Should I call her and apologize, Jackie?" she asked my sister. While I was laughing, I grabbed our mother around the shoulders and I kissed her several times on the cheek.

"Don't call that cheap old bitch up for anything." I never liked my Aunt Esther. When we were children she always reminded us of that mean old lady from *The Wizard of OZ* that wanted to destroy Toto.

It was about time our mother told her off. She was the cheapest relative we had. For Jacquelines wedding, which cost 100 dollars a head, she gave her a set of lousy pot holders as a present. My mother was the peace keeper in our family and the central figure in organizing holidays and get togethers. I couldn't stand most of my relatives and if not for our mother's almost blind commitment to family ties I probably would not see or speak to them again.

"Don't be disrespectful, Jacob," our mother said. "Your aunt isn't my favorite person in the world either, but she's still family and when you're around me I don't want to hear that crap."

"I'm sorry, Mother dearest," I said in a sarcastic tone of voice. "I'm happy you put her in her place, is all I meant to say. You've been putting up with her and the rest of them for years and you never lose your cool or tell them where to get off and I'm sure despite the guilt your feeling right now it must have felt pretty good to blow off a little steam."

My mother smiled at me and called me over to the couch to sit beside her.

"Stop that pacing. You're making me nervous. Come sit down and tell me about your trip to Mexico and your job in Florida."

"You would have loved it in Cozumel, Mom. The water was aquamarine and turquoise for about a hundred yards from the beach and then where it hit the wall and it dropped to depths of over a 1000 feet the water turned dark navy blue, almost black.

"The horizon where the ocean met the sky was a stark contrast between the dark blue of the water and the baby blue pastel of the noonday sky, and the beach was like talcum powder, bright white and fine as flour. At midday, you couldn't even look at it without sunglasses on, and a cool breeze was always blowing."

"That sounds wonderful, Jake," my mother said with just a touch of sadness and a longing in her voice. "Tell me about the diving. Was it as good as the diving in Grand Cayman that you told me about last year?"

My mother loved for me to describe my diving trips to her. She was always a great lover of the ocean and of tropical fish. In our home we always had decorative fish motifs on plates, shower curtains, and at one time even on the wallpaper in our downstairs kitchen. My mother and I would watch all the National Geographic specials together especially the ones featuring Jacques Cousteau when I was growing up and she always had a coffee table book of underwater photography in the living room on display.

Unfortunately, my mother was not the athletic type and suffered from terrible claustrophobia, so the idea of attempting to scuba-dive was as appealing to her as a 500 foot bungee jump from a bridge.

Her enjoyment of the underwater world would always be limited to photographs, videos and stories from her son, the dive traveler. Her enthusiasm for my stories and descriptions of the sea never dampened and she was my favorite audience when it came to showing my underwater photographs. She never got bored and she always made me feel like my photography was artistic. She would often compare my work to her favorites in the field like David Doubilet, who is also my personal favorite and Christopher Newbert. On this trip I didn't get to take any pictures since I was diving with 5 or 6 beginners from my company who were counting on me to watch out for them.

"The best dive of the trip was when the divemaster and I went out alone to a dive site called Punta Sur on the southern point of the reef," I began. "The current was very strong because the reef formation formed a point or a peninsula underwater and we had to descend rapidly to catch the entrance to the tunnels before we drifted out to sea.

"We did a backward roll into the water and swam as hard and as fast as we could to reach the sandy bottom below and to escape the strongest currents that were in the shallow waters. When we reached the bottom my dive computer read eighty-seven feet and I was already breathing hard from the descent. I followed Jorge, my divemaster, into the mouth of a large cave or tunnel entrance which became a chute that descended to over 120 feet by the time we reached the exit on the wall side of the reef.

"I love to enter these chutes which start in shallow water and wind down to deeper waters shooting you out over the wall like a giant slide.

You can look down into the dark blue infinity beyond the wall that descends for over 3000 feet. It feels like flying when you are perfectly neutral and weightless in the eighty degree water and the only sound you hear is your expelled air rising in bubbles to the surface.

"The color of the water changes from clear blue to a dark navy and eventually to black as dark and cold as midnight. I like to look out into the distance and see if I can spot any large animals such as whale sharks or manta rays that swim in the deeper waters off the wall. Jorge led me to shallower waters and as we rose to seventy or eighty feet some of the gray shading of the reef started to become colorized by the light from the surface which was able to reach it and illuminate it.

"We entered another cave whose mouth was ringed in large black gorgonian coral like a black veil covering the face of a widow and enormous purple sea fans and orange elephant ear sponges. The reef was teeming with schools of tiny blue chromies and yellow and white schoolmasters and several large groupers. As we entered the tunnel it continued to grow more narrow until it was only large enough to fit one man at a time in single file order.

"Jorge removed a light from the pocket of his bouyancy vest and he began to light our way through the twisting and turning cavern. When he shined his light on the caves ceiling you could see large patches of black coral. I looked at my pressure gauge and it read 1000 pounds of air left. My computer indicated seventy-three feet and we had been under for over eighteen minutes. Because of the depth and the current I was using up my air supply quickly, which always makes me anxious when I am in a tunnel with no visible exit. I decided to trust my dive guide and my own skills and experience. I figured I could always turn around and come out the way I went in."

By this point in the story I could see that my mother was completely enthralled, especially I knew from experience by the parts in the story that most frightened her, like being seventy feet under water in a cramped space. Conor and my sister had stepped out onto the terrace to admire the view of the Throgs Neck Bridge, and I could see by the way Jackie was shuffling around that she was anxious to get going.

"Maybe we should finish this in the car Mom. We have a long drive and we don't want to wear you out too early."

"Don't stop now, Jake. I'm really enjoying this and you don't have to treat me like an invalid. Your sister does enough of that for everyone."

"You know Jackie better than anyone, Mom. She's always been a worrier and she likes everything to go perfectly, according to her plan. Your being sick is something that has really shaken her. You two have become very close over the last couple of years since Erin was born and she's terribly afraid of losing you. We both are." I could feel the sadness that I always held at bay begin to wash over me as my eyes filled with tears.

My mother took both my hands in hers and said, "Jacob, I'm very proud of your adventurous spirit and your ability to just pack up and travel to far off places all by yourself. I've always envied you, even though I have always been afraid for you at the same time. You're finally becoming settled and you're successful at work. I never worry about your sister taking care of herself or Erin, but I've always worried about your future. You've never seemed to have any direction. I wanted to spend so much more time with you and your sister and someday I would have liked to have met your wife and to have held your children.

"I always wanted to go to Italy and see Florence and Venice. I have always wanted to shop in Europe," my mom said and laughed between her tears.

"I want to have my family all around me this holiday season, Jake. Promise me you will be here for the holidays." She was quiet for a moment and we looked into each others eyes. She broke my heart by saying, "I'm not ready to die, Jacob. I'm afraid." She began to shake and to sob while I held her.

I could feel my own tears streaming down my face and I could taste the salt in my mouth. "Please don't be afraid, Mom. There are alot of procedures we haven't even checked into yet. One of the doctors in the hospital told me about a procedure called the gamma knife at Loma Linda University in New Mexico that uses pinpoint laser surgery or radiation- I'm not sure which- to remove tumors without damaging healthy tissue."

Although Jackie had told me in the hospital that my mother was not a candidate for this procedure, we had all taken up lying lately to protect my mother from what she already knew, the truth. I changed the subject.

"Let me finish my story and then we will go upstate and we will have a wonderful day in the country," I said. "We finally reached the mouth of the exit and just as we were going to swim out a large green sea turtle swam by the opening. The cave was pitch black and the opening was a blue framed in black that was so bright it looked like neon.

"The turtle looked like it was set in a picture frame and I swam as fast as I could after it so that I could get a closer view, but although it looked like it was swimming very leisurely it swam off out of view very rapidly. We came out of the cave and settled at about forty feet and drifted in the current heading downstream as a couple of turquoise and yellow queen angelfish and a large grouper joined us and swam along side of us so that they could beg for the free handouts that divers sometimes carry in their vests, such as Cheese Wiz or crackers.

"The boat on the surface knew to follow our bubbles and to drift along with us on the surface. It always amazes me how the current can change speed according to your depth. If you swim up five to ten feet you are suddenly cruising faster and you can control your speed as you drift by ascending or descending into different speeds of current. It's Like changing the gears on your car. I have been 100s of yards behind a group of swimmers at my depth and have ascended into the quicker currents in order to catch up to them.

"You can almost visualize the comparison to a raging river in a jungle or a forest on the surface. It can be extremely exhilarating flying weightless through the water at what feels like thirty to forty miles an hour. I have met divers who have dove above falls like Niagara and flown at speeds approaching fifty to sixty miles an hour. We neutralized our bouyancy and floated five feet off the bottom while we spun in 360 degree turns floating vertically, standing straight up so that we could play with the angelfish and the groupers. Some of the groupers in the Caribbean are so tame from exposure to divers that you can pet them and almost scratch them behind their ears like housepets.

"Jorge took some cut up squid out of his vest and began feeding it to the grouper. He then handed a piece to me, and as I turned to face the grouper, it bit me on the hand in an attempt to grab the food. I have never seen anyone bitten by a grouper and the pain and burning in my hand startled me. Dark green and black, the colors of blood underwater were streaming from the puncture wounds in my palm and thumb, and I looked over at Jorge and gave him the thumbs up sign to ascend.

"When we got back on the boat, I was able to see that my wound was not as severe as I had thought and as Jorge and the captain of the boat exchanged words in Spanish they kept looking in my direction and laughing.

"I spoke some of the only Spanish words that I had picked up on my trip. Laughingly I said, 'Jorge no tiene propina,' which is a close approximation to "Jorge must not want a tip." It quickly ended the hilarity and his expression turned serious until I wrapped my arm around his shoulder and said muchos gracias for a great dive.

"Then we spoke all the way back to the dock about diving and about the beauty of Mexico's coral reefs. When I got back to the hotel for revenge I ordered a grouper sandwich for lunch and it was especially delicious."

The end of my story had the desired effect and my mom's mood was much improved. She laughed out loud and hugged me as my sister and Conor entered from the terrace. I was thinking about what Jorge had told me on the boat on the way back to the hotel. He had been very upset about the Mexican government granting permission to a cruise ship line to build a large concrete and steel port structure on the reef in Cozumel.

Blasting and digging had already begun to destroy large sections of live coral and despite several vigilant environmental groups lobbying against it, work had gone ahead as planned. I never considered myself an environmentalist and although I love the outdoors and especially the oceans I had always been too lazy or too apathetic to get personally involved. I sent checks twice a year to Greenpeace and to the Cousteau Society and felt that I was doing my part. This news, however, coming on the heels of such a spectacular dive to the very reefs that were now under siege hit very close to home and for the first time in my life I was considering doing something other than making a donation.

CHAPTER 7

"MIGHTIEST THING EVER BUILT BY A MAN, to run the factories for old uncle Sam." Lionfish was remembering the words to the song Woody Guthrie had written about the Grand Coulee Dam in 1941, when it was under construction. Lionfish was thinking about the information Stingray had presented to him when he first proposed this mission and the subsequent follow-up information he had given the team during initial briefings and lectures.

Lionfish and Stingray had spent three weeks in the Valley of the Great Whale in Northern Quebec, scouting the operation site and planning and organizing logistics and strategy. It was an ironic name for this valley since it was the plight of the white beluga whales that first attracted Stingray's attention to the area. These lovely white creatures live near estuaries at the edge of the sea where the fresh water from inland rivers mixes with the saltwater of the ocean. They share this environment with the Arctic char, the bearded seal and the Canada goose.

The whales had reportedly been dying off at an alarmingly high rate and at a surprisingly young age and further research had determined that there were unusually high levels of PCBs in their systems, causing lung disease, cancer, and ulcers. Stranger still there were traces of an insecticide called Mirex, which was manufactured inland and would have had to have been either washed downstream or been carried by an animal that was eaten by the whales to get into their systems.

The water inland from the bay was also detected to carry Selenium, a chemical which was killing ducks in the area. This operation would be RedTides first inland mission. The object as he and Stingray had discussed was to enlighten the general population to the inexorable connection between the pollution in the worlds rivers, lakes, and air, to the eventual destruction of our planet's entire water system including the world's oceans which had recently been shown to, in fact, be one continuous body of water.

Stingray had explained to the group months earlier during the initial stages of planning that if all the earth's water was contained in a one gallon jug that all the world's available fresh water would fit into one tablespoon, less than half of one percent of the total.

Over ninety seven percent of the earth's water is seawater and the demand on an overpopulated planet for fresh water is polluting the entire earth's water systems including its oceans at an alarming rate. It never ceased to amaze Lionfish how some greedy businessman swinging his driver on a lush green fairway in the middle of the Sonoran desert could be so blinded by his own selfish pursuits as to not even consider how they watered the grass or where the water came from. It takes enormous quantities of fresh water to keep a golf course alive and healthy in such a hostile and arid climate.

Not to mention the numerous insecticides and fertilizers that are used which eventually seep into the groundwater and finally mix with his own drinking supply, the very same water that his wife and children drink from their tap every day.

"*Maybe it was time for an education from Professor Lionfish*," he amused himself by thinking as he sighted and scanned his high powered Ziess binoculars on the 500 or so workers who were scaffolded around the curving concrete wall of the two-thirds completed dam they were building.

Lionfish and Stingray had become friendly with the local Indians of the Cree tribe who had lived and hunted in the area for over 5,000 years. The Cree were concerned about the large Caribou herds and about additional damage to their ancient burial grounds as well as additional impact to the natural resources in the area. Lionfish and Stingray were posing as photographers for a magazine with a known environmental bias and were readily accepted by the locals in the area. For obvious reasons they were keeping a very low profile and the cover allowed them to take pictures of the areas they would be penetrating without raising any undue suspicion. As Lionfish studied the area he became troubled by the number of employees who were still working and the heightened security in response to written protests from "environmental extremists," including his own organization. *How could he plant enough explosives to irreparably damage the dam site without having to kill hundreds of innocent construction workers who were only trying to earn a living?* he wondered.

He was convinced from the countless reams of data that Stingray had compiled that this dam would do little to increase employment in the area and that the long term environmental damage it would cause would have a ripple effect that would be felt from the inland waterways to the depths of the oceans, but he was still hesitant to kill innocent people. Most of the civilians RedTide had killed had been accidental collateral damage and on every operation, every contingency was made to avoid that cost.

Lionfish was going to need some type of a distraction to remove as many workers as possible from the site on the day RedTide planned their attack. Stingray had some ideas in that area and as usual Lionfish would defer to his greater intellect in the areas of technical planning. They were a perfect partnership and complemented each other very well by balancing and checking each other's strengths and weaknesses. Recently the group had been experimenting with non-lethal weapons such as gas and firearms which could stun and immobilize a target. Although Lionfish was skeptical about the practicality of using such armaments against a heavily armed opposition force, Stingray was enthusiastic about their partial use in less confrontational situations and was working on implementing their use on this current operation.

Lionfish had a long discussion a few days ago with one of the leaders of a small village at the mouth of a river along the Hudson Bay and as he counted the number of armed security personnel and sighted the location of the external cameras and alarm systems he recalled their conversation. The chief of the village recalled how Aqua-Canada the company currently working on the dam RedTide had targeted for destruction had previously diverted the sacred waterways and rivers including the Eastmain, the Opinaca, and the Caniapiscau to feed the 500-mile-long La Grande, increasing its flow ten times the normal amount to build two other hydro electric facilities.

The Eastmain had subsequently dried to a trickle. This river had been fished by the chiefs tribe since long before the white man ever set foot on the continent and now it was gone.

Numerous animals had been displaced including lynx, black bears and North America's largest herd of caribou. When all the projects Aqua-Canada had planned were completed an area smaller than Wyoming would have over thirty dams and 500 dikes.

The government's position was that Aqua-Canada was providing jobs and power but research showed that the jobs and electricity would be hundreds of miles from the area where the actual building would take place and the local residents would only have the environmental fallout from upriver factories and cities to deal with, much of which was already showing up in the local fish and in their drinking water.

The chief explained that the government was not concerned with a small populace in a remote area and that Aqua-Canada had already provided over twelve billion dollars to the economy and built roads and airports in the surrounding area. Environmentalists brought in by local tribes including the Inuit were calling the proposed destruction of the area monstrous and comparing it in scale to the destruction of the rain forest.

Once the dam begins to provide massive quantities of electricity to the area, factories move in at the invitation of the government. Metal and aluminum manufacturing which was already pouring chemicals into the area at other sites would now flood into the Great Whale Valley. The chief explained that they already had to limit fishing because of high levels of methylmercury, a nuero toxin which was showing up in the pike and lake trout they had been eating. There had been an increase in the levels since the flooding in the area increased decay of the local vegetation. Many native citizens had gotten sick from eating the fish. The chief was also concerned about the habitat of the caribou since the building of the new dam would flood the best feeding grounds in the north country.

Lionfish was concerned, he told the chief, with recent studies of the marine ecology that showed changes in the delicate balance of the sub-arctic regions waters. Lionfish explained that the food chain is dependent on spring blooms of algae and phytoplankton which are dependent on an exact blend of fresh and salt water. "If you change the mix even slightly you would disrupt a food chain that supplied local fishermen and Cree and Inuit Indians who traveled hundreds of miles to fish these waters. It could even affect fisherman as far away as Newfoundland.

The nature of water to move, dissolve, and carry substances is remarkable. Just look at the Grand Canyon in Arizona. The mixture of hydrogen and oxygen is referred to as the universal solvent and what it can't dissolve it grinds up into suspension and moves along. If you were to pour poison into the driest most parched desert, water would pick it up, molecule by molecule and because water is always moving somewhere it will carry it away. Heavy seepage from upriver factories into the air or ground will eventually reach groundwater that will carry the lead and iron oxides and other poisons into our oceans and drinking water.

Technically, water pollution can be divided into two types: point source pollution-waste dumped by factories or sewage plants and non-point source pollution-otherwise known as polluted runoff. In most cases, non-point source pollution is worse. Polluted runoff is what happens when you spill oil on the driveway and then hose it down. It happens when a lettuce field is treated with a herbicide and then it rains. It happens when someone throws a dead battery into a gully. It happens when a farmer's cow strolls through a stream. It happens when a gardener sprays his lawn with fertilizer. It happens when someone cleans their car with a solvent like ArmorAll and dumps or washes the liquid off his car and into the street. Water picks it all up and adds it to the system, oil, manure, lead, phosphorous, nitrogen.

Out of an EPA list of 18,770 impaired water sites, only 529 were polluted primarily by toxic point sources. Most are polluted by the average American citizen. Even the water in local springs and aquifers in remote and what were once perceived as pristine wildernesses were showing incredibly high levels of bacteria. This was more than just a mild case of acid rain. Recently in a remote wilderness in the Yukon territory a study of fish turned up a variety of chemicals including the insecticide Toxaphene, which was widely used in Russia. It obviously blew east and was collected by the rain. Recent pediatric studies from highly polluted areas such as Brownsville, Texas showed increasingly high incidences of birth defects such as Spina Bifida. Doctors in the area were convinced that it was caused by the Rio Grande, the most polluted river in the world.

The EPA had no control over what took place in horribly polluted countries like Russia and Mexico and their problems were our problems. It was no longer just a concern for the "tree huggers" and the "whale people."

In Washington state at the Hanford Site Nuclear Waste Storage facility they struggle to contain groundwater containing carbon tetrachloride, a proven carcinogen.

Lionfish suddenly realized that he had been lecturing this poor old man and that he was carrying on like a religious zealot. He was only supposed to be here on assignment for a magazine and although he was supposed to show a little concern about the environment he had to remain professionally detached.

He apologized to the chief and thanked him for his time and started to walk away when the chief walked up behind him and gently turned him around. The chief of the village asked him who he really was. He told him that he spoke like a scientist not a photographer and he told him that he was both very knowledgeable about their problems and that he seemed to be very passionate about the issues.

He then smiled and asked Lionfish if he was part Indian and commented on his complexion and his bone structure. Lionfish was taken aback by the man's questions and made his escape as quickly and politely as he could. He got in his truck and started the drive back to the fishing lodge that he and the other twenty or so men who had all arrived from different locations and with different covers were staying. He thought about his mother and how she herself had been so passionate about protecting the environment and as he looked out at the mountains covered in thick groves of lodgepole pine he wondered if she would have approved of what he was trying to do or if she would have been critical of his actions.

He told himself that although she would probably have disapproved of his methods, she would have understood his motives. It had been almost twenty years since she had been killed and he thought about her every day. Today he found himself missing her more than usual. The raid was planned for the twentieth anniversary of her death. Every year for the last ten years Lionfish had commemorated the anniversary with an operation of great significance. This was the best way he knew to honor her memory.

He was looking forward to getting back to the lodge and discussing what he had learned today with Stingray. He was the only one who could cheer him up when he got a bad case of the blues and it was time for them to start finalizing their plans for taking down the dam. He was anxious to hear Stingray's ideas for instigating an evacuation of the construction site. The truck containing the extremely powerful high explosives they had stolen was scheduled to arrive in five days and they needed to be ready to convert it into individual devices which would be compact enough for storage and transport down the face of the dam but powerful enough to destroy it.

Tarpon, their explosives expert, was arriving tomorrow and would have the difficult task of creating weapons which would meet their size requirements and also meet their requirements for destructive force. Lionfish had suggested one large weapon, detonated from a truck at the bottom of the dam, and Tarpon had instructed him that unless at least five or six individual weapons were placed at strategic structural points along the wall they would waste most of the force of the blast and wind up only blowing out the middle, as well as destroying the surrounding environment themselves.

Tarpon was working on something along the lines of a fusion device or a small thermonuclear weapon, but anything that would emit radiation was out of the question and it would be almost impossible to obtain the materials required to build it. Tarpon would have to devise something which would be manufactured using available materials such as plastic explosives and nitro-glycerin and could be built to cause a chain reaction similar to a fusion type weapon.

This would be a task which would be easier said than done and Tarpon was also working on a fuel/air type of weapon. They needed to take out the entire wall to make the type of statement they were trying to make and to delay future construction for an extended period of time. The damage would set Aqua-Canada back hundreds of millions of dollars and at least one to two years on their timetable for completion.

This would also allow more time for the Cree and Inuit Tribes to fight their battle in court. Shortly after the raid, Stingray would be appearing on the *Larry King Live* show and he would explain to the world, among other things, what was happening in this area of the world and why RedTide felt compelled to act.

Lionfish was dead set against the idea and was afraid for Stingray's safety. Every law enforcement agency in the world would be watching that show and looking for clues. Stingray might inadvertently say something that could give away their identities or their origins.

Yamaguchi would also be watching and if possible planning for a way to apprehend or kill Stingray at the broadcast. Stingray had finally convinced Lionfish of the necessity to educate the world about the problems that were spiraling out of control in the environment. The most dangerous thing of all, Stingray said, was not necessarily what was going on in the world but the rampant widespread ignorance of people who think that things are getting better or are under control because they see a smiling dolphin on their can of tuna when they shop at the local supermarket.

He had every assurance from the network that he would be safe and RedTide's own security people would be organizing the meeting. Lionfish would have ultimate control of the situation and would cover all the bases in protecting his lifelong friend. As Lionfish pulled into the driveway of The Elkhorn Fishing Lodge, he was listening to a song called "The Indifference of Heaven" by Warren Zevon on the tape deck, "A gentle rain falls on me and all life folds back into the sea. We contemplate eternity beneath the vast indifference of heaven."

Stingray was sitting in a wooden rocking chair, handmade from twisted pine branches on the back porch of his private cabin. He was staring out across the lake at the mountains that rose majestically at a steep angle from its shoreline. He was deep in thought as Lionfish approached and tossed a package into his lap.

"Hey big guy, you startled me. What's this a present? It's not even my birthday," Stingray said in his usual lighthearted manner.

"No numbnuts, it's the construction plans and blueprints for the dam site," Lionfish said as he raised his eyebrows repeatedly in an uncharacteristic comical gesture.

Stingray looked stunned for a moment and said, "You're a genius. How did you get a hold of these? Tarpon will be as happy as a pig in shit. Oh, and don't call me numbnuts, you overgrown poster boy for steroids or I'll jump out of this chair and slap the piss out of you."

"That's some language for a man with a Ph.D. in bio-chemistry. You're the genius and I'm just a grunt, remember," Lionfish said laughingly.

Stingray jumped up from his chair and assumed the stance of a late 1800s pugilist. He began shuffling around and poking at the air in front of Lionfish's face while shouting invectives at him. Lionfish was laughing so hard that he was doubled over until Stingray caught him on the jaw with an uppercut. Lionfish stood straight up with a scowl on his face which startled Stingray and made him take two steps back while hurling out rapid fire apologies as Lionfish approached.

"Don't fuck with me, you little runt. I'm not in the mood," Lionfish said as he grabbed Stingray around the legs and shoulders and with no more effort than it would take to lift a child he military pressed him straight over his head.

Lionfish began walking down the stairs of the cabin toward the lake while Stingray alternated between begging and threatening while swinging his arms in an effort to strike at his captor.

"Let me down, you fucking musclehead. I'm telling you for the last time. I swear I will find a way to kill you. Poison, or maybe I'll tamper with your scuba tanks. You know I'll find a way. This is your last chance."

"I'm going to let you down, very shortly in fact. Just be patient... we're almost there," Lionfish said, as he hurled Stingray into the lake.

The water was glacier fed and hovered at somewhere around fifty degrees. Stingray screamed when he surfaced and shouted curses between blue lips at Lionfish who was howling with laughter on the shore.

"I have to thank you, my friend. When I drove over here I was really in a foul mood and only you could have made me laugh today. Come on, let's get you inside next to the fire before you freeze your ass off. We can't afford for you to get sick little man," Lionfish said with a tenderness in his voice that he reserved only for his closest friend.

"Fuck you," Stingray screamed. You should have thought of that before you decided to play the schoolyard bully again, and don't call me little man. You know I hate that."

Lionfish wrapped his arm around Stingray's shoulder and spoke quietly as they walked toward the main lodge building and the cavernous fireplace, masoned from large river stones.

"Do you remember when we were kids and we would fight and Hannah would have to practically beat us with a stick to pull us apart. I was thinking about her today," Lionfish said.

"Hannah was a great lady, I miss her as well. I also miss the days when we were the same size, before you grew to be a giant and I could still hold my own against you," Stingray said. They entered the lodge and were welcomed by riotous laughter from their men as Stingray entered the room dripping wet and looking like a drowned puppy.

Tarpon arrived later that night and got to work immediately on the plans and drawings Lionfish had miraculously gotten his hands on. When Lionfish was asked how he had gotten them he responded that "in America anything was for sale, and that was the main reason why they were in this business to begin with."

Lionfish had an ironic, black sense of humor and was not in a talkative mood so Tarpon let it go at that. The drawings were a godsend and Tarpon was already close to solving some of the main problems he had been working on during the flight out that afternoon. Where to place the weapons was his responsibility. How to place them was going to be extremely difficult and would require special climbing and rappelling equipment, but that was going to be Lionfish's problem.

D Day was three nights away and Stingray still had not finalized his plans for evacuating the facility. If he didn't, then over 500 men were going to meet their maker very soon. Tarpon knew from experience that Lionfish would not alter from the scheduled day no matter what the consequences. That is why he always allowed himself extra time for planning. Two helicopters were being brought in this afternoon by truck and would need to be partially reassembled after their arrival. They were to be kept at an old run down farmhouse a quarter of a mile away, and Lionfish had bought out the entire fishing lodge six months in advance.

Tarpon had joined up with the group five years ago and by that time Lionfish had already become somewhat of a legend. The recruitment and initial screening had taken over six months and it had been two full years before Tarpon had been included in any training or strategic planning sessions. He was used strictly as a subcontractor and was paid only for the weapons he delivered.

He would be given his orders by coded messages left at a location he would receive by phone that day and then he would be literally kidnapped months later and delivered to the operation site on the day of the operation, blindfolded and confused. He was now RedTide's top demolition expert and he was well compensated, although he had to live his life in secret, with no more freedom than someone in a witness protection program.

His loyalty and silence were randomly tested by RedTide's undercover operatives, who sometimes posed as law enforcement agents and sometimes as corporate mercenaries trying to buy information.

Sometimes the stress and paranoia were more than he could take and Tarpon would complain to Lionfish that he was at his breaking point. At those times Lionfish would send him away on a trip around the world or would put him up on a Caribbean island to unwind, all expenses paid and all first class. Lionfish was a good leader and spoiled his men. They not only respected and admired him, they worshipped him and were extremely loyal. The biggest downside of his life was that he could never leave the organization and he would spend the rest of his life looking over his shoulder. Tonight there would be a final planning meeting between the team leaders and Stingray and Lionfish. Tarpon was hoping that he would please his boss and that his counterparts would have their parts worked out by then. He would be working all day tomorrow on assembling the explosive devices and would need to get a good night's rest before the tedious and extremely dangerous work of setting the detonators could begin.

"Welcome campers, to Operation Wrecking Ball," Lionfish began. "I trust you're all ready to begin this meeting and are refreshed from your travels," Lionfish said to the six men assembled in the private dining room of the lodge. There were news vans staged outside the lodge and various pieces of video and camera equipment arranged around the property as well as plastic ID badges to enhance the visual image that went along with the story Lionfish had told the lodge owners about doing a news story on the dam.

The two helicopter pilots known as Flying Fish 1 and Flying Fish 2 were in the room as well as Tarpon, Stingray, and the two team leaders, each of whom would command ten men each per helicopter.

"Stingray will speak first on the initial stages of the operation which will involve evacuating the facility and immobilizing the remaining men left on the premises," Lionfish said.

"Hello gentlemen and thank you for coming," Stingray began. "We are about to strike a blow for clean water and once again focus the world's attention on the ecological problems that plague this planet as no other organization before us has been able to do since the first introduction of RedTide onto the worlds environmental stage. I won't get too preachy since you have all been well briefed on the reasons for the selection of our current target.

"I have been experimenting with a non-lethal gas derived from the toxins of the Australian blue-ringed octopus and have been successful at refining a gas that will paralyze and immobilize a large group of men for up to two hours. It can be delivered by a gas cloud over a large geographic area.

"Step one will be to warn the Cree and Inuit Indians protesting at the site to leave the area. That will be handled by Lionfish first thing in the morning by a discreet meeting with several of their chiefs and leaders.

"Step two will be to call in a bomb threat twenty minutes before we strike. We have factored in that much time to evacuate the end of the day shift that totals around 450 men and to allow time before the night shift comes on.

"Step three is where the flying fish come in. Each aircraft will contain two large drums affixed with impact detonators of the gas that we are calling BLUERING. The drums will be dropped at the bottom of the gorge and the wind will carry it upward in a funnel which will engulf the entire structure. This has already been tested on a smaller scale by burning some figures in effigy along with the protesters at the bottom of the ravine three days ago.

"Each helicopter gunship will also carry ten heavily armed men, none of whom will be equipped with non-lethal weapons as I would have liked, a point I have conceded to our leader," Stingray said with a nod and a wink in Lionfish's direction.

"I will take over now. Thank you Stingray," Lionfish said and Stingray's exit was followed by a round of applause from the men in the room which visibly embarrassed Stingray who went to stand in the corner.

"In Step four, the helicopters will land on the top of the structure and unload the men and two large four wheeled dolleys which will be used to collect any and all unconscious workers left on the structure. They will then be lifted by helicopter for removal while me along with five other hand-picked men will rappel down the face of the dam and place the charges at the points on your drawings that Tarpon has indicated.

"Step five. The choppers will return from unloading the workers and remove me and the men from the structure. We will have only fifteen minutes. That is what the timers will be set for, so there can be no screwups at either end. The vans and other equipment will be abandoned and we will make our escapes by helicopter. You are all to carry your individual escape routes on your person at all times and you are not to discuss them with any other members of the team. Is that clear?"

"Yes sir, Lionfish Sir," the men responded mockingly.

"I don't get no respect," Lionfish said and he finished up by asking if there were any questions. No one raised a hand. "Since there are no questions, I want the team leaders to break out into individual groups with their men after dinner and review this plan until they can do it in their sleep.

"Now let's eat. The cook is grilling up a huge mess of baby back ribs and corn on the cob, and I for one am starving," Lionfish said as he opened the doors to bark out his orders to the cook. The cook had to do most of the work himself since Lionfish had sent away the kitchen staff and waiters a few days earlier. After dinner, Lionfish stepped out into the cool night air. On his way to see Stingray and Tarpon at his cabin, he felt a combination of exhilaration and anxiety. He always felt that way on the eve of a mission. He had grown fond of this place and the mountains and the native people he had met. He had spent his entire life in tropical climates following his mother around the world and had not spent any time in country such as this. He liked the cool temperatures and the pine scented fresh tasting air. He felt gratified that he was going to help the native people preserve the natural beauty of this area and to protect their way of life a while longer.

At first light, Lionfish strode into the encampment of the Cree chieftain he had spoken with days earlier. On the edge of the camp stood a lone teepee used only as decoration against a backdrop of the lake and mountains. The sun was just rising and the sky was a greyish blue, filled with pink and silver ribbon-shaped clouds. As Lionfish looked up, an American bald eagle circled over head and then dove for the mirrorlike surface of the lake. At the last second it raked its large talons across the surface and flew off with a trout in its claws.

Lionfish was transfixed by the amazing sight as a voice spoke in his ear and startled him, bringing him back to earth.

"Beautiful country we have here. You can understand why we fight so hard to protect her," the Cree chief said in a voice filled with remembrances of days long past.

"This is one of the most beautiful places I have ever seen," Lionfish responded. "I could easily see myself settling down in a place like this, if I were not so bound to the sea," Lionfish said.

"You are a mysterious man," the chief replied. "I look at you and I see a man of great strength but also a gentle spirit with an appreciation of beauty. I also see great pain in your eyes and I have heard you speak with anger in your heart. You speak like a chief, with wisdom and with knowledge and you demonstrate a great understanding of the natural world. You do not seem like a man who has found much peace in his life and I feel that you suffer from much inner turmoil."

Lionfish would have liked to have ignored the chief's words and in his usual sarcastic and cynically way to have likened them to the type of monologue he would get from a psychic healer after calling a 900 number. But he liked the man and although they had only spoken on several occasions he felt a bond with this kindred spirit.

"No one would ever describe me as gentle, chief. I have hurt many people in my life, whether it was justified or not and I will hurt many more before I'm through. I do appreciate the beauty in the world but I also see so much greed and destruction that it makes me sick, mentally and physically. Sometimes I get tired and I lose my faith, but I somehow manage to go on. You're a good man, that much is obvious. Tell me how you manage to keep your faith while the way of life your people have enjoyed for thousands of years is taken away?"

"Life is a perfect balance between good and evil," the chief said softly. "Every culture from the American Indians to the people of Asia speaks of this. Your bible contains countless stories of the battle between good and evil. We must continue to fight our battles as bravely and with as much determination as we can, while at the same time not losing sight of the beauty in the world and without losing ourselves and becoming like our enemies."

"If we allow ourselves to become corrupted by the wars we wage or to be made cynical by our efforts to protect what we hold precious then we have surely lost all," the chief said.

Lionfish turned back to the lake and said, "Thank you, Chief, for meeting with me today. I'm sorry the other chiefs could not join us but I am also grateful for this private conversation. I trust you and I must ask that you and your people not attend the protests at the dam today. Something is going to happen and I want your people as far away from danger as possible. As you probably know by now, I am not a photographer."

"I know who you are," the chief said, taking Lionfish by surprise. "I've known since our first meeting that you were not who you claimed to be. You have the bearing of a warrior, not an artist or a journalist. Please understand that we can do nothing to help you but neither will we betray you. Our fight must be one of passive resistance. It is the only way for us," the chief said.

Lionfish smiled and took the old man's hand in his. "We don't need any help, chief, other than your agreeing to keep out of harm's way. I must say good-bye now and thank you and your people for all your help these past weeks. I will miss this land and I wish you and all your people well. I will keep track of what takes place here after we leave and I assure you that we will take full responsibility for our actions and will leave your people blameless," Lionfish said.

"Good-bye my son and good luck," the chief replied. "Although I cannot condone your actions, my people thank you for your help and we will pray for your good health," the chief finished as Lionfish turned and walked away.

The operation would take place in less than twelve hours and Lionfish was running through things in his mind. He was also thinking about what the chief had said during their conversation and it reminded him of something his mother had once told him during a trip to the Galapagos Islands. She was explaining to him about Darwin and his *Origin of the Species*. She explained all about evolution and the need for all different types of life forms to exist in the world in order to maintain balance and order. She told him that even animals and creatures we normally abhor like leeches, bats and hyenas had an important role to play in the grand scheme of creation. Lionfish was only seven at the time and didn't understand what she had meant. He was now wondering what role nature could possibly have intended for man to play in the evolution of the planets ecology. Wherever man went he inevitably disrupted the balance of nature. All Lionfish could see was chaos and destruction if men were allowed to continue raping and plundering her at will. He would continue to play the role he believed nature had intended for him to play, as her guardian and protector. Today he would once again tip the scales in her favor.

The sun was beginning to set as the helicopters were warming up their engines outside the dilapidated barn where they had been housed for the last several days. All systems were go and the weather was ideal. In a few minutes the news vans containing the troops would be arriving and then the vans would be put in the barn and it would be set ablaze upon liftoff.

Stingray would be phoning in a bomb threat to the main headquarters of Aqua-Canada right about now with a stolen untraceable cellular phone and in a few minutes they would begin to evacuate the construction site and to call in the Royal Mounties. Bomb threats by RedTide were taken seriously since the organization was never known to bluff or to make idle threats.

Every eventuality had been planned for, even the response time of the local law enforcement agencies and the possibility of armed troops. The pilot checked his watch and it read 5:54 P.M., leaving six minutes until take off.

The vans were heading toward the helicopters when a police car pulled up behind them and they were forced to pull alongside the shoulder of the road. Stingray was in the back of the van with ten heavily armed soldiers and he began to sweat heavily and became very anxious. He was not supposed to have been in the van and was in direct violation of Lionfish's orders.

Stingray was supposed to have driven a rental car to the airport this morning and left before the operation began, but he wanted to stay through to the end so he could witness the first field use of his new gas bomb. He had managed to convince Sea-Wasp, one of the commanders riding with him now in this van as team leader, against his better judgment, to allow him to ride along.

Sea-Wasp knew Lionfish would gut him alive if anything happened to Stingray and as the officer approached the rear of the vehicle he released the safety on his Uzi machine gun.

"When I give the order, I want you to swing those doors open fast and fire at will," Sea-Wasp commanded.

"No," Stingray said. "I have a better idea. Let me handle this."

The men in the van exchanged nervous glances. Stingray was not a well respected leader when it came to the tactical deployment of forces and they were wondering what he had in mind.

"I'm in charge here Stingray, so sit down and be silent," Sea Wasp commanded. "I don't want you getting hurt or dirtying your hands with a policeman's blood."

"In case you've forgotten the hierarchy of this organization," Stingray explained, "I am second in command and for right now you will do as you are told," Stingray said in an uncharacteristic tone of voice to Sea-Wasp. "Trust me, I know what I'm doing."

The pilot checked his watch again and stepped outside the chopper to inform Lionfish that the vans were five minutes late.

"I know they're late, I have a watch," Lionfish said with an edge to his voice.

"Go back to the helicopter and wait. I'm sure everything is fine. They will be right along," Lionfish said, although he was thinking that they would not be late unless there were a problem.

Officer Kevin Williams was two feet from the back of the first van and had released the holster snap on his weapon when the rear doors of the van burst open and a man with a large automatic weapon jumped down from the back and aimed it in his direction.

Officer Williams knew he had no time to react and his last living thought would be about his wife and his daughter at home, just before he was gunned down. Instead of a barrage of bullets exploding from the weapon, a strange thick brown liquid emerged from the barrel and covered him in a thick, sticky paste. He fell to the ground and the more he struggled the more immobilized he became.

Strangely, his first reaction was relief to find that he was still alive and as he looked up at the heavily armed men in the van, the man who had showered him with the sticky goop he was now enveloped in leaned over and sprayed something in his face. Everything went black and he was unconscious in seconds.

"You see, I told you, you Neanderthals," Stingray said. "You don't always have to resort to deadly force. The non-lethal weapons I just used kept us from having to murder this innocent civilian."

"That's just wonderful, Stingray," Sea-Wasp responded. "But if he had his weapon drawn, or if he had backup, or if your experimental weapon had clogged or jammed you would now be lying in a pool of your own blood."

"Load him into the truck. We'll dump him with the other workers at the site," Sea-Wasp commanded.

Lionfish was looking anxiously up the road when the vans pulled into view. As the men unloaded from the back of the truck Lionfish saw them carrying the unconscious body of Officer Williams.

"What in the hell happened?" Lionfish asked Sea-Wasp.

"Ask him," Sea-Wasp responded, pointing toward the van.

Lionfish turned back to the van in time to see Stingray emerge from the rear. When Stingray locked eyes with Lionfish he smiled and shrugged his shoulders.

"What the fuck are you doing here!? We have made very precise arrangements for your departure. All hell is going to break loose once that dam goes down. What were you thinking, you stupid son of a bitch?"

Stingray had never seen Lionfish so angry and although he knew Lionfish would never harm him, he was a still a little frightened. But despite his trepidation about challenging Lionfish he was also determined to stand his ground.

"I'm staying to see how BLUERING works. It's never been field tested on more than one or two volunteers and if it were not for me this operation would not be possible," Stingray said as confidently as he could.

"Listen carefully," Lionfish said. "That chopper is already overloaded and now we have to carry the unconscious gift you brought for me. You still have time to get out of here and to take another flight. You can be at the airport before they shut it down. Now get going. Take one of the news vans. That's an order."

As the other men were loading into the chopper and pretending not to notice the exchange, Stingray said, "I am staying to help with the deployment of my gas. There's plenty of room, I checked with the pilot. And since when do I take orders from you, you self important egomaniac?" Stingray managed to get the last word out of his mouth, just before Lionfish struck him on the jaw.

Stingray was unconscious before he collapsed into the arms of one of the men standing behind him. "Nice catch, Orca," Lionfish growled. "Now put him in the chopper with me. Unfortunately he will have to come along, we're out of time. He'll have to escape with me," Lionfish said.

As he bent over Stingray, he rubbed his hand gently across his forehead and said "I'm sorry little man, I had no choice. Hopefully when you wake up you'll see it that way."

As the gunships flew into the Valley Of The Great Whale and approached the dam they could see that the initial stages of the plan were working out well. There were only thirty or forty men left on the platform and they appeared to be armed security officers preparing to exit the site last.

The helicopters dropped into the gorge at the base of the dam and dropped the four drums of BLUERING gas that Stingray had brewed. When the canisters exploded the men aboard the helicopters donned their gas masks. The helicopters hovered in place to intentionally swirl the gas around for a few seconds. The gas did just as expected and flew up the sides of the dam directly at the men above who began to drop to the ground immediately upon inhaling the blue colored smoke.

The gas was a bright blue and green cloud and as it swirled it looked like paint mixing with water. Lionfish was reminded of the scene in the movie *The Ten Commandments* with Charleton Heston where the plague sweeps through Egypt in a vaporous trail and kills all of Egypt's first born.

The helicopters touched down on the top of the structure and Lionfish and his demolition team sped to their assigned locations on the dam to tie off their lines and to begin the 200-foot rappel down the side of the mighty structure.

The other men quickly deployed and began loading the unconscious bodies of the security guards and workers onto the rolling carts. The bodies were piled six or seven high and looked like stacked cordwood. When all the guards and workers were loaded, the choppers lifted off to land at a safe site to unload them and to come back for more.

So far there were no problems or unexpected mishaps to throw them off their schedule. Lionfish was half way down the wall and was looking up to watch the action above. All seemed to be going well and he was relieved to see that Stingray's gas had worked so effectively. He would have to congratulate him, that is if Stingray ever spoke to him again.

Lionfish had reached his destination and could see that the other men had reached theirs. He checked Tarpon's drawing which detailed the exact placement of his weapon and then he began to attach the extremely powerful warhead Tarpon had constructed to the wall. He placed it in the precise location and in the manner that Tarpon had described and hoped that the other men were doing the same.

When the weapons were all set and were activated they would have fifteen minutes to climb all the way back up and to reach the single chopper, which would return for them. By now all of his other men had been removed from the site and only the demolition team was left to evacuate. The other men were smaller and climbed faster than Lionfish. They were already near the top of the wall. Lionfish was fifty feet from the top when a shot rang out. He felt a tearing, burning pain in his shoulder. He lost his grip on the rope and slid thirty to forty feet down burning and tearing flesh on his palms and fingers before he was able to get a firm grip again.

He looked up and saw a lone security guard in a gasmask looking down at him. The burning in his shoulder was intense and the pain every time he pulled himself up on the rope was excruciating. Before Lionfish could reach back to remove his weapon from his holster, the guard leaned over the wall and aimed his weapon directly into his face.

The chopper was landing 75 yards away on top of the wall. It had already picked up his remaining four men. The guard had killed one of

Lionfish's men and was now about to finish him off when Lionfish saw him propel forward and go toppling over the wall. He slammed into the concrete wall just a few feet from Lionfish and he could hear the loud cracking sound of breaking bones before the guard went tumbling end over end to the valley below.

When Lionfish looked up he saw Stingray looking down at him, screaming for him to climb faster. There were maybe six minutes left on the timer before the entire structure would be destroyed. The helicopter pilot had the good sense to know that he would never escape the fireball and shockwaves of the blast if he didn't leave now and he was defying logic by waiting for his leader.

Lionfish reached the top and he and Stingray ran to the helicopter. They jumped aboard with less than two minutes to spare. As the helicopter sped away from the wall the charges went off and the concussion and shock wave from the blast rocked the helicopter violently from side to side and propelled it forward on a column of superheated air.

They could feel the intense heat from the blast and were blinded by the bright orange cloud that seemed to engulf the helicopter. Lionfish was certain that at any second the gas tanks would ignite and the chopper would explode.

The noise was deafening. Whatever Tarpon had designed seemed apocalyptic in dimension. In a brilliant piece of flying, the pilot was finally able to stabilize the helicopter and as Lionfish looked backward to see the results of the explosion he made a mental note to reward the pilot with a healthy bonus check.

When he looked back all he could see was an enormous gray mushroom cloud of dust and debris rising hundreds of feet into the air. He could hear the loud, earth-shaking sound of the dam tumbling into the gorge below and knew that the destruction had been total.

The men on the helicopter broke into cheers. Lionfish had a pressure bandage applied to his shoulder and he leaned in close to Stingray to speak over the noise of the whirling blades. "I really didn't expect you to be speaking to me again, let alone saving my life."

"You were right not to want me in the way. I'm not a soldier. And besides you've always been an asshole and I've never let that interfere with our friendship before," Stingray said with a smile.

Lionfish thought about what they had accomplished today and despite their own casualties he was pleased with the results. He hoped there wouldn't be too much fallout from the blast to damage the surrounding area. He was mostly troubled by the fact that for the first time, Stingray had to kill a man. He hoped that he had not acquired a taste for adventure on this mission.

He was ready to go home to the warm healing waters of the

Caribbean and to rest and begin planning for their next mission. As he looked out over the valley he thought of a poem he had read some months ago by Kathleen Ross. "Because I see these mountains they are brought low, Because I drink these waters they are bitter, Because I tread these black rocks they are barren, Because I have found these islands they are lost. Upon seal and seabird dreaming their innocent world, My shadow has fallen."

CHAPTER 8

THE SUN WAS STREAMING THROUGH THE STAINED GLASS Grateful Dead sticker on the window of my sister's BMW, and it cast a spectrum of light across our mother's face. We had just crossed over the Throgs Neck Bridge into the Bronx along with the other six or seven million New Yorkers who also wanted to take a ride upstate to see the leaves change. There were another couple of million people riding along with us on the Cross Bronx Expressway who were probably on their way to New Jersey across the George Washington bridge to visit friends or relatives on this beautiful fall day.

One of the many things that aggravated me about living in New York was the endless weekend traffic, which can turn a plan for a relaxing day out, into a tedious, stress-filled experience. It is at it's worst in the summer when New Yorkers have only a dozen weekends, if it doesn't rain, to enjoy good weather, and millions of them travel in ten different directions from the Jersey shore to the Hamptons to their country houses in Woodstock, New York literally clogging every roadway and artery.

I once spent three hours on a Memorial Day weekend to travel only thirty miles on a one-lane road from Montauk, New York to reach the Long Island Expressway heading back into Manhattan.

"I'm tired of hearing you bitch about New York, Jake," my sister said. "It's dirty, it's dangerous, there's too much traffic. Every time you visit we have to listen to the same tired old monologue. If you hate it so much then stay in Florida with your 98% humidity and your geriatric neighbors," my sister yelled at me over the radio.

"You look ridiculous coming up here in December with your George Hamilton tan, and your skin is starting to look like an old leather sandal."

"I love New York, especially this time of year," our mother said suddenly looking up from where she had been staring silently out the window.

"I admit I miss the change of seasons in Florida and I miss the mountains," I said as I took my mothers hand.

"I don't want to listen to you two fighting all day," our mother said. "And you will wake up the baby if you don't lower the music."

Erin was sleeping comfortably in her car seat between my mother and I, and I thought how wonderful it must be to have no worries or adult concerns. Erin loved music and would dance in place almost the instant that one of her favorite songs was played. Her current favorite was "Bertha," by The Grateful Dead, and she enjoyed listening to music even more than she loved her favorite television shows, "Wishbone" and "The Big Comfy Couch."

We turned onto the Bronx River Parkway exit to escape the gridlock on the Cross Bronx Expressway, and we decided to take the Sprain Parkway up to the Tappan Zee bridge into Bear Mountain. My mother used to drive up to Woodstock every weekend for a few years to visit an artist friend and had always told us that this was the fastest route to the New York State Throughway.

Conor just popped in one of my favorite Warren Zevon CDs and we were all singing along to "Poor Poor, Pitiful Me." Our mother as usual was making up her own words to the song. We all began to laugh and I hugged her tight as we teased her for probably the thousandth time in our lives about inventing her own lyrics. She could not remember the correct words to even one song, not even from her favorite soundtrack from the movie *Funny Girl* with Barbra Streisand, which she played over and over again when we were children.

Still, it never deterred her from singing out loud and improvising as she sang. We were a family of singers and would all join in and sing out loud to our favorite musical artists on any long car ride or family trip. The family Von Trapp we were not and for the poor girlfriend or guest who happened to be visiting or was spending the day trapped in the car with us it could be a very irritating experience.

I still find myself singing out loud at traffic lights and am often embarrassed to look over to the left or to the right to see someone laughing at me from their car. I drive a convertible now, so I have to be especially careful not to sing out loud.

We were just rolling onto the start of Seven Lakes drive in Bear Mountain State Park and the views were spectacular. The leaves had reached their peak of season and as the paper had reported because of a very wet summer it was one of the prettiest fall seasons in years. The mountains were a cascading rainbow of golds and pinks and reds and we passed many old solitary trees that were covered in bright yellow or deep red leaves.

The road was carpeted in a pallete of wet fall colors and I looked forward excitedly to walking on the hiking trails that would also be covered in a soft spongy carpet of vivid reds and yellows. My mother wanted me to collect some colored branches and leaves for decorating her table at Thanksgiving and I could tell that she was already expecting me to fly up for her favorite family holiday.

The sky was bright blue, the dark rich blue of winter and presented a beautiful backdrop to the colorful mountains leaning up against it. We brought along blankets and some wine and a dozen good homemade sandwiches on fresh baked bread and laid them out in a field near the start of a well marked trail. I took my mothers arm and as she leaned heavily into me for support, we walked a few yards into the woods. We had only walked 100 feet when her breathing became strained. We had brought along the oxygen concentrator she used to help her breathe in the car and I volunteered to run back and get it. She sat down quietly on a wooden bench set back on the trail and took my hand.

"I'll be okay, Jakey," she said quietly, struggling for air. "Just let me sit awhile and catch my breath."

I looked back to our picnic site and could see Conor and Erin playing one of her favorite games. Erin closes her eyes and tries to catch her daddy, guided only by the sound of his voice.

"I get so much joy watching her do almost anything: play, sleep, even cry," my mother said as she too watched Erin running in circles and laughing.

"I know how you feel, Mom. She is so happy it makes you feel good just to be around her and to see her experience so many new things that we take for granted or have become bored with. I enjoy her innocent, unblemished appreciation of the world and its countless wonders."

"I'm so happy that I am getting to spend so much time with her before I die," my mother said, shocking me. "I love all my children but I think I will miss watching Erin grow up most of all," she said quietly, almost serenely, with the sound of birds and falling leaves around us. "I had a strange dream the other night, Jakey."

"Please don't call me Jakey, Mom. It reminds me of grandma's neighbor Jakey who was seventy years old and had a huge mole near his eye. He always scared me when I was a boy."

"I called you Jakey when you were small enough to sleep in my arms and when I look at you I still see my sweet little boy, until you open your mouth and say something sarcastic or cruel. And then you remind me of your father.

"Now let me tell you my dream. I was setting the table for Thanksgiving dinner and was almost done when I realized that I had forgotten sweet potatoes for your favorite dish, sweet potato pie. It was about 5:45 P.M. and the stores were just about to close, so I grabbed my car keys and rushed off to the supermarket. For some reason, I was driving across the Throgs Neck Bridge and it was beginning to snow very hard. I remember thinking that it was a little early in the year for snow on Thanksgiving day. I was watching the clock and I started to speed very fast and to weave in and out of traffic. I only had seven minutes to get to the store and, you know me, I wanted Thanksgiving to be perfect for my family so I floored the gas pedal. I hit a patch of ice and started to lose control of the car. I grabbed the wheel hard in both hands and felt like I could regain control when the rear of the car started to fishtail and I began to slide into oncoming traffic.

"I turned toward the direction of the skid and accelerated like you're supposed to do and the car hit some more ice, righted itself and then began to skid toward the guard rail. The front end slammed into the guard rail and the sound of screeching metal was deafening. The car burst through the rail and shot off the bridge over 500 feet above the water and I knew I was going to die.

"It felt so real, my dream. I remember the shock and the feeling of realizing that I was going to plummet into the icy waters below and I remember wondering if it would hurt and hoping that it would be quick and painless.

"As the car started to fall it got dark and the sky filled with billions of bright shining stars. The car disappeared and I was left floating free in space. My first thought was that I had died and that somehow I had been spared the final horrific experience of my death and the memory of my death, and now I was on my way to Heaven.

"I was surprisingly excited and was anxious to see what would happen next when I suddenly woke up at the dinner table and realized that I had fallen asleep in my seat. When I checked my watch I realized that it was three o'clock in the afternoon on Thanksgiving day and that your sister was supposed to be coming over at two o'clock to help me.

"I realized that I had been sleeping in that chair for almost twenty-two hours. I thought it must be all the painkillers I had been taking, and my lower back was killing me. Then the doorbell rang and your sister, Conor, and the baby walked in all dressed up for Thanksgiving dinner.

"'I'm sorry we're late, Mom,' your sister said. 'There was a horrible accident on the bridge and we have been sitting in traffic for the past two hours. Some poor woman committed suicide by driving her car off the bridge this afternoon on Thanksgiving day and the bridge is still backed up for miles.'

"I immediately had a chill that ran up and down my spine and when I screamed I woke up in my own bed in the middle of the night and I couldn't breath," my mother said as she finished her story.

"That's the creepiest dream I've heard in years, Mom. What the hell are your doctors giving you, LSD?"

"Jake, do you remember when you ran away from the Marines and no one knew where you were for over a week?

"Why didn't you call me to let me know you were alive? I couldn't sleep. I couldn't eat. I imagined every possible nightmare and was afraid you might have killed yourself. Your father was gone. I was hoping that you had finally grown up and that you were becoming a man and you did what you always did. You ran away and came home to your mother like a little boy, as soon as you ran out of money. You broke my heart, Jakey. Why didn't you come to me before you ran away so we could talk. I begged you not to join the service. I begged you to go to art school instead and to live with me. I tried to help you and you told me to mind my own business and to respect your wishes. You were acting like a grown up and you talked to me like you were a man but you came home after tearing out my heart, like a little boy, crying and begging for me to get you out of the Marines and to hide you. You almost killed me when you ran away. Why couldn't you call me and tell me where you were?"

I was stunned by my mother's words. She had forgotten some of the details of what had happenend. It had been almost ten years since that time and she had never brought it up and we had never really discussed it since then. It was a very confusing time for me and a painful memory. I still feel that I was right to have left the service but at the same time I'm ashamed of my cowardice and my failure to honor my commitment and to have completed my time in the service.

I still, to this day, after ten years, have this recurring dream that I have returned to boot camp as an adult, at whatever my present age happens to be in order to complete my contracted four years.

I felt a stabbing pain deep to my center at the sudden onslaught of guilt my mother was directing at me and I felt a little angry that she would hurt me now with this reminder at such an inappropriate time.

"I'm sorry I hurt you, Mom. I was a boy then. I was only 17 and although I tried for a short period of time to pretend that I was grown up and that I was a man, as you say, I was really just a scared and confused little boy. I didn't call you because I was ashamed and if you remember what I told you at the time, my original plan was to kill myself when I ran out of money. I didn't have the courage to see that through either," I said and I suddenly felt myself crying from the shameful memory.

"Jakey," my mother said, "Jakey, don't cry, please. I'm sorry I brought it up. I needed to get it out and I needed to resolve it and to have some closure once and for all. I do remember now that you had planned to end your life and I thank God you didn't do such a stupid thing.

"You think it takes courage to kill yourself. It takes more courage to live, when you're terrified of the future. Trust me. I love you and it would have destroyed me and your sister if anything had happened to you. When you turned yourself in and took all those bastards could throw at you including three months of hard labor I was proud of you.

"You were brave and you were strong and you've been strong for me these past six months. I'm prouder of you now than I've ever been. You have become a man, a good man. It might have taken longer than it should have," she said with a smile, "but you've always been a late bloomer." She smiled again at me and held me and loved me and forgave me as unconditionally as she always did.

I loved my mother more that day than I had ever loved her and I wondered how we would ever learn to live without her. I winced when I thought of a future without her there to celebrate my victories and to comfort me after my defeats. The doctor had recently given us some encouraging news about the shrinking of the tumors in my mothers lungs but Jackie quickly dampened my enthusiasm by explaining to me that it was at best a fifty percent chance that the tumors in her brain would ever be operable and that the best we could hope for was to extend our mother's life by six months to a year.

We walked down the trail for another hundred yards without speaking a word. When we approached a slight incline I could hear my mothers labored breathing. It sounded like a hoarse whisper in my ears and I asked her if we should turn around. The temperature had dropped suddenly and we could see our breath forming in small clouds with each exhale.

My mother seemed to breathe easier with the cold weather and she wanted to push on ahead. When we reached the top of the small rise we were greeted by a spectacular view of the Hudson River winding serpentine through the valley below in all its autumnal splendor. The sky was full of large, white cumulus clouds and the sky was bright blue.

It was a perfect fall day and although it had turned decidedly cold I was still looking forward to stopping in the city on the way home for a frozen hot chocolate at Serendipity, my mother's favorite restaurant.

My mother, the world's most heavily addicted chocoholic, had passed down the addiction through the umbilical cord to her children and she first introduced us to this chocolate lovers Valhalla in Manhattan almost twenty years ago when we were still very young.

The drive down the Palisades Parkway and over the George Washington Bridge would take longer and traffic coming out to Queens later would be hell but I knew there wasn't a person in the car who wouldn't be up for the ride considering the reward. We had been stopping in at Serendipity on our way home from various places for over twenty years and it had become a family tradition.

They made the best desserts in the free world and people would stand in line for hours just to try their mountainous hot fudge sundaes or most especially their frozen hot chocolates. It was almost sacrilegious in our family to order any thing else at our table and I remember once Conor receiving several barbed remarks after ordering a frozen lemonade drink.

I took over five different girlfriends who claimed to love chocolate to Serendipity over the years and can only remember one who wasn't blown away by their chocolate masterpiece. There is only one other eatery in all of New York that my family holds in as high a regard and that is the L&B Spumoni Gardens in Bensonhurst, Brooklyn. It occupies an entire block across the street from Lafayette High school where my mother and father both matriculated among some distinguished classmates, including Sandy Koufax in my father's class and Peter Max in my mother's.

L&B had stood there for over fifty years and I do not exaggerate when I say that they make the finest Pizza in the world.

When we got back to the picnic area the baby was sleeping and Jackie was giving me a disapproving look. I knew she would be upset with me for taking our mother so far from the car and her oxygen supply. We drank hot cocoa from the thermos and laughed about old family memories. My poor mother had grown up in a one-bedroom apartment with a pathological liar for a mother and a con man for a father. She shared a bedroom with her brother while my grandparents slept on a pullout sofa in the living room, which they kept covered in plastic during the day.

My mother used to always tease my grandmother about the plastic on the furniture. "What is it exactly, Mom" she would say, "that is so irreplaceable that you are trying so desperately to protect it? Could you imagine going into a museum and seeing all the fine furniture and artworks covered in dimpled, yellow plastic?"

My Grandfather was a part-time house painter who supplemented his income by getting run over by cars and suing the drivers. He was not ashamed of this sideline occupation and quite to the contrary he would often tell us all out loud about his dream of one day striking it rich. Someday he would make it to the top of his profession by being awarded a million dollars in a law suit.

He was a handsome man even in his late sixties. He had thick, wavy silver hair and bright blue eyes. He was somewhat of a Lothario in the neighborhood and his affairs were never discreet, often embarrassing and humiliating both my grandmother and my mother. He was a charming, charismatic man on the surface and presented this false front to outsiders, but he was a dangerous and sadistic man to his family. I was a favorite target of my grandfather's because I reminded him so much of my father, in both looks and attitude and he hated my father from the first moment they had met.

He worshipped my sister Jackie and would often spoil her with candies and presents while he deliberately neglected to include me and would brandish his favoritism like a weapon whenever we gathered at my grandparent's apartment.

His favorite game, which I'm embarrassed to say I fell for several times, was to encourage my sister to reach into his pocket by jingling a handful of change and then allowing her to scoop out over a dollar in quarters by digging her hands into his pants. It was only later in life that I suspected some sexual motivation for this game. When it was my turn to reach into his pocket for change I would approach him full of hope and imagined myself scooping out a bundle of the treasure that awaited me. When my hand was in his pocket he would grab my hand and crush it until I cried.

I remember one day, Jackie, our three cousins, and I were over at our grandparent's house, and my grandfather rushed into the room excitedly, announcing that he had gotten us all tickets to the Coney Island amusement park in Brooklyn. He said we were going to drive there right now. Our faces lit up at the news and we hurried downstairs, screaming with joy over the idea of flying through the air in a roller coaster and stuffing our faces with pink spun sugar until we were sick.

We all loaded into the car and my grandfather pulled away from the curb. He drove slowly while regaling us with stories of the many attractions and rides at the world famous amusement park, then he turned left at the corner. At the next corner he made another left and explained that the tickets he had were ten dollars apiece and that he had been tempted to sell them but he remembered his favorite grandchildren and decided we were more important, despite how hard money was to come by. As he said this he made another left and sped up to the next traffic light and then slammed on his brakes, slamming my three cousins in the back seat head first into the back of the front seat. My cousin Benjamin, who was the most sensitive of the bunch, started to cry and my grandfather explained as he made another left turn that he was only trying to prepare us for the bumper car rides we would enjoy once we reached the park.

When my grandfather made his last left turn his smile disappeared and his expression changed. When I saw the cruel, all too familiar darkness begin to cast its shadow across his face I realized too late what he had planned.

He quickly pulled into the exact same parking spot that he had just pulled out of five minutes earlier and ordered us all out of the car, explaining that he had momentarily forgotten it was Friday and that he just remembered he had to work tonight.

I was the only one who was not frozen in his seat with shock and I was the only one on the walk back to the apartment that didn't cry. I had recognized my grandfather for what he was much earlier than my peers and it was one of the reasons why he hated me more than the rest. I refused to play his game after that day and would immediately exit any room he entered.

It took my sister longer to grow to hate him, but eventually she too could see through his charm and could see the monster lurking beneath the surface. My mother would always defend him and she would explain that he had never hit either her or her mother and that he was a frustrated, unhappy man with a peculiar sense of humor.

My grandmother was even worse in her own way. She was an ignorant woman who would tell lie after lie or "stories" as my mother called them, about everyone, from the neighbors to the presidents of the United States, past and present, several of whom she had claimed to have met over the course of her life.

She would exaggerate about every aspect of her daily life and as we found out much later, once she was diagnosed and medicated, believed it all. She was very fearful and she was an incredibly negative human being and could give you fifty tragic consequences all in vivid detail to discourage any idea or experience you might suggest trying.

My friend Mike Cavelletti in our sales office calls people like my grandmother "dream takers" rather than "dream makers." My grandmother Bessie was also a very unkind woman who would criticize and degrade every person she came in contact with and was especially cruel to my mother.

She was also a persistent nag and would ask the same question over ten times, hoping each new time she asked that she would get a different response. In the end she would win and people would give in just to shut her up. One of my favorite memories is when she did the impossible and got my normally reticent and mellow brother-in-law Conor to blow his top and to yell at her. She had asked him ten different times and in ten different ways if he wanted a piece of cake. He continued to say no and she eventually resorted to form and explained to him in a lie that she had baked all day with just him in mind because she knew that pound cake was his favorite.

After Conor said no for the tenth time, my grandmother left the room and eventually returned from the kitchen and served him an enormous piece of the cake. Conor lost it and screamed at her that he was full and for the tenth time that he didn't want any cake. He apologized and rushed out of the room, embarrassed and angry at himself for losing his cool.

My grandmother was however an extremely entertaining person even though it was unintentional and my mother, my aunts, and my mother's friends would have us all rolling on the floor with stories about my grandmother and her idiosyncrasies.

A few years ago before my grandmother passed away, we let her join us in a game of Trivial Pursuit at my mother's apartment and my mother had to leave the room several times because she was laughing so hard. My grandmother would answer a question wrong and then upon hearing the right answer she would explain in her own pathological rationale how she had really given the right answer all along in a roundabout way.

At one point in the game, my grandmother gave an answer and then changed it three times, each time adding some new dimension to her original answer and we were laughing so hard we had cramps. My grandmother loved being the center of attention and became more and more vaudevillian when she answered a question, embellishing her answers with dramatic gestures and nuances while she dropped ashes everywhere from the end of her cigarette.

She smoked for over fifty years and for as long as I could remember she smoked them through these plastic aquafilters, which she swore would add ten plus years to her life.

When she answered Joseph Kennedy to the question who was the sixteenth president of the United States? we almost peed our pants. After we told her that she was wrong she asked if we meant the United States of America and when Conor asked her if there was another United States, my Aunt Deanna blew coffee out of her nose and had to go out on the terrace to compose herself.

My grandmother never knew we were laughing at her, and we felt no guilt because she was having the most fun we had ever seen her have. We also fudged most of the answers in order to let her win and she kissed us all in an uncharacteristic show of affection when the game was over.

We were sitting on the picnic blanket and my mother had just finished telling us about the first time she had gotten her period and the subsequent conversation she had with my grandmother. Although we couldn't help but feel sorry for my mother, we also couldn't help laughing until our sides hurt.

My grandmother explained to my mother that because of Eve's original sin in the Garden of Eden, God had cursed all her female descendants with their periods once a month and as an extra bonus women could look forward to excruciating pain in childbirth.

My grandmother explained that the reason that little girls did not receive their periods until they started to become women was because children were innocent in the eyes of the Lord and were not yet capable of sin. So this first period, my grandmother explained, was the beginning of my mother's becoming a woman. She also explained that when you reached menopausal age, although she did not use that word, God released you from having your period anymore because he felt that by that time you had suffered enough.

My mother had a phenomenal sense of humor and I believe it was that, combined with her strong spirit of survival, that saved her from the upbringing she received from my two psychotic grandparents, Irving and Bessie.

It was getting late and we packed up the car and headed for the city and our rendezvous with our frozen hot chocolates. My mom had taken her medication and was getting sleepy. Her eyes kept opening and closing just like Erin's who often fights sleep and wrestles to stay awake until the moment her eyes shut tight and she is sound asleep. When my mother and Erin opened their eyes we were just pulling up in front of Serendipity and my mother smiled, not at the thought of having her favorite dessert, but at such a strong visual reminder of so many happy family times together.

There was the usual mile-long line inside the small cramped hallway which served as a waiting area. The restaurant has a small boutique in which are sold a wide range of bizarre and eclectic T-shirts and other assorted paraphernalia and novelty items. The items range from leopard skin pill box hats to Yiddish board games and rhinestone coffee mugs.

The entire restaurant was decorated with original Tiffany lamps and the floor was covered with small black and white tile. Almost the entire staff of waiters are homosexual. Conor and I let my sister, mother, and the baby out of the car and drove into the indoor parking lot across the street from the restaurant on the other side of 60th street, just up the block from Bloomingdales department store.

When we got inside, my mother was sitting on a small bench and was obviously not feeling too well because the manager came up to me and asked me if she was feeling all right. She looked like hell, was pale and tired, leaning heavily against my sister who was trying to convince her to leave and go home.

"There's no way Mom can wait any longer," Jackie said. "The day has been far too long already for her and we need to get her home to bed. Just two weeks ago she was in the hospital, laying under an oxygen tent."

"Thanks for mentioning over and over again how horrible I look," our mother said. "I assure you that I look worse than I feel. You try chemotherapy for over six months and see how wonderful you look. I know I look horrible with this cheap wig and there are very few public places that I want to go out to any more, but I've been looking forward to this for weeks now, and I'm not leaving. The time will come soon when

I won't be able to go out at all. Two weeks ago I scared poor Jackie to death when my blood count was so depleted from the chemotherapy that I collapsed in the movie theater."

The restaurant manager, who was standing at the lectern nearby, overheard our conversation and turned and walked away. A minute later the hostess was seating us in the back of the restaurant at a large round marble table under an old Shell gasoline station sign.

Before I took my seat I walked over to the manager to thank him for his kindness and as I shook his hand, he covered both my hands, clenching them in his. He told me as his voice broke and his eyes became filled with tears that he had lost his mother to breast cancer only last year, and that it still felt as if it were yesterday.

I told him that I was sorry for his loss but I also felt it necessary to explain to him that my mother's cancer would soon be operable. I had a hard time even admitting that my mother had cancer. I felt grateful for his kindness and I also felt empathy for the man but strangely I also felt annoyed at his implication that we had something in common.

My mother was alive for Christ's sake and his mother had passed away. "This is a great table," I said to everyone as I took my seat. "I can almost taste it already." There were dozens of frozen hot chocolates flying past my head on the trays of the waiters who were shuttling them from table to table.

"It's a good thing I look so shitty," my mother said.

"We could try this at all the exclusive hot new restaurants in New York that no one can get into, and if there's ever a really long wait I can always rip off my wig and clear the room."

"You look fine, Miriam," Conor said as he kissed my mothers cheek.

"You are the most beautiful woman in this room and it's hard to look glamorous when you're not feeling well. Come to our house when Jackie's got the flu. It's scary," he said jokingly and he hugged my mom tight.

My sister gave Conor a loving look and then smiled and took his hand. I knew Conor meant what he said. He was as devoted to my mother as if he were her son by birth and would speak to her for hours about his hopes and dreams. My mother was somewhat of an artist herself and was very supportive and encouraging of Conor's sometimes misunderstood vocation.

We ordered our five desserts and fifteen minutes later they arrived at the table. The frozen hot chocolates were delivered in a large round glass dessert or ice cream dish and were topped with mounds of fresh homemade whip cream and shavings of very dark bittersweet chocolate.

The recipe in the Serendipity cookbook claims that there are over ten different varieties of dark chocolates from around the world used in the making of a frozen hot chocolate and the recipe looks like the blueprint for building the space shuttle, it is so hard to follow. No doubt, to add to the mystique of this world famous dessert.

My mother had her coat wrapped tightly around her and said, "This is the first thing in weeks I have been able to keep down. I was afraid it would be too rich for me, but I think my system has a way of compensating for chocolate. Your father used to say that if you cut me I would bleed dark, semi-sweet chocolate."

We all laughed and remembered a house and a refrigerator that was always full of frozen chocolate covered marshmallow sticks and huge refrigerated bars of Hershey's Special Dark.

"That was orgasmic," I said and I rubbed my distended belly with both hands. A disgusting habit at home that I picked up from my mother was too open my pants after a big meal right at the dinner table in order to get some relief from the uncomfortable bloating that often followed a holiday dinner. I remember when I was young being afraid that my mother would undo her pants in a restaurant and embarrass us all to death. Thankfully that never happened, although she often talked about it.

"Lets get going," Jackie said after picking up the check. "I'm exhausted and have a twelve hour day ahead of me at the office tomorrow. Besides we really need to put both of you to bed," she turned and said to my mother and Erin who's face was in the process of being cleaned with a wet nap by Conor.

This was Erin's first baptism by frozen hot chocolate into the family circle of chocoholics and she was in heaven, covering her face with a huge dark chocolate smile that looked like brown clown's paint.

On the ride home, both the baby and my mother fell instantly asleep and we all rode quietly in the car, reflecting on the day's events. When we got upstairs, my mother wanted to talk to us in the living room before she collapsed into her bed. I had this awful feeling in the pit of my stomach at the way my mother was acting and all my senses were registering trouble. As we all sat close together around my mother's couch she began.

"I spoke to Doctor Rubin, my oncologist, in his office two days ago and he told me that there are now several more tumors in my brain and that he and the other doctors at North Shore don't believe them to be operable."

My mother was trying desperately to be calm for our sakes, but her lip was trembling and she began too cry. We all rushed to her at once and as the shock and weight of my mother's last statement hit us we all began to vent our grief. I began to sob heavily as I held tightly to my family.

It was over, any last shred of hope I might have been foolish enough to cling to was destroyed and my mother knew the truth finally, better than any of us. The awful unavoidable reality was that my mother was going to die, and a huge part of us all would die with her. For two days, my mother had kept this news to herself, trying to decide how she would tell us, trying to protect her children when she was the one facing this disease by herself. How could I have ever questioned her strength, her courage, or her fortitude.

I spent most of my life seeing her as weak and passive. I was now witnessing enormous uncomprehendable courage and strength, and I felt ashamed. After my mother cried herself out and we put her to bed we talked about every possible cure, from the gamma knife in Loma Linda University to herbal medicine and we tried desperately to grasp at any idea or hope we could create. My mother explained that the tumors were too spread out and were deemed untreatable, although the doctors would try by torturing her some more with pinpoint radiation and chemotherapy.

Jackie decided to sleep with my mother, and Conor and I drove quietly home. I was thinking of my flight home in two days and was angry that the only way I could stay in New York now would be to resign my position. I was angrier still, that my financial burdens could not afford me that luxury.

Conor put Jackson Browne's "Late for the sky," one of our favorite albums into the CD player and ironically "For a dancer" was the first song to come on. This song always made me sad and recently for obvious reasons made me think of my mother and my fear of losing her.

"I don't know what happens when people die, can't seem to grasp it as hard as I try. It's like a song I can hear playing right in my ear, but I can't play. I can't help listening. Into a dancer you have grown from a seed somebody else has thrown, go on ahead and throw some seeds of your own and somehow between the time you arrive and the time you go, may lie the reason you're alive but you'll never know."

CHAPTER 9

THE WIND WAS HOWLING and snow was swirling in all directions making it difficult to see through the icy fog as Captain Samuel Stewart of *The Sea Leopard* walked along the ice. He passed by the mutilated and skinless bodies of over seventy baby harp seals as he made his way with five of his fellow conservationists toward the fishermen who were continuing the bloody slaughter only fifty yards ahead.

Captain Stewart's stomach was tightening and he could taste bile in his mouth. He had been waging a war against the horrific cruelty inflicted on the harp seals and other creatures of the sea for over twenty years and although he was a legendary figure and a hero in the environmental community he was deeply hated by the local fishermen of the area and had been violently attacked several times in the past.

Captain Stewart from 1975 to 1983 had led several major expeditions to stop this particular act of barbarism, two for Greenpeace, one for the Fund for Animals, and two most recently for the Sea Leopard Conservation Society. He had brought movie stars to the ice to witness the murders and had done more than anyone else to focus the world's attention on the suffering of these helpless creatures.

In 1983, he set up blockades and drove the fishermen from the ice. Two years earlier he was rammed by the Canadian Coast Guard and last year he was hospitalized after a mob of drunken sailors and fishermen broke into his hotel room and, under the eyes of the local law enforcement who did nothing to stop them, beat him unmercifully, breaking his ribs and fracturing his skull.

He won his greatest victory that same year by generating so much public support and political pressure that the import of seal pup fur was banned in Europe and commercial viability of seal hunting collapsed. This major victory lasted only twelve short years and although most of the world's population that had witnessed the previous slaughters on television still believe it had ended forever, it has begun again on the bloodstained ice of Canada's northern territories.

Last year in 1994, the Canadian Minister of Fisheries and Oceans Brian Tobin announced that Canada would set a quota of 250,000 seals for 1995 and 1996 and would pay subsidies to continue and encourage a renewed slaughter. The Russians and Norwegians had allotted even larger quotas, with the result that 1995 could see more seals killed in the North Atlantic than ever before in history. The new hunts could not even use the former rationality of using the meat for necessity, since the carcasses of the seals would be left to rot on the ice, and because of a huge surplus of pelts stored in warehouses in Norway there was no market for the once valuable fur.

As preposterous as it sounds in this most modern age of medical technology and pharmaceutical innovation, the prize to be collected by the butchers at work ahead in the distance was the genitalia of these helpless animals, who are often skinned alive while their mother's screams are silenced by the stomping boots and bullets of Canada's fishermen.

They are sold at markets in China and Taiwan as a remedy for male impotence. The demand is enormous and the powdered organs are sold for up to $200, to be mixed with dried tiger bones to make a potion to satisfy the sexual appetites of the Asian market. To support his position, the minister had blamed the disappearance of the northern cod on the seals despite the overwhelming evidence to the contrary of several marine biologists.

The art of politics is a fickle endeavor and as is usual with politicians, Minister Tobin's views blew with the wind. In 1994, in an edition of the *Ottawa Citizen*, Tobin said "We [Canada] will not consider a return to seal culling on the east coast, despite fishermen's claims that the seals threaten Newfoundland's endangered cod. Evidence of the impact of seals is not clear. There is no doubt in my mind that man has been a far greater predator."

Now that unemployment compensation for the fishermen was too costly to continue, Tobin needed to have a distraction from the many failed fisheries so he could achieve a higher office. Allowing the fishermen to slaughter the seals unchecked is a handy solution until the next election. To blame the seals is a coward's way to divert attention away from government mismanagement and the greed of the industrial dragger fleets that have depleted the oceans at a faster rate then they can replenish. Doctor David Lavigne, the world's leading harp seal biologist, believes that a massive slaughter of the seals may have negative repercussions on the cod.

"Seals typically consume a range of species, including some predators and competitors of commercially valued species," Dr. Lavigne was quoted as saying from his office at the university of Guelph in Ontario. "It is even possible that the seals could assist in the recovery of some commercially valued stocks; so reducing a seal population could actually be detrimental to fishing interests."

As inappropriate as it was, Captain Stewart had to chuckle at the image of Dr. Lavign presenting this data as a deterrent to twenty drunken fishermen violently swinging their clubs and covered from head to toe in the blood of the baby seals they were brutalizing.

Captain Stewart had taken that route by trying to educate the local fishermen and discovered through time and experience that the killing was more about tradition and an outlet for the anger and helplessness that the fishermen felt about their inability to earn a living and the shame of living on government handouts.

The seals became a scapegoat for the pent-up hostility that the local fishermen dealt with everyday. Captain Stewart had watched with horror the expressions of hatred and menace on the faces of the local citizens as they repeatedly killed and tortured the beautiful harp seals. Captain Stewart was trying to think of creative solutions to the current economic problems that were fueling the current bloodshed. He had noticed years earlier that the harp seal pups had hair follicles that were transparent in color and hollow in structure. It is very similar to polar bear fur. The baby seals have this hair for only three weeks, until they put on enough blubber to keep their bodies warm. Their transparent hairs absorb the heat from the sun making for tremendous insulation.

Captain Stewart felt that if these hairs could be collected there might be a practical use and possibly an economic alternative to the hunt could be found. His team had been collecting these hairs in large amounts and sending them to corporations in Canada and the United States and several firms had expressed interest in investing. This current expedition was being funded by a large outerwear manufacturer in the United States that was going to use the baby seal in its marketing campaign to promote the products it manufactured as environmentally conscious. Captain Stewart began to recruit men from among the townspeople to help comb the baby seals and to collect the hairs for sale to their patron company.

At first he had up to six young men and women working for him, until their parents and their peers began to pressure them and to question their loyalty. The young men were told by their friends that combing seals was not manly work, as if clubbing to death a helpless newborn seal pup were the barometer by which to measure manhood. Little by little, his employees began not showing up for work and what he thought was a brilliant idea and one he thought would be well-received began to fail.

He was doing the work alone now and running into the fisherman who were at cross purposes on a daily basis. Their confrontations were becoming increasingly more violent and he knew he could no longer stand by helplessly and watch the killing. As he drew closer to the men up ahead he warned his men not to provoke the fishermen and to keep their hands to themselves. He was about to forget his own instructions when he saw through the clearing fog a sailor standing above a baby seal with its head in a noose strangling the life out of it and shouting to his friends.

Captain Stewart rushed forward without thinking and struck the sailor in the side of the head with his fist. He was too late to save the panic-stricken mother, who another fishermen had just shot through the head.

The fisherman he struck fell to the ground and the other fishermen became instantly quiet and turned menacingly toward him and his men as they entered the area.

"You cowardly son of a bitch!" Captain Stewart spat down at the man at his feet. Captain Stewart was screaming and he was shaking from rage. "Get up and let's see how you handle someone who can actually defend himself."

While he was looking down he was attacked from behind by several men who threw him to the ground and kicked him with their heavy boots. His men were attacked on all sides and were greatly outnumbered. A full-blown riot had broken out and it appeared as if Captain Stewart and his men were going to be seriously injured or killed.

There were two women on Captain Stewart's team and they were being held by two fishermen while they received special attention from several others. The leader of the fishermen, a huge man of approximately 6'5" tall and over 250 pounds, asked his men to drag the captain over to him while he instructed the others to strip Captain Stewart's people bare and to throw them into the icy waters where they would quickly die from exposure.

The captain was dragged over to the apparent leader of the mob. He was bleeding heavily from his nose and mouth and he had to be held up by the men who were leading him forward.

"My name is John Le Clerc," the giant fisherman who was leading the mob said. "My family has fished these waters for over 100 years and has been killing seals since our first days on this continent. You and your group of wealthy bleeding heart Yankees come here and try to tell us how to live our lives. You organize boycotts and destroy our livelihood and interfere with our way of life. Most of the people in your country wouldn't know a seal if it walked up and bit them on the ass. Who the hell do you think you are?

"It's time to make an example of you and your friends so the world can see what happens to people who stick their noses in where they don't belong," the big man shouted, his face only two inches from Captain Stewart's face, the stink of cheap liquor on his breath.

"By the time they find you and your friends floating around at sea you'll look like a bunch of ice cubes in a glass of gin," the leader of the fishermen said to the uproarious laughter of his men, who were slapping at the heads of Captain Stewart's men and tearing at the clothing of the women in his group.

With tremendous strength and dignity, Captain Stewart raised his head and spat a wad of bloody saliva into the face of his tormentor.

"You and your men are the lowest form of cowards and can only feel like men when you've drank up enough courage to bludgeon helpless animals. Now you abuse men and women that you outnumber ten to one," the captain said.

Le Clerc's face turned bright red with rage and as he wiped the spittle from his face he grabbed a heavy club and raised it high above Captain Stewart's head to strike a deadly blow.

At the moment he was about to swing, the loud crack of a rifle shot sounded in the camp, freezing all activity and it stopped Le Clerc's hand in mid-air.

"Let him go!"

A deep voice from out of the icy fog resonated through the area and echoed in the swirling snow.

Everyone turned in the direction of the sound as the wind parted the gusty powder and revealed a tall man dressed from head to toe in white including a white ski mask. He stepped confidently into the circle of men and commanded, "Turn Captain Stewart and the others loose, now, and you may still live to fish these waters again."

His manner and his voice were so powerful and compelling, not to mention the phantom-like way that he had entered the area that the men holding Captain Stewart instantly responded and released their hold on him.

Le Clerc regained his composure and said, "Who the fuck are you?" to the man in white standing two feet from him. Then he turned to his group and shouted, "What's wrong with you bunch of pussies? This is one man. I don't care if he is dressed up like a fucking polar bear. He's with the rest of these whale hugging assholes and he made the mistake of showing up late. Now grab his sorry ass and the rest of them and dump them in the water like I said, or I'll bust your heads myself."

The fishermen seemed to agree with Le Clerc's reasoning and after the initial shock of the stranger's entrance wore off they recognized that as Le Clerc had said, the stranger was only one man.

They immediately leapt into action and three of them armed with clubs rushed the stranger at the same time. As the first one swung his club the tall stranger ducked and snapped a kick with lightning quickness and surprising power into the man's sternum and there was a loud cracking sound.

The stranger rushed forward and kicked one of the oncoming men in the side of the head while throwing a hard straight-arm across the throat of the third man, crushing his windpipe and landing him hard on the ice.

One of the fishermen reached behind his back and drew a 38 S&W revolver and aimed it in the direction of the tall man in white. As his finger pulled back on the trigger, a shot rang out from the fog and the fishermen flew backward holding his shoulder. The sound of twenty automatic weapons being cocked simultaneously rang out in the camp and a large circle of men dressed in white like their leader stepped into the fray.

"Enough," the tall man shouted as he stepped up to the self appointed leader of the fishermen. "Your man on the ground there is lucky my men are all expert shots and that I gave them orders not to kill or the seabirds in the area would be snacking on his brains."

"Who are you?" Captain Stewart asked the tall leader of his rescuers, although he thought that he already knew the answer.

"My name is Lionfish and these men are members of RedTide," Lionfish said out loud to the assembled group.

There was an audible gasp from some of the men in the group and the fishermen's attitude immediately appeared to turn from anger to terror.

"I want you and your men to clear out of here immediately and if you ever come back the next visit we make will be to your homes to burn them to the ground," Lionfish said to Le Clerc.

"We may leave today, but rest assured we will be back and when I'm gone then my sons and their sons will return until every one of those stinking seals are exterminated," Le Clerc responded.

"You and your men are cowards like Captain Stewart said and you turn my stomach. If it were in my power it would be you who would disappear from this area forever," Lionfish said as he grabbed Le Clerc by the throat.

Le Clerc was a powerful man and he pushed Lionfish back and away from him and then rushed forward to fight him. As Lionfish removed his hood he shouted to his men, "Keep everyone back. Let's see how our friend fares against an animal that isn't helpless."

"One on one, Le Clerc. No one will interfere. You have my word. If you win my men will not sink your ships to the bottom of the sea as we had intended."

Without warning, Le Clerc stepped forward and threw a surprisingly swift right cross at Lionfish who easily ducked beneath it. Le Clerc followed it up with an uppercut that caught Lionfish squarely in the abdomen. Lionfish had just enough time to steady himself for the blow and bore down hard flexing his abdominal muscles to receive the impact.

It was like slamming his fist into a concrete wall and Le Clerc was stunned to see his blow had little effect upon his opponent. Lionfish threw an uppercut of his own with all his power and followed through landing the blow squarely in Le Clerc's solarplexus. The big man dropped to one knee and vomited into the snow while gasping for air. As he stood he drew a knife from his rear pocket and concealed it while charging at Lionfish.

Lionfish caught the glint of sunlight on the blade and as Le Clerc swung wildly toward his chest Lionfish caught his wrist and while twisting it backward and upward broke it in three places.

Le Clerc dropped the knife and fell to both knees facing Lionfish and he screamed in pain as he held his wrist. Lionfish saw the nylon rope which the fishermen used to strangle the seal pups dangling from Le Clerc's pocket and he reached down and grabbed it and as he stepped quickly behind Le Clerc he tightened the noose around his neck.

Lionfish began to strangle Le Clerc and he had a look in his eyes that would live in the nightmares of the fishermen.

"How does that feel?" Lionfish screamed at Le Clerc. "Is it too tight? Tell your men what a baby seal feels as it's being strangled to death. Take a good look you men, because if we ever have to come back here you will see this again and again and you might be the next one who will be gasping for his last breath."

Lionfish drove his knee into Le Clerc's back and slammed him into the ice face down without ever loosening his grip on the rope around his neck. Le Clerc's face was blue and his eyes were bulging from their sockets. Suddenly Lionfish felt a kick in his side and he loosened his grip on the rope seconds before Le Clerc would have died.

As Lionfish released his grip he began to tremble from anger and a sudden rush of adrenaline. Lionfish looked up in amazement to see that it was Captain Stewart who had delivered the kick that had saved Le Clerc's life.

The men in the group were horrified by Lionfish's attempt to murder Le Clerc, most especially the conservationists whom RedTide had rescued.

Lionfish regained his composure and approached Captain Stewart, who was standing among his people with a look of shock and repulsion on his face.

"Come now, Captain, you've witnessed the slaughter of hundreds, maybe thousands of animals at the hands of these monsters. Twenty minutes ago they were about to throw you and your entire group into the water to freeze to death. Don't look so surprised by my actions. You know RedTide's reputation."

Lionfish paused to settle his breathing. "Who are you to judge me? You yourself have rammed ships, possibly sinking them and the men aboard them. Today we accomplished more than your group has achieved in years of struggling."

"You are wrong, son," Captain Stewart replied. "What you almost did was murder a man and I have no more respect for you than for the man you left lying there on the ice," Captain Stewart spat out at Lionfish.

"Despite your own self-important views you have not helped our cause at all. To the contrary, you have now linked us with terrorism and probably have set us back ten years in terms of the public opinion on which we depend," Captain Stewart said as he turned to assemble his group to make their way back to his ship.

Lionfish grabbed the captain by the shoulders and spun him around. As their eyes met a look of recognition passed over Captain Stewart's face and he said to Lionfish, "I know you, don't I? You look very familiar to me. Where have I seen you before?"

"You don't know me, Captain, but you knew my mother a very long time ago."

"Who was your mother and how did I know her? I know your face and it somehow reminds me of happier times."

"I've told you far too much already, Captain," Lionfish responded. "There are people who would torture and kill you for the little I have just revealed. I am behaving like a fool and have probably already put you at risk. I'm sorry you disapprove of my actions today, Captain Stewart. You have always been a hero of mine and I don't have many left.

"Remember that we saved your life today and probably the lives of your seals for a good long time to come."

"I am grateful for your timely appearance today but again I do not support you or your group and when the media arrives I will say so publicly," Captain Stewart said. "Now you better leave. The Coast Guard and the authorities will be arriving shortly."

Lionfish narrowed his eyes and hesitated for a moment before he said, "Captain, if you feel that way, then why did you invite us here?"

"What did you say, son?" the captain nervously shouted to Lionfish as he grabbed his arm. "I never asked you to come here!!"

"We received an encrypted message on the World Wide Web at our secret location at "Cybershop," an internet catalogue site we use to communicate. You asked us to come and help your team at this location and on this date. Only the elite members of my team holding the highest security clearances and a few trusted friends and conservationists know how to reach us through that site."

As the recognition that he had been set up registered in his voice and on his face, the sound of a helicopter and approaching snowmobiles could be heard through the frozen shroud of fog that Lionfish now prayed would provide cover for him and his men.

"Retreat! Now"! Lionfish screamed at his men as they turned and ran for their snowmobiles, which were hidden in the fog. It would be over a fifteen mile run to the icebreaking ship which was waiting for them to make their escape. That was a lot of ground to cover by snowmobile with an enemy helicopter covering the distance at ten times the speed. Lionfish would have to be creative about using the terrain and the weather to their advantage.

Back on the helicopter, MacGregor was feeling optimistic that his latest plan to finally trap and kill his elusive enemy was at hand. He had been brilliant in the design and execution of his plan and was looking forward to giving the much awaited news of Lionfish's capture to his benefactor.

"Get us in closer, I can't see a goddamn thing," MacGregor shouted to the pilot over the thundering sound of the blades. It had been his idea to wait until RedTide revealed themselves inside the circle of fishermen, instead of searching for their approach route in this miserable weather. Visibility was poor and he wanted to catch them in the open.

Unfortunately, the weather had delayed liftoff and MacGregor had been hesitant to deploy the snowmobiles without air cover. Now RedTide was on the move and once again he was in the chase position. Out on the open ice there would be nowhere for them to run, and with the helicopter constantly identifying their position escape would be hopeless. Nonetheless, MacGregor reminded himself not to underestimate Lionfish again.

"Fagan, can you hear me? Check in," MacGregor radioed to his team leader below.

"Do you have visual contact yet?"

Down below, the ten black Arctic Cats of MacGregor's crack squad burst through the circle of fishermen and conservationists at over sixty miles an hour, sending men and equipment flying in all directions. The men were dressed in all black snow suits and wore silver polarized goggles to protect against snow blindness and drove in pairs, a heavily armed gunman riding on the back of each snowmobile.

"I can hear them, but I still can't see them sir," Fagan said into his radio as he drove with one hand on the handlebars, squeezing the throttle to its fullest.

"Do you have a visual yet, sir?" he asked MacGregor.

"I am just over your position and I can't see below," he answered. "We can't get in any lower because of the wind and the low mountains of ice and snow," MacGregor responded over the static on the snowmobiles mounted speaker.

A wind from the east blew in strong suddenly and the area began to clear as the sun burst through the clouds. From above, MacGregor could now see the enemy below on ten green and black snowmobiles riding at breakneck speed single file through the ice and snow below. His men were also in single file and were closing the distance rapidly. MacGregor felt his pulse quicken as he realized that the end of his almost two year struggle to destroy RedTide was at hand. It had cost over a million dollars to buy the necessary information from the editor of a small conservation rag in order to set this up but it was worth every dime.

MacGregor had been following a lead supplied by Blowfish for over three months. It seemed that the editor and Lionfish had a falling out over some philosophical differences and the increased violence, and on top of that his magazine was on the brink of bankruptcy.

Yamaguchi had visibly flinched when MacGregor told him the amount of the bribe. After he had finished laying out his plan, Yamaguchi was uncharacteristically enthusiastic and he promised a one million dollar bonus if he captured Lionfish alive. MacGregor instructed his men to try only for wounding fire if possible but that they were to shoot to kill if necessary. He would not let them escape and err on the side of caution, million dollars or not. The landscape below was beautiful but treacherous and there were many caves and crevasses to negotiate and open water all around.

It would be crucial to lead MacGregor's men into as many traps as possible and to use the environment to his advantage, Lionfish knew. They had painstakingly chosen this escape route, although they had not counted on air cover from their expected opponents, the Coast Guard. He felt guilty at exposing RedTides's men to unnecessary danger. And Lionfish wondered where the security leaks were coming from.

Lionfish knew that Yamaguchi had unfathomable resources to draw upon in money and in contacts worldwide. He had underestimated the depth of his lust for vengeance and his ability to penetrate RedTide's security. Lionfish spotted a fifty foot bridge of ice ahead and directed his men toward it as he dropped back to last position. The enemy bullets were hitting the ice just behind his snowmobile, the automatic weapons fire dangerously close. As the last of his men flew over the ice bridge spanning a 150 foot deep crevasse below, Lionfish followed, dropping two explosive charges timed for one minute each into the snow on the ice to hide them. Two enemy snowmobiles had already cleared the bridge when the explosives went off. The air thundered with the sound of the explosion and two snowmobiles exploded in balls of flames, spinning into the air and dropping below into the crevasse with the shredded remains of their passengers.

As the blue and green ice of the bridge dropped below, the remaining six snowmobiles slammed on their brakes while the lead two drivers slid to a stop with their front ends hanging over the edge. MacGregor was blinded by the flash and the helicopter was buffeted by the shock waves of the blast.

"Son of a bitch!" MacGregor screamed as he pounded the dashboard of the helicopter.

"Turn right and look for a place to cross," he shouted at the pilot. MacGregor spotted a large drift of snow formed like a ramp at a narrow place in the crevasse only six feet wide and with little time to search for an alternate route he instructed his men to jump it.

The snowmobiles hit the top of the ramp at over fifty miles an hour and easily leapt the divide, landing with a crashing sound as their belts touched down on the other side. One passenger was thrown from the back of a snowmobile in mid flight and tumbled into the chasm below with a scream. MacGregor had expected casualties and was not as upset by the losses as by the fact that Lionfish had managed to separate his forces and to distract his air cover. He soothed his worries with the realization that there was really nowhere for him to run and that he was only delaying the inevitable, as MacGregor reached behind him for his high powered rifle and scope.

He instructed the pilot to ascend so he could get a better overview of the battlefield and the gap between his men and the enemy. As the helicopter got higher it entered low cloud cover and visibility worsened. He was forced to descend. Lionfish spotted a long tunnel through the center of a giant mountain of ice and led his men through it. The tunnel was only wide enough to fit two snowmobiles side by side and he instructed his men to line up in twos. The tunnel was dimly lit and the ceiling was lined with 4-6 foot icicles or stalactites, which were dripping water over his group and decreased visibility as the water covered their goggles.

The inside walls were smooth and had the bluish color of the glacier. The tunnel was very long and had many curves at the end so the exit was not visible. Lionfish could hear the reverberating sound of the engines in his ears and could not shout out orders or commands. The two leading enemy snowmobiles entered the cave just sixty yards behind and began to fire heavily in RedTide's direction. Bullets began to blast into the walls of ice along the sides of RedTide's last two snowmobiles chipping huge chunks and shards of blue ice into the men aboard.

Lionfish pointed his weapon at the ceiling of the cave and signaled his men to shoot in that direction. His men began to fire behind them at the icicles on the roof and the stalactites shattered dropping to the floor below. As the lead enemy snowmobile turned slightly, following the curve of the tunnel, the driver spotted the avalanche of deadly ice missiles falling in front of him and slammed on his brakes. It was too late to stop and the water and ice on the cave floor was dangerously slick. His braking speed carried him into the rain of daggers. One five foot long spear of ice impaled the driver through the chest cleaving him wide open. His passenger was bludgeoned to death by falling ten to twenty pound hunks of ice as the snowmobile crashed head on into the tunnel wall.

The driver behind turned the corner as the last of the ice crashed to the ground and quickly fishtailed around the dead men, avoiding a rear end collision. Lionfish spotted a separate tunnel branching off to the left and told the men who were riding solo on their snowmobiles due to casualties, to pair up. This left one snowmobile empty to be used as a diversion.

When the driver of the remaining enemy snowmobile looked ahead he could see a fork in the cave and a separate tunnel turning left and he stopped his engine so he could hear the RedTide snowmobiles. He detected that they were just ahead down the tunnel to the left. He accelerated his snowmobile to maximum throttle as the gunman behind steadied his weapon to fire. When he spotted the empty snowmobile perched on an iceboulder spinning its belt in midair at the edge of the tunnel opening it was too late to stop, although he tried. The last thing the driver and his passenger saw as they shot out of the tunnel opening over eighty feet above the water below was MacGregor's helicopter hovering above them.

MacGregor winced as he saw the snowmobile come flying out of the hole in the ice. Lionfish and his men could see the proverbial light at the end of the tunnel as they sped around the last bend. Lionfish could see the first of his men exiting the tunnel, when suddenly the driver and his passenger on the first snowmobile flew off the back. The passengers back was blown open from the high velocity round that entered the driver's chest and exited through the passenger's back.

Both men were killed instantly and were blown off the snowmobile, which proceeded ahead without them for fifty feet, leaving both dead men behind in the snow. MacGregor smiled and gave himself a mental pat on the back for his fine marksmanship.

The chopper hovered fifty feet from the tunnel exit and waited for Lionfish and his men to exit as MacGregor's remaining men entered the tunnel entrance.

"Come out without your weapons and your hands in the air and I will let you live," MacGregor announced over the helicopter's external speaker system.

"My orders are to take you alive and you have my word you will not be harmed.

"My men have entered the cave and it will be minutes before they are upon you. If you stand and fight men will die on both sides, but in the end you and all your men will be slaughtered. You are in a no-win situation, Lionfish. Order your men to surrender."

As MacGregor spoke his last warning a driverless snowmobile came flying from the exit of the cave and headed straight toward the helicopter.

"Up, you son of a bitch, NOW!" MacGregor screamed at the pilot. As the helicopter ascended to fifty feet the snowmobile exploded directly below it sending up a huge plume of fire that touched the bottom of the chopper and engulfed the underside in flames.

The helicopter was lifted an additional fifty feet into the air by the shockwaves and the superheated air below and MacGregor was relieved that the fuel tanks did not ignite. The pilot steadied the aircraft as Lionfish and his men sped out of the tunnel and flew down a steep bank of snow and ice in the direction of the water. The underside of MacGregor's chopper was still on fire and he could only look on in desperation as Lionfish made his escape.

"Land in that snow drift to douse these flames before we go off like a roman candle, you stupid bastard," MacGregor shouted to the pilot.

The pilot landed in a ten-foot deep snow drift and the flames quickly went out. MacGregor's men exited the cave and the remaining six snowmobiles circled the steaming helicopter. MacGregor opened the door and told Fagan and his men the direction in which RedTide's forces had headed. Fagan and his men took off while the charred helicopter lifted off again.

When the chopper was airborne, MacGregor spotted RedTide's forces entering a small cave at the water's edge. Their snowmobiles were parked outside of the cave and MacGregor could see some equipment including a Comsat communications dish standing outside in the snow. MacGregor concluded that Lionfish had decided to make a last stand at his base camp where he could resupply his ammunition and radio for help.

MacGregor was surprised at Lionfish's choice for a camp, with his back to the freezing water and no way to retreat. He had regarded Lionfish as a better general than that, and he had certainly not been a disappointing opponent thus far.

MacGregor could see that his men had formed a semicircle around the mouth of the cave and were positioned behind their snowmobiles with their weapons at the ready. This was a band of battle experienced ex- marines and mercenaries, but MacGregor's intelligence had told him that RedTide was made up of mostly ex -Navy SEALs and Special Ops personnel.

He knew this firefight would not be a cake walk and held out little hope of seeing his bonus. "Land right next to my men just outside their perimeter," he instructed the pilot. As soon as the helicopter touched down he leapt from it and ordered his men to the cave entrance on either side.

"On my command open up with everything you've got. NOW!!"

MacGregor's men opened fire in unison and fired hundreds of rounds into the cave as they rushed in. When they entered the cave it was empty. MacGregor looked around and saw two snowmobiles, a worktable and some discarded weapons, and nothing else. There were no other entrances or exits visible in the cave other than the one he and his men had entered.

His eye caught something in the corner of the cave tucked in on it's side. It was a scuba bouyancy vest with a Drager rebreathing unit on the back. These systems were brand new and had not yet been released in the United States. The sons of bitches had swam away. But that was impossible. He had been in the air and he watched as RedTide's forces had entered the cave. He had never seen them exit the cave or enter the water. The backpack he was holding felt unusually heavy and the tank that held the odorless Nitrox gas used on this system had an unusual smell to it.

He recognized that smell a moment too late as he dropped the unit to the ground and ordered his men to run quickly from the cave. The special explosive device, manufactured by Tarpon back at his workshop, detonated, filling the cave instantly with a gelatinous highly flammable substance similar to Napalm yet infinitely more powerful.

A huge ball of flame curled up around the entire cavity of the cave incinerating the men standing inside instantly before rolling out of the opening across the ice to ignite the remaining snow mobiles and then finally engulfing the helicopter, causing it to explode.

The men at the cave exit were set ablaze and hurled into the air before landing in the icy waters beyond. MacGregor ran ten feet from the mouth of the cave and was close to the edge of the ice as the fireball reached him. He could feel the intensity of the heat and smell the chemicals. His hair and clothing were set ablaze as he was lifted into the air and projected out into the water. Lionfish looked up from the controls of his underwater scooter when the ice above turned bright red and orange. He and his men would have to swim two miles in the frozen waters of the North Atlantic to finally surface at the boat.

He had lost only four men, and thanks to exhaustive planning, they had made their escape with the majority of his forces intact. Two days earlier, he had his men stow the heated dry suits, scooters and rebreathers in the cave and cut a hole in the ice to make an escape hatch. He had them install hooks in the underside of the ice lid so that it could be dragged into place when they entered the water. He hoped that the constantly swirling snow within the cave would cover the opening. He knew that careful inspection would reveal the hatch but the explosion would solve that problem. He had to hope that MacGregor would make the mistake of being drawn in by a cornered opponent and that he would make the added mistake of landing the helicopter on the ice near the cave instead of at a safe distance.

He hoped that the loss of MacGregor today would finally put an end to Yamaguchi's relentless pursuit of his organization. He was reluctant to launch a counter offensive against the man and to assassinate him. He had hoped that Yamaguchi would eventually lose interest and his hunger for vengeance would abate.

The cost today had been too high and this was the second time that they had made a narrow escape from Yamaguchi's trap. Something had to be done to tighten security. Despite the heating units inside their dry suits, Lionfish was freezing in his extremities and around his mask and when he checked the thermometer on his gauges it read 28.7 degrees Fahrenheit, the coldest that water could be without freezing.

The air temperature above was -50F when they entered the water. Lionfish looked up at the blue ceiling of ice above him and he realized that they had swam from the relative safety of a 10 foot ceiling of ice over their heads to a thickness of over one hundred feet. The visibility in these waters can exceed 500 feet and normally navigating within view of a hole in the ice above for escape is relatively simple in a part of the world where the ice can reach a thickness of over 9000 feet.

As he looked out into the deep blue of the frozen sea he thought once again about the warm waters of his beloved Caribbean and he remembered a verse from, "The Rime of the Ancient Mariner."

"The ice was here, the ice was there, the ice was all around, it cracked and growled, and roared and howled, like noises in a swound."

He looked ahead at the single file line of men on their motorized scooters and hoped the units would continue to function in these temperatures as Stingray had promised. It would be a long cold swim without them and soon there would be a full-scale search on for them. They didn't have the luxury of time. Lionfish heard a splash in the water at the edge of the ice and reacted instantly, looking in the direction of the disturbance and saw a group of harp seals entering the water all around him and his men. They were looking for fish.

They swam around circling him and his men with grace and beauty and an entertaining playfulness. They reminded him of what today had been about and he felt reassured about his purpose. He was amazed at how fast they moved, leaving a trail of bubbles in the frigid aqua water. He had been told once that because of an unusually high oxygen level in their blood that seals could hold their breath for over an hour without surfacing.

As he and his men swam away he remembered the first time he had met Captain Stewart, almost thirty years ago. He was six years old and on a trip with his mom who was at work in the Dry Tortugas studying sea turtles. His mother introduced him to someone she had described as a great man and a hero in marine biology, Captain Samuel Stewart. Captain Stewart was charismatic and charming and he was larger than life. Like Lionfish's mother, Captain Stewart had not treated him like a child but was respectful and courteous.

It was ironic that by setting a trap for Lionfish today his enemies provided him with the opportunity to meet Captain Stewart once again and to pay him back for his kindness. Without meaning to, they allowed Lionfish to help Captain Stewart's cause today and to save his life. Despite Captain Stewart's harsh judgment of Lionfish's actions, he was proud of what he and his men accomplished today and Lionfish knew that someday Captain Stewart would recognize their contributions.

Later that evening in his cabin, safe within the boat, Lionfish sat drinking some coffee. His cup was half filled with bourbon and he looked through his mother's old diary. He had no idea at the time, of course, when he was first introduced to him that his mother had been carrying on a love affair with Captain Stewart for over five years before he was born. His mother was a lonely woman who traveled over 200 days a year doing field research. Lionfish's father had ran out on them both when he was born and his mother never discussed him, either who he was or what he had been like.

Lionfish didn't blame his mother for the affair and wondered why nothing permanent had ever come of their relationship; they seemed to have so much in common. According to his mother's diary it had been a torrid, passionate affair. Captain Stewart was married and would not leave his wife, despite the unhappy circumstances of their marriage. Lionfish and his mother lived alone and she was married only to her work until the day she was killed on that fateful night just after Lionfish's sixteenth birthday.

Since that day, Lionfish had been haunted by his mother's death. It cast a shadow over the man, darkening the edges and draining the color from his life. According to articles in several newspapers, Captain Stewart was now a widower. As Lionfish closed the book and drifted off to sleep he wondered how different his life would have been, had his mother lived. He dreamed that night that he was six years old again and that he was diving for the first time while his mother held his hand and introduced him to all the wonders of the sea.

CHAPTER 10

I WAS RUNNING FULL OUT and the weapon in my hands was feeling heavier by the second. My men had circled around the enemy as I had instructed and we were closing in on them from two sides, forcing their backs against the water and removing any possible route of escape. I signaled for the six men in my squad to slow down and to follow me through the densest section of trees at the top of a small hill overlooking the enemy. We were heavily camouflaged and as we peered through the bushes to get a visual sighting we were virtually invisible to our targets below.

I could see below that there were four enemy soldiers, and to my surprise and delectation the top ranking officer of their group was with them, standing right out in the open. He was doubled over and breathed heavily from his half mile run to evade the other half of my squad, which had herded them to their present position.

I whispered to my men to each pick a separate target so that we could fire simultaneously, killing all four men at once and eliminating the risk of return fire. I indicated that I would take out their leader with a head shot and I aimed my rifle and waited a few more seconds for what I knew would be the highlight of my day. I sighted my weapon directly on the front helmet of my target just above his brow and squeezed slowly on the trigger while holding my breath.

"Now," I said just loud enough for all my men to hear me, and we all fired at once. The other four men standing near my target were hit directly in their chests and spun around. My shot caught my target dead center on his helmet an inch above the rim, and splattered a huge blob of yellow iridescent paint that spread out in the shape of a large sunflower. The paint ran down the face and onto the protective goggles of my regional sales manager, Al Chadwick. Al turned and began to scream and curse in my direction. Me and my teammates were laughing out loud and began to tease our deceased co-workers mercilessly.

"Stein, you asshole. No headshots," Al bellowed at me. He was clearly embarrassed and even more pissed off about losing the contest. "You were told that by the instructor and by me three times. You could have blinded me and those fucking paint pellets can crack your skull at close range. What the fuck is your problem?"

"I'm sorry, Al. I was aiming for your left shoulder," I lied, "but you were moving around and I was close to sixty feet away when I took that shot." I slapped him on the back and tried to charm him as best as I could.

This paintball competition had grown from an idea my co-workers and closest friends at the office and I had one day while eating blintzes at our favorite breakfast restaurant. I was teamed up with my usual gang of misfits, John Kaszinski, Danny Fraschilla, and Frank Freda. Two or three mornings a week, we would drive over to Twin Bagels, the only good New York bagel place in Florida. We would have a leisurely two-hour breakfast before we grudgingly hit the streets, to once again give our monotonous pitch to yet another cardiologist about the return on investment of purchasing his own cardiac ultrasound machine.

We were all pretty bored and burned out with the business. The monotony and the constant stress and pressure to make quota were brutal and every month became a renewed battle to save your job. Most people in office jobs across America in what are supposedly sales support positions see field sales people as spoiled egomaniacal children who have too much free time and make far too much money.

In every company I have worked for there has always been a resentment between the inside office people with their set hours and fixed incomes and the outside salespeople. Unfortunately most senior managers handle this derisiveness poorly and the company ultimately pays the price for this prejudicial attitude.

The truth is that there are very few people who would want to live the life of a salesperson and have to deal with the daily scrutiny and performance pressures. I was arguing with one of the bean counters in the office one day about the salesman's quarterly bonus program and she made a snide remark about salesmen being greedy and overpaid.

I had just had the same conversation on the phone with my sister earlier that morning. Jackie was always putting down my profession. I told my sister that although her husband was a great artist if he were a little better at selling his work he would be doing a hell of a lot better. This was a sensitive subject and she hung up on me.

Now, I asked this bookkeeper why she didn't go into sales herself since it seemed like such a great way to earn so much easy money. I asked her how she would like it if at the end of every month her performance was reviewed by her boss in the accounting department, the CFO of the company. At the end of each and every month she would be reviewed and if her performance had slipped or was not up to par the Chief Financial Officer would put her on probation.

It did not matter if the previous month she had saved the company hundreds of thousands of dollars, or if the previous year she had been Employee of the Year, or if she had twenty years of loyal devoted service to the firm. All that mattered was that she did as good a job every single month, and it would have to improve every month as her performance quota was raised so that she now had to do an outstanding job each and every new month.

If she had a bad month then she had to make it up the next two months by doing a spectacular job at work and had to document that she had saved the company twice as much money in order to make up for her previous loss.

Every month her work would be compared to the other accountant's work, and if she didn't do as well as they did she would be publicly ridiculed and her performance would be displayed on a bulletin board for all the world to see, and would be published in the company newsletter.

This treatment would continue for her entire career as an accountant even if it lasted thirty years. And when she got older and could not add as quickly or lost some of her skills she would be cast out with no money and limited prospects, having to compete against people half her age at half her salary.

There is no other profession as cruel in its accountability, and no other profession as inhumane in its short-term memory for recognition, as sales. I explained to her that it is the salespeople that drive a company. That it is the salespeople who will make or break a company. You can have the greatest products in the world, fantastic customer service, and the world's greatest accountants, but without customers you may as well close your doors.

That is why salespeople are compensated so well. High risk and high reward, I explained to the clerk who had offended me. When I was done with my lecture did she thank me for enlightening her? No. She told me that she now understood why the other people in the accounting department thought I was such an asshole.

Well, the office people were right about one thing. Although my friends and I were by far the most talented group of salesmen at LifeForce Technology, we were also the laziest. Luckily, our natural talents and persuasive charms and our ability to instantly find some point of mutual interest and establish rapport with almost any individual made us all relatively successful.

When I say successful I mean that we all earned over seventy-five thousand dollars a year and rarely suffered the indignity of being put on probation. Probation for a salesman working in a highly competitive environment with over twenty different, yet equally enormous egoes all vying for attention and recognition is the equivalent of being put in stocks and displayed in the town square as a pedophile.

LifeForce was the largest medical dealer in the southeast and sold everything from Batman Band-Aids, to Pediatricians, to high-end capital equipment such as ultrasound and treadmills to cardiologists. I was recruited from my prior company by my current sales manager, Al Chadwick. Al met me at the American College of Cardiology convention in Anaheim two years ago. Al had heard through the grapevine that I was a rainmaker and that I had consistently ranked as my former employer ACD, Advanced Cardiac Devices, top salesperson month after month.

I became ACD's Rookie of The Year in my first seven months with the company, beating out salespeople with ten times my experience in the industry, and followed it up by becoming Salesman of the Year the following year and doing over 160% of quota. At the awards banquet, I was awarded a gold and stainless steel Rolex Submariner, one of my most prized possessions and as a diver something I had coveted for many years.

Al pursued me with the same persistence and aggressiveness that had made him a top rep in his profession for over ten years and offered me full relocation, a $10,000 sign on bonus and a guaranteed eight percent commission my first year, doubling the standard four percent commissions that most reps received.

His investment paid off, despite a rocky beginning. Two weeks after moving to Florida a category 5 hurricane slammed into the east coast and destroyed a full third of my territory. I had no network yet in Florida and still had not completed full training. The first month I would get lost exiting my own neighborhood and relied heavily on maps to coordinate my time within my territory.

One night, I was watching the news about the destruction and was listening to interviews with some of the survivors when I had a brainstorm. I created a disaster relief and recovery plan for physicians whose practices were hit by Hurricane Donna. I began concentrating my efforts and prospecting in those areas. I designed, with the help of LifeForces marketing people, a one-page flyer which outlined the discounts available to physicians who needed to replace equipment they had lost due to the hurricane. It explained that my company would coordinate payment directly with their insurance companies, freeing up their precious time to deal with other more pressing problems. I offered a large discount considering the circumstances and accepted only two thirds of the money that was reimbursed by the physician's insurance companies, in most cases allowing the balance of the funds to go directly into the physicians pockets.

There were literally hundreds of doctors who had set up makeshift practices in trailers outside in the parking lots of hospitals and within three months I had surpassed the top salesmen at LifeForce by almost fifty percent of quota and had earned over $75,000 in commissions.

One day, Al installed a large brass bell with a long rope tied to its clanger in the sales room and implemented a policy, or rather a game, whereby a salesman who closed an order for the day would announce it to the company by walking into the room and clanging the bell to signify his sale. We all thought it was ridiculous and corny at first but eventually looked forward with great excitement to walking into the office and ringing that bell for all the world to hear.

Everyone would look up to see who had sold something and at the end of a good month when the bell was clanging like mad I had to admit it created a lot of excitement. One of my greatest moments in selling was the day I walked into the offices of LifeForce Technology and stood there and rang that bell five consecutive times for the five sales I had closed in that one day, establishing a new company record.

Every office worker, from secretary to accountant, stood around and cheered while I smiled proudly from ear to ear. It was only my second month with the company and I had found a way to turn the hurricane to my advantage. Like Al always said, "In times of adversity a loser complains about his troubles and sees only darkness, a winner recognizes opportunity and seizes it." Or there's his abbreviated version, "Winners find a Way."

These days, however, all I could see was darkness with no way out, no clever solution or creative way to solve my problem and find the light. I suppose that would make me a loser in Al's eyes and a small part of me was hurt at the thought of Al thinking of me in that way. There was another part of me that promised to break his neck if he gave me another pep talk about how lucky I was to have the kind of mother I had for as long as I had her and how a lot of people have never known that kind of love. I knew that what Al said was true but I also knew that he was about as sincere as a ten dollar hooker complimenting your sexual prowess and that the only reason he ever said anything kind or encouraging was to manipulate you or as he put it, "to motivate you."

My intimate knowledge of Al and the fact that I knew that he always had an ulterior motive only caused me to resent his attempts to console me about my impending loss. My friends, however, were a different story. My first day back in the office they spirited me out of the office and took me deep sea fishing with several cases of Hieneken.

We fished all day, occasionally calling clients from our cellular phones with the sound of the sea crashing around the boat in the background and Danny yelling for another beer. John, Frank and Danny told me that I should take a leave of absence and that if Chadwick fired me they would all resign the very next day. My eyes filled with tears when I looked up and saw my friends and the genuine love and concern in their eyes. We were as close as any group of men could be, especially salesmen. We would cover each other in the office and we would share sales in order to make sure that we all attained quota every month. This is virtually unheard of in a profession that encourages isolation and vicious competition while at the same time preaches about teamwork.

We talked on the boat about one of our favorite topics, the greed and avarice of the physicians we sold to. Medical sales can be very disillusioning for people that think that doctor's care for anything besides their own financial statements. When we sold equipment all we talked about was return on investment, cost, the volume of tests times Medicare reimbursement minus the monthly lease equals huge monthly profits.

We rarely talked about diagnosis or treatment of patients. When I sold an ultrasound machine I would tell the doctors that this was a machine that would take the five dollars he invested in each test and turn it into a hundred dollar bill, and when I proved it to them by showing them insurance reimbursements and their own monthly testing volumes, based on their own records, their eyes would almost pop out of their heads.

The machine I sold was technically inferior to my competition's, but it was cheap, "diagnostically adequate," and it paid the same amount for the tests it performed as machines twice its cost. Where was the incentive for doctors to buy the best with reimbursements on a steady decline?

Doctors got rich by performing unnecessary tests and procedures that were not deemed risky, and because people who had insurance were too apathetic to read their bills, and the insurance companies did nothing to police it, they got away with it.

That was all right with me. The medical companies whose products I sold were grossly overpriced and they were making a 1,000 percent profit on the drugs and equipment they sold. I knew pacemaker and catheter reps who were making 250,000 dollars a year.

Everyone was getting rich at Medicare's expense. I knew sales people at clinical laboratories that double-billed for Ferritins and other tests and indulged in other forms of double-dipping and they gave enormous kickbacks to physicians and clinics that used their services.

When Al was selling ultrasound in radiology he made over 200 thousand dollars a year, every year. We were all getting rich at the insurance trough.

Now supposedly the government was aware of the overspending and the abuse and it was going to do something about it, ostensibly to protect the consumer and to keep Medicare from going bankrupt. All that will do is open the door for a new brand of crook and allow new types of health care companies like HMOs to deliver healthcare in new packages, while they exploit this new window of opportunity and grow by thousands of percentage points and get richer than ever. Hospital buying groups like Columbia will become enormous conglomerates and will buy up all the non-profit community hospitals and will lower services while raising their profits. In the end, the doctors and the hospitals will still get rich and the consumer will receive the lowest quality of healthcare in America in over twenty years. The average American will have little or no say in how he is treated in the future and will have to take what he can get.

The first time I noticed the effects on the consumer were when I became one and I got my bill for my Malaria treatment from the hospital. It was over 12,000 dollars for a one week stay at the hospital. Doctors were sending me bills with ten consultation fees of seventy five dollars. Every time they poked their heads in my door, they charged me. If they looked in on me to ask me how I felt, they charged me. I had a CAT scan of my abdomen when they checked my liver and they double billed me for a pelvic scan that I know they did not do. When I inquired at the billing department they said, "Don't worry, your insurance will cover it."

When I finished my story about the hospital bill, John told us all a story about a cardiologist in Hallendale who asked him to write up a lease on an ultrasound machine for ten thousand dollars more than it would really cost him, and instructed John not to tell his other three partners in the practice. This way he could get a ten thousand dollar kickback on the lease and his partners would wind up paying the total cost of the machine with no expense to him personally. John, the most ethical salesman in the office, refused and when he finished his story Danny asked him why he didn't throw the lead his way.

Then Frank told us a story about his visit last year to see a urologist. Frank was worried that he might be impotent. He quickly explained that he was seeing a girl in her twenties and that it had turned out to be a simple case of performance anxiety.

The urologist gave him two little Velcro bands to attach to his penis at night. It seems that a man will involuntarily get two to three erections a night while he is sleeping and if you are healthy you will wake up the next day and the bands will have popped off.

Frank told us that he found the bands the next morning across the room under his dresser and we all laughed so hard I thought I would pee my pants. The doctor sent Frank a bill for 400 dollars and called the test a "nocturnal penile tumescence test," no doubt to impress the insurance company. Frank was outraged and called the doctor to tell him so.

"How could two little pieces of Velcro cost 400 dollars?" Frank asked. The doctor told Frank that they cost him over twenty dollars apiece. He then told Frank that he was over his deductible and that his insurance company would pay for it and that he should not be concerned.

Frank threatened to report him for fraud but in the end wound up selling him a 50,000 dollar piece of equipment instead. What a character. Only Frank could threaten fraud charges one minute and then charm the man into writing a check the next. Frank told us that he recognized in the doctor's unmitigated display of greed a perfect candidate for a sale and told the doctor that if he wanted to make some real money then they should have lunch together to talk about some diagnostic equipment, like a penile doppler.

Frank was the one who had brought us all together and he was the most charismatic man I had ever known. He was fifty-three years old and looked forty. He had once been an actor, playing Diver Dan on a popular TV show in the sixties. At a sales meeting in New York, Frank took us to the Players Club and showed us a picture of himself with Henry Fonda.

We played poker and smoked cigars all night long and showed up the next day at the convention booth hung over and exhausted, but we were still able to close more business than any convention group before or since. Frank was incredibly charming and was the best-dressed man in the office. He only wore suits made by people whose last names ended in I, like Armani or Canali.

Although he was by far the most immature person among us and was often the leader and instigator of our daily trips abroad to play hooky during working hours, his age and his personality gave him a distinct air of credibility and wisdom when calling on a customer.

If Frank told you something you believed it and I would marvel at how educated board certified specialists would nod agreeably at what I knew was the biggest load of bullshit I had ever heard.

He had a dated pencil thin mustache and looked like Errol Flynn, who he said was his favorite actor.

Danny was an Italian boy from Brooklyn, New York, where his family owned a plumbing supply business. When Danny would brag that they were the largest distributor of Speakman shower heads in the northeast we would all respond in unison, "Big Fucking Deal." Danny was about 5'6" tall and was heavily muscled from years of weightlifting, probably to overcome his insecurity about his height. He had a huge heart and would often defend even our most unpopular and obnoxious co-workers at LifeForce.

One day, Danny and I were parked at a traffic light on the off ramp of I95 in Hollywood when a young black girl knocked on my window to beg for money. When I refused, she told me that she was homeless. She also told me that she was pregnant. When I asked her if the baby was mine, Danny punched me in the arm and immediately handed the girl a five dollar bill.

All the way back to the office he lectured me about what a sarcastic insensitive prick I could be. I explained to him that the girl was probably shooting up his five dollars as we spoke and he got even madder. But as big as Danny's heart was he also had an equally large temper and would frequently try to engage Al in a screaming match about subjects ranging from commissions to territory re-alignments.

Al who is the master manipulator and knows everyone's hot buttons and pet peeves knew what drove Danny crazy. He would just sit there and infuriate Danny even more by using two of his favorite weapons against him, quiet patience and patronizing calm.

The more upset Danny would become, the quieter and more rational Al would become. I would literally have to drag Danny from the office for fear he would strike Al at any second. Danny was very self conscious about his appearance and in particular his premature balding. He was only twenty-seven years old and had already lost most of his hair. He had once talked about hair plugs, until Frank who Danny idolizes and is also balding, talked him out of it.

Danny's passion was deep sea fishing and it was one of the main reasons he moved here from New York five years ago. It was Danny's dream to own his own fishing lodge in the Florida keys. I was quite certain that this excursion today was Danny's idea. Even though the boat had a qualified first mate, Danny insisted on running around checking our lines and baiting our hooks himself until finally he got so drunk he passed out below with his head only six inches from the noxious odor of the marine toilet.

Danny's best quality as a salesman was that he was almost immediately likable and people trusted him. The down side to his personality was that he was not a strong closer and found it hard to be confrontational with people, especially people he liked. Consequently he was always struggling to reach quota.

John, Frank, and I would often blitz Danny's territory after we ourselves had hit target and would often push him over the edge of quota by going in on closing appointments and double-teaming fence sitters, literally forcing a decision. This had to be handled very tactfully with Danny, who was very proud and often hard to coach because of his insecurities and his defensive personality.

I heard John laughing behind me and when I looked up he was taking a picture of Frank, who had been nude sunbathing on the forward deck. Frank was standing with his back toward us and the only thing he was wearing was a Panama hat. John had by far the best sense of humor in our group and he could always make me laugh no matter how foul a mood I was in. John was a strikingly handsome man with thick wavy black hair and bright green eyes. He had a boyish, infectious smile and deep-set dimples, with a strong square jaw and high-set cheekbones. He was a giant among us, standing close to 6'3" tall and weighing over 210 pounds.

He was a top ranked basketball player at St. Johns University until a career-killing knee injury in his junior year destroyed his chances of entering the NBA. John is a natural athlete and could handily beat me at any sport, even the ones that I had played for years and had introduced him to. We both took up golf at the same time almost a year ago and while I still struggled to break 100, John was playing in the low 80s. He joked with me about having to find a new partner to play with, but in reality he never lost patience with me and he was always encouraging and supportive. His personality was so charismatic and magnetic that on sales calls the women in the offices we visited would flirt with John shamelessly.

He never had any trouble getting past the guardians of the gates who often have the charm and personality of prison guards. I had seen the coldest most professional office managers carry on like school girls while John was giving his sales pitch. The thing I admired most about John was that he took it all in stride and was the most down to earth person I knew. He was so comfortable with himself and so sure of who he was that he had no need to be self congratulatory or to make others feel inferior. I have known many men with half as much to be proud of who were egocentric and shallow. I often wonder how I would behave if I had been blessed with so many gifts.

The rarest quality of John's in today's world is that he was also extremely loyal to his friends, his employer, and especially to his wife of ten years, Julie, who he still seemed to be madly in love with.

In all the time I've worked with John I had never seen or even heard about him so much as flirt with another woman. John was one of the finest people I knew and I was proud that he considered me his friend. John was also from New York, Smithtown to be exact.

It is strange how all the New Yorkers in the office seemed to have gravitated toward each other. The commonality of our backgrounds made relating to each other easier, I suppose. My friends and I had a rare friendship among men. We often spoke openly about our fears as well as our desires without fear of judgment or criticism. Like all men we teased each other mercilessly when we screwed up and we were extremely competitive with each other, but we also supported each other and forgave each other our weaknesses and frailties.

On the plane ride down from New York, I had the misfortune of sitting next to a group of rowdy twenty-year-old men who were returning from a ski trip to Vail. They were drinking continuously and were making lewd remarks about the stewardesses, their co-workers, and even each other's wives.

I felt like I was trapped in the middle of a beer commercial and expected any minute to see the flight attendants come dancing down the aisle in bikinis dispensing Budweisers. Their conversation was a typical one among extremely macho men. They talked about who got the most "pussy." They talked about who could eat the most, with the winner bragging that while in Vail he had eaten two entire pizzas by himself. They talked about breaking things, including equipment and their own bones, another favorite topic of modern-day, thinly-disguised Neanderthal man.

I listened to five minutes of dialogue about jumping snowmobiles and tumbling headfirst down double diamond trails they should not have been on. I was already feeling stretched to my limit and I got up to change my seat. I'd had enough of the Flight of the Testosterone.

As I got up to move my seat, one of the most obnoxious men in the group asked me if they had been disturbing me. I assured him that they were not and that I personally was having too bad a week to appreciate their merriment without at least half the beers they had comsumed.

I was very lucky to have found such a safe environment and the comfort and friendship of such good men. We drank all the beer and the first mate, after some haggling with Frank, sold us some pot and we smoked a joint or two, watched the sunset and sang along with "The Boss" who was playing "Thunder Road" over the boat's loudspeakers.

It was a perfect "work" day in Florida and one of the last carefree days I would enjoy for some time. Tonight on CNN Larry King was going to interview one of the leaders of RedTide and we were all going to watch it at my house. I had just broken up with my girlfriend Mariela, a secretary who worked in our office. Mariela was a Cuban receptionist with long brown hair and long tan legs and perfect round firm breasts, but unfortunately she had the IQ of an eggplant.

She was leaving me messages every day on my answering machine that alternated between cursing me out and telling me she missed me. I had gotten bored of her two weeks before I left for New York. Two days before I left I had met Linda, the blond sales girl who manages the rental office at my apartment complex. Linda was the most beautiful woman I had ever seen and I didn't want Mariela to come around the complex any more and risk my running into Linda with my girlfriend.

Mariela was okay in bed but she had a lot of hang ups and seemed only to want to have sex to please me, which to most men would be acceptable, but quickly bored me. Linda was only twenty-four years old but she was powerfully seductive and very exciting. I had been flirting with her for weeks, with little or no recognition except for polite conversation. I would have been happier if she had at least taken me seriously enough to have been offended. Then one day I ran into her out at the pool on her day off. I pulled up a lounge chair across from where she was sitting so that I would be close enough to check her out in her bikini, but not be so close that she might think I was going to hit on her again.

I decided to give up before I began to look pathetic and to be polite and civil. Linda was lying on her stomach with her top undone and she was wearing a baby blue thong bikini that was riding high between her thighs. She has long thick blond hair and blue eyes and an even brown tan. She has very small but nicely shaped breasts and a perfect round firm behind.

I could see the light blond hair on her behind which looked like peach fuzz illuminated by the strong afternoon sun and as she shifted her body I could see the blue band of her suit between her legs, barely covering her.

I wanted her so much I felt dizzy. I began to fantasize about rubbing lotion all over the back of her thighs and up between her legs. I jumped in the pool to cool off and she tied the top of her suit and rolled over. When she saw me doing the backstroke across the pool, trying hard to appear as if I hadn't noticed her, she called me over to talk. I came over slowly, trying to play it cool and said, "Hi Linda. This is the last place I would have expected to see you on your day off."

"I live here, Jake. Besides I had errands to do around the house, which brings me to the reason I wanted to talk to you. I was wondering if you could help me hang some speakers in my house. I have the brackets and the cable and it should only take a few minutes."

This girl has some nerve, I thought. *She practically ignores me for over a month and then she asks me to play handyman. Let her get her fucking boyfriend to do it.*

"Why don't you get your boyfriend or one of the handymen on staff to do it?"

"The only one working today is Carlos and he has a major air conditioning repair job to do. And I don't have a boyfriend anymore. I have a small party tonight Jake, which of course you are invited to and I need the speakers mounted."

Then she smiled that perfect toothy white smile and I would have installed ten miles of chain link fence in the hot sun that afternoon if she had asked me to.

"When do you want to me to do it?"

"How about right now," she said. "Let's go." She jumped up and wrapped her matching sheer blue sarong around her hips. I followed her back to her apartment, staring at her from behind and praying to the gods above to let something happen. I had been in situations like this before and my *Penthouse Forum*-corrupted imagination produced fantasies that never played out the way I had hoped. I would wind up hanging speakers for two hours on my day off, then later I would have to watch some guy like John make out with Linda at her party while I sat and suffered silently in the corner.

After twenty-five minutes of standing on a ladder my back was killing me and I told Linda who was still in her bathing suit that I needed to walk around and stretch my back muscles. When I came down from the ladder she had a towel and she began to wipe the sweat from my neck and face. She was standing only a few inches from me and the sexual tension was electric. Every nerve in my body felt stimulated. I decided to take a risk and to do something courageous and totally out of character for me and I kissed her on the mouth.

She leaned into me and responded. I ran my hands over her breasts and kissed her neck and chest. We moved quickly to the coach where I removed her top and kissed her nipples while I gently ran my hand up her thighs between her legs. I kissed her over her stomach and slipped her bathing suit off while I tenderly kissed her beautiful young body.

I could smell her sweet feminine scent mixed with the fresh smell of chlorine from the swimming pool. She rocked her hips and moaned quietly as I pulled down my shorts and climbed up between her legs. I can't remember ever feeling so excited and so happy at the same time. My desire for her was on so many different levels. I had dreamed about this for so long and it was better than I had imagined.

Then suddenly she stopped me and asked me if I had anything on me.

"I'm wearing a bathing suit," I said, hurt and disappointed. "Do you think I carry condoms to the pool?"

"I'm sorry, Jake. We can't, and you know I'm right. There will be other times," she said and then she kissed me and we held each other until we both fell asleep naked on her couch. She meant what she had said, there were other times—one to be exact—before she reconciled with her ex-boyfriend, a guitar player with a popular local band.

We only had sex that one time but to this day I still find myself daydreaming about it. Linda was the most beautiful woman I had ever been with and the lovemaking was fierce and passionate and adventurous. I fell in love with her that afternoon and would wince with pain every time I would see her and her boyfriend together at the apartment complex.

She barely acknowledged me after that magical day and would stop to talk to me just as long as she had to in order to be civil and polite. Eventually I wound up calling Mariela back. I told her with heartfelt sincerity that I knew exactly how I had hurt her and how she must have felt. Mariela was not nearly as beautiful or as sensual as Linda, but her heart was pure and she would never hurt anyone intentionally so I invited her over to watch the interview with my friends and I. I had never seen the *Larry King Live* show before and really had no interest in the politicians and Hollywood has-beens that frequented his show. However, it was receiving more hype than the 30 second, forty dollar Mike Tyson fights that aired on Pay Per View and I was fascinated by the group RedTide. I longed for that kind of adventure in my life and for the kind of passion and zeal that men like them brought to their cause. I could identifiy with their love of the ocean and the world below and it was probably the one cause in life that I could ever feel that strongly about. I promised myself for the tenth time that I would do more than just talk about helping and that someday I would do more then just slap a World Wildlife Foundation sticker on my car or on the front of my refrigerator.

Someday I would get involved, as soon as I could find some time. My phone started ringing. I let it ring through to my answering machine in order to screen the call. It rang four times before the machine picked it up and then I heard my sister's tortured voice crying and screaming for me to answer the phone. I ran toward the phone tripping over the couch and I banged my knee on the coffee table. I heard my sister say just before she hung up that my mother had died.

I stood paralyzed, frozen in time by the shocking impact of my sister's words. I clutched the portable phone tightly in my hand and I began to tremble from head to toe. I couldn't catch my breath and I let out a high-pitched violent scream as I dropped to my knees and came completely apart. I curled up on the floor in a fetal position and cried for two straight hours until the doorbell rang announcing my friend's arrival.

I called my sister and, instead of us consoling each other, we fought. I attacked her for leaving such news on my machine and for not waiting until we could speak live. She retaliated by reminding me of where I was when my mother passed away. I made arrangements to fly to New York immediately. I felt dead inside and for one brief moment in time I was distracted with the logistics of planning my departure. I focused on the details of my trip. I made reservations and I packed while my friends surrounded me and offered comfort. My pain had lessened in the midst of my busy work to become a continuous dull ache in my chest.

Mariela arrived later and held me all through the night. Her presence was a great comfort to me. I promised myself that I would always appreciate what I had and that I would stop longing for what I could never have and for what I probably would not want if I wasn't so shallow and selfish.

I never appreciated my mother for who she was. I punished her for who she was not and who I thought she should be and now I missed her so much that I didn't think I would be able to live without her. Someday I would become the sort of man that she would have been proud of. The time had arrived for me to change my life and as I cried myself to sleep in Mariela's arms thinking about the future, when I closed my eyes I dreamed about the past.

CHAPTER 11

"LIVE FROM THE CNN CENTER in Atlanta, this is Larry King. Our guest tonight is a man who is known only as Stingray to the general public and to the various law enforcement agencies around the world who are pursuing him and the other members of the infamous fugitive organization in which he is a leader.

"The organization is known as RedTide and is an environmental terrorist group responsible most recently for the total destruction of a large dam in northern Canada.

For his protection I will be speaking with Stingray by satellite from a remote location which only RedTide's security personnel are aware of.

"Good evening, Stingray, and thank you for joining us. Let's start with a simple question first. I would like to know how you arrived at the name RedTide for your organization and what the significance is, if any, in the name?"

To the right of Mr. King where a guest would normally be seated was a large 26" monitor which showed the darkly lit image of a man disguised in a knit cap and wearing a beard. This interview had been arranged almost a year in advance and RedTide had been meticulous in guaranteeing the safety of one of its founders. Stingray was in an RV camper driving in some unknown foreign country thousands of miles away and the interview was being conducted via satellite signals that would be relayed and bounced over 10,000 miles through over 15 different sites before they finally reached the CNN center in Atlanta.

The latest communications devices and digital technology were being employed to scramble the signals and to render them virtually untraceable. The cost was staggering but CNN was gladly footing the bill for what would be the highest rated interview in over a decade.

This week, the body of Gregory Jugan the editor of *Oceanus*, a small conservation and underwater photography magazine was found drowned in a 100,000 gallon tank of raw sewage at a treatment facility in Island Park, New York. His legs had been tied to a length of chain attached to a 200 pound weight at the bottom which allowed only his untied arms and hands to break the surface and to claw for air.

Although RedTide had not claimed credit as of yet there was much speculation that they were the responsible party and tonight's ratings were expected to go through the roof.

"I would like to thank you for speaking with me tonight, Mr. King," Stingray began. "I understand that you and your network have been receiving a great deal of pressure from the FBI for your cooperation in arranging my security and have also received a great deal of negative criticism as well from the public for meeting with me this evening.

"In answer to your question, there has been much speculation as to the origin and the significance of the name RedTide. Our friends at Greenpeace believe that we chose RED, because it is the opposite of the GREEN in their name. Red which symbolizes "STOP!" and is considered the opposite of green which symbolizes "GO!," is seen by them as a direct insult to their organization. I have heard it speculated that the name RedTide represents an ocean of our enemy's blood, which will wash ashore as a warning to others.

"As a scientist I can tell you that a so called RedTide is caused by billions of dinoflagellates of various species; such tides are sometimes dangerous because they can poison both humans and fish. RedTides have occurred off the west coast of Florida and in the coastal waters of New England and Southern California, Texas, Peru, Eastern Australia, Chile and Japan. In 1948, such a tide killed fish, turtles, oysters, and other marine organisms in the Gulf of Mexico near Fort Meyers, Florida. The blue green algae called trichodesmus sometimes in dying off imparts a reddish color to the water. The Red Sea is so named because of this phenomenon.

"It is widely believed that one of the plagues that Moses wrought on Egypt to free his people was nothing more than a RedTide. Although I did not create the name for our organization, I believe it is an appropriate choice."

"That is very interesting information and you are obviously a highly educated man Stingray," Mr. King said. "Why do you belong to such a violent organization when there are so many other effective and productive ways in which a man with your obvious intellect could contribute?

"For the past several years you have contributed, albeit anonymously to the research and development of numerous pharmaceuticals derived from sources found within the oceans that have helped mankind begin to find cures for its most debilitating illnesses.

"It is widely known throughout the ranks of law enforcement that you have never been directly involved with the violent, more destructive elements of RedTide's organization. I recently heard that you had been offered amnesty if you should decide to cooperate with the government."

"You are wrong, Mr. King," Stingray said. "I am very closely associated with the violent side of RedTide's organization and have always been an extremely active participant in the planning of most of their operations. Although until recently I had never participated in any hostilities and I have always tried to encourage non-lethal intervention whenever possible. I still strongly support RedTide's actions."

"Did your organization murder Gregory Jugan, and if it did, why?" Mr. King asked. "Mr. Jugan was a known supporter of RedTide."

"First of all, I resent the use of the word murder and your earlier use of the word terrorists in describing our organization. Mr. Jugan was a traitor in what is an ongoing war to protect this planet and he put many people's lives at risk for his own selfish pursuits. The accepted penalty in this country for treason especially during wartime is death, is it not? Every day I see and hear more and more people on television and in the newspapers calling for the use of the death penalty in cases involving cop killers and serial killers. In invoking this sentence I have never once heard the states attorneys or federal prosecutors referred to as murderers. In this most educated and enlightened of times I hear the death penalty referred to as capital punishment, not murder. The state uses the threat of capital punishment to stop the killing of innocent civilians and to deter violent offenders. RedTide is also trying to stop the killing, by whatever means necessary.

"It is ironic that today species are disappearing faster than ever before. More species will have gone extinct from the years 1980 to 2000 than in the past 65 million years, and yet people call the members of my organization murderers and terrorists for trying to stop the killing."

"I would like to take some calls now," Mr. King announced. "Hello caller – – – – –-(Silence). Who do we have on the line?"

"Hi Larry, I love your show." With extreme patience and good humor, Larry King asked the caller her name and if she had a question for Stingray.

"My name is Barbara and I do have a question for Stingray. I read in the papers that you are supposed to be a marine biologist or a scientist of some kind. My mom is seventy-eight years old and she suffers from Alzheimer's. It has been devastating for my family watching my mother lose her dignity, and sometimes she doesn't know her own grandchildren. I read in the *Times* that you had anonymously submitted your research for finding a cure for Alzheimer's disease to Johns

Hopkins and that the FBI had seized it for evidence and would not allow its use. Is that true and do you believe that a cure is possible?"

"In fact what you are saying is accurate," Stingray responded. "I did submit some preliminary findings for a possible cure utilizing the venom of the Australian blue-ringed octopus and that information was seized. My work however will continue and if and when I discover a cure for this debilitating illness I will present it to the scientific community. Of course, it will have to be judged by the community, including the FDA, as to its legitimate benefits and its safety, and if it is judged to be effective then I hope that the law enforcement agencies will not interfere with its use.

"The ocean like the rainforest is a virtually unlimited pharmacopoeia which may yield the answers to finding cures for age old illnesses and new viral strains that are destroying the lives of our loved ones and have touched virtually every family or household in America.

"The ocean is yielding an increasing number of previously unknown chemical compounds manufactured by animals such as jellyfish. Scientists hope that one day these substances may cure cancer, lung diseases, including emphysema, and asthma, and inflammatory ailments such as arthritis and psoriasis. About half of all drugs known today are derived from plants or animals, including quinine, quinidine, digitalis, cortisone even aspirin which comes from tree bark. Over the last 200 years or so we have not had the technology to study marine organisms systematically the way we have studied terrestrial organisms. Now we have that technology.

"Sharks have a mysterious immunity to cancer that we cannot begin to understand, but we need to study them in order to find a possible cure. Instead, out of fear and ignorance we hunt them down and we massacre them until eventually we will have driven them to extinction.

"The definition of extinction is the death of birth, did you know that, Larry? The ocean's uniquely marine resources are rapidly declining because of the changes caused by human activities that are modifying coastal waters and in some cases destroying the reef habitats that harbor the greatest diversity of life and marine organisms.

"I was in the Philippines last year searching for a certain type of jellyfish to be used in my studies of Alzheimer's Disease and I watched in horror as native fisherman poured cyanide all over the reefs in order to catch tropical fish for the aquarium trade. Tropical fish also now fill a billion dollar a year Asian appetite for picking out live fish to eat. The cyanide is used to stun larger fish but ends up killing smaller ones and kills the reefs in days. They are dumping tons of the cyanide yearly and what I witnessed was the ecological equivalent of clear cutting a forest.

Maybe the cure for your mother's disease lays on one of those reefs.

"If you knew that in some remote Brazilian acre of rainforest was the cure for your mother's illness and the bulldozers were approaching to destroy your last hope of saving her, what would you be willing to do? I imagine the least you would be willing to do would be to write to your congressman or to send a small donation to the World Wildlife Foundation so that they could purchase that acre and preserve it.

"I will dedicate my life to trying to find a cure for Alzheimer's Disease and I promise you that if I do it will come from the sea. Please help me to protect it until I do."

"Hi, Larry. My name is Paul and I am in Seattle, Washington. I used to work at a mill up north until it was closed down. I was out of work for over a year before I got some work as a machinists apprentice with Boeing."

"Very good sir, now what is your question for Stingray?"

"I want to know how he can go around destroying property and putting people out of work? Has he ever had to feed his hungry kids with nothing in his pockets but change and no where to go for help, and does he really think a bunch of fish or a spotted owl are more important than the economy or the future of this country?"

"I am sorry for your particular situation Paul," Stingray began, "but you have to try harder to see the big picture. Our goal as an organization is not to put you out of work but to save this planet for you and for your children. In the North Pacific region where you are from, hydropower, pollution, and logging have devastated salmon spawning streams. Logging wounds, from clear cutting, bleed sediment into the watershed of places like the Escalante river in Vancouver Island, British Columbia where streams bear the brunt of clear cutting.

"Logging erosion has paved rivers with gravel, smothering prime salmon and trout spawning habitats. Before water sprays from a fountain in downtown Portland it flows through the 102 square mile Bull Run watershed. It has been shown that erosion caused by logging has jeopardized this water supply for over 720,000 people. You mentioned feeding your children, well, we are trying to protect your children from eating fish loaded with mercury or insecticides that run off into the water from agriculture and erosion caused by clear cutting the land.

"This year alone, warnings about polluted fish rose by twenty percent, according to the EPA. Forty-six states issued warnings about fish taken from various waters, including Maine, Massachusetts, Michigan, Missouri, New Jersey, and New York.

"More than half the warnings concerned mercury poisoning, with PCBs, chlordane, dioxin, DDT, and more than two dozen other chemical substances making up the rest. The size and the quantity of fish to eat is diminishing rapidly. The average weight of a swordfish caught on a line 20 years ago was 265 pounds, now it is 65 pounds. The population of stellar sea lions in the Gulf of Alaska and the Bering Sea has declined by over eighty-five percent because the food that they subsist on, the pollock, is either polluted by oil spillage or is being over fished by Alaskan fisheries.

"Recently a student at the Ryerson Polytechnical Institute in Toronto performed an experiment whereby he developed film using only water which was taken from the Love Canal and Lake Ontario. The water contained iron, diesel fuel, paint, and dyes, the same substances found in darkroom chemicals.

"We have hard data which shows over and over again that the food we eat and the water we drink is being threatened by a corporate culture intent on increasing profits, no matter the cost to society, and by a government which is so paralyzed by partisanship and so corrupted by private interest lobbyists that it is selling your children's future out from under them.

"In parts of the world and in our own country the water is not safe to drink and the air is not safe to breathe. There is a direct link between pollution and birth defects, cancer, and infant mortality.

"In Brownsville, Texas, next to the Rio Grande, which was recently labeled the continent's most endangered river, and in Chernobyl the statistical data proves convincingly that the world's children are in danger.

"If you knew for certain that the land fill in your neighborhood could be killing your children would you fight to close it down, even if it meant the repositioning of its workers? I believe you would kill to shut it down if that was the only way to protect the people you loved.

"It is my organization that is standing shoulder to shoulder with you, gun in hand, as polluters and land developers approach to threaten your family. If you would only open your eyes and look you would see the truth.

"That mill which you worked in closed because your government allowed the wood from federally protected old growth forests to be cut down and to be shipped overseas to be milled in Japan. We lose a valuable national heritage and the mill closed anyway.

"If not for RedTide and the other numerous conservation groups that oppose these practices, and use whatever resourceful defenses they can mount, including the plight of the spotted owl, there would be nothing left for you, your children, and your children's children."

"Thank you, Paul, for your call," Larry said. "Next caller please. We have Rita from Woodstock, Vermont on the line."

"Hello, Larry. Hello, Stingray. I want to read you something I found in my *National Geographic* about an experimental project called bioremediation. It is a project that is designed to promote the growth of microorganisms naturally present in the environment that break down oil. Technicians sprayed nitrogen-phosphorous fertilizer mix onto an oil laden shore of Green Island in hopes of stimulating oil eating bacteria. It says that this technique was shown to work in Alaska and that it has been used against toxic waste and could help double the cleanup of oil. I want to ask Stingray if he thinks the government should mandate that companies that are proven to pollute as a side effect of the industries they operate should have to contribute to future R&D for ways to help nullify the damage they do, or if the government should offer tax incentives or inducements to companies which produce techniques to aid in the cleanup of the planet?"

"That is an excellent question, Rita," Stingray responded. "I thank you for bringing up the subject. Yes, I do believe that the government should not only impose large fines and even imprisonment against companies and executives that knowingly violate EPA guidelines, but that conversely they should reward those companies that voluntarily find solutions by the way of tax incentives and subsidies.

"Those forward thinking companies like Ben & Jerry's of Vermont that are taking responsibility for cleaning up their own mess should be rewarded. This is a less cynical subject Larry and I would like to go on if you don't mind with other examples of techniques that are currently being developed and employed to stem the tide of overwhelming damage that is perpetrated on a daily basis.

"On Cape Cod and in Louisiana they are using greenhouses to purify sewage. They found that many of the chemicals used in conventional waste treatment actually added to the problem. John Todd, an environmental inventor, moves sewage by gravity through a series of tanks in a greenhouse where hundred of plants and animals break it down naturally.

"In April, the town of Harwich, Massachusetts began to use Doctor Todd's system to handle a third of its septage, concentrated waste from septic tanks. In a step by step process, bacteria digest the organic matter and convert ammonia into nitrates on which algae and duckweed thrive. Zooplankton and snails feed on the algae, fish eat the zooplankton, and floating plants soak up the leftovers. Bulrushes, cattails, and water hyacinths render toxins harmless by breaking them down into constituent parts.

"Now in Florida, California, Mississippi, and Louisiana open air lagoons process sewage alongside conventional systems.

"Other examples of companies sensitive to the environment are the Lawrence Livermore National Laboratory. At their explosives weapons test site, they use a small camera mounted in a tiny remote operated vehicle they call a MOLE for Miniature Optical Lair Explorer to peek down holes used by burrowing owls, San Joaquin kit foxes, and American badgers to avoid harming or disrupting them.

"In New England where fishermen are sensitive to the diminishing catches and the depletion of the ocean's fisheries they are developing aquaculture as a solution to the inability to meet the worlds demands for seafood and the economic hardship for our fishermen. Aquaculture is predicted to produce one half of the worlds supply of fish by the year 2025."

"Thank you, Stingray, and thank you, Rita, for a more optimistic viewpoint," Larry King said. "We have Belinda on the line from Soho, New York."

"I just want to say that I think what your organization is doing is admirable. I watched the French government on TV three months ago, preparing to detonate a nuclear warhead in the South Pacific where I had spent my honeymoon. I became so angry I was sick to my stomach. I turned to my husband and told him I wish someone would stop them. Where was our government? Where was the world government? The French need a nuclear warhead like the Israelis need another Arab neighbor. My husband said the way the French surrendered to the Germans in WWII, the only possible use they could have for such a weapon would be to have something valuable to trade when Paris became occupied. I saw a week later on CNN that RedTide had first evacuated and then blew up the French embassy in Washington and then you threatened to blow up one embassy worldwide a month until the testing was stopped. When I heard that I applauded. God bless you."

"We have Stephen from New Jersey on the line."

"Larry, I just want to say that the woman who was just on the phone is a fool. Did she forget that two guards at that embassy were killed in that blast and that the only thing the thugs and terrorists who call themselves RedTide accomplished was to postpone the testing for a couple of months. The French have rescheduled for March and swear that nothing will stop them and that they will not submit to terrorism. I have a son in the Marine Corps standing guard right now at an embassy in Germany, and I worry that some fanatic zealot in Germany with a grudge against America will kill him in a similar explosion. Once we support terrorism of any kind we open the doors to anarchy and destroy any shred of security or safety we might have. A civilized society cannot function in such a way. Every time you or your family stepped on board a plane and every time your wife and children went to the grocery store you would be in danger. I hope the FBI tracks you and your group down and that you are prosecuted to the full extent of the law."

Stingray rubbed his temples and responded in a very even and controlled voice. "I respect your opinion, sir, and I am sorry about any collateral damage that has been caused in our war to protect the environment, but make no mistake we are at war.

"When you watched your television at home during the Gulf War did you cheer like most Americans at the video play by play of men and machines that were being destroyed on a daily basis. Many of those men were ordered to stand their ground by a tyrannical government. They were put in the line of fire against overwhelming odds. Americans sat in the comfort of their homes and watched the gruesome violence with relish the way they watch Monday Night Football.

"The Iraqis were our common enemies. The monsters who raped Kuwaiti women by the thousands and spit upon our flag. We could feel good about that war. What about the children who were killed in the relentless bombings over Bagdad? Did anyone really believe in the surgical precision that our government tried to sell to us when they described the air raids on that city.

"The truth is that people are not capable of relating to pain or suffering unless it is their own. Honestly ask yourself this question: What hurts you more, the death of a beloved family pet that you raised from a puppy and loved dearly for years, or a news report about a busload of kids in a city 2000 miles away that went off a bridge?

"Which is a worse tragedy? Which hurts you the most? Which makes you cry? Most people will support a war if they believe in the cause. The Iraqis believed in their cause, they just happened to be on the wrong side. It is too abstract to think of soldiers dying and bleeding to fight for something that so many Americans so easily support from the comfort of their Lazyboy recliners.

"What happens when the soldier is your son or your husband or your father or even your best friend and he is bleeding to death in the sand, screaming out in pain for his mother his wife or his child?

"If we had to choose which battles to fight based on that criteria, how many less wars would we be willing to support? How many of us would then be willing to sacrifice the life of a loved one in order to protect Kuwaiti oil reserves, most of which were destined for Japan. How many would be willing to fight for democracy in a country, which is decidedly undemocratic.

"I am not a pacifist, quite to the contrary. I supported the war in Iraq, but for my own reasons. I am also not a hypocrite. I will kill to protect what I love, and I will kill to protect what I believe in and so will most of us.

"RedTide is never happy to do so and we take great pains to avoid it at all costs. We do not plan attacks or bombings when they are likely to endanger the greatest number of people possible but put ourselves at great personal risk to prevent such things from happening. The people we have planned to kill were evil men that endangered hundreds of thousands of lives and deserved to die, and we have no remorse about eliminating them, but neither are we insane indiscriminate killers."

Lionfish was watching the interview from a cabin nestled in the trees high above the rocky seaside and was nervous and agitated about the exchanges between Stingray and the television audience. He had argued relentlessly about doing this interview, to no avail. Stingray felt the need to purge himself of whatever guilt he had been carrying around with him these past ten years. He had become sullen and withdrawn after the incident on the dam and was throwing himself into his research, working sometimes fifteen hours a day in an attempt to assuage his guilt by finding some remedy for Alzheimer's disease in the venom of sea urchins and jellyfish.

He had already made several contributions in this area, although they had to be made through a chemist at Stanford University who was posing as a front for Stingray, until it was discovered by the FBI and he was arrested. Now Stingray was afraid that his work would be discarded and ignored and that he would be remembered only as a criminal and a murderer.

Lionfish had two vans full of armed men. One in front and one in back of the camper, which was running flat out on a desert highway in the Baja peninsula. He had removed the last leak in the organization and, although he was nervous, he felt confident that nothing would go wrong tonight. Even so, he would not be in radio contact again for another twenty minutes and he needed to blow off some steam. He called to his two dogs, a black lab mix and a German shepherd to come outside and he began a three mile sprint along the beach with the dogs running at his heels and with a full moon illuminating the surf.

He was barefoot and was wearing only a pair of cut-off desert camouflage pants frayed at the ends and faded from many night swims in the ocean. He could feel the stress leave his body as his muscles began to loosen up and he lengthened his stride. He looked down and smiled at how easily his four legged companions matched his pace and as he turned around at a rock arch hanging over the Caribbean Sea he decided to race Indigo and Neptune back to the house. He was sweating heavily and his long hair was blowing into his eyes. When he finished he dropped to his knees and wrestled with the dogs, who had refused to accept his challenge. They would never pass him even though they could easily but would only race alongside him, refusing to go against their training.

Lionfish ran out into the ocean and swam to where there was a small patch of coral. He dove under the water and grabbed onto a piece of staghorn coral to keep him down and waited for thirty seconds before a giant Barracuda he had named Methuselah crept up around his side. The fish was six or seven feet long and had been here on this reef for as long as Lionfish could remember. The moon was illuminating the reef fully and he could see a green, yellow and pink parrotfish sleeping inside a mucus bubble it had blown around its body for protection.

The light from the moon was dancing up and down the sides of the Barracuda's silver body, and Lionfish was feeling at peace for the moment. He had no way of knowing that 2000 miles away things were beginning to unravel.

"On the line from Stockholm we have Anna. What is your question Anna"?

"Hello Stingray. I am very active in the environmental movement here at home and my area of special interest is the protection of the dolphin population around the world. Can you tell me from your experience and observations if things are getting any better?"

"Dolphins are also a very special area of concern for RedTide as well and our founder, the man the world knows only as Lionfish. He has been working in the area of dolphin protection for over fifteen years. Our organization began early on by focusing its energies in this area and although some strides have been made to protect the dolphin, in the past few years we have lost a distressing number of these highly intelligent mammals.

"People see a dolphin on a can of tuna in their neighborhood supermarket and are relieved by this very clever piece of marketing and believe in their hearts that the world is safe for dolphins now because Starkist has limited some of the unsafe fishing practices it employed in the past. Nothing could be further from the truth.

"The problem is that dolphin-safe requirements exclude many nations from selling in the U.S. markets, even those that have done their best to comply. Some think this was a ploy by U.S. canneries to capture the market. Latin American fleets are likely to turn in frustration and simply ignore the restrictions on dolphin killing, since they see no reward in it and it lessens their catch.

"In the past decade alone, millions of these animals have been drowned in commercial fishing nets, which accounts for seventy percent of those killed, and the rest are poisoned by polluted waters. The oceanic drift net fishery, an enormous, highly unselective industry, lays out unimaginable lengths of gill nets into the open seas each night. The nets made of an almost invisible synthetic fiber hang like silent walls. Everything that swims into them tangles and dies.

"In 1990, the US marine mammal commission estimated the aggregate length at over 25,000 miles, enough to circle the earth. Drift netting has produced no safeguards at all. Asian countries such as Japan,

Taiwan, and South Korea use the nets to feed their unquenchable appetites for squid and other seafood from the Pacific and Indian oceans. In the Atlantic, several European countries fish only for albacore tuna.

"Marine mammals that have never known obstructions are now forced to swim a deadly maze of nets. The modern nets are made from nylon. They can never rot and if pieces of these nets rip free they float through the oceans neutrally buoyant like ghosts sweeping up everything in their path, becoming eternal purposeless killing machines.

"Their death toll is uncountable. The drift net is the most indiscriminate killing device used at sea and has been deployed since the 1980s. Monofilament nets up to forty miles long—vast enough to encircle Manhattan—hang drapelike from floats entangling everything that swims by.

"The nets are hauled aboard ships where fish are stored and the unwanted bycatch *including dolphins* is discarded. Thankfully a United Nations ban will ban commercial drift nets by the end of the next year.

"The purse seine net introduced by the tuna industry in the 1950s and pioneered in the U.S. devastated dolphin populations. Captains would seek out dolphins, which were known to travel with tuna. They would encircle and haul dolphins and tuna aboard killing thousands of dolphins. A newer procedure called backdown used by careful seiners now kills only hundreds, a number still too high for RedTide.

"If you don't mind Larry I would like to lecture a bit on the plight of the dolphin since it is such an important subject and the purpose of my visit today is to educate the world to our message and our purpose.

"Whales, dolphins and porpoises make up an order known as Cetacea. There are thirty-seven species of dolphin throughout the oceans and inland waterways of the world in both warm and cold waters and in rivers and bays. They range in size from the majestic killer whale, which is technically a dolphin reaching up to thirty feet in length, to five-foot creatures such as the rare black dolphin of Chile and the pink river dolphin of the Amazon, which are being driven to the brink of extinction by deforestation and inhabitation of people along the river who pollute.

"The pink river dolphin is so rarely seen that it is already spoken of as legend. Scientists such as myself classify six other species of cetaceans as porpoises, small beautiful animals that live half as long as the dolphin. There is also a large game fish called Mahi Mahi that is really not a dolphin, but is often called dolphin fish. So when you order this in a restaurant the joke most often told by waiters to put your conscience at ease is that you are not about to eat Flipper.

"In reality, there are about half a dozen countries in the world that do eat dolphin meat including Peru, China, the Philippines, and Sri Lanka. One thing is evident: For the past two decades dolphins around the world have come under increased pressure. In 1990, there was a worldwide symposium on cetacean mortality in passive fishing nets and traps. This was sponsored in part by the United Nations. The symposium revealed that more than a million dolphins and porpoises are still killed each year in nets. Most are accidental bycatch of fishermen combing the seas for fish.

"The main culprit is the gill net, made simply of twine and knots and used since ancient times. Fish poke their heads through the net and get their gills entangled as they try to withdraw. Dolphins also die when their beaks, teeth and fins get caught and they quickly drown. Porpoises which swim in murky water are especially hard hit and their numbers are in serious decline.

"Don't get me wrong. Since the passage of the marine mammal act in 1972, the numbers have dropped. In the U.S. tuna fishing industry the amount of dolphins killed has decreased from hundreds of thousands to only tens of thousands. Only three of thirty-five U.S. tuna boats still use some dangerous fishing methods, but what about worldwide devastation and pollution?

"Right now, republicans in the House of Representatives are moving to repeal import restrictions on tuna that have been credited with reducing the killing of dolphins. The legislation would lift the embargo against tuna caught by methods that are not dolphin- safe and would end the dolphin-safe labeling requirements for canneries.

"Representative Randy Cunningham from California argues that lifting the ban is necessary to help revitalize the fishing industry and that the ban is no longer needed, given current fishing techniques. However conservationists with the Earth Island Institute and the World Wildlife Fund counter that lifting the ban would undo decades of dolphin protection without helping the US economy.

"We must continue our worldwide pressure to enforce against dangerous fishing practices. After a ban on commercial whaling, hunters in Japan quadrupled their yearly harvest of Dall's porpoises up to 40,000 in 1988 alone. Over harvesting in Japan has made some of their dolphin stock almost disappear.

"Recently fifteen dolphins beached themselves on the shores in the Philippine town of Lukok north of Manila and were clubbed to death by local residents who wanted to sell their meat in the local market. Local police did nothing to stop it, and when asked why, said that the villagers were equivalent to fishermen at sea. Before RedTide stopped it, the waters of Futo harbor ran red with the blood of slaughtered dolphins trapped and butchered in the bay. The fishermen of Futo were no different than many others trying to wrest a living from the seas. They regarded the dolphins as just another type of fish. We tried to explain to them that dolphins are not fish, that they are mammals, smaller relatives of the great whales, and are among the most intelligent animals in the world, along with the chimpanzee and the elephant.

"Their memory capacity matches our own and they are loving familial animals with tremendous loyalty and integrity. You will find few pangs of conscience among commercial fishermen, unfortunately. Almost every society has gotten used to killing fish or what they perceive as fish.

"Although the statistics are appalling for dolphins drowned or harpooned there is another even more insidious danger, pollution. The oceans are threatened in the bays and along the coastlines, especially in the Black, North, and Baltic seas. Agricultural runoff and industrial waste have introduced toxic chemicals, and the refuse of civilization, fishing gear, polystyrene cups, plastic bags, and kitchen trash from ship's galleys are found everywhere on the beaches of the world, from Miami to New York, and from South America to Australia, and kill up to a million seabirds, 100,000 sea mammals, and countless fish each year. And it is getting worse.

"A U.S. fish and wildlife survey of albatross babies found that ninety percent had plastic in their digestive systems. Roughly eighty percent of marine pollution comes from land, including sewage from cities, tourist development in fragile coastal areas and farm chemical runoff which causes "eutrophication" an explosive growth of algae that uses up the oxygen in the water and kills marine life.

"PCBs may be directly causing the death of whales and dolphins in the Mediterranean and Atlantic, and strangely the highest concentrations of PCBs occur in Arctic waters thousands of kilometers from their probable source. Pesticides from soils around the globe are carried on winds to the Arctic and Antarctic, where they end up in the ocean to be eaten by fish, whales, seals, and ultimately humans.

"Recently, the International Whaling Commission reviewed research concerning the effects of industrial pollutants on cetaceans. The studies suggest that chlorine-containing compounds may be having a lethal effect on marine animals. During the past decade there have been five massive die-offs of marine animals traced to strains of morbillivrus, the virus that causes distemper among animals and measles in humans.

"The events took place along polluted coastlines, increasing the possibility that it was caused by organochlorines such as PCBs and pesticides. Recent studies of harbor seals in the Baltic Sea show high levels of these organochlorines. Additional studies prove that these compounds are interfering with the reproductive systems of marine animals, reducing testosterone levels and blocking the activity of hormones, and have decimated whole populations like the Beluga whales of the St. Lawrence estuary.

"In the Amazon the rare and almost extinct fresh water dolphins are threatened by a water shed endangered by dam projects and by deforestation and agricultural runoff. In Sarasota Florida, the mangroves and seagrass meadows that supply food to the local dolphins are disappearing from pollutants. Studies show that even the Jet Ski, a noisy pestilence upon the seas is endangering the safety and security of the Sarasota dolphins and is driving them from the area. The clash between man and wildlife is most evident in Florida, where each week more than 10,000 people move into the state. The endangered Manatee is hard pressed to find food among the vanishing sea grass beds while avoiding deadly propeller blades. In 1989 alone fifty-one manatees were killed by boats.

"We spend an inordinate amount of money, Larry, on space exploration when we have barely begun to unlock the mysteries of our own inner universe or inner space at home, the ocean.

"In Monterey, California last week, a fishermen pulled up a never before seen 200 foot giant squid from a mile deep. The Marianas Trench is over 30,000 feet deep and we have no idea what creatures live down there. Creatures that glow in the dark and are completely translucent have been seen at higher depths."

"Thank you, Stingray. That was very enlightening," Mr. King said. "There were a lot of things you mentioned that I myself was not aware of. I want to ask you about your recent attacks against Aqua-Canada and the destruction of their most recent dam project. Your group put a lot of people out of work and I, like many people, was surprised at the inland attack. Why did you do it?"

"I won't take up as much time answering this question since RedTide has already released numerous public explanations of this action. The waterways of the world, the rivers, the lakes, and oceans are all linked together, and as I have explained to the caller from the Northwest, oceans and waterways are also dramatically effected by what happens on the land as well.

"Dams are notorious destroyers of the environment and man's most dramatic display of his arrogance in trying to control and harness and ultimately subvert nature. The delicate balance of nature is forever destroyed when a dam is put in place along a river, often flooding a valley.

"The optimism of an era when dams spurred both the economy and recreation is now tempered by fear of irreparable damage to the land and the wildlife. Man's unquenchable thirst for fresh water to irrigate his lands and water his lawns and golf courses has resulted in a virtual

Armageddon on the environment and the future plans for additional projects is frightening.

"In the U.S. alone, which has already developed about half of its hydropower potential, the federal energy regulatory commission has issued licenses for 192 new dams that are not yet built. The relatively undeveloped rivers of this country's last unspoiled frontier, such as Alaska are a primary target. Tom Cassidy, a lawyer for American Rivers, was recently quoted as saying, "The four horsemen are driving a truck up the Alaska highway and its an eighteen-wheeler double-wide.

"Only nine percent of this nation's rivers are undeveloped and many of those are marked for projects. My organization will continue to interfere and to block the progress of these projects whenever and wherever possible, but we need help.

"I ask the people watching and listening tonight to research and investigate any proposed dam project in their areas and to find out how it will effect your environment. Then carefully weigh the benefits against the consequences of such a project. If you find the truth to be that this project will jeopardize the future of the local environment, then I ask you to pick up a sign or a banner and protest against its construction.

"If you don't agree with our methods and are against picking up a rock or a stick to fight for your beliefs, then pick up a pen and write to your government representatives. The main message I want to get across tonight is that there is still hope for this planet and for the environment but only if people—" BOOM!!

Just then there was a blinding flash of light behind Stingray and a blast of static over the studio speakers and the monitor went black.

"I'm sorry folks we seem to have lost our satellite link to our guest," Larry King said. "We will try to reconnect. Please be patient and we will return after this announcement."

Devil Ray, the driver of the front van was blinded by the sudden impact of over a dozen high beams and search lights shining in his eyes and slammed on the brakes of the van, driving the six armed soldiers in the back into each other.

"This is the FBI!! Throw out your weapons and get out of the van slowly, one at a time with your hands in the air, and lay down on the pavement. Fold your hands behind your heads," a voice crackled over a loudspeaker mounted in one of the vehicles blocking the road in front of RedTide's convoy.

"What the fuck do we do now?" the driver turned and asked Blacktip, the squad leader for the Marine Iguanas and one of Lionfish's most trusted lieutenants.

"You know as well as I do that we never surrender. That's a standing order," Blacktip responded. "Get ready to put this vehicle in reverse when I say. I will order my men to fire with all they have and we will run as fast and as hard as we can for as long as we can."

Blacktip picked up the radio and gave instructions to the other vehicles to synchronize their movements on his command, and he had his men get ready to open the large removable sunroof designed for just this situation.

"We will count to ten and then we will begin to fire on your vehicles," the anonymous voice in the shadows called out. "The area is covered by over twenty Mexican police vehicles and by FBI helicopters. Escape is not an option. I urge you to surrender. Our orders are to apprehend you alive if possible and I give my word you will not be harmed."

"Now!!!!" Blacktip shouted over the radio and all three vehicles slammed into reverse with all the power their engines could provide. Simultaneously, three men burst through the opening in the roof and fired on the vehicles in front of them while a man in the window of the RV fired a high caliber, tripod-mounted machine gun above and behind them toward the barricade of FBI vehicles.

Men dove for cover as RedTide's expert marksmen sprayed automatic fire into the windshields and into the bodies of the men who were slow to react to the onslaught of heavy weapons fire.

The RV lacked the pickup and maneuverability of the other two vehicles and as they did 180 degree turns in the road, the rear van slammed into the back of the camper and it jostled the gunmen on top and halted their attack. An FBI agent armed with a shoulder held rocket kneeled down and fired into the back of the retreating vehicle.

The van exploded into a ball of bright orange flame and ejected two soldiers through the roof, on fire and mutilated from the blast. Blacktip had just enough time to apologize to his leader for his failure when he saw the rocket fired in his direction. He was killed instantly by the explosion.

The blast propelled the RV forward and set the rear on fire including the soldier who was manning the machine gun, and as he held his bleeding face in his hands he collapsed in flames in the aisle of the camper.

The RV sped on a downhill run as the vehicles chasing them from behind began to gain ground. Seahorse, the driver so named because of his former life as a rodeo cowboy, cursed quietly as he turned to Stingray for guidance. "What should we do? There's no way we can outrun them in this piece of shit. I got my foot on the floor and we're barely doing seventy. I say we stand and fight."

Stingray wiped the sweat from his eyes and looked down at the burnt corpse of his fallen comrade, who was now covered by a blanket, and he tried not to wretch from the smell of burnt flesh. His nerves were raw and he was summoning all of his courage in order to be brave and not fall apart.

Lionfish's orders made it absolutely clear that he, especially, never be captured alive. His face was itching from the phony beard but he would not take it off until they were out of sight of the enemy.

"Turn off on the next dirt road. This thing is slow but it is heavy and it is equipped with all-wheel drive. We will try to lose them in the desert. Head east toward the mountains. We'll ditch the camper in the dark and walk out through the canyons where the cars can't follow."

There were six men in the front van, including the driver and their leader, Whitetip, a man with over twenty years of special operations experience and fiercely loyal to Lionfish. Stingray got him on the radio and revealed his plan. Whitetip knew instantly what he had to do and he ordered the driver to swing the vehicle around and behind the camper. Despite Stingray's objections Whitetip decided to stay behind with his men to set up an ambush and to buy Stingray some time.

He ordered four of his men into the rocks and then blocked the road with the vehicle, parking it sideways across the middle line, blocking both lanes. He then sent two men up the road behind them to lay in the brush so the enemy would be caught from behind once they passed, creating a crossfire. All his men were wearing night vision goggles.

The RV swung left off the paved road and out into the desert across a one-lane dirt road lined with ruts and hollows, and bounced violently from side to side. They shut the lights and drove very slowly, steering by the light of a full moon and they listened for their pursuers.

Four FBI cars and the five remaining Mexican police cars which were filled to capacity with soldiers came into sight of the parked van and as they slammed on their brakes, Whitetip and his men opened fire killing over twenty men before the others could spill out of their vehicles and take cover behind some rocks.

The firefight could be heard for over twenty miles in the clear desert air, and Stingray clenched and unclenched his fists as he thought about the inevitable fate of the brave men who had laid down their lives for him without hesitation. The RV was burning out of control and the flames had reached halfway up the front of the bus.

Stingray was afraid of two things: that it would soon explode, and that it could be seen for miles. He ordered his men out of the bus to proceed on foot and before the driver jumped from the vehicle he lodged a boot onto the gas pedal and sent it out into the night speeding ahead without a driver. It went off the road, crashing through an obstacle course of saguaro cactus and rocks.

As the firefight raged on and RedTide's men exhausted their ammunition, the bus came to a ravine and flew out into space before it crashed and exploded onto the rocks below. The explosion lit the night sky and drew the attention of the men on the road who wondered if the passengers had escaped. Stingray and the two surviving men with him made their way slowly in the dark through rough-hewn countryside alive with the sounds of coyotes and crickets.

The road was covered like an oil slick, with the blood of dead or wounded soldiers on both sides. As Whitetip made his way between the cars to work his way up into the rocks he passed two men who were face down in a pool of their own blood, and he could see the yellow FBI lettering on their nylon windbreakers reflected in the moonlight.

When the last of Whitetip's ammunition was exhausted and he had done all he could to stall Stingray's pursuers, he climbed up higher into the rocks with Minnow, the sole survivor other than himself and they made their escape.

They had bought Stingray over twenty minutes and he had never been prouder of his men, who had paid for that precious time with their lives. He hoped that the helicopter would follow him into the desert but he knew that they had come for Stingray and that they would follow that path.

The FBI man in charge of this operation looked around in disgust at the carnage and ordered his remaining men to head out in the direction of the explosion while the helicopter used its high powered searchlight to scour the desert for the man he had come for.

The sun was coming up and the sky looked pink and turquoise as the red and orange of the mountains and canyons came into view. The beauty of the surrounding landscape was lost on the men who had been walking all through the night without food or water. Stingray had lost his beard, and his face was black from ash, and he was already sweaty from the morning heat. It was only 7:15 A.M. and it was already over eighty degrees. When he looked around he realized that they were now standing on a table-shaped mountain over 1,000 feet high and that there was only one direction to head, south.

They made their way around the edge of the mountain and walked along its steep rim. As Stingray came around the outside of a large stone precipice, the helicopter came into view. It was perched on a flat section of the mountainside and it seemed to be waiting for them. Two men scrambled over the edge of the rock above them and dropped down thirty feet behind them. They were trapped.

"Welcome gentlemen," a voice called out over the helicopter's PA system. "We've been waiting for you. Please drop your weapons. This time, as you can see, there is nowhere to go but down."

Stingray recognized the voice. It was the same one from last night.

Suddenly, the door of the helicopter opened and out stepped a tall man in an all black suit with horrible scars running from below his collar, up his neck and across the entire left side of his face.

"Allow me to introduce myself, Gentlemen. My name is Colin MacGregor, and this, he said as he passed his hand across his face, this is a present from a mutual friend of ours.

"I've brought a present for you," he said as he waved to his men. They dragged Whitetip and Minnow from the helicopter. Both of them had been severely beaten. As his men dragged them to the edge of the ravine, MacGregor said, "Now, which of you three gentlemen is the infamous Stingray?"

After several seconds with no response, MacGregor nodded to his men and they threw Minnow from the cliffside. Stingray was frozen with shock and he began to tremble as the men next to him rushed forward. Two of MacGregors men fired at their feet and they stopped their advance.

Stingray was racked with terror and he had broken out in a cold sweat. MacGregor walked up to Whitetip. Although he was badly beaten, he still stood erect and proud. His hands were bound behind his back.

"You should be very proud of your men," MacGregor said. "They are very brave. If I had ten like them, this whole thing would have ended long ago. It's a pity that I will have to kill them."

"You aren't fit to serve beside men, let alone lead them, you cowardly mercenary whore," Whitetip said, then spit into MacGregor's face.

MacGregor wiped his face with surprising calm and then he kicked Whitetip in the chest and sent him flying backward over the edge and out into space before he crashed onto the rocks below.

Stingray never heard him scream. He grabbed his men and held them in place.

"I'm Stingray," he said as he stepped forward. Then the man on his left stepped forward and said "I'm Stingray," followed by the man on his right.

"Ah what brave lads," MacGregor laughed out loud. "It warms my heart to see such profound loyalty. This is better than the movie *Spartacus*, except that none of you are Kirk Douglas and I certainly won't ever be mistaken for Sir Lawrence Olivier."

He walked up to the three men and looked them each in the eye. Then he stepped back, removed a small automatic weapon from his pocket and shot both the man to the left and to the right of Stingray in the forehead.

"You sick bastard!" Stingray cried. "Why did you have to kill them all? You twisted grotesque butcher."

"I'm afraid there wasn't enough room in the helicopter and my patience had reached its limit. I knew you were Stingray. Now climb aboard the helicopter with me. I promise you won't be harmed. You have my word."

Stingray turned slowly around and leapt from the cliffside.

MacGregor ran forward. He screamed in anger and frustration as he looked 1,000 feet below at Stingray's crumpled body. Once more his enemy had done the unexpected and had found a way to escape him, even in death.

As he turned back to the helicopter he could not help but admire the awesome resolve of these men and for the first time he wondered if he could beat them. He had lost over forty men and he had failed to capture Stingray alive as his employer had instructed. His only consolation was in thinking of how the news would be received by Lionfish, and as he looked out through the window of the helicopter he slowly began to smile.

CHAPTER 12

"ALIVE, YOU FOOL!" Yamaguchi screamed in rage. "I said I wanted him alive so he could lead us to Lionfish." MacGregor had just given his full report of the events in the desert. "This man was a scientist, not a soldier, and he is of no use to us dead.

"You told me yourself he was Lionfish's Achilles heel and our best hope of drawing him out in the open. You told me Stingray would be the only bait strong enough to draw Lionfish out into the open."

"I apologize, Yamaguchi San," MacGregor pleaded, "but as you have just heard, his death was completely unavoidable and I am as disappointed as you are by our failure to capture Stingray alive.

"The good news is that after two years of dead end leads and failure after failure we have finally eliminated one of our primary targets. You can also take comfort as I do in the fact that Stingray's death will be devastating to Lionfish personally and to the organization as a whole. They have lost one of their primary tacticians and our intelligence tells us that Lionfish will be exposed and vulnerable without a man he has depended on since RedTide's earliest beginning.

"I believe for the first time his judgment may be compromised and that he may finally make the mistake that will deliver him to us," MacGregor finished.

Yamaguchi's anger appeared to subside momentarily. He turned and walked down the short mahogany stairway that led to the ten-acre Japanese gardens, which were his pride and joy. This was the place on his estate where he spent most of his time since his son's death. He walked over to a bench by a pond filled to capacity with red and gold coy and sat down. He waved to MacGregor with his back turned for him to come and join him. As MacGregor walked over to join his employer, Akiro Yamaguchi stared down into the water and thought about his son and realized that today's news did little to ease his suffering or assuage his guilt. The pain was still there and it had not diminished in its intensity or in its ability to cloud his mind and compromise his thinking.

In business, Yamaguchi had always been regarded as a ruthless competitor, and as an employer he was known to be intolerant of poor performers. But he was also known to be a fair man and a man of unquestionable integrity.

He had always had contempt for men who could not control their appetites and ruined their lives and their businesses with women and gambling and other western vices. He disapproved in general of people who could not control their emotions and he knew from experience that in business one of the most dangerous indulgences was to allow one's personal feelings to influence his decisions. Now, he had hired mercenaries, and had himself in effect become a killer. Now, he was intentionally practicing business in ways which were purposefully designed to damage the environment and eventually his own reputation.

He went to bed every sleepless night with his heart full of hate and arose each morning feeling the same way. He could not find peace at work or at home. He thought that vengeance would cure his sick heart but he took little satisfaction in the death of a man he had been told was a scientist and was also known not to be a man of violence.

Yamaguchi clenched his fists and fought to regain his composure. He must be strong and see this through to the end. He could not rest until he destroyed Lionfish and his entire organization. It was a point of honor and he hoped that at the conclusion he could make peace with his son's memory and find the man he had once been.

He heard MacGregor approaching on the path of fine sea pebbles and asked, "Where is the body?"

"We had to leave the area quickly, Yamaguchi San. The body was 1,000 feet below us in a ravine and it was not accessible by helicopter. Besides, the authorities were probably on the way, based on our informant's information, and we could not risk entering the country with a dead body. I am sure you can understand that, Yamaguchi San."

"How do you know the man was Stingray?" Yamaguchi asked. "You have never seen a photograph of the man and you had no way of verifying his identity?" Yamaguchi said as he clenched his jaw and turned and fixed MacGregor with a fierce, hard stare. MacGregor was a man who had been in many battles and he was not easily frightened or intimidated. But he felt a chill run up his spine when he looked into Yamaguchi's eyes and he had to turn away and look at a large, very old Cherry tree near the edge of the pond when he responded. "Our informant explained to us that Stingray would be in the camper and we were monitoring his voice over the television. It was the same voice as the man who leapt from the cliff and identified himself as Stingray. He was also the recognizable leader of the group and his men on the road and on the cliffside died trying to protect him. I have no doubt that it was Stingray, and although we did not check the body to see if he was dead, no one could have survived that fall."

"Do you have any idea what I am worth, Mr. MacGregor?"

MacGregor was surprised by the question and the sudden change of subject and replied, "It is my understanding that Yamaguchi San is worth over three billion American dollars."

"I am worth closer to five billion American dollars to be exact, but today I feel that I have nothing. I built this company with my own hands and it was my intention to leave it to my son, who was my only heir. Now I will die alone with no one to continue my family name and with a legacy of death and destruction for those who will run my empire when I am gone.

"For over a thousand years my family has had a long, proud heritage in this country. Before the war, my family was very wealthy and we were regarded as nobility, or what you would call royalty in your country. My mother was a cousin to the emperor himself and my father was a very successful businessman. I grew up wanting for nothing and I received a first class education in the United States. One of my fondest memories from my youth is the time I spent at Yale University and it was a proud day when my son also graduated from that fine institution. I entered the war as an officer and a pilot flying Zeroes for my country and for my emperor and I killed hundreds of men on the ships that I helped sink in the Pacific Ocean.

"I was one of the most highly decorated officers in the war and when I returned home on leave I was regarded as a hero by my people, yet I never felt proud of my actions. I remembered flying low over my enemies and when I watched in horror the sinking ships and the hundreds of men that were drowning in oil and were burning alive, I felt ashamed.

"I helped kill thousands of Americans, some of whom I might have known during my years at university. I could hear their screams as I flew low over the wreckage, even over the engine noise of my airplane. Sometimes I can still hear their screams ringing in my ears and I awaken in the night covered in cold sweat and trembling.

"After the war, I learned that my family had lost everything and I came home to find that my father and mother had taken their own lives and that my father's business was destroyed. I drifted for a while and finally found work in construction as a laborer, ironically working beside American engineers who were helping to rebuild my country with American dollars.

"I eventually worked my way down to the sea where I found work on a fishing boat for a very old man who had lost his only sons in the war, and when he died he left me his ship. In ten years, I had seven boats in my fleet and I was building the world's first commercial factory fishing vessel. That ship which I still have, was followed by six more over the next five years and I then expanded to cargo vessels. It took me over twenty years to earn my first billion dollars and I was very proud of what I had accomplished, but it meant nothing compared to the birth of my son.

"I tell you not as a sentimental man, but to illustrate the depth of my commitment to this project that the proudest day of my life was the day that my son was born, and that I would give up everything I own tomorrow to bring Nobuaki back to me."

Yamaguchi stood and faced MacGregor and said, "I want an end to this soon. Do what you have to, spend what you must. You have no limit, but end this soon. Bring me the man known as Lionfish so that I may ask him why my son had to die. I want to hear his answer just before I cut out his heart, or I promise you, Mr. MacGregor, that it is you who will disappear before the year ends.

"I assure you that I am not a man to make idle threats. I do not want to see you or hear from you again until you can deliver this man to me," Yamaguchi finished, then he quickly turned and walked away fighting to control the trembling in his hands and the nervous tick which had developed in his left eye over the past two weeks.

MacGregor did not like to be threatened by anyone, not even Yamaguchi, but he understood the man and the depth of his grief and he also knew from working together over the past two years that he meant what he had said. Yamaguchi was one of the strongest men that Colin MacGregor had ever known, but the strain of the past two years and his sense of honor combined with his grief were taking their toll. He seemed to have aged tremendously in just the past two months. It was time to bring this to an end.

MacGregor was unsure of his next move and could only hope that with the death of Stingray, Lionfish would come out of hiding to find him in order to exact his own retribution and vengeance. He had spent over seven million dollars in the past two years on payoffs to informants and on bribes and payoffs to newspaper reporters and to FBI and various law enforcement agents.

It was a lucky break that they had discovered Stingray in the desert, but their informant at CNN was now dead, found in his home with his throat cut and his tongue removed. The FBI computer expert who had helped trace them through an advanced tracking system, which he had designed for the FBI, had also disappeared.

Lionfish had an elaborate system of informants and an extremely sophisticated intelligence system. He had killed MacGregor's contacts almost as quickly as MacGregor had bought them, then he publicly condemned them in the press as a warning to others. It would be very difficult for MacGregor to find someone willing to work with him now, no matter what the price. MacGregor was tired of waiting for opportunities to present themselves. It was time he created an opportunity for himself. Instead of waiting for Lionfish's next move, MacGregor needed to create a mission for RedTide so irresistible that it would draw them out and into his trap. He needed to find a place that Lionfish felt connected to on a personal level and when he began to destroy it, Lionfish would have to come to save it, but where? And why? Those would be the crucial questions that would have to be answered before he could begin to set his final trap.

As frustrating as the current situation was, MacGregor would once again have to wait for a good lead or a visible chink in Lionfish's armor. He would make one more giant push to find an informant, maybe a disillusioned or disenfranchised ally of RedTide, and he would spend whatever was necessary to find his answers. MacGregor had an instinctual, almost prescient, feeling that the end was very near and he knew that the next time Lionfish and he met that one of them would die.

CHAPTER 13

"IT'S NOT YOUR FAULT," Lionfish said for the tenth time in over a month. "He volunteered for the assignment and I think it's about time you gave yourself a break and stopped beating yourself up over it. I respect your sensitivity and how much you care, but you of all people should know after all the time we've been fighting this war and all the friends we've lost the risks that go along with this kind of a life.

"Schoolmaster knew the risks and he accepted them. Would you be happier if I had let you go along on that trip to Baja as you had intended? Would you be happier if it was you that had died out there in the desert instead of him?"

"His name was Paul," Stingray said quietly. "Could you please stop using our ridiculous codenames for five minutes. There's no one else around, Tom. Paul was once a college professor and he was also a scientist like me. He wasn't one of your goons and he never should have been put into such a potentially dangerous situation. What's happened to your fabulous security precautions and your network of spies? It seems to me that an awful lot of people are selling us out these days."

"Goddamn it, Tom, what happened out there?" Jerry's voice was breaking and he was trying to hold back tears. Lionfish was worried about him. Since his stand-in and protege had been killed at the ambush in Baja he had become reclusive and lately he had sudden crying jags that were followed by deep depression and long silences. Lionfish had thought of everything to protect Stingray's safety that night but he couldn't do anything today to ease his pain.

He had asked Schoolmaster to pose as Stingray that night while Stingray answered the questions from a remote location by satellite and RedTide dubbed the audio. Schoolmaster was a gifted young chemistry professor who had graduated from MIT and had joined RedTide after he had become disillusioned with his work at Genisys, a large pharmaceutical firm that specialized in genetic research and re-engineering.

He had blown the whistle on the company when he learned that their new product, which he had helped develop to treat Alzheimer's disease, contained low levels of toxins that over time could produce dangerous, even potentially lethal side effects.

The company's top executives and chemists claimed that his data was incorrect and they threatened to terminate him if he spoke out. The drug had passed FDA approval and that was good enough for them. The company refused to wait to release their cure to the public. He and his team had literally begged for some more time so that they could find some way to change the formula without altering the efficacy of it.

It had already cost the company tens of millions of dollars in R&D and upper management was anxious to introduce it to the market. The company had already claimed publicly for weeks that it had produced a miracle drug in the treatment of the degenerative disease and they refused to halt production.

Paul Willet, later to be known as Schoolmaster within RedTide's organization went to the producers of "60 Minutes" and blew the whistle. He came to the attention of RedTide, and Stingray in particular, when the show aired on television in the fall. Stingray reached out to Paul when he learned that he was terminated from his employment with Genisys. He contacted him through an associate of the attorney who was handling his lawsuit. Paul and Jerry instantly became good friends and Paul's respect for Stingray's work bordered on hero worship. The two were inseparable and spent up to twelve hours a day locked up in Stingray's lab, sharing their dream. They coordinated their efforts in the pursuit of a cure for Alzheimer's disease.

"What a waste. What an awful waste," Stingray said to Lionfish. "His contribution to the project advanced my work by years. He was one of the most brilliant minds I had met in some time and he was fully committed to the project and to the organization."

Paul had been selected for the desert mission because of his uncanny resemblance to Stingray and the fact that their voices were almost an exact match. If the satellite audio dubbing had failed to work during the interview, Paul would have been able to answer the more scientific questions posed to him more competently than any other member of the organization.

The other members of RedTide were soldiers and mercenaries and could never complete the illusion. If captured they would reveal to the enemy instantly that they were not Stingray and that he was in fact not present in the camper van. Except for veteran leaders, Lionfish selected members for the assignment who were relatively new to the organization and had either never seen Stingray or had only seen Stingray from a distance.

The only people who new of the masquerade were Blacktip & Whitetip so the other members of the team would readily accept orders from the impostor and would behave in a fashion that would convince anyone watching that it was actually the real Stingray that they were protecting. If captured, Paul's scientific demeanor and his professorial appearance would also complete the illusion.

Lionfish had no reason to believe that there would be a problem considering the months that he had spent painstakingly going over every detail and all the time he had spent planning. There were numerous failsafes that he had devised and implemented. He would not admit it to Stingray but he was relieved that at the final hour he had decided to use Paul as a stand-in instead of actually sending Stingray as they had originally planned.

MacGregor and Yamaguchi had once again surprised him with their relentless pursuit and the level at which they had corrupted his intelligence network. They seemed to have found a way to compromise one informant after another. Lionfish began to seriously consider a counterattack, and he made a mental note to begin to devise a plan for the assassination of Akiro Yamaguchi and his hired mercenary.

"I'm sorry, Jerry. Please believe me. My primary objective was to protect you, and I did, although we did sustain unacceptable losses. The 'goons,' as you called them, who lost their lives fighting to protect you were good men and both Blacktip & Whitetip were longtime friends of mine. I mourn their loss as greatly as you grieve for Paul."

Jerry turned and walked to his room. Before he closed the door he said. "I'm not sure I can do this work anymore. I'm tired of the killing and I can't make myself believe the rationalizations anymore. They say that patriotism is the last refuge to which a scoundrel clings. I'm afraid I don't believe anymore in our cause. I've lost my faith. The cost is too high. I just want to be left alone for awhile." Then he closed his door leaving Lionfish alone to wonder whether the organization could survive without his brother, whether he could survive. They had always had each other to lean on when their doubts outweighed their faith. Now Lionfish needed to be strong enough for the two of them.

He sat down on the porch steps and put his head in his hands and wondered for the first time since they began their long journey whether they would make it to the end.

CHAPTER 14

HERE IT COMES AGAIN, anger so hot and so blinding in its all consuming hatred of anyone who even appears to be happy. I'm on a boat full of vacationers who are celebrating their liberation from the glass and steel offices and carpeted cubicles where they serve their sentences as accountants and lawyers and secretaries. I watch them laughing and joking with each other and I begin to hate them.

I feel it welling up in my heart, increasing its beat as it drives my pressure up making my nerves raw as it floods my body with adrenaline. It's a physical change that I can feel as my brain fills with chemicals that leave a bad taste in my mouth, like dry bitter tea.

It doesn't matter how hard I try to conjure up serene mental images or concentrate on pleasant happy memories, my mood never changes. I've been sucked into a black hole and there's no escaping its pull. I can't seem to get close enough to pleasant memories of my mother to actually feel anything except pain.

Even the spectacular view in front of me cannot seem to distract me from my misery and guilt. What would I do to bring my mother back? I ask myself over and over again. Would I swallow my pride? Would I be a better son, a better person? Would I grow up? Would I appreciate what I had and stop taking people for granted? Would I stop being angry and learn to forgive? Would I try to be less judgmental and more understanding? I would do anything I tell myself, but now that she's gone I realize that I could never do any of those things while she was alive and that now it's too late.

I'm on the run now, but I already know as Jackson Browne says in one of my favorite songs that, "No matter how fast I run I can never seem to get away from me." I am in a boat skimming along the surface of the bluest, cleanest water I have ever seen. The group of tourists here in the boat with me are almost all exclusively divers and have just finished pointing and yelling at a school of dolphins that were in front of the boat. The dolphins were leading us on a merry chase through the warm, gentle waters of the Caribbean just off the coast of Honduras. It was a beautiful sight but I barely noticed them.

How I despise my fellow travelers here on this boat with me and almost everyone I see these days, especially those that seem to be the happiest. Last month I took an indefinite leave of absence because Al refused to allow me to resign. Since then I had been walking around in a fog, always on the edge of erupting and I started looking for trouble and was hostile and irritable with everyone. I started going to bars and I got in a few arguments with some of the patrons. I think I wanted to get in a fight and at certain times I was definitely asking for it. It was almost as if I were seeking physical punishment for the agonizing guilt and mental anguish I was feeling since my mother's death.

One day I was out jogging to relieve the mind splitting stress headache I was suffering from days spent crying and countless sleepless nights. I was running along the sidewalk and a black Porsche convertible driven by some rich spoiled kid in his early twenties flew out of a driveway without looking and cut me off. The driver had no intention of stopping for me. At the last minute, the driver saw me and he slammed on his brakes. Luckily, the anti-lock brakes kept the car from skidding. It stopped but the bumper hit me gently in the shins. I was so angry that I exaggerated the impact and threw myself backward onto the hood which covers nothing but trunk space, since it is a rear engine vehicle. I caved the hood in completely with the full weight of my body.

The driver started to leap from his car and as I rolled off the hood he began to curse at me, screaming about his daddy's car. Then he threagthened to kick my ass. Just as he got one leg out of the car I slammed my knee into the door and trapped him in the car. His leg was caught in the door like a vice and I yelled in his face like a madman with spit flying from my mouth. I told him that he was lucky that I wasn't suing him and that if he didn't stay in the car I would kick his teeth down his throat.

I turned and continued my run home but my heart was beating dangerously fast so I jogged slowly. I was so terrified and confused by my own rage and I felt so desperately unhappy that when I finished my run at the front door to my apartment, tears were running down my face to mingle with my sweat.

The day I resigned from LifeForce Technology my friends and I drank our way through a three-hour lunch. At first, Al tried to talk me in to working through my grief but when he saw the lifeless look in my eyes he changed his mind. Then he surprised me by telling me that I would always have a job with him and that if he didn't have a territory for me when I returned he would create one. Then he did something completely out of character. He hugged me.

On the drive home that day I was still feeling pretty loaded from all the beers I had drank. At a stop light I rolled down my window to listen to a father in a convertible LeBaron next to me who was screaming at his son. The man was out of control and was insulting and abusive. I could see the boy sliding lower and lower in his seat, receding inside himself. I could see him flinch with every miserable word his father hurled at him.

The child was maybe eight or nine years old and I had an instant flashback to my father and me working together in the yard when I was just a boy. I could almost hear my father's voice telling me what an imbecile I was because I couldn't tell the difference between a Phillips head and a flat head screwdriver.

I remembered standing over him with a Phillips head screwdriver in my hand daydreaming about sinking it into his neck all the way to the handle, and I shuddered at the memory.

I screamed over traffic to the man in the LeBaron that he should give his son a break and that he should try taking his frustrations with the world out on something else. His response was to tell me to mind my own fucking business or he would take his frustrations out on my head. I yelled back at him that I wasn't an eight year old boy and that if he got in my face he would be concentrating his future energies on his physical rehabilitation. I told him that I had stopped being afraid of bullies when I graduated high school and joined the Marines.

My last attempt to get into trouble happened earlier today at the airport in Miami. The woman at the airline check in desk asked me if I had been asked by any strangers to carry a package for them. I was in a particularly bad mood and I thought that had to be the stupidest question I had ever heard. I responded that a dark-skinned gentlemen in a Turban had asked me to carry the bag that I was now holding to Honduras for him. He asked me to give it to his mother when I landed at the airport. I lifted my small carry on bag to my ear and I said, "I think it's a clock."

Needless to say my attempt at humor was not well received by the security personnel who warned me that I could be detained and fined for even joking about such things.

Two weeks earlier, when I was planning my escape, I researched several dive locations. I ended up choosing my current destination for its solitude and for its advertised privacy and its remote location. I read about this exclusive dive hotel in the Bay Islands off of Honduras in an issue of *Rodales Scuba Magazine*.

It is limited to only twenty-five people, mostly couples, and is exclusive to advanced certified divers. I received, along with the brochure for the hotel, a five-page conservation newsletter published by the owners and a release form I had to sign that would allow the dive and hotel operators to canccl my stay and to eject me from the island if I was caught damaging the reef or bothering the marine animals.

I was intrigued by the literature and by the description of the pristine diving in this part of the world, not to mention the description of the hotel and the private beaches. The name of the hotel is the Aegis Inn, which I learned later on means "to protect" in Latin. The dive operation was called Neptune Divers.

The hotel was built on a small island off the coast of Honduras called Arrecife, which means "reef" in Spanish. The whole island is only eleven miles in diameter and is hilly and lush with tropical vegetation. It has no roads, no phones and no electricity. The hotel which has the only buildings on the island gets its electricity from solar energy and gas powered generators.

Our plane landed on Roatan, a neighboring island and we were now in a boat shuttle, which was overloaded with dive gear and luggage on a thirty-minute ride to Arrecife. The trip here was a nightmare and took over fourteen hours from Miami. First, I stopped in Belize, then San Pedro Sula, then La Cieba, which was lush and mountainous. In La Cieba we transferred to a twenty-year old twin prop flying cigar tube that pitched and rolled all the way to Roatan. In Roatan, our gear was transferred to this dilapidated, oversized canoe they now had the twelve of us crammed onto.

I was sitting at the front of the boat writing in a journal I had started to keep when the hotel came into view. The buildings were barely visible. They were nestled deeply in the trees on the hillside. There was a long wooden dock which ran out of the treeline where a thirty-foot stairway from the main house above descended. There was a 150 yard crescent shaped beach with three or four thatched wooden bungalows at the edge of what looked like a small rainforest. There was a waterfall at one end of the beach near a rock arch, which formed a giant tunnel over the beach, and I could see a small house at the opposite end of the beach, separated from the hotel.

I guessed that this house must have been either a private hotel suite or it was the manager's quarters. As we pulled up alongside the dock I could hear the sound of hundreds of exotic birds. The sound resembled the wild parrots I often heard near my building at home.

Two large dogs came running down the dock to greet the new arrivals. One was large and was jet black and looked like a Labrador retriever and the other one was a German sheperd. I reached down to pet them and I noticed that their coats were matted and that they had welts from tick bites.

I had to admit that just from what I had seen already the place was charming. I had told the reservations people back in the states that if I liked it I might extend my stay for up to a month.

On the dock was a small hut that was the dive shop and there was a blackboard outside on a wall with the next day's dive destinations written on it. Boat #1 was going someplace called Frenchman's Cove and Boat #2 was going to a wreck called the Black Pearl. I was beginning to get excited. I knew there was nothing that could heal my heart and my soul better than the coral reefs and warm waters of the Caribbean.

During our last conversation, Jackie told me that I was in denial and that I was running away. I said, "No shit," but she pressed on. She told me that I could not ignore my grief and that I would have to face it head on and deal with it.

I told her that I agreed with her but that I was looking forward with all my heart to running away and that for awhile I was going to do everything that I could to deny facing our mother's death. I refused to deal with it for as long as I could get away with it. This place would be perfect for what I had in mind. I would dive all day and I would drink all night. I would take moonlight swims and keep to myself. I would lay on the beach and write notes in my diary. I was going to write about my travels and my adventures if I found any.

We were walking up a long steep stairway made of what appeared to be teak to the main building, and I could see our luggage was being brought upstairs by a rudimentary conveyor belt operated by ropes. When we got to the main building I could see that it was a 360 degree circle which was made entirely of hardwoods and thatch. The main building contained the bar, a living room or lounge area, and a dining room, which held only two large tables for communal dining.

There was a large outside sundeck which hung over the cliffside and was supported by large timbers. There appeared to be a night club of some kind along the cliffs beside the sundeck. There were ten to fifteen tables and an area up front with a microphone stand for the performers. There was an easel with a sign which announced that tommorow night the world famous duo of Tom & Jerry would be arriving straight from their Caribbean tour and would be performing at the Aegis Inn.

Despite my melancholy mood, I had to smile. Off to the side, attached to the building and suspended over the jungle, were two large screened cages and in one were two enormous rainbow macaws and in the other cage was a toucan. I had never seen a toucan and the bird was spectacularly beautiful. The building was completely open on all sides and was built into the trees like a large treehouse. There were several hummingbird feeders hanging in the windows and I could see one was being used by a little green and yellow bird, which was suspended in mid air.

Like the tiny bird, the outbuildings of the hotel including the kitchen and the guest rooms were also suspended in the thick canopy of the trees. They were interconnected by a network of boardwalks, which I saw the next evening were dimly lighted.

There were a number of stairways that wound there way down to the beach. I found out several days later that above the hotel were several trails which all led to private beaches and rivers where couples could be alone all day to picnic or skinny dip. The trees were full of exotic flowers, including orchids, and the smell of the jungle humidity and the flowers reminded me of a nursery or a greenhouse.

This was an extremely romantic location, but just the same I was happy to be alone. In the trees I could see several large iguanas and I hoped that unlike the small lizards at home they couldn't find their way into the rooms. I would have a heart attack if I woke up in the middle of the night with a twenty-pound lizard in my bed.

A woman came into the room and announced that she was the manager of the hotel and that she was also one of the head divemasters. She told us that her name was Sam and that in a few minutes we would all be shown to our rooms. She told us that we would need to return to the main house for orientation for both the hotel and the dive operation at 7 P.M. at Atlantis or we would not be able to dive in the morning. Atlantis was the name of the club deck and lounge I spotted on the way in.

She explained that, believe it or not, The Atlantis Lounge was one of the most popular spots in the Bay Islands and that on weekends, especially Saturday nights; people boated here from Roatan to listen to music and to dance. She told us that we better be early if we wanted a table.

She also told us that there were no phones or TVs in the rooms and that there were no alarm clocks. Instead there was a large brass gong hanging outside the kitchen which she pointed out would be rung at meal times and at 8 A.M. to wake everyone for breakfast and for morning diving.

She led us to the bar where a heavyset native woman with a pleasant smile poured us all complimentary pina coladas from a pitcher and introduced herself as Carmen. Sam was a very attractive woman, although she was not what you would call classically beautiful. She had a hard, weathered look and appeared to be in her early 30s. She was approximately 5'7" tall and was blond and very tan. She had light blue eyes which were heavily lined from many years of working in the sun, and she also had deep set lines in her forehead and around her mouth.

Her teeth were perfectly even and were bright white and she had a very toned athletic body. She was strangely attractive, but she looked tough and hardened by life and I never particularly cared for women that looked as if they could take me in a fight. She was wearing a pair of faded, tight fitting denim shorts and a loose fitting white gauze blouse.

She had on no make up and looked like someone who never did. I looked around the bar and I noticed for the first time that it was built in the shape of a boat. It even had a main sail post in the middle with lines and riggings, and fixed every ten feet along the outside were cleats. Above the bar were photos and drawings of tropical fish and carvings in dark wood of whales and seabirds. There were also hundreds of stickers from dive shops from all over the world that had visited the island. I noticed at the end of the bar was a small blackboard which stated that tonight's dinner was going to be Mahi Mahi.

I called Sam over to where I was standing and said, "Hi, my name is Jake. I noticed that the board over there says that tonight's dinner is fish. Is there a menu or is that the only choice. I don't eat fish. One more thing, it appears that the dinner is some kind of a communal arrangement. Is there some way that I could arrange to eat privately?"

She looked me in the eyes and said nothing for a moment. I couldn't read anything in her expression when she said. "Did you read the brochure we mailed you, Jake? It explains in the brochure that all meals are to be eaten together with the other guests. There are only fourteen guests here this week and you will be diving with these people everyday. Since you are alone you will also be buddy diving with some of them. It might be a good idea to get to know them and we find that dinner is a relaxed time to discuss the day's diving and to share past diving experiences."

"Let me take this one step at a time, Samantha," I said with just enough attitude to offend her. "I'm assuming that's your full name. I chose this place because I wanted to spend time by myself in an out of the way location with no outside disturbances. I don't like a camp atmosphere on vacation. If I were looking for that I would have gone to Club Med." I was beginning to lose my patience.

"Number two. Since you brought up the brochure. The brochure said that there would be a choice of two entrees at dinner, or that there would be a buffet-style dinner served. I can-not and I will not eat fish.

Number three. I don't mind diving with the group, and I promise to trail closely behind, but I do not want the responsibility of diving with a buddy. I especially don't need someone that I do not know and that I do not trust watching out for me.

"I have over ten years experience in diving and I am also a certified divemaster. I brought two separate cameras with me and I like to stop and take macro photographs. Sometimes I will stay in one spot for over ten to fifteen minutes. And what about the unlimited shore diving your brochure promised? One of the reasons I came here is because there's a 1000 foot wall just 50 feet from the beach," I said, pointing toward the sea.

"I don't want to have to look for a buddy every time I want to go for a shore dive. I also don't want to be tied to a string of different buddies for what might be a month's stay on this island and have to change them every week when they go home."

I could see her jaw clench and I realized that I had started off on the wrong foot with the manager of what was to be my new home for the next thirty days. With controlled calm and just a slight hint of annoyance she said, "Mr. Stein, I realize in dealing with American travelers that it sometimes takes a few days to decompress from your trip and to get acclimated to this style of hotel. This is not the Hyatt or the Hilton, and things are a little bit more relaxed in the service department. That is the charm of this place and why people come back again and again. I will see about getting you something else to eat for tonight's meal and if you like we can set you up outside in the club area by yourself or you can dine in your room.

"As for your request about diving alone. I am one of three divemasters on this property, but I cannot make a decision like that myself. I will have to talk to the owners and they will not be arriving until tomorrow night. For tomorrow's dive you can buddy up with me, if that's all right with you, until we can straighten things out. I encourage you to relax and I promise you the best dive vacation you have ever had. Is that fair?"

"Fair enough," I said. "I'm sorry to be such a pain in the ass."

After our conversation, I turned to follow one of the local workers to my room and I overheard Sam saying something to the bartender behind my back. I couldn't make out what she was saying but I did catch the words "American" and "complainer" and I felt my blood pressure increase. I started to chew my lip.

What did she mean by her comment "American travelers." Unless I mistook her accent she was as American as apple pie, and she sounded like a southern redneck to boot. That "embarrassed by the behavior of her fellow Americans" attitude reminded me of a friend of mine in high school, Linda McCormick. After finishing school Linda traveled for three years around the world and came home with a phony Australian accent. My friend had turned into a travel snob. She complained constantly about the ethnocentric behavior of the Americans she encountered during her travels.

I followed along behind my "bellman" on a winding boardwalk that was suspended in the trees to my cabin, which was built in and around a gigantic tree filled with large red flowers resembling orchids. Flowers were cascading down over the roof and around the sides of the building and filled the cabin with a natural perfume. When we got inside, I saw that the floor was made of large beams of polished wood and that the bed was shrouded in mosquito netting. The toilet and shower were in a little shack attached to the side of the main cabin, and the shower had large wooden louvers that ran up the walls from floor to ceiling for ventilation. It would be like showering outdoors but with privacy and I looked forward to a hot shower.

There was a front porch with a hammock, and from the hammock you could see the ocean through the thick veil of trees which blanketed the hillside. I thanked my "bellman", a short native dressed in little more than rags, then I lay down on the bed, which was thin and lumpy.

I closed my eyes and breathed deeply and tried to relax. I could hear the waves crashing against the shore and in the distance I could hear a waterfall crashing down upon the rocks. I had to agree with Sam that this was not the Hyatt, but I also had to admit that it was one of the prettiest, most romantic locations I had ever been to. I also heard that the diving was supposed to be phenomenal.

There were twelve other people besides myself at the hotel. There were three French couples who had arrived together and that barely spoke English and there was a Japanese couple that spoke no English at all.

There was a couple from L.A. that came through Miami and had traveled with me all the way here. The husband was the president of a printing company and was pompous and arrogant. He spoke to his wife in front of strangers as if she was an idiot and I hated him instantly. I would make it a point to steer clear of them while they were here.

There was a tall, thin pasty-faced girl from Seattle who seemed to be alone, although she told everyone within earshot that her fiancee would be meeting her here. I did not see a ring and I suspect he does not exist. So far, she is my favorite.

Suddenly, I heard panting outside my door and when I got up and opened it the two hotel hounds walked into my room as if it were their living room and made themselves right at home. One curled up on the floor and the other smelly beast made a beeline for my bed, where, without hesitation, he leapt upon it and rolled over on his back. Instead of being angry, I laughed for the first time in over a month at the gall of these animals. After scratching the Lab's stomach, I threw him off my bed with a gentle slap on the rump. I collapsed into the bed where I fell instantly to sleep, my snoring blending in with the snoring of my houseguests to form a lovely harmonic chorus.

CHAPTER 15

BONG!, BONG!, BONG!! "What the hell is that?" I asked myself as I rolled over and wiped the gunk from my eyes. I threw my legs over the side of the bed and I heard a groan of complaint as my feet landed on the 100 pound black Labrador that was curled up beside my bed. I realized after awakening from my disoriented stupor where I was and I opened the front door and ushered the dogs out of the room.

I checked my watch and realized that I had slept straight through the night without hearing the dinner gong. Over twelve hours of sleep and I felt more tired than ever. I had a major case of jet lag. I missed last night's dinner and more importantly the orientation.

I dressed hurriedly and filled my mesh dive bag with my regulator and the rest of my gear and headed for the main house. When I entered the house and approached the breakfast buffet I could hear Bill the Blowhard sounding off to an enormous couple that must have arrived late last night about a shark feeding he had gone on in Fiji.

I made the mistake of turning in the direction of the table he was sitting at and he waved me over. I filled my plate with some mango and kiwi slices and a bran muffin and walked over to the table.

"We missed you last night," Bill said, throwing his arm around his wife Donna.

"Me and my photo assistant went snorkeling under the dock last night to see the eagle rays and it was amazing. When the lights under the dock are on the rays come in ten to fifteen at a time and swim around under the dock in circles through the pilings.

"I slipped quietly into the water with just a snorkel and I've already shot two rolls of Fuji Velvia. You have to check it out tonight, Jake."

Bill is one of those people who knows you for thirty seconds and presumes that you are already close friends. "Sounds great, Bill," I said. "I can't believe your stamina. All the way from L.A. in one day and you're already in the water your very first night," I said, looking at his wife who looked like she hadn't slept in a week.

"This is Jean and Frank," Bill said, introducing me to hotel guests number thirteen and fourteen. "They arrived by boat from Roatan late last night after their flight got delayed into Honduras.

The new arrivals were both wearing matching Stingray City tee shirts from Grand Cayman and together had to weigh over 600 pounds. They were very friendly and said they lived in Indianapolis. I sensed that they were just about to tell me their life stories, so I excused myself and walked back to warm my coffee, which was surprisingly good, despite the fact that it was also very strong. I passed one of the French couples and they pointed at the Cousteau Society tee shirt I was wearing and said something I could not understand. I recognized the word "Bon" and they were smiling so I nodded and smiled back. I turned around a little too quickly to make my escape and slammed into Samantha, spilling my coffee all over the Duke University sweatshirt she was wearing.

"Jesus, I'm sorry, Sam. Let me clean that up."

I ran to the bar to get some club soda. I used a dry rag from the bar and I was able to get most of the coffee out. The whole time I was cleaning the bottom of Sam's sweatshirt she didn't say a word. She finally lost her cool and grabbed the material from my hand and said, "Enough. That's fine. Thank you, Jake. By the way, you missed orientation last night and technically I'm not supposed to let you dive today, but we are going to the Black Pearl and it is one of the best wrecks in this area. I don't want you to miss it, so I'm going to do you a favor. Meet me at the dock in fifteen minutes and I'll give you a quick run through of the dive program and you can get your dive license."

"Thank you," I said, although I didn't appreciate her tone, "but I already have a license to dive."

Samantha smiled. "You need a separate license to dive here, Jake. I'll explain later."

I was grateful she wasn't going to hassle me about diving today. It was pretty clear that we were not going to be starting local island fan clubs for each other. As I approached the stairway going down to the dock, she said, "Oh by the way, I spoke to one of the owners last night by radio and he said that for insurance reasons he would not be able to let you dive alone. He told me that he would explain it to you when he arrived tonight. He said he would see you at the show."

I nodded that I understood and I walked down the stairs to the dock. I was going to have to do some selling tonight when I met with the owner. This was bullshit. I should have been told before I came here that this was the policy. I was going to hammer this guy tonight and I would get my way in the end. I was sure of it.

I went down to the dive shack and got the lead I needed from one of the workers. The tanks were already on board the boat. There were two identical twenty-seven foot dive boats which were in surprisingly good condition and they had a shaded area below the flying bridge to stow cameras and to keep your gear dry. There was a beautiful painting on the front of the boats of a hammerhead shark inside of a shield above crossed swords. It looked like the kind of Army insignia that Special Forces used. There was the identical painting on the front of the other boat. Written below the paintings were the words "Hammer Time."

"Jake, are you ready?" I heard Samantha ask as she walked up behind me. I turned around and saw that she had changed into a tight fitting sleeveless black and pink neoprene vest with the Body Glove logo over her left breast. It was zippered down past her cleavage just above her belly button. She was wearing a pink bikini bottom and her stomach was as well defined as a professional body builder's. Her arms were also well- defined and athletic.

By the condition of her body I guessed that she was either a very serious athlete or that she had been an aerobics instructor back in the states. Her legs were well defined as well and resembled the legs of a bicyclist or a triathlete. Maybe not beautiful, but she sure as hell was sexy.

"Do you compete in any races?" I asked. "You look like working out is something more than just a hobby."

"Is this you being nice, Jake?" she asked with a sarcastic grin. "Believe it or not, there was a time in my life when all I did was smoke and drink. I started to work out as a matter of survival. Then eventually I guess I wound up substituting one addiction for another. Now I compete in triathathlons throughout the Caribbean and in the United States. I ride my mountain bike on the trails around the island."

I could see that she was uncomfortable with the conversation and it got quiet for a long moment. "This is your license to dive this island," she said and she handed me a plastic chip much like a casino chip that was attached to a pull tie so I could secure it to my BC. It was white and had a picture of Poseidon on it. He had a fierce, warlike expression and his trident was raised high in the air. He was riding a chariot that was being pulled by a team of dolphins. It was a very striking piece and I hoped I would get to keep it as a souvenir. It had three Latin words written on it and when I asked for a translation Sam told me that it meant "Do no Harm."

"The owners of this island take conservation pretty seriously it seems," I said. She turned to me and replied, "They take it very seriously Jake, and so will you by the time you leave here."

She told me I would not get the license to continue diving until I was checked out on this morning's dive. Then she gave me a twenty minute briefing of the rules and regulations concerning diving and a stern warning about touching the reef and about watching my bouyancy. She told me the owners did not encourage photography since photographers were notorious for kicking the hell out of the reef. That is why the hotel had no photography equipment and no facilities for developing E-6 slide film.

I noticed that Samantha's bathing suit was a Brazilian cut and when she turned around I saw on her left cheek a tattoo of a yellow and blue queen angelfish. I also noticed that she had a number of scars, one on her left leg and two identical slashes across her lower back which looked like they had been deep wounds. I wondered what had gotten a hold of her. Since I was convinced that this was one very tough lady I knew that it had to be something large and very strong.

I was not bringing my camera equipment on this morning's dive. I never carried my camera on the first dive of a trip since I wanted to first become accustomed to the new surroundings and I wanted to be free to just look around and explore. Sometimes I will dive one dive with the camera and one dive without it. Although I love underwater photography I find that spending a whole dive looking through a lens can be like work and that sometimes I can become so focused on composition that I wind up missing things around me outside the camera's field of vision. Obviously Bill did not share my view since he was coming down the dock with two large pelican cases full of equipment.

His poor wife was loaded down as well and they looked like they were on assignment for *National Geographic*. The rest of the morning's divers were also wandering down to the boat and I could see the heavy-set couple from Indiana walking slowly and carefully down the stairs in matching red and blue dive skins. Samantha quickly loaded everyone on board and we got under way. On the way out to the northernmost point of the island Samantha gathered the group around a white board and with an erasable marker she drew a profile of this mornings dive, including a good drawing of the wreck's position in the sand and the direction of the current.

She said that the current might change and that she would update us when we arrived at the site. I had read about the wreck of the Black Pearl in last month's issue of *Skin Diver* magazine. It was an American freighter that had an explosion in its engine room that tore a whole in the side and sank her in minutes. It rested in the sand just twenty-five feet from the bottom of the shallowest section of the wall and was sitting upright in ninety feet of water. It had two large stacks and a tower that were intact and rose just fifty feet from the surface. The ship was totally encrusted in coral and anemones and was home to two large moray eels and a school of barracuda. There were also large groups of tarpon that were known to swim in and out of the large holes that were cut into the ship by the local dive operators.

The best thing about this dive was that you could combine a wreck dive and a wall dive at the same time. If Samantha allowed me to, I was going to use my computer so I would get another fifteen or twenty minutes of bottom time. It was very distracting to see her walking around the boat in her thong bathing suit and I wondered how her employers let her get away with it. It seemed unprofessional to me, although she seemed very competent to run this operation.

She was climbing the ladder to the flying bridge to talk to the captain, a twenty-five year old native when she stopped and turned around to check something below. She caught me staring at her rear end and I quickly turned my head to watch Bill grease the O-rings on his Aquatica housing.

I thought about her tattoo. It's a funny coincidence that of all the fish in the sea the queen angel is my favorite. Bill had two separate and complete cameras with him, one with a 15mm wide angle lens and one with a 105mm macro lens. Both were Nikon F3s and both were in Aquatica housings. The whole set up must have cost him tens of thousands of dollars. I guess the printing business was pretty good. I only had a Nikonos V camera with a Nikonos strobe, but I got some great pictures with it and it was virtually idiot-proof when it came to proper exposure.

Bill explained to me that the SLR feature made it easier to frame subjects and that having two separate cameras with him made it easier to capture any subject near or far since he could not change either film or lenses underwater. This made sense but I personally could not imagine carrying all that equipment underwater and I wondered what joy his wife got out of being his photo assistant.

I was sitting next to one of the French couples who, as it turned out, did speak English. The husband was explaining that his wife was a new diver and that she was very nervous about seeing a shark or a barracuda. I told the woman that it wasn't sharks she had to be afraid of; it was decompression sickness if she wasn't careful.

I told her that there was a recent study at a technical university hospital in Germany that showed that amateur divers were likely to have brain lesions from tiny strokes caused by gas bubbles when a diver surfaces and that the long-term effects were memory loss, depression, and other behavioral problems.

I stood up and Samantha who had overheard the tail end of our conversation gave me a dirty look before she took my seat beside the couple in order to calm them down. I took a seat at the back of the boat and turned to look out on the water as a flying fish leaped out and skimmed along the surface.

It was a beautiful day and the sun was already burning strongly in the sky. I turned my face toward the sky and closed my eyes and as the early morning sun warmed my face I thought about the day of my mother's funeral only one month ago. Over 300 people had attended the funeral of an abandoned housewife turned cosmetician on a cold rainy day in Huntington, N.Y.

My mother had touched the lives of so many people with her warm, loving soul and her good-natured, generous spirit. When we were growing up we were always amazed at how easily my mother made friends and how long she kept them. She would bring her car in for auto body work and months later would still be continuing a friendship with the owner of the garage. As a matter of fact, Sal was at the funeral and he was visually upset when he came over to offer his condolences to my sister and me.

The irony is that neither Jackie nor I have ever been able to make friends very easily, and because of our judgmental, unforgiving nature we don't keep the ones we make very long. Jackie gave a beautiful eulogy and at the end she became so overcome with grief that I had to help her to her seat. I was numb and cold throughout the service and was appalled to see that my mother was dressed according to Jewish tradition. She was lying in a simple pine box, and instead of wearing her wig her head was covered in a white linen hat. Jackie who cannot speak two words of Hebrew and uses Cliff Notes for her Seder insisted on a traditional service, even though my mother had not been in a temple since she was a little girl, and had also been one of the vainest people I knew. My mother would have been appalled at being seen publicly without makeup.

We fought about it but Jackie as always was the winner. She used her tongue like a scalpel to apply guilt with surgical precision in order to break down my resistance. I didn't cry until two days later when we were sitting Shiva at my sister's house and I was in the bathroom.

The smell of the lotions and perfumes in my sister's bathroom triggered an overpowering olfactory memory and a devastating response in me. I remembered sitting on my mother's toilet dressed for a date while my mother stood over me blow drying my hair. I was so self conscious about the curly black mop on my head that I detested. My mother was the only one who could get my hair to look wavy for at least the night and I remembered her teasing me about my insecurity and us laughing together.

I remembered leaning my head against her belly and thinking how much I loved her and not being able to tell her because of the circumstances that had shaped our relationship at that time. I could never forgive her for being a human being and for being so lonely and so heartbroken about my father's betrayal that she looked desperately for love in the arms of any man who would have her. I couldn't forgive her for what I thought was her weakness and her lack of self-respect. I couldn't forgive her for not being the kind of mother I had, before my father had left.

My father broke my mother's heart and I didn't have the maturity or the selflessness to comfort her or to try to understand her and I hated myself for it now. I suffered terribly because I realized that I was never there for her. I ached and I cried there in my sister's bathroom and the pain I felt remembering how much I loved our mother and how much I missed her was shattering in its intensity.

I felt a hand on my shoulder and I realized that tears were running down my face so I quickly wiped my eyes and turned around.

"Are you okay, Jake?" Samantha asked.

"I'm fine," I snapped, as I stood and walked quickly away.

"I got some diesel fumes in my eyes. When the hell are we going to get there, I asked? Your brochure also said short boat rides. We could be half way to Tahiti by now."

I was embarrassed and angry at myself for losing control in public, especially in front of Samantha. At my outburst, Samantha's initial look of concern immediately disappeared and a look of mild anger replaced it. I was sorry but I preferred her anger to her pity. She followed me to the front of the boat and said, "We are just a couple of minutes away from the sight now, Jake. That's why I came over. Since we are dive buddies for today we need to run through a couple of things, including buddy breathing and the location of your octopus. I will lead on this dive, so follow me closely. Since we are both on computers we will surface when we have 750 PSI in our tanks. I normally make everyone surface with 1000 PSI, but since you are a divemaster we'll try to squeeze in some additional bottom time.

"Ernesto, the captain is also a divemaster and he will lead the rest of the group after he finishes mooring the boat. Does that sound okay, Jake?" I just nodded.

"I see you have a Scuba Pro AirII system, so I assume you will give me your regulator if I have a problem."

I told her that was fine and we ran through the dive profile again. I was grateful that she was being so accommodating, especially since I had been acting like such an asshole, but although she was being professional she was not making any attempt to hide her dislike for me.

The boat tied off at a permanent mooring that floated above the wreck's tower. Someone started yelling excitedly and everyone turned to look in the water to see what all the excitement was about. A small school of hammerhead sharks were twenty feet below the boat and were circling around the top of the wreck. It was the first time I had ever seen such a thing and my heart was racing. The fat couple from Indy was frightened about the prospect of entering the water and the husband told Samantha that they would prefer to wait on the boat.

Samantha explained to them and the rest of the group that we were all going to wait until the sharks left the area and that there was no need to be frightened. She said we should all relax and appreciate the beauty and the rarity of such a wonderful sight. She explained that there was a time when these waters were teeming with hammerheads, blacktips, and bull sharks and that due to overhunting a view such as this was now exceptional.

She then made another speech about conservation and bragged that because of the conservation efforts of the Aegis and of Neptune Divers many large animals were now returning to these waters. Bill had his hands in the water and was hanging his wide angle camera over the side. He was snapping away like a madman when Samantha pulled him back in. I could see by the look on his face that she had not made a friend and he reluctantly sat down to reload for the dive since he had only shot sixteen pictures off of a roll of thirty-six exposures.

Samantha sat down next to me since it was the only free spot and I said, "If I were them," pointing to the heavyset couple, "I would definitely stay out of the water. They are probably what sharks dream about at night when they're sleeping."

Samantha turned to me and said, "The Martins are two of my favorite customers, Jake. They have been coming here every year for six years. They rarely complain and they are a pleasure to be around. They are also avid divers and are very competent in the water, despite what might be their physical limitations on land."

I cut her off in the middle of her speech and said, "Diving is great for fat people, weightlessness for the weighty."

I thought that was a very witty remark. Samantha finally lost her patience and stood up and said, "Look Jake, it's obvious that you are going through something very heavy and I'm sorry about that. You're a customer and I don't mean to be disrespectful, but your constant rudeness and your shitty attitude are getting on my nerves.

"We will dive together this morning and that's the end. After that I will still be available to help you but we won't be diving together again." Before she left she said, "There's a great Bruce Springsteen song that reminds me of you. I can't remember the name but in it he says, It's a sad man, my friend, who's living in his own skin and can't stand the company. Every fool's got a reason for feeling sorry for himself and turning his heart to stone.

"Bad things happen to everyone, Jake and we can't stop them from happening but we sure as hell can control how we react to them and how we treat other people. That's the true test of character," she finished and then she walked away.

I was stunned and my face became flushed. I couldn't believe she spoke to me like that and I was fuming. I was going to complain to the owners about her when we met this evening. I would be paying close to ten grand for a month here and I wasn't about to tolerate any disrespect from the hired help.

Finally the hammerheads disappeared and Samantha gathered the group for yet another tiresome briefing, then we began to suit up for the dive. First, everyone entered the water before us while we stood around sweating and then Samantha and I finally got in the water. The water was over eighty degrees and the visibility was over 150 feet. I could see the entire wreck ninety feet below me. The incline of the wall ended right before the boat's stern.

The divers below me were already at the stacks, except for one of the French couples who appeared to be having problems with their buoyancy until Ernesto came over and assisted them. Samantha was in a steep descent and was heading straight down. She was descending quickly without having to clear her ears or adjust her mask.

I caught up to her and she put her fingers side by side giving me the sign to stay together. I made a face at her and hoped that I would not have to chase her all over the wreck. She was wearing a black wetsuit with green flourescent arms. Her hair was flying behind her and it looked long and flowing underwater. I could see every muscle in her legs as she kicked her oversized spear-hunting fins back and forth.

We circled around the tower and it was covered with both hard and soft corals. A large school of tiny blue fish were dancing in one large circle around the mast and their shape kept changing as they moved in unison from point to point. We swam down the length of the tower and across the deck to a large smokestack. Samantha swam to the top of the stack and entered it. She disappeared inside but I was reluctant to follow her. I could not see her inside, neither could I see daylight, and I had mild claustrophobia underwater, when it came to entering a wreck, unless I could see the way out.

It was obvious that she was fucking with my head and that she was testing me, so with the comforting thought that she knew this wreck inside out, I entered the stack. I was nervous as hell and I made a mental note to add to my complaint the fact that as a guide she had left me behind and had led me into possible danger. The stack was fifteen feet wide and in the dark I occasionally banged my tank against the sides, which caused an eerie sound reverberating off the sides all around me.

I was thirty feet down when I began to see light and I breathed deeply in relief. I came out into what was left of the engine room and could see Samantha waiting at a large opening that had been blown out of the side of the ship. She pointed behind me and I turned to see ten large tarpon. Their silver bodies were shining in the darkness from a shaft of light from above that danced across their skin. They were hovering in one spot packed closely together.

It was a beautiful sight and I stared for several seconds before I swam over to Samantha. It was a great experience swimming down the shaft and I motioned to Samantha that I now wanted to swim back up. She shook her head no and led me out of the hole in the side and I noticed that all of the sharp edges from the explosion were smooth where they had been welded down.

The dive operators had done a wonderful job of creating a safe and enjoyable site out of this artificial reef. When we exited the ship we were facing the wall which was only several kicks away, and Samantha led me up the wall to sixty feet. She stopped at a large outcropping of brain and pillar coral and reached her hand into a hole, being careful not to touch anything.

She pulled her hand out and seconds later the largest green moray eel I had ever seen appeared with a head that was shaped like a large dog's. It opened its mouth wide, showing rows of razor sharp teeth. To my surprise and my utter joy the eel swam into Samantha's arms and she began to stroke it like a household pet as it wrapped itself around her. She looked like a mermaid with her beautiful blonde hair swirling around her.

She called me over, put her hand on top of mine, and while the eel wrapped itself around the two of us she ran my hand over its body. I was exhilarated and made a conscious effort to control my breathing. The eel felt silky smooth and I could feel the power in its body as it moved from side to side. I looked at Samantha and was smiling from ear to ear.

Her face showed no expression so I stopped smiling. She let go of the eel and it swam off to its hole and disappeared inside. I spotted a large white anemone with purple tips and swam closer to take a look at it. I wanted to look very close to see if there were any shrimp living in it. I saw movement among the tentacles and spotted a white and purple spotted anemone shrimp the size of my pinkie nail sitting on one of the anemone's tentacles.

I reached out my hand to brush aside one of the tentacles in order to get a better look and Samantha grabbed my hand. She shook her head no and tapped the dive medallion attached to my BC as a reminder of proper reef etiquette. Samantha then led me back to the wreck and we swam along the outer railings just below deck and found two large barracuda blocking our way. We stopped and the barracuda swam toward us, then over us, passing just a few inches above us.

For the next fifteen minutes, we swam in and out of several openings in the wreck through the galley and down some hallways, and eventually came to the bridge where I grabbed the large wooden pilot's wheel and spun it around pretending to steer the ship. I was feeling great and this was becoming one of the best dives I could ever remember.

Samantha signed to me, asking how much air I had left. After checking my gauges I held up ten fingers to signal that there was 1000 PSI remaining in my tanks. She told me that she still had 1,900 pounds remaining and I was impressed by her incredible lack of air consumption. She then led me back out to the reef and we came upon Bill and his wife, when I saw by the angry look in Samantha's eyes that he was doing something wrong.

Samantha took off like a sea lion and swam quickly ahead of me toward Bill and his wife. When I finally caught up to her she was ordering them through a combination of sign language and dive signals to get their asses back on the boat immediately. I stared at Bill, who looked like a fox caught in the henhouse. When I looked at his camera I saw what he had done.

At the end of the lens housing was an attachment that looked like a rod with an alligator clip on the end of it. Attached to the clip was a piece of a purple sea fan and on the fan was a perfect flamingo tongue which was clean and white and was covered with large yellow spots. A flamingo tongue looks like a snail shell. It is usually found on sea fans and is a very beautiful animal especially when it is contrasted against the background of a bright purple sea fan.

Every underwater macro photographer has at least one shot of this subject and we all look for the one perfect mantel to get a picture of. It appeared as if Bill had found one and was not going to take any chances on composition or exposure. He had broken off the piece of the fan with the snail attached and then ascended to a depth where there was more available natural light and he clipped his subject to the ideal focal length to get a perfectly focused and exposed photograph.

Samantha was livid and she looked as if she was about to pull her dive knife and turn Bill into chum for the hammerheads. Bill removed the fan from the clip and dropped it to the bottom of the sea. I guess it was his intention to get rid of the evidence and this appeared to infuriate Samantha even more. Then Bill and his wife swam back to the boat as Samantha had instructed and I followed behind.

When we got close to the boat we saw that a large school of hammerheads had returned and were swimming in a circle above us. From below, they were silhouetted against the sky. It was a phenomenal sight and I wished for the tenth time on this dive that I had brought my camera. Bill had the same thought and he raised his wide angle camera toward the surface.

He was about to snap the best picture of his life when Samantha put her hand over the bubble shaped port on the camera housing and blocked his shot. The hammerheads broke up the circle when the engine started and swam away in a group. Now the expression on Bill's face became menacing and we all surfaced and made our way over to the ladder. I was glad that Samantha's attention was temporarily focused on someone else, and I was curious to see what would happen when we got back to the hotel.

It was a long quiet ride back once word spread about what had happened. Bill approached me and asked me to back up his story about finding the sea fan already broken and reminded me how rudely and unprofessionally Samantha had been treating me during the day.

Bill knew that Samantha and I were not friendly and he encouraged me to lodge the complaint that I had been thinking about before our dive. When we got back to the hotel I took a hot shower and ran through the dive again in my head. It was spectacular and Samantha was the most extraordinary woman I had ever seen. The sight of her with that eel was magical. She was so comfortable and confident in the water. It was also very gracious of her to show me such a good time considering what a jerk I had been and how she must have felt about me. She could have gone through the motions and taken me on a quick spin around the wreck but she went out of her way to provide me with the best dive possible.

Despite my wounded ego and my normally defensive nature I knew I deserved to be told off by her earlier on the boat and I respected her for doing so. I also admired the way she had stood up to Bill in order to protect the reef. Bill was an asshole and he deserved what he got. I, for one, would not miss his presence on this island.

There was a knock at my door and I was told by one of the maids that the owner of the hotel was on the radio and that he wanted to speak to me. I dressed and walked quickly over to the main building. I was ushered into the manager's office where Bill and his wife and Samantha were already waiting. I could hear a man's voice on the radio's speakerphone talking to everyone in the room and Samantha interrupted him to tell him that I had arrived.

"Good afternoon, Mr. Stein, and welcome to the Aegis," he began.

"I am very sorry to have to bother you during your vacation and I was reluctant to involve you in this matter, but you were present at the time and I am being presented with two conflicting stories."

"I trust Samantha implicitly, but as you know, being a salesman and a businessman, 'the customer is always right' so I have a dilemma. Mr. Kritzer says that he picked up the broken sea fan from the reef and that someone must have torn it on an earlier dive with their fins. He also says that when you all surfaced, both he and his wife were spoken to disrespectfully by Samantha and that later on the boat Samantha had threatened them.

"Mr. Kritzer says that earlier in the day he witnessed and overheard you being spoken to disrespectfully by Samantha and that you were close enough on the ride back to have heard Samantha cursing at them and threatening them.

"Once again, I apologize for this uncomfortable situation and when I arrive later tonight I would like to speak to you in person about this unfortunate situation. I have to ask you, is what Mr. Kritzer says about your treatment by Samantha earlier today accurate and could you please tell me what you saw or heard earlier today in regards to this matter with the sea fan?"

I looked over at Samantha and she was cool as could be. Her face showed no expression whatsoever and she exuded total confidence.

"I was with Samantha when we came upon Mr. and Mrs. Kritzer on the wall. The fan was already in the clip and although I could not say with absolute certainty that it was already damaged, I can say that based on my experience and all of my years of diving that I find it highly unlikely that a perfect flamingo tongue on a seemingly healthy piece of sea fan just happened to be there.

"Of course this is all speculation on my part but I also have to wonder why the tool with the alligator clip was there in the first place.

"What other purpose could it have served?

"I am a photographer and I don't carry one and I have dove alongside professional photographers and none of them carry anything like it.

"What I can say with absolute certainty is that Samantha never cursed or raised her voice or threatened the Kritzers in any way, although she was obviously upset. She handled herself very professionally and was never disrespectful.

"As for my own experience with Samantha, I have no complaints whatsoever, which I can tell you is saying a lot for me." I noticed that Samantha smiled.

"Samantha took me on the best dive I have ever been on today and she handled herself on the boat with the group better than any divemaster I have ever seen." I turned to Samantha with an apologetic look and I smiled.

"Thank you for your help, Mr. Stein. I look forward to seeing you tonight and to talking to you about more pleasant subjects like this island's reef systems and your plans for the rest of your trip," the voice on the radio said.

" No problem" I said, "and please call me, Jake."

"Thank you, Jake."

I left the office and talked to Carmen at the bar before going to watch the sunset on the deck. There was a puzzle on the bar with two connected horseshoes, which you had to disconnect somehow. I tried it over and over with no success and watched Carmen solve it in seconds again and again while she laughed at my unsuccessful attempts and my growing frustration.

Finally two hours later, after my third mudslide, I figured it out and to celebrate, Carmen gave me a fourth drink free. By the time I reached the sun deck there was already a crowd and I was feeling pretty light headed. The sun was a large orange ball hanging just inches above the water and the sky was red, blue and purple and full of long billowy clouds.

The sunset was magnificent and as I stared at the horizon with the rest of the group a seaplane suddenly appeared in view and touched down gently 100 yards from the dock. The plane pulled up alongside the dock just as the lights came on and I could see and hear the dogs barking excitedly as they raced down the dock to meet the plane.

Just as the sun finished its descent into the ocean and I missed the fictitious green flash for the thousandth time in my life the plane doors swung open and a tall man, followed by a shorter man, climbed out.

"Quite an entrance," I heard Samantha say in my ear. "I think they time it that way on purpose for the benefit of the guests."

"Who are they?" I asked.

"They're tonight's entertainment, Tom & Jerry, the famous Caribbean duet," she said with a laugh.

"Thanks for your help today, Jake. I appreciate it," she said.

"All I did was tell the truth, nothing more. I want to thank you for today's dive, especially after the way I behaved. I swear to you that I'm not as much of an asshole as I appear to be."

"Well then, you're one hell of an actor," she said with a serious expression, and then she smiled and I knew she was kidding.

"What happened to the Kritzers?" I asked.

"They're in their room packing. They'll be gone tomorrow morning."

"How do the owners get away with that?" I asked. "Don't they get sued and how do they stay in business?"

"Remember, I told you when it comes to the environment the people who own this place don't fool around and they stay in business because there are a lot more divers out there who appreciate what they are trying to do and how they feel than people like the Kritzers, who think everything on earth was put here to better serve them.

"As for law suits, there have been plenty of them, but the people who come here sign an ironclad agreement and the hotel refunds all of their money, even their airfare, although we are not obligated to."

"Well, I am certainly looking forward to meeting the owners," I said.

"I was curious during today's conversation how he knew I was a salesman. I never filled out that information on my application."

"I'll tell you a secret, Jake. They know everything about you. They told me today that of all the guests that are here this week they are most looking forward to meeting you."

CHAPTER 16

THE SHOWER only provided about fifteen minutes of hot water before it ran out and the warm water was replaced by a blast of what felt like glacial runoff. I turned my back and leaned my head forward and let the pulse of the inconsistent water pressure massage the back of my neck and shoulders and wash the salt water from my back. Today was a good day and I was looking forward to seeing Samantha again at tonight's show. Especially after our first civil conversation on the sunset deck, as I now referred to the lodges main patio. I was more than a little curious by her comment that the owners "knew all about me" and the way she changed the subject when I pressed her for some elucidation.

I was beginning to feel really relaxed after only a day on this island and I could actually go more than an hour now without thinking about my mom. I felt a little guilty for allowing myself to have a good time and to forget, if only for a little while.

I turned and let the water spray my face and I washed my hair, which felt like straw, from a combination of the salt water, sun, and sunscreen. I looked down between the wooden slats in the walls surrounding the large open shower stall and I could see the lights from the beach and I could feel a cool tropical night breeze on my wet skin.

This place was heaven and I couldn't think of anywhere I'd rather be tonight. I was going to wear my white linen Ralph Lauren slacks with a baby blue silk Hawaiian shirt that I had brought with me. Probably a little dressy for this place but it was Saturday night and I was attending a live performance in the club. Besides I wanted to impress Samantha.

During our talk on the patio she was smiling and laughing a lot and I think I've turned her around on her feelings about me since the first miserable impressions I made on her. I finished showering, then I shaved and put on some cologne and went back to the cabin and got dressed.

Through the open window of my room I could hear music beginning to play at the main building, and I checked my watch which read 8:52. I heard other guests filing past my bungalow on their way to the club. I hurried out the door and made my way past the iguana cages and entered the bar where I was surprised to see a crowd of close to seventy-five people who were laughing and drinking.

The show was scheduled to begin at 9:30 and the place was already packed. There appeared to be a lot of locals and Carmen was speaking Spanish with a group of about six people she seemed to know very well when I interrupted her and ordered a mudslide. I took my drink and walked out on the patio and saw below me at the dock that there were at least ten to twelve boats of varying sizes tied up along the pier. Samantha was right. This was a big event, the appearance of Tom & Jerry in the islands.

I got a kick every time I read or heard their names, and had told Samantha earlier that Tom & Jerry was the original name of Simon & Garfunkle when they first started out. She laughed and told me that she didn't know that but that it made sense since they sang a few of their songs. It was a clear night and despite the light pollution from behind me I could see the sky was full of stars and a cool breeze was blowing in from the ocean.

The Eagles "Hotel California" album was playing and I began to involuntarily play air guitar along with Don Felder and Joe Walsh. By the time the song reached the climactic guitar solo at the end of what I consider to be one of music's best guitar jams I had my eyes closed and I was strumming right along.

I kept my hands low and in front of me so that no one could see me but I guess the swaying of my head gave me away. Samantha walked up behind me and said with a laugh, "Hey Jake, maybe we can get you up on stage tonight to back up the boys."

My face was bright red when I turned around and then I almost choked on my drink when I saw Samantha bathed in the light of the torches that surrounded the patio. She was wearing a 1950s style, silk beach dress, which was decorated in the style of an Hawaiian shirt, but in very subdued pastel colors. It had short sleeves and a deep V-neck and fell to mid-thigh.

Samantha's hair was blow dried so it was full and long and the color in the lamplight looked like spun gold. To my amazement, she was wearing make-up as well, but only a tiny amount. She looked luminous.

"You look incredible," I blurted out. She looked uncharacteristically embarrassed for a moment.

"Thanks, Jake. You're a gentleman even if you are full of shit. What are you drinking? It looks pretty good."

I explained the origin of the mudslide and the ingredients and she told me her two favorite drinks were club soda and cranberry juice. "You were right, Sam. This place is packed. Who would have thought?"

"You'll see, Jake. These guys are pretty good and when they're done, we play 70s disco music including Donna Summer and The Hustle. It's corny as hell but people love it. The tourists especially. We get people here from the hotels on Roatan and Guanaja and locals from all over the islands, although most really can't even afford what it costs in gas to make the trip."

I heard a loud commotion at the bar and noticed that there was a small group of very large men who were drinking quickly and getting louder by the minute. Carmen looked agitated and Sam excused herself to go and speak with them. They wore rough work clothes and they had numerous tattoos on their hands and forearms. I had just screwed up enough nerve to join Samantha when she stepped up to them and said a few words. They left the bar and took over a large rattan sofa near the end of the patio. Sam leaned over the bar and said something to Carmen.

"What was that all about?" I asked when she rejoined me.

"Just some local construction workers from Roatan who have been working on the new 500-room resort, which is scheduled to open on the island in July. We get them over here some times, although I've never seen this group. For awhile we weren't too popular with that lot since we fought tooth and nail to block the building of the resort and we helped to delay its start for over ten months."

"Good thing they didn't give you a hard time or I would have had to give them a beating," I said with a smile and then I flexed my right arm in a comical impression of a bodybuilder. I twisted my wrist from right to left so that my bicep would dance up and down my arm.

"My hero," Samantha said, and she squeezed my bicep hard between her thumb and forefinger.

"Ouch, that hurts," I said, and it did. Samantha told me she had to mingle with the other guests and that since the show was about to begin she needed to herd everyone into the club. I made my way past the French group, who all waved hello to me and entered the club only to find that it was standing room only and that all the tables were taken.

I saw Samantha waving to me from the corner of the room and she ushered me over to the only empty table left. She explained that it belonged to the owners of the hotel who were arriving tonight and that they had asked that I join them. I took my seat and my curiosity was again aroused. I had no idea what I had done to distinguish myself, except behave like an ass, and I could see no reason why I was receiving such special attention when so many of my fellow guests appeared to be standing against the back walls.

Samantha walked to the front of the room and took the microphone. She smiled and in the bright stage lighting her teeth looked as white as ivory.

"Good evening, everyone, and welcome to the Atlantis Lounge. For your entertainment tonight we bring you direct from their world tour, Tom & Jerry."

The room exploded with applause and the two men I had seen arrive on the seaplane entered from the kitchen and took their places behind their instruments and began to play. One of them played an electric acoustic guitar and harmonica, which he wore around his neck like Bob Dylan, and the other one played what looked like a small standing electric keyboard or synthesizer.

They immediately began to play Jimmy Buffet's "Volcano" and everyone sang along. The keyboards sounded like a five-piece band and their harmony and vocals were excellent. The song was a perfect introduction for the night's festivities and even I got into the spirit and sang along.

I couldn't take my eyes off of the man who was playing the guitar, and I noticed that several women around me were also staring at him and laughing among themselves. It was only my own strong homophobic feelings that kept me from examining him any longer than I had, but I had to admit that he was the handsomest human being I had ever seen outside of a television soap opera.

He stood about 6'3" tall and I would guess he weighed about 200 pounds. He had long wavy, dark blond hair like Samantha's, although it was at the moment covered by a straw cowboy hat, and he had a deep dark tan. He had a square jaw like a movie star's and high cheekbones. He also had deep dimples in his cheeks when he smiled. His eyes looked gray with a slight tint of blue.

He was wearing a dark navy blue bowling shirt open, and he had on a white ribbed tank top T-shirt underneath, which was tucked into his faded denim jeans. He wore open-toed leather sandals on his feet. He looked powerful although he was not too heavily muscled and appeared lean and lithe like an Olympic gymnast or a swimmer.

Through the thin material of his cotton T-shirt you could see the definition of all the musculature in his abdomen and he had the elusive washboard stomach, or "six pack," that every man sweats hours in the gym trying to earn.

I felt almost instantly inadequate and began to do a quick self-evaluation of my own appearance. I stopped when I got to my stomach where I could feel my jeans cutting into my waistline. His partner appeared average by comparison. He was about 5'9" and weighed about 165 pounds. He was balding on top and was wearing wire frame glasses.

He looked like Anthony Edwards, the actor who plays Dr. Green on the Television program "ER."

The tall man had a deep, resonant voice, which was a little rough like Springsteen's, and the smaller man had a sweeter more melodic voice. They complemented each other very well and covered every possible range as they sang six more songs without stopping, from Cat Stevens to Bob Marley.

Finally they took a break and the big man took the microphone. "Is everybody having a good time here at the Aegis Inn?" The room exploded with applause mixed with cheers and whistling. "My name is Tom and my partner here is Jerry. Many of you here know us and can vouch for the fact that as ridiculous as it may sound, those are our real names."

Tom held up his hand to quiet the laughter and continued. "On the flight over here Jerry was in one of his pensive moods and as we passed over the reef system he started to lecture me for the thousandth time about conservation and he gave me a brief history of the planet.

"He did tell me something interesting which I wanted to share with you tonight. About six hundred million years ago the first amphibians crawled up onto land, something resembling a lungfish, and they began to breathe air for the first time. Jerry's history lesson about evolution reminded me that we all originated from the sea. Most of us in this room are still trying to return as often as possible." All the divers in the room began to hoot and holler and to wave their hands in the air.

"Well, a few million years ago the first amphibians also chose to return to the sea. The whale and the dolphin long ago began as land animals and they eventually returned to the sea. Land mammals today in utero float in a body of salt water and they are able to breathe in liquid. At around 4 weeks of age we even grow something similar to gills early on in our development."

"The sea is where we began. It is our heritage. It is our past, and it is also our future. Love her and respect her as we do and teach others to do the same."

When he ended, he began to strum slowly on the guitar and then he began to sing "A pirate looks at forty" by Jimmy Buffet and Jerry joined in with a beautiful piano accompaniment. Then they sang "Mother mother ocean" and it was corny as hell. In any other venue other than a starlit outdoor patio at a Caribbean seaside resort filled primarily with divers it probably would have been laughable, but the room was visibly moved. People sang along and couples held hands and even I, the world's greatest cynic sang along.

Tom had a soulful voice and when he finished, everyone including me, enthusiastically applauded. They began to play some up beat rock and roll tunes and some reggae music by artists like Jimmy Cliff and people got on their feet and danced. Samantha walked over to my table and sat down.

"Having a good time?"

"I have to admit these guys are pretty good and they are playing some of my favorite artists, including James Taylor and Van Morrison. Tom is a pretty attractive guy, don't you think?" I asked, curious to hear her answer and feeling a little insecure. I was wondering about the nature of their relationship.

"I never really noticed," she said in a sarcastic tone, then she looked at him and said with a smile, "I guess if you're attracted to a man with rugged good looks and a perfect body who also happens to sing and play the guitar you might go for Tom."

She looked at me to see my reaction. When I appeared sufficiently stricken she finished by saying, "But honestly, Jake, Tom's not my type and I can tell you from personal experience that his only interests are Jerry and his work."

"They're gay?" I asked in shock, while they played Dave Mason's "We Just Disagree" in the background. Samantha laughed.

"Oh, Jake, they're brothers, Tom and Jerry Peterson." She stood up and started to walk away, but I stopped her by asking, "Tell me Sam, what is your type?"

She turned back and looked at me and I thought I must not have really seen her when I first arrived on the island. At this moment, I thought she was the most beautiful woman I had ever seen. "You are, Jake. You're my type, because you're sweet and because you make me laugh." Then she quickly walked away.

I felt like I had just downed a double shot of Cuervo Gold. My cheeks flushed and I felt light-headed and I caught myself smiling like an idiot. I started thinking too much again and I wondered if she was just teasing me but then I decided that Samantha would never be that cruel. Tom & Jerry finished playing "Mexico" by James Taylor when Jerry spoke to the audience.

"I want to play a very special song for my brother, who also happens to be my best friend. The name of this song is "Blood Brothers" by Bruce Springsteen and the words have a lot of meaning for me."

Jerry began to play the piano extremely well. I was impressed by both of their talents and I wondered what had brought them all the way out here to play music over 2000 miles from the U.S. mainland. Like all Springsteen songs it was well written and powerful, and I could identify with many of the lyrics.

"We got our own roads to ride and chances we gotta take. We stood side by side, each one fighting for the other, we said until we died we'd always be blood brothers. Now the hardness of this world slowly grinds your dreams away, making a fool's joke out of the promises we make, and what once seemed black and white turns to so many shades of gray, we lose ourselves in work to do and bills to pay. And it's a ride, ride, ride and there ain't much cover, with no one runnin' by your side, my, blood brother.

"On through the houses of the dead past those fallen in their tracks always movin ahead and never looking back. Now I don't know how I feel, I don't know how I feel tonight, if I've fallen 'neath the wheel, if I've lost or I've gained sight."

I was thinking it would be easier to believe that these two were lovers than brothers when I looked at them side by side. When they got to the second verse of the song and Jerry began to sing the part about those fallen in their tracks it made me think of my mother. My eyes were tearing when Samantha came up behind me.

"Don't be sad, Jake. Please not tonight. I'd like to see you have a good time tonight, all night," she said as she sat down beside me and took my hand in hers.

"I'm having a great time, Sam, really. Thanks for your concern." I smiled and put my other hand on top of hers. "When are the owners coming?" I asked. "I thought I was going to meet them tonight. I feel a little guilty hogging this entire table while people are standing."

"They're already here, Jake." She pointed toward the stage. "Tom & Jerry own the Aegis Inn and the entire island."

"Them?" I said in genuine surprise. "Does everyone else here know that?"

"Most of the regulars and returning guests and, of course, the locals know it. Tom & Jerry travel most of the time so they're only here off and on a few times a year. I manage the hotel most of the time, if I'm not with them on a dive trip somewhere. And when that happens we leave Carmen in charge.

"Tom & Jerry are independently wealthy and they like to travel to dive destinations all over the world. Sometimes they even take the staff along as a bonus. They really are a couple of jokers and they like to make a grand entrance. They'll play for a couple of hours and then they'll announce to the people who don't already know it that they are the owners of the property and their hosts for the evening. Then they'll end by buying a round for the house."

Like Samantha said after they played "Tupelo Honey" by Van Morrison and Jimmy Cliff's "The harder they come, the harder they fall" to close out their final set they told everyone that they were their hosts for the evening. Tom said that they would be on the island for at least a month. They welcomed everyone to the Aegis Inn. Tom gave another tiresome environmental warning about diving safety, then he bought everyone a drink.

They walked off the stage to thunderous applause and went back into the kitchen. A couple of minutes later, Tom walked out alone and I saw that he had removed his hat. I saw that his hair was rather long, almost shoulder length and was thick and wavy. He made the rounds and talked to friends and locals and hotel guests. Then he walked toward my table.

"Are you taking care of Mr. Stein?" he asked Samantha when he got closer. Then he grabbed a chair and took a seat. "Please, Tom, call me Jake. And I couldn't be happier," I said as we held out our arms and shook hands. "You guys were terrific. Played all my favorites, except for Jackson Browne."

"Are you a Jackson Browne fan, Jake?" Tom asked. "I'm a big fan myself, which is why I refuse to butcher his music. I wanted to apologize again about the upset with the Kritzers and for involving you in our problems. I promised Sam that I would make it up to you. Samantha tells me that you are an excellent diver so I'm going to break my own rule and I'm going to let you dive without a buddy for the rest of your stay with us, on two conditions. My first condition is that you dive with me tomorrow so that I can check you out. I have a special treat for you, Jake. I'm going to take you to my own private reef, an area that only I know about. The second condition is that when you dive alone you keep at least one person in your range of view at all times, no more than thirty feet away, does that sound okay, Jake?"

I was startled by his offer and I was intrigued and excited about the prospect of diving some unknown pristine reef. I was looking forward to spending some time with Tom and getting to know him. I also liked the fact that Samantha had told Tom that I was a good diver. That meant a lot to me.

"That sounds great, Tom. Thanks for your generosity and for the flexibility. I promise to be careful." He smiled and revealed a set of perfect white teeth, then winked at Samantha. I felt a twinge of jealousy and wondered again about the true nature of their relationship. To me, Tom seemed like the kind of man who would be irresistible to women, and they worked together for long periods of time on this tiny island. Who wouldn't feel a little intimidated around a man that resembled Tarzan and I wondered if Samantha had been able to resist his charms over the years.

"Tomorrow morning at 8:00 meet me at the dock and we'll take off. You don't get airsick do you, Jake?" Suddenly Tom turned around to speak to a couple at the next table.

"What does he mean airsick?" I asked Sam.

"You're in for a rare treat. Tom has only taken a few people to his secret hideaway and they were so amazed that when they returned they could hardly speak. It's rumored to be the best dive in the islands," Samantha said.

"That's great," I said. "But does he intend to fly us there?"

Samantha laughed out loud, "Of course. But don't be nervous, Tom is a great pilot."

Suddenly, there was a loud crash of glass and someone was screaming at the bar. The four drunken construction workers who Sam had trouble with earlier had returned to the bar and were yelling and pushing some of the guests, who quickly removed themselves from the area.

Carmen looked overwhelmed and then one of the men called her a "fat bitch" and she began to cry.

I saw a look on Tom's face that gave me a chill as he raised himself out of his seat. In an instant his visage changed. He tightened his hands into fists as he approached the bar.

"There are four men over there, Sam. Should I go with him?"

"Don't worry. Tom can handle it. Stay where you are."

Tom walked up to the one with the biggest mouth and the biggest body and moved in very close until they were toe to toe. The man who was at least two inches taller than Tom also outweighed him by at least 50 pounds. The man picked up the bar puzzle that was made from two solid horseshoes and with a smile he directed at Tom he twisted them apart with his bare hands breaking the metal links that bound them together.

Tom reached out and took the man's meaty right hand in his right hand as if he was shaking it and then he leaned in and whispered something in his ear as he began to squeeze it. I could see the man's hand turn white as the bands of muscle in Tom's forearms tensed and flexed. The man squeezed back and his face showed great exertion. He turned bright red. He was sweating profusely and the veins in his forehead were throbbing.

Tom had a calm, almost serene look on his face. Although I knew he was exerting great force I could see no visible signs of effort other then the flexing of his powerful forearm. The man's hand was as white as bone and looked bloodless and his fingers were beginning to twist and overlap. He appeared to be in great pain and then he dropped to his knees. Tom kept squeezing his hand until the man begged him to release his grip.

Tom released his grip and the man fell to the floor, holding his hand and whimpering. Two of his friends moved toward Tom when a local man nearby said something to them in Spanish and they suddenly looked frightened and backed away.

They helped their friend to his feet, but Tom would not allow them to leave until they all apologized to Carmen. When they left, Tom reached for Carmen's hand and he gently kissed it. He was once again the smiling charming host. I was intrigued and was also a little frightened by this very unique man.

As Tom walked back to the table his chivalry was rewarded by a loud round of applause from the entire room. He blushed, then made his apologies to everyone for the disturbance. He worked his way back to the table, where I followed him and sat down.

"I'm sorry about that, Jake," he said. "Sometimes the locals show up here with a chip on their shoulder because of the stand we took on the construction of the new hotel on Roatan. They drink a little too much and things get out of hand. I'm always sorry when our guests have to see something like that but I don't want to exclude the locals from our hotel."

"That guy certainly had it coming, and I thought you handled it brilliantly."

"Thanks Jake. I noticed you moving toward us at the bar. Were you coming to help me?" I felt a little put on the spot by his question. I didn't want to lie but I also didn't want Tom to think I was a coward.

"I honestly didn't know what I was going to do, but because of the odds I felt compelled to do something. I was praying the whole time I approached the bar that nothing would happen. To tell you the truth, I don't know how much help I would have been, but at 4 to 1, I didn't like the odds."

"You're all right, Jake. You're also honest, which is a rare quality these days. I've got to get some sack time now. I'm exhausted. I'll see you bright and early at eight down on the dock." He said goodnight and then he left the room as people patted him on the back and shook his hand.

I was looking forward to tomorrow and to spending some more time together. I liked it here and I already felt very much at home. Maybe I would extend my trip, and if I got friendly with Tom maybe I could hire on here for awhile as a divemaster.

I had forgotten to ask him and Samantha how he knew that I was a salesman and what she had meant by her comments on the sunset deck, especially about the owner's knowing all about me.

CHAPTER 17

I AWOKE ANYWHERE BETWEEN 7:00 AND 7:10, according to my Rolex watch. It always ran a little slow and looked better than it actually worked. My head was feeling a bit cloudy from the three mudslides I had drank last night and my throat felt scratchy from inhaling all the second-hand smoke that was floating around the club.

I was excited about the prospect of diving at a remote, virtually inaccessible site but was also more than a little apprehensive about flying the first thing in the morning and landing in the middle of nowhere alone with someone I hardly knew. I was thinking about the possible effects of flying shortly before a dive and all of the possible side effects, such as decompression sickness, or the bends. I assumed that Tom would fly the plane at a very low altitude in order to avoid pressurization. I rose reluctantly from the bed and let out a great yawn, then I stretched my arms, shoulders, and back and walked over to the porch to look outside.

I was surprised to see that a heavy fog was covering the island and had spun through the trees like cobwebs. There was a fine mist falling and the trees were glistening. Their leaves were covered in tiny beads of water and shined like glycerin in the pale yellow light that was just beginning to burn its way through the haze.

When I listened closely, the jungle was actually quite a noisy place. There were thousands of birds all with a different sound that were constantly singing in the trees. I could hear the waves crashing. Then there was the incessant humming and chirping of the insect world, which at night sounded as if the entire species of the hillside had plugged into amplifiers. At night the volume seemed to increase tenfold in its decibel level. When I lay down and rested my head on the pillow the sound would fill the room. It's funny how I could become accustomed to certain sounds. What a city boy might find comforting in a familiar way might be the sound of sirens and clanging garbage cans and car alarms that would scream their warnings at 3 A.M. It was the absence of those noises which used to keep me up at night when I first moved to Florida. I would lay in bed and the quiet would drive me crazy. I would listen for the sound of the train on Dixie Highway as it made its way down south, dropping off chemicals and consumables along the way. The train tracks were over five miles away from my apartment but at 11:30 at night it sounded like it was running through my living room. I was sleeping better here than I had in over a month and I could feel the physical manifestations of the past year's stress were beginning to drain from my body.

In the last year I had suffered with muscle aches and pinched nerves and had fought off over half a dozen colds as my mind wreaked havoc on my body. I lost interest in exercising and because of the increase in my drinking I had gained over fifteen pounds. I was eating better now and the short jogs I had started last week were already tightening my waistline.

I wondered what type of workout Tom did to keep so incredibly fit. I was surprised that his brother was so unathletic looking by comparison. In fact I saw almost no likeness whatsoever between the two. I wondered if they had different fathers. It must not have been easy for Jerry to have grown up with a brother who appeared to be physically perfect and who stood a good six inches taller than him. Jerry seemed more introverted. He was very quiet and after the performance he seemed to have disappeared.

Tom appeared to be his exact opposite in every way. He was energetic, extremely charismatic, and he seemed genuinely happy and enthusiastic about meeting his guests. I was sure our trip this morning was canceled because of the weather and I decided that I would wait until 8 or 8:30 to go up to the main building and grab breakfast.

I thought that I would just go out on the boat with the rest of the guests later when the fog burned off. I figured that Tom and I could buddy up on the boat dive for my check out dive so that he would let me fly solo. I couldn't understand why I felt nervous about spending time alone with Tom. I was a little intimidated by him and I felt a little uneasy in his presence, but that wasn't it exactly. It made no sense to me and I was angry at myself for feeling like some high school nerd who felt uncomfortable or unworthy around the high school football hero. But that wasn't really the reason for the feeling I had either.

Was I afraid of him? I felt drawn to his almost magnetic charm and I liked the idea of hanging out with such an experienced diver. But I had this same foreboding feeling when Sam had told me that the owners knew all about me. I had a prescient, almost instinctual, feeling that something was going to happen. I didn't know what it might be, but my gut told me that it had something to do with the strange enigmatic man I had just met.

I was brushing my teeth and I had just told myself not to think so much when I heard a scratching sound outside at the front door. It was followed by a low whining noise and with my mouth full of toothpaste I stepped out to the front door of the cabin and opened it. The dogs burst through the door before I had opened it more than a foot, and in their excitement they knocked me down. I was sitting on my ass with toothpaste drooling from my mouth when Indigo, the German shepherd, began to lick my face. I looked up when I heard laughter and saw Tom standing on the boardwalk outside my cabin.

"I'm sorry, Jake. I came to see what happened to you and these damn dogs follow me everywhere I go. I've never seen them take to anyone the way they have you, and I trust those dogs' instincts more than I do most people's."

I mumbled something incoherent as I rose to my feet and then I went into the bathroom and rinsed out my mouth. Tom didn't enter the cabin but waited for me outside the door, which I thought was rather polite, considering he owned the place. Was I wrong in assuming that he wouldn't fly in this weather?

"I'm sorry, Tom. I looked out the window this morning and I figured that you wouldn't fly, and that we would probably go out with the others on the boat after the fog cleared away."

"The fog is laying pretty low, and we'll be above it in less than a minute. I'm still going up in about ten minutes so unless you've changed your mind-which I'll refuse to accept anyway- you better grab your stuff and get a move on."

"Tom, I don't know," I said sheepishly. "You haven't given me any details about this trip and I've never dove from a plane. Are we landing in some remote location? Are there currents? How far away is it? What if we can't find the plane when we surface?"

Tom made a face full of sarcasm as if he were being excruciatingly patient and said, "Do you have any more questions Jake? Do you want me to file a flight plan with you? Do I need to provide drawings of the dive site?"

He laughed and put his hand on my shoulder.

"Relax. You're on vacation. I've been diving since I was 6-years-old and flying since I was eighteen. That's a long time believe me, and if you don't trust me, trust Samantha. She likes you and she told me last night to watch out for you today. Try to remember that you're on vacation and lighten up."

I felt foolish and was about to say something, but then I became momentarily distracted by Tom's comment about "Sam liking me," and her expression of concern for my well being.

"Don't make me carry you, Jake. It would be embarrassing for the both of us."

"Just give me two minutes to grab my gear and I'll be right down to the dock to meet you."

"Sounds good. You're in for an experience you'll never forget and when we get back you'll thank me," he said. Tom got down on his knees and with one arm wrapped around each dog he told them in a voice that a parent would use to talk to a small child that they should stay with me to make sure I found my way down to the dock on time. He walked away, whistling all the way down the path to the main building and disappeared from my sight.

I packed my dive gear and slapped a Transderm/Scop patch on my arm to fight possible motion sickness or nausea, although I really should have done it last night in order to allow the drug time to enter my system. When I got to the dock, Tom was finishing up his flight safety check and two of the hotel workers were bringing out our tanks. The dogs ran to Tom and he took a tennis ball from his pocket and tossed it into the water. Both dogs raced to the end of the dock and leaped three feet to the water, then they swam furiously, racing each other for the ball.

"That should keep them busy for awhile" Tom said. "Jake, take your BC and your regulator and gauges and hook them up to one of those tanks. We are going to strap them to the top of the floats outside the plane so that we can slip them on quickly when we arrive at the sight. Besides, there really isn't enough room to stow them in the plane."

Once we were done getting ready, Tom instructed the men to strap our tanks down and to load our gear into the plane and then we got on board. When we were seated Tom fired up the engines and we coasted away from the dock and began to immediately pick up speed. The fog was still pretty thick and I was a little nervous since we seemed to be rushing blindly ahead through the water unable to see any boats that might be in our way. When the engines were screaming and it seemed like the plane would shake to pieces, Tom looked at me and gave me the thumbs up sign and smiled. I smiled back and gave him an affirmative thumbs up and then we lifted out of the water and into the air.

I could feel my stomach drop and it felt like a hand was pressing on my chest as the pressure of lift off and the angle of our climb pushed me into my seat. My anxiety had abated and I was feeling exhilarated and excited about my first flight in a seaplane and the adventure of taking off to an unknown dive destination. Suddenly, we broke through the cloud cover and I glanced at the altimeter that read 1,100 feet. The sky was bright blue and I could feel the sun on my face. I glanced over at Tom as he was putting on a pair of gold aviator shaped RayBans with green lenses. We were wearing heavy green headphones with a built in microphone so we could communicate. He reached under his seat and took out a nylon CD wallet and handed it to me. I picked out one of my favorite Dire Straits albums put it in the player and skipped ahead to the "Sultans of Swing" and the music began to play on my headphones.

"Good choice, Jake. On this song Mark Knopfler plays one of the best stratocaster leads ever recorded." As the song played we sang along and I became so relaxed in front of a man who actually plays the guitar that I embarrassed myself by beginning to play lead air guitar right along with Mark Knopfler.

When Tom saw me he laughed and I turned bright red. He took both of his hands away from the controls, which momentarily alarmed me, and then he joined in. We were now at 3,500 feet and Tom turned the plane so that I could see the island. It looked beautiful from the air. It was only partly covered now by the white blanket of fog, which was swiftly clearing away. The island looked small and dark green and I could see two small mountains, or rather two very large hills poking through the fog. The island was surrounded by a coral necklace which created a turquoise lagoon that circled the entire island and it looked like a giant swimming pool from the air. The string of coral with its numerous atolls opened right where the hotel was situated and where the wall dropped steeply from that side of the island. I could see the reefs and the darker blue water where the wall dropped off to over ten thousand feet.

"Why didn't Jerry come along today?" I asked.

"Jerry likes to dive every so often but most of the time his hobbies tend to be more cerebral and his diving is usually work related," Tom replied. "He likes to work on his experiments and to go off on his own and read. He reads two, sometimes three books at a time and he devours science journals the way most kids read comic books."

"He seems so different from you," I said, cautiously trying to get a read on the sensitivity of the subject. "It's incredible to me that you two are really brothers."

For a moment Tom looked sad and pensive and then he said, "We had different fathers Jake, in case you were wondering. Besides being my brother, Jerry is also my partner and my best friend. Unfortunately, he got all the brains in the family."

I thought that Tom was probably being modest about his own intellect and looking at Tom I also thought that if asked, Jerry would probably rather have what Tom had inherited. It's funny how no one is ever satisfied. When I was young I was so frustrated and insecure about the tangled heap of curls on my head that when I was sixteen I actually went to my mom's salon and had my hair straightened or reverse permed I think they had called it. While I was in the salon I was seated between two young women who were each paying over sixty dollars to have their hair permed.

"Jerry seemed to be in a bad mood last night," I said, feeling that it might have been too presumptuous of me to make such a personal comment about Tom's brother, a man who I had never spoken to.

"Jerry's going through something pretty heavy right now. Like you he's very sensitive and when he's feeling down he withdraws. I've learned that it's best not to push him, and to leave him alone to work things out on his own. One of the reasons we cut our so called tour and came home early was to allow Jerry to spend some peaceful time alone with his work. He has several various projects he's working on and he really needed to clear his head. We came home for many of the same reasons that you had for coming here, Jake. You probably needed to get away from the pressure of sales and wanted to decompress as far from home as possible."

That was the third familiar type of comment that Tom had made during our conversation. He mentioned the fact that I was sensitive. He stated my reasons for taking this trip and again he made a reference to my occupation. It was time to get some answers.

"Tom, you mentioned something just now that reminded me of something that Samantha said last night that disturbed me. How do you know what I do for a living and if I'm sensitive or not sensitive. The reason I took this trip was to dive, just like the rest of your guests."

I felt myself getting upset and I began to raise the tenor of my voice. "Sam said you knew all about me. What's that all about? Do you make it a habit to investigate all of your guests? What are the ulterior motives of that French group that's here this week? Are they foreign drug smugglers? Maybe they're a group of swingers who've come here for a tropical orgy."

"Relax Jake. I think Samantha was just pulling your chain when she told you that. First of all, Sam told me that on a couple of occasions you seemed very sad and that you were keeping to yourself and that you had even requested to eat alone. Samantha is very sensitive to the moods of our guests. Aside from it being her job to keep the guests happy, she has taken a liking to you.

"I think your sensitivity is obvious to anyone who meets you and talks to you for more than fifteen minutes. I can tell you that it is one of the things that both Sam and I like about you. As far as what you do for a living, you told one of the guests, I think it might even have been the Kritzers, and they told Sam.

"We see alot of people here and Samantha has good instincts and tremendous powers of observation. Believe me, aside from our obvious concerns about the environment we don't really care what you do for a living or why you came here. Our only concerns are that while you're here you respect the reefs and your fellow guests. Above all else our primary concern is that you have a good time. Now lighten up and stop being so paranoid or I might just leave you behind when I take off today."

When Tom was finished I felt like a complete idiot and was tempted to open the door and jump from the plane.

"I'm sorry. I guess I'm not fully adjusted yet to a non-threatening environment where people don't have some ulterior motive for being friendly. I'm coming off of a very stressful period in my life that's made me even more hyper-sensitive and sometimes my mouth gets ahead of my brain. Please don't be offended."

"I understand," he said with what I thought was genuine warmth. "You and Jerry are a lot alike. Your mannerisms and your reactions to situations are very similar. I've learned over the course of time to not just listen to what people have to say but to look in their eyes and to listen to their hearts. When I'm dealing with people, even if its people I just met I can usually tell what kind of people they are in just a few minutes. We're here. Look east."

I looked downward and toward the east and I saw an unusual reef formation. It was in a long oval shape, narrowed at the ends and looked like a giant eye in the middle of the sea with only one narrow opening on one end which appeared to be the only entrance and exit into a large lagoon. It looked like a giant swimming pool stuck in the middle of the ocean. Tom explained that it was the top of a volcano and the pool was the cone.

The water inside the eye was bright blue and from this height the bottom seemed to be pure white sand. The water on the outside of the eye was a dark navy blue, which usually indicated great depths. It did look like a narrow opening in the top of a volcano that rose thousands of feet from the sea floor.

"I call this site The Aquarium. Its unofficial name is Neptune's Eye but you'll soon see why I call it The Aquarium when we swim inside. You're in for a real treat, LITTLE buddy."

"Tom, do me a favor, don't call me little buddy. It makes me feel like Gilligan from "Gilligan's Island." Tom laughed and told me that he used to watch that show when he was a boy but that he never realized the connection until just now. He told me that Jerry also hated it when Tom referred to him that way.

I was so excited. I felt like I did when I first started diving before I got so spoiled by diving the Caribbean and started to take its beauty for granted. Angel fish and sea fans are beautiful, don't get me wrong, but after you've seen a thousand of them they just don't hold the same sense of wonder that they did the first few times you saw them. I think that's why people who have dove for many years are always looking for the next great thrill or the next great exotic location and dream of traveling to Palau and The Red Sea. I myself have explored diving with dolphins at UNEXSO in The Bahamas or traveling to Micronesia to swim through heavily encrusted World War II wrecks.

We began to descend rapidly and the plane touched down gently on the water. Tom maneuvered the plane to the mouth of the reef and shut the engine. He opened the door and took a deep breath.

"We are over 160 miles from the nearest island. Way too far for a boat trip from any of the hotels and resorts. Some of the live aboards will sometimes show up here but this spot hasn't really been discovered yet. I'm sure as soon as some writer from *Skin Diver* shows up that shortly afterward it will be surrounded by divers who will eventually destroy it.

Wait here while I tie us off. About a year ago I put in a permanent mooring to protect the reef."

Tom slipped off his shirt and I noticed over half a dozen scars on his back and on his right shoulder blade. I knew from pictures that I had seen in the past and from movies and television that some of them were bullet holes and my curiosity about the man intensified. Tom grabbed a roll of thick nylon rope out of the back seat. Then he stood out on the float and tied one end of the line to the strut. He stood up and looked out past the propeller. Without a word, he dove into the water and disappeared below the surface. I couldn't believe that he went in without even wearing a mask. How could he see anything?

It seemed like he was down forever and I began to become anxious. I checked my watch and looked around the outside of the plane. After a minute, when he still had not appeared, I stepped out of the plane on my side and moved to the front of the float. I leaned against the plane for support and scanned the area. I checked my watch again and a full minute and 40 seconds had elapsed. Then I saw bubbles about ten feet from the plane and Tom's head broke the surface, his hair flowing into his face, covering his eyes.

"You scared the hell out of me," I yelled. "What the fuck happened to you? I thought you drowned!"

"The mooring is down about thirty to forty feet and I lost my bearings for a second," he responded. "Then on the way up to the surface three gigantic manta rays appeared and I followed them for a little while to see where they were headed."

"You're full of shit," I said, knowing full well that he probably wasn't. My heart was pounding when he said, "Grab your gear. They swam inside and if we hurry we can see them before they leave. Now move your ass."

Tom climbed quickly aboard and untied his tank and BC and slipped them on, all in the time it took me to untie my gear. He was standing on the other side of the plane and so he could not help me with my gear. I struggled for balance as the waves rocked the plane from side to side and I felt queasy. I slipped on my booties and my fins and eventually climbed into my BC. We did a quick buddy check and tested our gear and then we did a giant stride entry into the water. Tom gave me the thumbs down sign and I reached for my dump valve and began to descend.

I had never seen manta rays in the wild and I was so excited that I had to make a concerted effort to control my breathing. Since I had just seen Tom do a free dive without tanks for almost two full minutes I knew I was going to consume my air in half the time he did. Tom had descended to about fifty feet and was swimming toward the opening in the reef at the top of the volcano. It looked like a bright blue window. It was framed by the coral around it and stood out in stark contrast to the deeper darker blue water that surrounded the outside of the opening. The opening was surrounded by a rainbow of colored corals and sponges. There were large staghorn and elkhorn corals and large barrel sponges of various sizes and color.

Inside, I could see large schools of fish and there were several grouper and barracuda and forty feet beyond the opening I saw a green sea turtle. I could indeed see why Tom referred to this place as "The Aquarium." It was incredibly unique and inside it did in fact resemble a giant fish tank. We reached the opening and Tom gave me the okay sign and I signed back that I was fine. Tom pointed off to his right and my eyes almost popped out of my head when I saw three enormous manta rays swimming in the distance.

I guessed that they were each at least twenty feet across. Tom put two fingers together, giving me the sign to stay close and to follow him and then we swam off toward the large animals. Manta rays are harmless creatures despite their intimidating size and appearance. I had friends who had seem them in Cabo San Lucas and in Kona, Hawaii, and I had always envied them for having experienced what is one of the world's rarest dive experiences.

The mantas turned toward us and swam quickly in our direction. On their backs were large remoras, which resemble baby sharks. They usually accompany the manta rays and swim piggyback in order to feed off their leftovers and to clean and remove small parasites from their bodies. They got to within twenty feet of us and Tom smiled when he saw the expression on my face. They were about to pass over us when Tom took me by the hand and pulled me up above their flight path.

He held his fingers out and imitated a swimmer kicking his feet very fast and pulled me forward. I had an idea of what he wanted me to do but I couldn't believe it. I swam as hard as I could to intercept the manta rays and when one of the largest animals passed below me and I was matching its speed I descended and grabbed on to the tails of the two remoras that were attached to its back and I hitched a ride. I kicked my feet and held them gently so that I wouldn't be noticed by the ray and so I wouldn't dislodge them and when I looked back I could see that Tom was quickly disappearing behind me.

It was the single greatest dive experience I had ever had. After a couple of minutes, the mantas headed for the exit and I let go of my ride. I heard a knocking sound and turned to see Tom swimming toward me as he banged his dive knife against his tank. He gave me the okay sign again and I responded by enthusiastically signing OKAY!! with both hands. We swam around in The Aquarium for another several minutes and played with groupers and watched turtles swim by us, accompanied by a variety of schooling fish in all different sizes and colors.

I checked my gauges and I still had over 1700 PSI in my tank. I held up ten fingers followed by seven to Tom and he led me out of the opening and down the wall. We explored inside the nooks and crannies of the reef and found lobster and other smaller invertebrates.

We saw flamingo tongues and flaming scallops and anemones in colors ranging from pink to purple. The wall was covered in orange and yellow sponges and with barrel sponges bigger than a man.

I looked at my gauges again and saw that I only had a little over 600 PSI remaining. I asked Tom what he had left and he signaled that he had 1500 PSI. I gave him the thumbs up sign to surface and he nodded okay and we swam toward the plane, ascending as we swam. We surfaced at the plane and I pulled off my mask. "THAT WAS UN-FUCKING BELIEVABLE!" I screamed. "OORAH!!!"

Tom laughed and swam to the float. He removed his BC and tank while he was still in the water and lifted it onto the float, then climbed out of the water.

"Was it worth the flight?"

"You were right. I promise you I won't ever doubt you again and you can consider my answer YES!, to any future invitations."

"I had the kitchen pack us some lunch. Club sandwiches I think. And I have another surprise for you."

I climbed aboard the float after removing my gear and I sat back against the plane's strut and hung my legs over the side. Tom was rummaging around inside the plane and suddenly the Crosby Stills Nash & Young album "Deja Vu" started blasting from the plane's speakers. Tom suddenly appeared with a small cooler and sat down beside me and when he opened the lid I saw that it was full of ice cold Coors beer.

"I could kiss you," I said.

"I like you, Jake, but if you come anywhere near me I'll be filing a missing persons report with the Honduran authorities upon my return to the hotel."

I was so dehydrated from breathing compressed air that I swallowed my first beer in three gulps and then I let out a thunderous burp and quickly began to devour the turkey club sandwich that Tom had brought along. It was covered with bacon and mayonnaise, just the way I liked it and I thought to myself, like the TV commercial says, *It doesn't get any better than this.*

In the past, whenever I saw that commercial I always thought it was ridiculous and would say so over and over again. It shows three men alone in the woods without a woman in sight and they're all saying how life couldn't be any better. I used to joke to my friends that they were either gay or that they hated their wives and girlfriends.

"Are you going to be okay to fly?" I asked Tom when I saw him quickly finish his second beer.

"Jake," he said, "have you ever had a couple of beers and then drove home? Do you think flying a plane is any different? It's actually safer to fly drunk than to drive. There's nothing to crash into. Besides I could be barely conscious and I could still fly this plane sideways through a barn door."

"You're quite a guy, Tom," I said sarcastically. "I'm in awe of you."

"Fuck off, Jake, and don't forget how you got here."

I looked out on the water and thought about where I was. I was sitting on a plane in the middle of the Caribbean over 150 miles from the nearest land, next to one of the prettiest reefs I'd ever seen. The sky was blue and full of clouds and flying fish were leaping from the water. I was sitting in the sun drinking a cold beer and listening to CSNY.

"This was the best day I've had in years. Thank you, I really appreciate it."

"At the Aegis Inn, we aim to please," he said and then he reached into the cooler and brought out a small Zip lock bag that contained three joints.

"Do you party?"

"Once in awhile, at concerts, or when I'm out fishing with friends." Tom lit the joint and leaned back against the plane and sang along with David Crosby.

"It increases my paranoia," he sang out loud as he handed me the joint. I leaned back against the plane and closed my eyes and felt the sun on my face.

"What would happen if the plane didn't start?" I asked.

"You never stop worrying, do you?"

"If the plane didn't start we would drift aimlessly for days, maybe weeks hoping to run into a passing boat. If we didn't die of thirst or exposure we would eventually be picked up." Then he paused for effect and said, "or we could call someone on the radio."

"You've had three beers and now you're smoking a joint, Tom. Would it be out of line for me to ask you again if you're capable of flying us out of here. I only ask because personally I'm so wasted right now that I would probably have trouble peddling a bicycle."

"We'll wait another hour or so before leaving and maybe we'll go snorkeling. That should give me enough time to clear my head."

"I was surprised you let me ride that manta ray today, Tom. If Sam had seen a guest doing that she would have read him the riot act and then evicted him from the hotel."

"You were gentle like I knew you would be, and I don't make a habit of that sort of thing. Just the same, he said with a mischievous smile, let's keep it a secret."

"When you went to attach the anchor line you must have been down for close to two minutes. How did you hold your breath at 30-50 feet for so long?"

"In another life, I had to train to stay under water without air in case of an emergency or to sneak up on people. Later, I participated in some free diving competitions in the Caribbean and I once trained for over a year with Jacques Maillioux on West Caicos."

"My deepest dive on a single breath hold was 220 feet. Not good enough to compete seriously, but it was a great time in my life just the same."

"You trained with *the* Jacques Mailloux?"

"Yup, The one and only Jacques Mailloux, womanizer and braggart. I spent one full year training with him in the Turks and Caicos islands. He was already an old man but he could still stay underwater on a single breath hold longer than any man I had ever known and longer than the twenty-year-olds who traveled from around the world to challenge him."

"At over sixty Jacques was still a very attractive gentleman and he probably still is. When I was with him he was just becoming famous. A film by Luc Besson called *The Big Blue* had just been released about his life but he was already a legend in the islands. He had an enormous appetite for women and most could not resist his considerable charm.

"He told me once that he had slept with over a thousand women in his life and that married women were by far his favorite target. He said that they presented a greater challenge and he was turned on by the element of danger that a jealous husband presented.

"Although Jacques is a legend in the islands he is an even greater legend in his own mind. He told me one day on our way to a remote dive site that he believes that he is reincarnated from a dolphin and that he has a supernatural connection with the species. He insisted that during the making of the film this connection be written into the script. I thought he was crazy until I witnessed something miraculous happen that day.

"While we were on the boat, a tourist spotted a pod of dolphins swimming ahead of us and Jacques leapt to his feet and ordered the captain to stop the boat. He did as he was told and when the boat stopped the dolphins swam in circles around us. They jumped into the air and screamed in high pitched tones.

"The five tourists aboard began to prepare to enter the water when Jacques stood up and like a Roman Emperor ordered them all to sit down.

"'No one enters the water but me!' He screamed. He had absolutely no authority whatsoever and was simply a guest on the boat like everyone else, but they all obeyed. Jacques went to the back of the boat and began to do the deep breathing exercises and meditation that were a part of his preparation for a deep free dive. After five minutes with the entire boat watching his powerful silver-haired chest heave in and out he jumped into the water and descended immediately without a mask or fins and disappeared below the surface.

"To the amazement of everyone aboard, including myself, the dolphins who seemed to be waiting for him the entire time followed him below. I have to admit I was impressed and after two and a half minutes Jacques and the dolphins finally emerged from the water with Jacques laughing out loud. He started yelling something in French to the captain who didn't understand a word.

"Jacques came aboard and grabbed a round sled used for water skiing that the captain had showed the group earlier and instructed the captain that he would ride behind for awhile with his friends.

"In a few minutes he was riding behind the boat at over thirty miles an hour with water spraying from behind the sled. The dolphins raced behind and along side of him.

"I tell you, Jake, it was one of the most amazing sights I have ever witnessed and I had seen quite a lot by then. The tourists were awe struck and were snapping pictures and shooting video like mad. When Jacques came aboard, everyone cheered and he took immediate advantage of the moment to press himself on a blond woman of perhaps thirty years who was alone on the boat.

"Although she was wearing a wedding band, she was staring at Jacques in wonder. He was quite a character. He was tall and tanned and had bright blue eyes and silver hair and an accent like Maurice Chevalier.

"Women did find him irresistible. He taught me a lot in the year I was with him and, although for the most part he found me to be a disappointing student and I found him to be shallow and egotistical, we did share a deep love and an appreciation of the sea."

Tom finished his story and if it had been anyone else telling it I wouldn't have believed it. I knew Tom had no need to lie to impress someone and that he only told the story because he found it entertaining. I remembered the movie. I had seen it at a time when I had a major case of the hots for Roseanna Arquette and I had heard that there were some nude scenes in the film.

It was a decent picture and at that stage of her career Roseanna was breathtakingly beautiful. "That's an amazing story," I said. I stayed at a small dive resort in Provo once called the Blue Turtle with a *National*

Geographic photographer who was there on assignment. He told me that he had once met Jacques Mailloux."

"He described him just as you have. He said in a heavy Tennessee accent that he was a "Poon hound" and that he didn't like him very much."

"I tell you Jake. I've been around dolphins most of my life. My mother was a marine biologist who studied them for over twenty years from the Amazon to the Indian Ocean, and I've never seen anything like what I witnessed that day. It was supernatural."

The pot had worn off and I was feeling sleepy from the dive and dehydrated from the beer and the sun and I asked if we could get going. I asked Tom again if he was okay to fly.

"I feel better than I have in a long time. I'm sure I could probably hold the plane steady for the thirty minute trip home." We stowed the gear and in ten minutes we were in the air. Tom spotted another group of manta rays and flew down over the water to just over 100 feet and followed above them, like a rancher herding his cattle by plane.

It was a beautiful sight to see. I counted twelve rays and they were all swimming in a close formation just below the surface. They looked slightly blurred beneath the rolling turquoise waves. We climbed quickly to 2,500 feet and after several minutes Tom pointed to the island up ahead. The fog had completely burned away and the island looked emerald green, covered in its thick blanket of trees and vines. I could see clearly now the two large peaks that reached around 1200 feet in elevation at opposite ends of the island with a sway-backed valley in between. The only wall dive on the inside of the lagoon was only fifty yards from the front door of the hotel, and looked from the air like a dark blue runway that ran straight through the break in the coral that circled the island.

"It's beautiful. Not a bad place to call home."

"We like it, Jake. It's our sanctuary from the rest of the world, although we never allow ourselves to forget that what happens in downtown Detroit effects us here. Speaking of home, Jake, where are your home and your family?"

"I lost my mother to cancer recently and the only family I have left is a sister in New York. My dad ran out on us when we were just kids. Like you said earlier, that's part of the reason why I came here, to relax and to recover and to forget for a while if that's possible."

"I'm sorry, Jake," Tom said and he grabbed my shoulder and squeezed it.

"I lost my mom when I was sixteen and I never knew my father. My mother told me he was a great man but I had my doubts considering that he never showed any interest in contacting either me or my mother. It sounds like we have a lot in common. My mother was a great lady. Her name was Hannah. Like I said earlier, she was a marine biologist and her specialty was the study of cetaceans or dolphins. When we weren't traveling around the world, her home base was at the Miami Seaquarium and Jerry and I grew up around sea lions and dolphins.

"I learned to dive when I was six years old and by the time I was thirteen I had already dove most of the world, including the Galapagos islands and the South Pacific. I never formally attended school and, aside from Jerry, my mother was my only real friend.

"My mother tutored me along with other friends of hers who were all either scientists, biochemists or professors and I took tests and matriculated by mail. I was never much of a student anyway. I was easily distracted and I spent most of my time daydreaming. Jerry was a different story entirely. He loved school so much that he would rarely travel with us. Instead, he chose to stay at home with friends of our mother while he attended school.

"He quickly outgrew public school and when he was ten years old he went away to the Chadwick Institute in New England on a full scholarship. It was a special school for gifted children and it was funded in part by large American corporations that had the foresight and the business savvy to invest early in young minds, hoping for future recruitment to their corporations.

"As a matter of fact, Jerry did go to work after his post grad years for a genetics firm which paid for a large part of his early education. Our mother gained some fame and notoriety as the Dianne Fossey or the Jane Goodall of dolphins and she had a story written about her and her work in an issue of *National Geographic*.

"She later went to work on a freelance basis for the magazine and they funded many of her projects. My mother was a very active and vigilant protector of the environment and was instrumental in helping to pass most of the protective bans and dolphin safe legislation we have today.

"In 1976, my mother helped to expose and bring to justice a large American corporation that was illegally dumping chemicals in the waters off of the South Carolina coast. At the trial she showed data from dolphin autopsies she had performed that showed large amounts of mercury and PCBs in their bodies.

"When I was a boy of perhaps thirteen my mother found a baby dolphin that was caught in a net next to its dead mother that had strangled in the lines. Together we raised it at the aquarium until it was strong enough to be set free to join another family. I named her Coral and would swim in the tanks with her at night when no one was around.

"I loved that Dolphin and I cried the day we tied a transponder to her and let her go. My mother and I fought for a week about it, but she convinced me that it was the right thing to do. Six months later, Coral was found dead, drowned in a fishing net and I told my mother that I would never forgive her for making me turn her loose.

"I was fourteen and was already bigger than most of the men we knew, but I behaved like a little boy and I cried myself to sleep for weeks afterward. My mother continued to become more and more well known as the protector of the cetacean world, and she often helped with the investigation and eventual prosecution of numerous foreign and domestic firms that were either polluting the waters or were illegally net fishing.

"She was on the cover of *Newsweek* in November of 1979 for obtaining film of a large American tuna company fishing boat that had just hauled in a half a dozen dead dolphins among its catch.

"Six months later, she was killed walking to work from our apartment by a hit and run driver. It was only one block from the aquarium.

"The driver was never apprehended and although many people, including the FBI, suspected foul play, the case was closed after only six months. Two months later, I lied about my age and with a forged parental consent form I joined the Navy. One year later, I became the youngest person ever to graduate from SEAL training at the age of seventeen.

"Jerry started college at only sixteen, and went on to graduate school directly afterward. We only saw each other once or twice a year when I was on leave. Most of the time I traveled on secret assignments and couldn't tell him where I was. I finished college eventually while I was in the service and I went on to finish Officers Candidate School by the time I was 23.

"Jerry went on to make millions of dollars as the creator of numerous chemical and pharmaceutical products. That's where most of the money for the hotel came from. We became close again after I had left the service and Jerry had become burned out and disillusioned in the corporate world of science and research. We both decided to find a more meaningful and productive use for our time, and when we can we try to carry on our mother's work in environmental studies and protection."

Tom stopped talking and he stared ahead out the window of the cockpit. "I can't believe how much I'm talking. I sound like one of the old ladies who used to live in our building in Miami. I've never told anyone except for a few close friends my life story, Jake. Although I know you less than twenty-four hours I trust you. We both lost mothers that we were very close to and I guess that connection brought it all back for me and started me babbling. I hope I haven't bored you or made you uncomfortable. Pot always loosens my lips and gets me talking,"

Tom's life story was fascinating to me and I now had a greater insight into his passionate feelings about the ocean and the motivation behind the strict rules and regulations of the hotel.

"I'm glad you told me, Tom. It's funny but when you're grieving you feel like you're the only one in the world who's ever suffered, and it's a very lonely feeling. I miss my mother so much," I said feeling myself grow sad, my eyes beginning to moisten.

"Like you, Tom, my mother was also my best friend and she was the center of our family. She was the glue that held us together. I feel that without her I have no center, no compass. I feel as if my family is going to break apart now and fly off in different directions. All our traditions, our rituals, and our almost daily interaction happened in my mother's living room or around her dinner table. My mother's phone line was like some umbilical cord that fed us emotional nourishment and now it's been permanently severed. My sister and I are not very close and since my mother's illness she's become even more bitter, angry and resentful. I could never call her and speak to her the way I spoke to my mother. I'd receive very little sympathy or tenderness from that quarter. The only thing we really ever had in common was my mother's love and our family history and now that's over."

"Jake, what you're feeling now is natural. If time won't heal the pain and those feelings it will at least dull it and provide some perspective. You won't ever forget the loss of your mother or stop hurting, but you will learn to survive. Eventually, you'll figure out how to find happiness through the pain and it will lessen to a dull ache. I also don't think you should be so hard or unforgiving with your sister. She's also suffering and she's all you have left now.

"It's unreasonable to expect the same kind of unconditional love from her that you received from your mother. If that's what you're looking for," he said pointing to Ebony and Indigo as we pulled up alongside the dock, "then buy a dog.

"Jerry and I drifted apart after our mother's death, partly because we were both hurting and because we couldn't deal with all the feelings of abandonment and the anger and the resentment we were both feeling. This may sound strange, but it's partly because of how close we were growing up that we drifted apart after my mother's death."

The dogs were barking and crying outside for Tom when he turned to me and said. "I think it was a good idea your coming here, Jake, and you're welcome to stay as long as you wish. If you're staying indefinitely I think you should call your sister and talk to some friends back home. Maybe we can find something for you to do around here so that you won't go broke while you're figuring out your next move."

"Thanks, Tom. I had a great time today and I love it here. Right now I can't think of anywhere else I'd rather be."

"Anytime you need a friend to talk to, come knock on my door."

We unloaded the gear and I washed the salt from my body at the outside shower on the dock. I saw Tom running up the stairs to the lodge with the dogs. There were over 400 steps to the top. He was carrying over 50 pounds of gear in his arms and was taking the steps two at a time all the way to the top while the dogs chased him and barked like mad below him.

I went to my room and I prepared for dinner. I showered and lay down in my hammock and smelled the strong scent of orchids that were carried on the early evening breeze. I thought about my mother and I tried to imagine her voice and face. I was afraid that I would forget her someday. Not who she was or what she meant to me, but the clear picture of her sound and her image.

Lately, I had found myself imagining that she had become a ghost who traveled around with me or had become my guardian angel or spirit. I believed that she had become my connection to God and to heaven and that if I spoke to her and told her my hopes and my dreams she would hear me and she would pass along my wishes with a strong personal recommendation to God.

If anyone could nudge God it was my mother. I was never religious and I had never been Bar-Mitzvahed. I had grown up never really having attended any services, but since my mother's death I had started to hope that there was a God and a heaven and that my mother was there now. It eased my pain to think that one day I might see her again in heaven.

I could feel the pain surfacing again like the rebreaking of a bone or the opening of a deep flesh wound which had almost healed and once again I fought it with all my will. My mother always forgave me and intellectually I knew that she always would but I needed to hear the words from her, the words I would never hear again over the hundreds of months and thousands of days that I would walk the earth. The sun was setting and the sky had turned a pale shade of purple and I closed my eyes and drifted off to sleep. As the world turned black around me I wondered about the future and felt lost.

CHAPTER 18

I WAS SITTING ON THE BEACH writing in my journal and looked up in time to see Ebony, Tom's big wet black Lab, trouncing all over my beach towel. "I'm going for a hike with the dogs to the other side of the island.

Do you want to join us?" Samantha asked. I was excited at the prospect of hiking through the jungle to a deserted beach with Samantha and quickly accepted her invitation. I started imagining us skinny dipping in a private turquoise lagoon and I grabbed my things and sprang to my feet.

"Tom wants me to talk to you about the possibility of working around here for a while. We're short one divemaster and we could use the help. He would pay you, of course, and room and board would be included."

Samantha had a red faded bandanna around her head, and her hair was pulled back from her face. She was wearing a halter bikini top and baggy gray sweat shorts and she looked breathtaking to me. As usual she was not wearing an ounce of make up, and her eyes were bright blue and sparkling. Her hair was a hundred shades of brown and blond and it shimmered in the sun.

"Does that mean you'd be my boss?" I asked as I scrunched up my face with a repulsed look.

"It sure as shit does and when I say jump I expect you to say how high, and move your ass when I call you. I'll probably make you haul tanks half the day and then you would spend the afternoons cleaning boats before I allowed you to lead any dives," she said and then laughed.

"I don't know how I feel about working for a woman. I don't know if I would be comfortable."

"Well Jake, think of me as a man and maybe you won't feel as threatened." She pinched my cheek like my grandmother used to do when I was five. I swatted her hand away and I took a fighting stance and said, "Don't mess with me, Sammy. I move like the wind, and thinking of you as a man will be a piece of cake since you act like one most of the time."

She looked genuinely offended and then in the blink of an eye I was laying on the beach on my back with the wind knocked out of me while Samantha strode away to where the trail began. I never even saw her move and I was both stunned and impressed at the speed in which she swept my feet out from under me while she struck me in the chest.

I jumped up and ran after her and said, "Look Sam, I was just kidding. If anything I'm uncomfortable around women I'm attracted to and I always have been. Sometimes I overcompensate with my inappropriate sense of humor."

"Forget it, Jake," she said in a soft voice. "You just touched a nerve. It's ancient history. Let's just walk quietly for a while." The first quarter mile of the trail led straight up through the jungle on a well-worn narrow dirt path which was covered with heavy foliage. The dogs would keep running on ahead, then they would stop to lay down in the grass and wait for us to catch up. They appeared to know the trail very well and looked very much at home in the jungle. *What a great backyard*, I thought, *Doggie Heaven*.

When we came to the top of the hill, Samantha turned to me and with a mischievous grin said that she was sorry for knocking me down. She said that it was inappropriate since I was still a hotel guest and that she hoped she had not hurt me. I noticed that she was barely breathing. I was sweating bullets and was huffing and puffing like a steam locomotive.

I said between gasps of air, "Next time—-I'll be ready for you——and —you won't be able to sucker punch me. Seriously, where did you learn to move like that? I'm impressed."

Samantha ignored my question and, pointing at the horizon, she said, "Look at the view, Jake. Isn't it beautiful?"

I looked behind me and realized when I saw the ocean below us that we must have climbed over 1,500 feet straight up. We were at the highest point on this little island and I could see for over 180 degrees. At the Northern most point of the island I could see a little appendage of land perhaps 100 yards long that was attached to the main island by fifty feet of sand. There was what looked like a cave or a rock arch above the divide.

At high tide, if the currents would allow, you would probably have to swim to get to the northern most tip of the island. It looked like a beautiful beach but it had to be at least a two and a half mile walk from where we stood. Samantha told me that was where we were headed when I pointed it out to her.

"That's a long walk from here, Sam." She began walking ahead down the trail and without turning around she said, "It's not as far as it looks. I ride my mountain bike there a few times a week. If you get tired we can stop along the way. About a mile from here is a swimming hole with a waterfall. It's a pretty spot and we can take a break and grab some lunch. I grabbed us two box lunches on my way to see you this morning. It's fried chicken I think, and some fruit."

"How did you know I would be going?" I asked, as I studied her from behind. I could see the muscles in her calves and thighs flexing as she stepped over fallen tree limbs and rocks. Her legs were incredible. Each band of muscle in her thighs and hamstrings stood out and her back, shiny with sweat, was a deep honey color from the sun. I could see every muscle in her neck and shoulders and although her physique was perfectly shaped and looked powerful she still looked very feminine.

"I didn't know for sure if you would come or not," she answered. "I figured I would give your lunch to the dogs if you didn't."

I grabbed a small dark piece of fruit that was hanging near me on a tree and I hurled it at her back. My aim was high and it bounced off the back of her head.

"She stopped dead in her tracks and turned around to face me when we both heard a shot echo through the trees and across the mountains.

"What the hell was that?" I asked.

"Poachers," Samantha said. Then she took off her backpack and told me that I should stay put and wait for her to return.

"Wait a damn minute!" I shouted. "That was a gun we just heard and you are unarmed. And what do you mean poachers? What would they be hunting on this island? It's only ten miles around and I haven't seen a living thing since I got here, except for birds and iguanas."

"Jake, I don't have time for this now. Jerry and Tom own this entire island and there is a very small population of wild boars, which they have managed to save that still live here. Every so often men from the other islands come here to hunt. They only come every once and a while and they are usually either very stupid or very desperate. They are never dangerous or threatening, since most of the locals in these islands are terrified of Tom. Now wait here like I said. That shot came from only about half a mile east of here. I'll scare them off, then I'll be right back. I'm responsible for you and I don't want you to get hurt. Please wait here."

Before I could say another word, she literally exploded through the trees and was gone in a flash. I was frozen in place for a full two minutes. My heart was racing and I felt like I was going to hyperventilate from the rush of adrenaline that my fight or flight instincts were flooding into my body. I almost jumped out of my skin when the dogs who looked like an angry pack of wolves came crashing past me and began to follow Samantha's trail.

I started to run in the direction of the dogs and I was getting cut up from the thorns and branches that were hitting my face and arms. I heard Samantha yelling to the dogs to freeze. I slowed down my pace and walked slowly in an arc around the direction of the voices. I could hear a brook and I was glad it was there because it seemed to be covering the sound of my footsteps. I crept slowly for another twenty feet, then saw Samantha.

She was standing on one side of the brook and she was holding the dogs, barking like mad, by their collars. Sam was screaming what sounded like Spanish obscenities at two men on the other side of the stream. I recognized them. They were in the bar the night Tom had humiliated their friend. They were standing over a wounded boar which was breathing heavily and was laying sideways in the brook with blood pouring from its nose and mouth.

One of the men stood about 6'3" tall and had an enormous beer belly. His partner was about 6 feet tall and very skinny. Both men were dressed in dirty, tattered clothing and looked like peasants.

The smaller man looked nervous and was speaking very rapidly in Spanish but his fat partner had a menacing look, his eyes yellow and bloodshot. They were both carrying rifles and the fat man had his aimed at the dogs. I guessed that he had threatened to shoot the dogs and that was why Samantha was holding them.

Samantha pointed to a large rusted "No trespassing" sign that was nailed to a tree and started to scream something in Spanish. I could recognize Tom's name, "Tomas," mixed in with her words, and the smaller man stepped back from the brook with an expression on his face that looked as if he had just seen the devil himself. He lowered his weapon.

I was hopeful that they would now turn and leave. I was breathing deeply and sweat was pouring from my face and was running down my back. The fat man laughed out loud and raised his weapon and aimed it at Ebony.

Later, I would not remember much of what happened next, and Samantha would have to fill in the blanks. I think I must have moved on some internal autopilot, driven by my overwhelming love for animals.

Without thinking, I grabbed a heavy log that was laying beside me and ran the five feet between me and the gunman. I was screaming like a maniac as I ran toward him and swung my weapon. As the man lowered his rifle and turned toward me, I swung the log at his head. I missed his head and wound up hitting him in his right shoulder instead. The log snapped in two and the man dropped his rifle. His partner ran like a gazelle through the trees and was gone from sight in the blink of an eye.

I had accomplished my goal and had saved Ebony's life but was now about to be torn to shreds by a three hundred pound madman. He was fuming and his eyes were full of violence as he grabbed me by the shirt and raised his arm to strike me.

I raised my forearm to block the blow when Samantha grabbed the man's wrist and spun him around. What I saw next I had only seen before in Saturday afternoon, Chinese action movies, and I thought that I must have been dreaming.

Samantha moved with lightning speed. She kicked the man in the chest, then in the side of his head. He was at least six inches taller than she was and she was stretched full out in a standing split when she snapped the last kick with brutal force against his head. He was thrown sideways, bounced off a tree and hit the ground with a thud.

"Grab his rifle, Jake," Samantha said with amazing calm as if she had been doing this sort of thing her entire life.

I picked up the man's rifle and handed it to her and she walked over to the wild boar, which was breathing very shallowly and she shot it in its head. Then, in an instant, she grabbed the rifle by its barrel and she swung it against a tree and it snapped in two.

She bent over the man and checked his pulse and his respiration and slipped something into his pocket. It looked like the dive medallions we were given during orientation and I was puzzled by this last act.

She stood up and said, "He'll live, but for about a week he'll wish he hadn't."

Then she said, "Let's go, hero. Our swim is waiting."

"Let's go," I said, incredulous. "What do you mean 'let's go?' What about this man? Are we just leaving him here? What about the police? Don't we have to notify them? Shouldn't we at least report this to Tom & Jerry? We can't just go finish our hike like nothing happened. What's wrong with you?"

I felt like I was suffering from a mild case of shock and Samantha was acting like we had just finished a round of golf.

"I'm sorry, Jake," she said. "Look, this isn't New York or Miami. This kind of stuff happens here every so often, so I guess I'm more accustomed to it. This guy was drunk. You can smell it ten feet away. He was riding on a temporary wave of courage born of cheap alcohol.

"He'll wake up and then he'll limp home and sleep it off. I guarantee he won't be back here again and he won't be telling any of his friends about this either. The men around these parts are muy macho and he isn't going to want anyone to know that an American woman kicked his butt.

"There really are no official police around here. Tom & Jerry are the only true authority on this island. I'll tell them about it when we get back to the hotel, especially about how you saved Ebony's life.

"Tom loves those dogs more than anyone except for Jerry and he will be very grateful to you. Let's walk it off and try to relax and enjoy the rest of the day."

What she said sounded logical but still seemed to me to be bizarre and inappropriate. I said okay and the dogs began to run on ahead again. After about a mile, we came to the waterfall. It was about 120 feet high and was very wide so that it fell with gentle force and would provide a cool shower in the damp, sultry jungle.

It was surrounded by wild flowers and purple orchids, and on one side we found a patch of soft grass to set up our picnic. I lay down on the grass and put my hands behind my head.

Samantha stood above me and said, "How about a swim, Jake? You look hot and sticky.

"In a minute, I just want to relax for a second or two."

"You're the boss," she said, then began to disrobe.

She unbuttoned her shorts and lowered them around her hips. She was wearing a red and yellow flowered, thong bikini. It had thin red strings that tied the sides together, and others that made up the entire back of the suit. Despite my exhaustion and the stress-filled afternoon, blood began to flow to specific regions of my anatomy and I turned on my side so that Samantha wouldn't notice.

I was praying that she would not stop at her shorts. She turned around to face the water and gave me only the briefest glance at her perfect derriere before she dove in. I stood up quickly and undressed down to my shorts and followed her in. The water was surprisingly warm and it felt like heaven.

We laughed and splashed each other, then climbed up under the waterfall. We stood back behind the falls in a little alcove and we looked out through the wall of water. The falls gave a blurred slow motion perspective to the jungle and the flowers. It looked like a Van Gogh painting or like a watercolor of the forest. It was a very natural special effect.

I turned to look at Samantha and I noticed that her top had been displaced by the rushing water as we passed through the falls. Her left breast was exposed. Her nipple was brown and small and it was erect from the cold air and water. Her breasts were perfect and round. I couldn't seem to catch my breath.

Not since Linda had I felt such a strong magnetic pull toward someone, such an overwhelming attraction. I looked at Samantha and I felt an incredible fount of desire.

"Jake," she said.

"Yes, Sam."

"What if that man had been aiming that gun at me? What would you have done then? Would you have risked your life to save me?" She looked up at me with a tenderness and a femininity which was in stark contrast to the Rambo routine I had just seen in the woods. My heart felt as if it would burst from my chest.

I moved closer to her and touched her face gently with the back of my hand and told her truthfully that she was the most amazing person I had ever known and that, although I never considered myself particularly brave, I would do anything and everything I could to protect her.

She traced her fingers across my lips and said "I think you underestimate yourself, Jake. I think you're just beginning down the same road of self-discovery that I traveled down ten years ago. I think you'll be surprised to learn just how strong and brave you really are."

She leaned into me and her chest touched mine and our lips met. I ran my hands across her back and through her hair. We embraced. I turned and my left shoulder broke the plane of the waterfall and showered us both with cool fresh water.

I leaned over and sucked the beads of water from her breasts and ran my hands along her thighs and gently cupped her rear in my hands. We made love behind the falls and it was the most romantic, sensual, and passionate experience I could ever have imagined.

We were laying naked on a blanket she had carried with her in her backpack. The dogs occasionally interrupted us by forcing their way onto the blanket. They tried to nuzzle us for attention until I ordered them away. I turned to her after perhaps an hour of blissful silence. "Tell me something. How did you learn to fight like that? I've never seen anything like that before."

I gently ran my fingers over the scar on her back and I asked her where she had gotten it. She turned her back on me and I moved closer and spooned her. I cupped her breasts in my hand and gently kissed the back of her neck as I stroked her hair. She didn't say anything for a while and then told me that she had run away from home when she was fifteen. Her father was a drunk and he had abused her and her mother. When she started to become a woman, he began to touch her in ways that made her prefer his beatings. That's when she took off.

She worked as a waitress for awhile, then as a topless dancer in a dive in Houston. She married at seventeen to a man who was a little too much like her daddy. He beat her so bad once that she had to be hospitalized for over a week. He had broken bones in her face and her body. "That's why my face is such a mess," she said.

I turned her around when she said that and I told her that she was the most beautiful woman I had ever seen, and I meant it with all my heart. She told me that when she recovered she ran away and joined the Army where she eventually entered advanced infantry training. She had to threaten to sue the Army in order to be allowed to receive Special OPs training alongside the men. She never wanted to feel helpless or defenseless again in her life. She became the first woman to receive Special OPs training, but would never be allowed to fight in a war. She met Tom five years ago, and he was the one who really taught her how to fight.

She had been very highly respected among the Berets she trained with, in hand-to-hand combat and self defense, but when she met Tom she realized that she still had alot to learn.

I felt a twinge of jealousy at the way she mentioned Tom's name and ability but I quickly buried it. Tom was one of those men who could intimidate just about anyone, and you couldn't help feeling slightly inadequate when you thought of him in comparative terms.

"Tom seems so mellow and laid back," I said genuinely surprised at this revelation about a man I knew almost nothing about. I was shocked when he told me that he had been a Navy SEAL. He sings Cat Stevens songs and walks around in a straw cowboy hat. I've heard him speaking in baby talk to the dogs."

Samantha laughed and turned toward me. She was surprised that Tom had told me about his days as a SEAL. She said that Tom must really like me. I ran my hands down her back and over her bottom. Her rear was incredibly firm and I felt a surge of electricity throughout my body.

"Jake, Tom was probably the best SEAL there ever was. He's one of the most dangerous men I've ever known but he can also be one of the gentlest. He's saved my life over half a dozen times. One of those times was when I got this scar you asked about. Now please, no more talking. I've told you far too much already. Tom would kill me if he knew. Let's just hold each other and enjoy the rest of the day."

We made love once more at the waterfall and again on the hike back to the hotel. We never did make it to the beach that day but promised each other that we would try again sometime next week. On the trail back, I noticed a large concrete building that was tucked in the woods at the top of a small hill. It had a large steel door, which looked like it could take a direct hit from a missile. I asked Samantha about it and she said it was a tool shed and a workshop and then she told me that it was strictly off limits to hotel guests and to most of the staff.

When we got closer to the hotel I joked again about having to work for her now and she told me that I could look forward to many special perks on the job. We parted at the main building and she asked me to please be discreet around the hotel grounds and I reluctantly agreed. I knew it would take great effort to keep my hands off her. I whistled and sang all the way back to my room, where I collapsed into the hammock on the front porch. I was deliriously happy and it seemed as though my initial plan when I came here had worked. I wanted to forget and now I couldn't remember anything before this afternoon and I couldn't think of anything but Sam. I fell asleep to the songs of the wild birds and the roar of the ocean below me.

CHAPTER 19

I was laying on my back feeling the strong afternoon sun on my face when I heard Samantha's voice calling to me from the beach. I had swam out to a large carpeted wooden raft that was anchored to the bottom of the lagoon. It acted as a small island in the middle of the bay that fronted the hotel. It was a good forty yard swim and my arms felt heavy. I had only just begun to settle my breathing down. It had been weeks since Samantha and I had first made love at the waterfall. Since that time we had been inseparable and Samantha had started to take me running with her. The afternoon runs with Samantha these past two weeks had done alot to improve my stamina and I had lost over fifteen pounds since my arrival to the island.

"Jake, let's go. It's time for our run," she screamed over the sound of the waves that were breaking against my little floating oasis.

Shit, I thought, running was about the furthest thing from my mind at that moment. I just wanted to lay there, listen to the waves and soak up the sun. Besides, by the time I swam all the way back to the beach I would already be winded and I would be tired even before our run began. The week after Sam and I got together I accepted a divemaster position with the hotel and during the day Samantha and I tried to be as discreet as possible about our relationship. Once I had even accused her of going overboard in trying not to show me preferential treatment when she asked me to fill and load over sixty tanks on board the boats for three straight days in a row.

She laughed and told me that since I was the new guy I had to pay my dues by handling the majority of the dirty work for awhile. Tom sent one of the hotel workers down to the dock one afternoon to summon me to his office and when I arrived he was wearing a telephone headset and was talking on what looked like a laptop computer with a small radar dish hooked to it.

He explained that it was a satellite phone he used for secure transmissions to his broker in the States. He swiveled around in his favorite chair. It was a faded and well worn tan leather and wooden antique. Tom told me that it had come from a midwestern bank and was made in the late 1800s. Behind his desk was a standing, Tiffany-style stained glass lamp of a design that I didn't recognize. It portrayed a coral reef with varying shades of blue for the ocean and there were turtles and green moray eels and colored corals and sponges around the bottom rim. Lit from inside, the colors were vibrant; it was a beautiful work of art. The base was designed in the form of a tree with the roots ending at the bottom, and it was made of bronze. In some places the bronze was greenish blue from oxidation. I asked about the lamp and was surprised to learn that Tom had made it. He told me that he had a workshop in the shed I had seen at the top of the hill during my hike with Sam. Tom told me that this hobby helped him to relax. I told him I couldn't imagine what he would need to relax about, his stressful life as the owner of a Caribbean hotel. He laughed, reached behind him, and took down a book from a tall rattan bookshelf next to his desk. He threw it to me.

"Stress is a relative thing, Jake," he said. "You should read this book now that you're in the hotel business. It's very funny."

I turned the book over and read the cover. It was *Don't Stop The Carnival* by Herman Wouk. I had been told about this book before. I think it was Jackie who had told me a few years ago that it was very good.

"Thanks, Tom." But this can't be the reason why you called me to your office." I was constantly surprised at the amazing insights I got into this increasingly curious and intriguing man. Tom stood up and I saw that he was wearing a pair of faded denim cut - off shorts and his usual footwear, a pair of Teva sandals. He was also wearing a Miami Dolphins cap and a white tank top from a clam bar in Key West called "Eat it Raw."

He walked up to me and looked down from his high altitude to stare me in the eyes. Tom was at least five inches taller than me. Tom told me that he knew that Samantha and I were seeing each other. I asked him if he had a problem with it and he smiled and shook my hand.

"I've known Samantha for a long time, Jake. She's been through a lot and hasn't had an easy life. This is the happiest I've ever seen her, and you're not the same person who showed up here four weeks ago either. Hell no, I don't have a problem with it. I think it's terrific.

"I just wanted to let you know that I knew, so that you two wouldn't feel like you had to keep sneaking around. I don't know what you were thinking anyway. This isn't the Hyatt Regency you're working at.

"The only thing I ask is that you control your passion when you're around the hotel guests. One more thing, Jake. I was going to wait to surprise you, but I might as well ask you now. How would you like to go to Cozumel at the end of the month with Jerry, Samantha, and me?"

"Are you kidding? I was there last year and I loved it. Is it a vacation?"

"Jerry and I are performing at a hotel called La Cieba. We're also going to meet some old friends and do a little diving. I think we can work you into the budget. We'll call it your one month anniversary bonus."

When Tom invited me, I had no idea that he had intended on paying for me. It wouldn't have mattered to me anyway. I would have gladly paid for myself. A trip to Cozumel with Sam and Tom sounded fantastic.

"I've barely seen a glimpse of Jerry these past two weeks. Is he okay?"

"Jerry's actually been very busy working on a new project and his work is the best medicine for his recent depression. Cozumel was his idea, actually, and he seems to be in a much better mood the past few days. Thanks for asking. I appreciate your concern."

If Tom was a mystery to me, his brother was an even bigger source of curiosity and speculation. Since they had landed on the island I had only seen him at meals twice and had only spoken with him once, down at the dock. He had just come out of the water from snorkeling and was carrying a sealed plastic bag that contained a small Portuguese man-o-war.

He walked right by me, looking as if he were a million miles away. I said "Hello Jerry" to the back of his head, and he turned around and walked up to me. He asked me some very strange questions.

"Jake, have you ever known anyone that suffered from a debilitating illness?"

"What would it have been worth to you to have been able to provide them with a cure? Would you risk your life or the lives of others to save them? Would you ever presume to be so arrogant?"

Considering that we had never spoken a word of casual conversation, his questions threw me off balance. I was about tell him that I didn't know what I would do when he quickly turned and walked away.

"Please don't take this the wrong way, Tom, but your brother makes me a little uncomfortable. I don't think he likes me very much. Are you sure it's okay with him if I come along with you to Cozumel? Sam and I could always run things here while you're gone."

"Jerry hasn't liked himself lately, Jake, it's got nothing to do with you. When I told him I was going to invite you along he had absolutely no problem with it. I need Sam along on this trip and she would be alot happier if you came along. So, if I were you, I would talk it over with her and then get back to me."

"I'll talk it over with Sam but I can tell you now the answer is yes. Thanks, Tom. I mean it. I'm only working for you a little over three weeks. It's very generous of you to invite me along."

"My pleasure. It will be fun having you there. Now get back to work before your boss gets mad and assigns you to washing out gear all afternoon."

I smiled at the memory of that afternoon in Tom's office and the subsequent times that Tom and I had spent talking and diving together since our trip to The Aquarium. We had developed a friendship and I was surprised to find that despite his intimidating presence he was also a very sensitive person and had a great sense of humor.

Sam called to me again and I rolled over on my side away from the beach and pretended that I was sleeping. I was hoping that she would leave me alone and that she would go running by herself or would go for a ride on her mountain bike.

"Jake!!!" She yelled again. "Get your ass over here. I know you can hear me. If you're not here in five minutes you can forget about seeing me tonight."

I stood up and reluctantly dove into the water and swam to the beach. There was an undertow that day and when I finally washed ashore I was choking for air like a beached whale. I knew I was going to be in for an even more miserable afternoon than usual. Our runs consisted of me chasing Samantha halfway around the island. There was also the usual added humiliation of having her stop every half a mile so she could wait for me to catch up.

The first three times we ran together I could barely keep up with her. My ego was tormented by the added knowledge that she was taking it easy on me by easing back from her usual pace.

"Why don't you go on ahead without me," I said when I stood up and approached her." I don't feel like running, and besides it looks like rain." Dark clouds had begun to quickly roll in from the other side of the island and it did look like a thunder storm was imminent.

"Running in the rain is great. And I might just let you catch me today."

"In the unlikely event that I do catch you and that I can still breathe without a respirator, what would be my reward?"

Samantha looked around to see if anyone was looking and she grabbed me around the shoulders and gave me a very passionate kiss. She pulled away from me and said, "I'd like to make love again in the woods like our first time. In the rain under a canopy of trees, our bodies all hot and sweaty from our run, the cool rain washing over us and steaming from your back as you enter me."

"Let's go," I said. "I feel a sudden surge of energy."

Samantha laughed as we began our jog up the hill. This was the part of the run that I hated the most. The first quarter mile was straight uphill. By the time I got to the top my legs were burning and it took me another quarter mile to settle my breathing and to get into a rhythm. We crested the hill and we were near the tool shed I had seen on our first hike. It was the place where Tom supposedly worked on his stained glass. I heard the heavy metal door open, and as I looked back over my shoulder I saw Jerry emerge from the building.

It had gotten ominously dark. I heard a crack of thunder in the distance and a minute later a flash of lightning lit the darkened hillside. "Maybe we should....cut it short...today," I said between breaths.

"Don't worry. The odds of us getting hit by lightning are very slight."

Sam took off and pulled ahead of me. Thankfully, we were beginning to head down hill. We got to a part of the trail where it levels out. Samantha had beaten the trail down over the course of the last year with her mountain bike and you could see her tire tracks in the dirt. When we were about two miles into our run, the sky opened up with a torrential downpour. The water falling upon the thick canopy of trees beat against the leaves above our heads and it sounded like thousands of tiny drums beating in the jungle.

We were drenched to the bone in seconds and I yelled to Samantha who had slowed down and was now only five feet ahead of me. "I'm soaked," I said. "My feet are wet and my shoes are squishing with every step."

The rain was blowing hard and was in my eyes making it hard for me to see. Samantha ran beside me and said, "Okay, we'll head back, but it's only water, Jake. I think it feels great."

Suddenly, she jumped in the air and landed in a mudpuddle. She angled her feet when she landed to intentionally splash me with muddy water. A large wake of muddy brown water landed on my legs up to my knees and soaked my shoes.

I could hear her laughing hysterically as she hit the afterburners and quickly pulled out ahead of me. With great effort I sprinted after her, cursing all the way, until I was along-side her. I leaped a foot into the air and grabbed a handful of branches that hung above the trail directly in front of her path and I shook the tree violently.

A bucketful of water fell from the tree and hit Samantha directly in the face and chest. She shook her head to clear her eyes and leaves flew from her hair.

"That's hysterical Jake," she cried, "but I'm already wet." Suddenly Samantha doubled over and screamed in pain as she grabbed her ankle. "I twisted my ankle. Damn it!!" She cried.

I quickly ran over to help her. I started to bend down to examine her foot when she threw a handful of mud in my face.

"Now that's funny," she screamed, then she ran for her life. Dark reddish brown mud was running down my face and into my mouth. I wiped it from eyes and started after her. We had reached another hill and I knew it would require a heroic effort on my part to catch her but I was driven on by the thought of vengeance. I crested the hill and was huffing and puffing.

I could see Samantha was slowing down in the slippery mud and that she was trying to keep her balance. I recklessly increased my speed and when I was within a foot of catching her I dove for her waist like an NFL linebacker trying to keep Emmit Smith from the end zone.

My timing was a little off. I could feel her back with the tips of my fingers as my hand brushed against it. An instant later I landed face down in a foot of muddy water. I sat up in the puddle feeling utterly defeated. Samantha walked up to within a few feet of me and taunted me to come and get her.

"What a sad sight you are. I'll see you back at your cabin after I use up all the hot water."

She was off again, running down the trail. I stood up feeling wet and cold. I could feel mud had worked its way into every orifice on my body. I shook out my shorts and released a stream of mud back into the river that only minutes earlier had been a trail.

I was extremely uncomfortable but I was also steaming mad and my competitive nature refused to allow me to give up. I ran as fast as I could, knowing that Samantha was going to have to take it slow going down the hill toward my cabin. The final quarter mile to the cabin was very steep. I decided to live dangerously, throw caution to the wind. I proceeded recklessly down the hill at breakneck speed. I was crashing through trees and jumping over rocks and fallen limbs. I was within reach of her and I was screaming like a madman. I increased my speed and with the final reserve of strength I had left I launched myself at her.

I was going too fast and when I tried to brake I found I couldn't stop. I grabbed Samantha, wrapping her in my arms and my forward momentum took her off her feet and sent us both tumbling down the trail.

We fell on our asses and tumbled backward head over heels through the mud. We slid over fifty yards downhill before we finally came to rest just inches from an enormous boulder. We looked at each other in silence. I think we were both momentarily in shock. Then we both started laughing and Samantha said, "Are you fucking nuts? You could have killed us."

I was so winded I could barely catch my breath. My laughter sounded muffled and wheezy. "There's..... no way....I was... letting you get away with that. I ..was fed up after three weeks of...having to swallow my pride. I'm tired ...of... chasing you around...this fucking island. Having mud thrown in my face was the final humiliation.... I was going to suffer ... at your hands."

Sam leaned over and kissed me on my muddy lips, then she stood and she said, "I'll race you back to the cabin. One more big push. Let's go."

"You're impossible," I said. "I don't even think I can walk and I'm going to need a turkey baster to wash out some of this mud from the places it's worked its way into."

"You're disgusting Jake. Come on and we'll take a nice hot shower together. I'll help you wash off the mud in those hard to reach places."

We ran back to the cabin and burst through the door laughing and feeling great. We fell into bed, covered with leaves and mud, and made love for over an hour. The sheets were filthy and we had mud in our mouths and on our lips as we kissed each other and explored each other's bodies. We took a hot shower and we took turns washing each other's hair, then I grabbed the blanket from the floor and we both climbed into the porch hammock.

I traced my finger along the tattoo on Samantha's bottom and asked her about it. She told me that the queen angelfish was her favorite fish and that "Angelfish" was a nickname a friend had given her a long time ago. We fell asleep holding each other and listening to the sound of the rain falling through the trees. I couldn't ever remember a time in my life when I felt so happy. As I closed my eyes and drifted off to sleep I realized that I had fallen in love.

CHAPTER 20

"IT'S TIME TO SNAP OUT OF THIS DEPRESSION and rejoin the living." Lionfish said. "It's become self-indulgent and we can't afford it." He had followed Stingray back to their home at the top of the hill and confronted him when they reached the front porch. "Paul wanted more than anything else to make a contribution and to do some good and you can help him accomplish that by finishing the work you began together."

Lionfish grabbed Stingray around the shoulders and, looking him in the eye, said, "It's time to get back to work. We need you, Jerry, and I miss you. Next week we're all going to Cozumel to begin reconnaissance and preliminary inspections for our next project. I need you whole again and of sound mind. This is a crucial time in the life of the organization. Our people are worried and morale has suffered because of our current losses.

"As the leaders we need to present a stable and unified front to the others. This next mission in Mexico against the cruise line and the pier they intend to build will be a simple one. It is just a warm up for our major assault in the Florida Everglades this spring.

"It's essential that we have a victory in Mexico for the future of the organization. We are now receiving national recognition, due in large part to your interview with CNN. People are beginning to ask questions they never before asked and are starting to look beyond their front lawns to the problems in their communities, problems they didn't even know existed.

'That's because of you, Jerry, and what you've taught them. I can raise a rifle and fire a shot that will get them to look in our direction but it's you who holds their attention and stimulates their thinking and their collective conscience.

"Without you and your influence in this organization we are in jeopardy of becoming strictly a militant group of environmental fanatics. The organization needs you. I need you."

"I feel better now, Tom. I've had some time to sort things out and I'm ready to get back to work. Besides how could I not feel better after that inspiring pep talk," Jerry said with sarcasm and then he smiled for the first time in weeks. "I thought any minute you were going to lead a cheer. Go RedTide!!"

"Fuck you, asshole." Tom was happy to see that there was hope that things could begin to get back to normal. Tom grabbed Jerry and hugged him tight and said, "Welcome back, buddy. Why don't you take the day off and go diving with me and Jake today?"

Jerry's expression changed to one of concern and he said, "What's the deal with you and Jake? You're not planning on bringing him on board are you? He's a salesman, not a soldier. He's not an environmentalist and he's not a scientist. What would he do? More importantly, how do we even know we can trust him?"

"I like him, Jerry. I like him a lot, and I trust him. He's also an ex-marine. And although he only spent a few months in the Corps he's been through boot camp and he's had infantry training. He knows how to handle a weapon. As a matter of fact he qualified as an expert marksman with both the M16 rifle and the 45 caliber pistol.

"I've been feeling him out about his views on the environment and I like what I hear. He just lost his mother and he only has a sister left in New York. I also think he's in love with Angelfish, so I know he has no intention of leaving us anytime soon.

"If he came on board I could teach him to fight, at least well enough to defend himself. And he's been working out and running with Samantha almost every day. Any idiot can fire a weapon but with proper training and practice I think I can turn him into a decent soldier. More importantly he's loyal and he has a good heart and I know he's eager to assume a more substantial and meaningful role in the world.

"He's already told me that he's through being a 'sales whore,' as he refers to his job back home, and that he wants to do something more self-satisfying and gratifying with his life. He mentioned the possibility of getting a teaching degree to me the other day."

"What's wrong with you Tom?" Stingray snapped. "You don't know anything about him and even if he is for real, there's a big difference between teaching children and shooting at people and blowing up their property.

"I urge you to take it slow with Jake and not to say anything that would give us away. He's vulnerable now during this time of grief and he's not thinking straight. Throw his infatuation with Sam into the mix and he doesn't know if he's coming or going. Last month he was in

Miami earning six figures driving his Corvette to cardiologist's offices to sell them EKG machines. This week he's a divemaster in Central America, working for room and board.

"He knows where we live and he knows where our main base of operations is. I for one do not want to have to pick up and move again. It took us a long time to set up this cover and to work out an arrangement with the Honduran government, not to mention the four million dollars in cash we spent to buy this island and the hotel.

"I'm not telling you how to do your job, Tom," Stingray continued more cautiously when he saw the hostile look on Tom's face. "I know that his situation with both his dad and his mom reminds you of Hannah and that you feel a bond, a kinship with Jake. I know you don't have any friends outside of me and the soldiers you surround yourself with. I recognize your loneliness and the burden of leadership. I empathize and I understand your wanting to spend time with Jake. I like him also. He's a nice guy. I just don't think we can afford any more mistakes. I can't believe I'm saying this to you of all people, but I want you to think with your head and not your heart."

Lionfish walked to the window and he looked down at the dock where Samantha and I were washing out the guest's gear in the 200 gallon aluminum rinse tanks that stood along-side the wall of the dive shop. I had no idea at the time that they were having a conversation that would alter the course of my life and would lead to the most important decision I would ever have to make.

Samantha had just turned the hose on me and she was spraying me in the face. She was blinding me with the spray as I approached her to grab it out of her hands. As Lionfish looked on, she steered me toward the edge of the dock and I lost my footing and tripped over a spooled up rope that was laying on the dock. I toppled into the water, headfirst.

Lionfish laughed and turned from the window toward Stingray. "You're right, Jerry. And of course I'll be careful. No one except a few senior high-ranking RedTide officers knows about this island or about our covers. No new recruit in the history of the organization has ever been told of this location." Lionfish's expression changed and the darker side of his personality appeared.

"We'll see how he behaves in Mexico when we visit the Greenpeace protest sight along the town pier. I'll talk to Angelfish to see what her thoughts are. We'll take it slow with Jake and time will tell if his desire to do something meaningful with his life is for real or if it's a passing phase.

"My instincts tell me that Jake can be trusted. I like him far too much to allow myself to tell him anything that might later put me in the unfortunate position of having to kill him."

CHAPTER 21

We arrived in Cozumel at 3 p.m. yesterday afternoon on a small private jet that Tom had chartered out of Roatan. Samantha, Jerry, Tom and I flew to Roatan on the seaplane. Jerry was in a good mood for the first time since my arrival on the island and we talked all the way to Mexico about his background in marine biology and biochemistry. Jerry, I learned had graduated from Cornell University at the top of his class at the age of 19 and went on to receive his doctorate at Johns Hopkins by the time he was 21. I asked him why he had left the world of science and commercial research. It seemed to me, I told him, that someone with his talents and education should be making big money working for a large pharmaceutical company or for the government. He laughed out loud which drew the attention of the group. It was the first time I had seen him do such a thing and when he smiled he looked like a little boy instead of the troubled melancholy man I had seen sulking around the hotel for the past month with his head buried in a book.

I felt more comfortable speaking with him now, although I was out of my league on most of the subjects we discussed. The plane Tom chartered was a five-year-old Gulfstream jet that once belonged to the owner of a large furniture manufacturer in the United States before his company went belly-up.

It was well appointed and was definitely what you would call a first class ride. We were all sitting in highback, thick black leather chairs, which could swivel 360 degrees once they were unlocked from their liftoff and landing position.

Tom spent alot of time in the cockpit speaking with the pilot and co-pilot and he seemed to know them very well, although when I asked him if they were his friends he told me that he had only met them for the first time today. He told me that they had been recommended by a friend in Belize. He barged into the cockpit and barked out orders with such familiarity that it appeared as if they were his full time employees. I was surprised to see that they never threw him out of the cabin or told him to kiss their asses.

Although Tom was physically intimidating the pilots both looked like Marine Corps drill instructors and they were tall and well-built. They looked like they could hold their own against big Tom and I told him so when he returned to his seat.

Tom gave me his most charming and seductive smile and he told me that the two of them together wouldn't have a chance, not even if I jumped in to help them. Samantha turned to me and chimed in that although Tom was kidding he was probably right. Her comment annoyed me greatly.

We had not really spoken to each other since the night before last and I had avoided making eye contact with her on the flight from Arrecife to Roatan. I suppose I was trying to punish her by ignoring her but in the process I ended up torturing myself, especially since she didn't really seem to be affected by my coldness toward her.

We had a fight on the dock at 4 A.M., two nights ago, after a wonderfully romantic night of diving nude together during a full moon. All during dinner that night I kept looking for Samantha but she was nowhere to be found. I checked with the entire hotel staff and no one seemed to know where she was. This was very strange in such a small place and it was especially unusual for the manager of the hotel not to be accessible. After dinner, I went to the bar and had a couple of vodka and cranberry juices. I had given up mudslides because of the calories. I was feeling agitated and I drank my cocktails quickly. I had been looking forward to spending the night with Samantha. Lately I was fighting feelings of neediness and the urge to smother her since she had warned me a week ago that there would be times when she would need to be alone, and that at those times when she needed some space I shouldn't feel threatened.

Despite her mature explanation and her warning, I was feeling threatened and I was hating myself for being so co-dependent. I knew Samantha was a loner. She always had been. She came from an abusive dysfunctional family and went directly from one abusive relationship to another. She had an elaborate defense system in place and she explained to me that she would let people only get so close to her before she pushed them away.

She told me that I was already further inside her walls than any man she had ever known. She made it sound like a siege. I imagined that I had already swam the moat and I was scaling the outside walls of her castle. Now was the time when the hot oil would come flying down from above to repel the invader. I was afraid that her disappearance tonight meant that she had made her escape through my lines and was now on the run.

I ordered another drink from Carmen and she came over to me and said, in broken English, "What's the matter, Jake? You look like your dog just got run over by a car. No more drink for you, Sam's orders. She gave me this to give you instead," Carmen said holding up a small pink envelope.

"She told me not to give it to you till 10:30. Maybe I wait, it's only 9:45," she said looking at her watch.

I smiled for the first time that night and replied, "Carmen you know I love you and if Samantha hadn't gotten to me first, right now me and you would be covered in oil and would be in my room rolling around in the sheets. Now don't let your jealousy get the better of you. Hand over that note."

Carmen and I had become good friends despite the language barrier and we had some very meaningful conversations about her four children and her desire to go to the United States. She told me that her husband had worked for Tom & Jerry for over five years before he was killed in a scuba accident. She never provided details about the accident and she would become uncomfortable and would change the subject whenever I tried to get more information out of her. She told me that Tom & Jerry had provided her with housing for her and her family and that they had both told her that she would have a job with them for the rest of her life. She was devoted to them both and she was extremely loyal.

"I don't know, Jake," she said, enjoying my discomfort. "Sam say over and over 10:30, not before."

"Don't make me jump over this counter, woman," I said, raising my leg and putting my foot on the bar.

"Okay, Senor Macho, here is the note." As she started to hand me the note she sniffed it and said, "Muy Calor." Then she dropped it to the counter as if it were on fire.

I grabbed it quickly and walked away with the sound of her giggling in my ears. I sat down at one of the rattan sofas near the largest window in the room and quickly tore open the envelope, being careful not to tear the letter inside. The note was short and simple. It was written with a black calligraphy pen on rose-colored, heavy weight paper similar to the card stock used for invitations and business cards and it was sprayed with Sam's perfume. It simply said:

> "Go to your cabin.
> I have a surprise waiting for you.
> Hurry."

The final instruction to hurry wasn't necessary. The second I had finished Samantha's note I was on my feet and I was speeding down the boardwalk to my cabin. Halfway there I ran into the Kellers from Austin, Texas who wanted to engage me in a conversation about the bull shark we had seen together on the morning's dive. I had guided them and four others to Diablo Canyon on the west side of the island.

It was their first day on the island and they were very excited and I had a difficult time breaking away from them. My anticipation for what awaited me in my room increased by the second. I told them that I had to fix a problem in one of the cabins and I made my escape. I knew Sam would be pissed off at me for being rude to our guests and I made a mental note to have breakfast with them the next morning.

I burst through my cabin door, expecting to find Sam in a negligee on the bed and looking lusty holding a bottle of Moet. Instead I found an empty cabin with a trail of flower petals that led to the bed. In the middle of the bed was another envelope that was surrounded by a circle of flowers. I was becoming frustrated but was incredibly excited and I grabbed the envelope off of the bed and tore it open with such ferocity that I tore off a corner of the card inside. Again, Sam had written a simple note with specific instructions for me to follow.

> "Take off your clothes and put on the trunks I left on
> top of the bureau.
> Go to the Jacaranda tree at the westernmost part of
> the beach.
> Hurry, I want you."

My blood was pounding and again my imagination had us sharing a picnic under the full moon after we made love in the surf like Deborah Kerr and Burt Lancaster in *From here to Eternity*. I did as instructed and I changed into my swim trunks. I took nothing else with me and I jogged down the trail to the stairs and in the full light of a large silver moon I ran toward the Jacaranda tree, only to find to my disappointment that once again Samantha was nowhere in sight. I saw a reflection coming from the tree. When I got close I saw that Samantha had tacked another envelope to the trunk, along with a silver foil heart. She had put it there to catch the moonlight in order to draw my attention to the note. I was about to explode from frustration and I tore the note from the tree. I laughed when I read the first line. In only a month Samantha already knew me so well.

> "Relax Jake and take a deep breath.
> Some things are worth waiting for.
> Turn around and you will see a kayak waiting for
> you.
> Paddle one half mile north and look for a light on
> the beach.
> I'll be waiting."

I knew the beach that Samantha was talking about. Although I had never been there I had moored the boats offshore to dive the reef that sat just offshore. The beach was only accessible by boat or by hiking through the woods on a treacherous downhill trail that was also unmarked. Many of the hotel's guests risked the danger in order to spend afternoons skinny dipping and picnicking.

I went to the kayak and began paddling frantically to what I hoped was my final destination for the evening. It was a beautiful night. It was cool and breezy and the water was calm. The moon was large and full and the air was so clear that you could see all of the detail of the moon's surface. Its light was so bright that you could see clearly for hundreds of feet, and the whitecaps looked like silver foam as they danced across the top of the dark sea.

The trip to what the guests called "Lovers Beach" was closer to a mile and my arms were starting to get tired. I saw a flickering light, which I guessed correctly was a campfire 100 yards ahead. I paddled ashore and pulled the kayak up alongside Samantha's small motor boat and noticed that our dive gear was inside. Samantha had brought all of my gear and had it all hooked up and ready to go. I was excited about the idea of a moonlight night dive and I hurried toward the fire. Samantha was standing behind the fire and looked luminous in the bright yellow glow of the flames. Her hair was long and flowing and the golden strands flickered in the dancing firelight. She walked toward me and I could see she was only wearing a sheer flowing silk Sarong. It was tied around her breasts like a dress and there was nothing underneath.

When she stepped in front of the fire it silhouetted her and showed her long legs and her beautifully shaped thighs. I could also see the curve of her hips beneath the sheer fabric. I practically lunged at her. My heart was racing and my desire was intense and ravenous. I ran my hands over her body feeling her nipples harden beneath the silk and we lay down and made love, first on the blanket and then in the sand.

When we were through, she rolled over on her back and I tickled her between her shoulders and gave her a gentle back massage. We laid side by side for awhile and then we ate French bread and cheese and we drank the one glass of Merlot Samantha would allow us to have before our night dive. Around midnight, when the moon had reached its apex, we put on our dive gear and nothing else and entered the water. We swam out to the reef and quickly descended to thirty feet. Samantha signaled for me to shut my light and when I did I could see the moon's rays slicing through the water and illuminating the reef in subdued, washed-out pastel colors.

I looked up and I could see the moon. It was blurred by the motion of the waves but it still looked bright and beautiful from underwater. Silver light was dancing up and down Samantha's naked body and her hair was flowing around her. She looked the way she had the first time I saw her underwater during our first dive together and again I thought how like a mermaid she appeared. She was strong and lovely and looked mythical in the warm weightless environment where she felt so much at home.

We descended to fifty feet and found sleeping parrot fish of all different colors and varieties and a nurse shark that was sleeping below a ledge. Samantha took my hand and we pet the shark gently along its side. The skin felt rubbery and smooth and the shark never moved. It continued to sleep as we swam away.

Samantha waved her arms up and down and told me to do the same. The phytoplankton in the water became stimulated by the motion and illuminated in tiny silver bursts like thousands of microscopic flashbulbs all around us. I pulled my regulator from my mouth and Samantha did the same and we kissed. We locked our lips and opened our mouths fifty feet below the surface and I felt exhilarated and completely happy.

We dove the entire time without our lights. We navigated entirely by the light of a moon in a cloudless sky and when we finally swam ashore I took Samantha in my arms and thanked her for the single greatest dive I had ever experienced. She laughed and told me that the hotel had considered putting it in the brochure as a way to increase business but Jerry was against it.

She told me that it was something that divemasters reserved only for special guests. We were cold and Samantha's skin was covered in goosebumps. We added wood to the fire and huddled beneath a blanket and talked for hours about traveling, diving, past lovers, eventually getting around to the subject of my mother.

I had accomplished what I came here for, to hide from my pain for awhile. I was so happy the past few weeks that I had forgotten my grief for a brief moment in time but when I told Samantha about a day when my mother and I were looking at underwater photographs and my mom, even though she was terrified of the water, urged me to become certified to dive, I began to cry.

I told Sam that I felt guilty and selfish about feeling so happy so soon after my mother's death. Samantha held me and comforted me until I fell asleep in her arms and when I awoke the moon had nearly set and it was time to go. Samantha towed me back to the hotel dock and we sat quietly for awhile and watched the spotted eagle rays swimming below the light and through the pilings. There were over twenty of them and some were juveniles. Samantha told me that she wanted to sleep alone in her own room tonight since she had a meeting with Tom & Jerry at 8:30, which was only four hours away.

I kissed her and looked her in the eye and said, "Tonight was like a dream, Sam. You're an incredible woman. You're strong and independent but you're also sensitive and incredibly feminine and passionate. I think you're the most incredible person I've ever known and I've fallen in love with you."

It seemed like an hour before she responded. It took me a long time to muster the courage to tell her how I felt, and I hoped that she would tell me that she felt the same way.

"Jake, don't," Samantha said. She took my hand and looked at the ground. "I think you're a terrific guy. You're the first man I've ever known who thought about me first and put my needs before his own, and you make me laugh all the time. I love being together, but I'm not in love with you, Jake."

I felt like a fool and I wished that I could take back the words I had just spoken, or just disappear into thin air. I became upset and said some things in anger that I wished later that I could take back. Then I walked away to my room without saying good night. That was two days ago and we had not spoken more than a few words between us since then. It was obvious to everyone on the plane, that we were fighting. I was miserable but I didn't know how to approach Samantha or what to say and my pride was suffering greatly. I should have been happy just to spend time together and I knew I was not behaving maturely, but old patterns are hard to break.

In my family we never learned how to communicate outside of shouting ugly hurtful words at each other. Sometimes when the damage was done and the words were already spoken and couldn't be retrieved it was difficult to forgive or to get over the hurt. We would often go as long as six months without speaking to one another. I had hoped that after my mother's death I had learned something about communicating more effectively and that I would make the most out of the time that I had left with the people I loved. Since my mother's death I had told myself repeatedly that if I had another chance with her I would do things differently, but now I wondered if that were true or if I was doomed by my history and my personality to repeat the same mistakes over and over again.

I looked over at Samantha and she caught me staring. She looked me in the eye from across the cabin. Her expression was slightly angry but it was also a little sad and I mouthed the words, "I'm sorry" to her. Her expression softened and she mouthed "me too" and when we finally landed and arrived at the La Cieba Hotel we went straight to my room and we made up for over two hours. She told me to be patient with her and to try and understand her and I told her that I would, and for the first time in my life I felt that I had meant it. Maybe the impossible was happening and I was growing up after all.

Later that evening, we went to the bar to hear Tom & Jerry perform. I was embarrassed and saddened when at one point in the show

Tom played Jackson Browne's "These days," which he dedicated to a fellow Jackson Browne fan who knew all about loss.

After the show Tom introduced me to three men who he described as old friends from his Navy days. Their names were Jack Miller, Jorge Calderon, and Peter Hanson. They all had the same Marine Corp insignia tattooed on their arms. Jack was a tall black man, an affable person with an honest open face, a warm smile and a handshake like a bear trap. Even bigger than Tom he stood about 6'5" tall. He was heavily built and had arms that must have been twenty inches around.

Jorge was a relatively small man and I was surprised since I assumed that all Tom's military buddies would be big and tough looking. Jorge was about my height, 5'9" and slight of build. He was aloof and when I tried to engage him in a brief conversation about how he and Tom had met he ignored me and walked away to the bar to get a refill on his beer.

Peter was about Tom's height, and was also lean and muscular like Tom. He and Tom looked more like brothers than Tom & Jerry did. When Samantha arrived from changing in her room all three men hugged her and kissed her hello and Jack lifted her off of her feet and spun her around. I felt a jolt of jealousy but quickly let it pass. If Jack had decided to kiss her passionately on the lips there wasn't much I could have done about it so I told myself that they were just old friends and I put his greeting in its proper context. I was surprised to see that even Jorge warmed up upon Samantha's arrival and he kissed her on the cheek and smiled for the first time. Tom started teasing Samantha and me about our "love affair" and soon all of them were at it except for Jorge, who seemed to grow increasingly angry.

I was blushing like a kid in front of a group of combat veterans and I forced myself to try and act cool in front of them. Jorge became nasty and started to say some offensive things to me about Sam and my relationship. Even though I was intimidated by the group I felt compelled to respond.

"Hey man, why don't you watch your mouth," I said. "Maybe you should slow down on the beers." Jorge was on me in the blink of an eye and had me around the collar.

"Fuck you, puta," he said spitting the words in my face. "I could drink all night and I could still kick your ass without even breaking a sweat."

I assumed incorrectly that since Jorge was my size and perhaps he was even a little lighter that I could handle him but his grip was as powerful as a man twice his size and I couldn't get his hands off of me. I was choking and although I was reluctant to strike him and to escalate things I had no choice, so I hit him with an upper cut in his solarplexus.

My blow didn't exactly knock him over but it did get him to break his grip and to take a step back. My heart started pounding in my chest when I saw the menacing expression on his face and I put up my hands expecting any second to receive a serious ass kicking. He took a step foward. He raised his fists and he began to scream at me in front of a poolside bar full of tourists.

He screamed, "Samantha won't think you're so cute when I get done breaking up your face, you little faggot," and I just about wet my pants.

He lunged at me and out of nowhere Tom appeared and stepped in between us.

"Enough, nino," Tom said, and I thanked God for his appearance.

Jorge's face changed for an instant and he looked confused. At first, he seemed surprised, then became angry again. "Why did you bring him along if he can't even protect himself?

"You won't always be around to protect him Tom. Now get the fuck out of my way and let's see what your girlfriend can do on his own."

I had to say something if I was going to retain any dignity at all and be able to look Samantha in the face again. From what I had seen her do in the jungle to that poacher I was sure that she could take this guy and I couldn't let him humiliate me in front of her. How had I gotten into this situation anyway? This was supposed to be a friendly vacation with some of Tom's friends. I couldn't believe Tom could be friends with this psycho.

"Get out of the way, Tom, I'm warning you," Jorge yelled.

"I'm not afraid of this loud mouth," I said, not believing that I had allowed the words to escape my mouth.

"You heard him, asshole. Step the fuck aside," Jorge bellowed. Then he made the mistake of pushing Tom hard in the chest with both his hands. He shoved Tom backward only a step or two. I heard Jack, who was standing behind Jorge with his arms crossed enjoying the show say, "Oh Shit" and then I saw Tom take a step forward and clench his fists.

"Now you've got more trouble than you can handle, little man," Tom said.

For a moment I saw a flash of fear on Jorge's face and then it was gone. People like him are too insane to know when to use good judgment and aren't really afraid of very much. That's what makes them so dangerous.

"I'm not scared of you like everyone else is, Tom. Size don't mean shit to me if there aint nothing above the shoulders. Fuck You!," Jorge screamed, then he moved with amazing speed. He jumped into the air aiming a roundhouse kick at Tom's face.

Tom made almost no movement and I thought I heard him laugh

as he blocked Jorge's kick absorbing the blow with his forearm. Jorge threw a quick right hook and Tom caught his wrist in his right hand. Tom held his wrist for a second, then let it go and slammed a backhand with his fist closed against the side of Jorge's head.

The noise of the impact was unbelievably loud. It was like a rifleshot or two boards slapping together and it sounded amplified as it echoed around the bar. Jorge dropped to his knees with a puzzled expression on his face and then fell with a thud onto his chest. He appeared to be unconcious. My jaw was wide open. I had never seen anything like it and I looked at Tom in amazement. He'd dispatched a recon Marine, albeit one who was half his size, with little more effort then I would need to take out a Girl Scout.

Jack and Peter walked over and Peter said, "Short fight." Then Jack said, "Jorge never learns. Some day he's going to have to learn to control that Latin temper or he's going to get himself killed." Then Jack turned to me and said, "Tom didn't tell you that Jorge and Sam used to be an item, did he? He should have warned you."

Tom carried Jorge to the pool over his shoulder and then he threw him into the water. Samantha walked over and said, "Shut up Jack. You've got your facts wrong. We were never an item." Then she looked at me and said, "And that was over three years ago."

"I'm proud of you, Jake, for standing up to him," Peter said. "I could see you were scared shitless but you didn't back down. Good for you," he finished and he raised his glass.

"Here's to, Jake, our newest brother in arms. After tonight we might even make you an honorary Marine."

Then Jack and Peter clinked beer mugs and Jack said, "To Jake," and he chugged the full glass in one swallow. Then released a thunderous burp. "Marine Corps salute." Then he winked at me and walked off toward the bar with Peter and Tom. They left me and Samantha alone.

"This is very weird. This whole evening feels surreal," I said. "Tom and Jorge are friends, and Tom just slapped him into La La land. I don't know about you, but my friends and I don't usually try to kill each other. And what's this crap about you and Jorge. It would have been nice if I knew I was going to run into a jealous ex-boyfriend who also happens to be a trained killer with a bad temper."

I was fuming and Samantha said calmly, "Relax Jake. Jorge and I slept together once, three years ago. We were both drunk and I was lonely and it just happened. Nothing ever came of it and I told him it wasn't going to happen again. He's never mentioned it once since then and we've become good friends over the years. I had no reason to expect him to be jealous and there was no reason to tell you about it." Then she hugged me.

I kissed her and she said, "I was proud of you, Jake, for standing up to Jorge, even though it was macho and stupid and it's not at all what I expect from you. I know you did it for me but I don't want you to ever do it again. Jorge would have hurt you bad just to make a point and Tom knew it. That's why he stepped in.

"Let the others play macho man. They're like a bunch of kids, a gang of big, violent, stupid children. That's not what attracts me to you, Jake. It's your sense of humor and your tenderness. Leave the fighting to men who've spent their lives fighting. Promise me."

"I promise you that I will try to avoid violent confrontations whenever I can, but if I have to fight to protect something I care about, then I will."

"Fair enough," she replied. "Now let's get some sleep. We're going to the Greenpeace protest first thing in the morning."

I had been looking forward to it all day. It would be the first environmental protest I had ever attended and I strongly believed in the cause, to save Cozumel's Paradise Reef. It was being destroyed in order to build a pier for additional cruise ships to enter Cozumel.

Tom had told me all about it on the plane and he gave me some pamphlets to read. I told him that I was familiar with it already and that I had already sent a fifty dollar donation to Greenpeace to protect the reef. I mistakenly thought that he would be impressed.

I was hurt when he laughed and said sarcastically, "I'm sure your fifty dollars went a long way to dissuading the cruise ships from continuing their fifty million dollar project, Jake." Then he laughed and tousled my hair and said, "At least your heart's in the right place. Maybe we can find some way to put your good intentions to better use when we reach Mexico."

It was only 7 A.M. and the pier where the ferry boats to Cancun and Playa del Carma docked was already overflowing with people. Members of Greenpeace had already chained themselves to construction cranes and to the props of a Mardi Gras cruise line ship and they were spray painting protest slogans across its hull. I commented to Tom that I thought they were heroic and that I admired their commitment.

Once again, he surprised me by responding that he thought that they were a bunch of self-serving fools and that they were doing nothing today but promoting themselves and their organization. He said in the end the new pier would be built, the reef would be destroyed, and Greenpeace would have accomplished nothing more than to delay construction for a day.

He told me that he had worked for Greenpeace for over five years and that at one time he was a high-ranking member of the organization. If I checked their records I would find that they had really accomplished very little, except he admitted, in educating a small portion of the public.

The rest of the public was mostly too apathetic to care and they usually threw Greenpeace flyers into the trash without even opening the envelopes. There were a few more people who liked to plaster their Volvos with environmental stickers to promote their own yuppie, politically correct self-image, and some who eased their consciences by sending a couple of bucks in the mail.

He told me that he knew for a fact that in boardrooms across the country, executives laughed at them and regarded them with very little respect. They were considered a minor nuisance. I asked him why we had come today if he felt this strongly about it, and I said that I was shocked to hear this type of digression from a man who runs his hotel by the strictest environmental guidelines.

He told me that he did what he could to protect his little part of the world and he reminded me that the reason we had come on this trip was to dive. Today's visit was merely for entertainment. Then he asked me if I had all of my camera equipment ready for photographing the reef. He was especially concerned about the speed of the film I would be using to photograph the pier during our night dive. He instructed me to take as many pictures of the protest as possible, although he would not say why.

There were many guest speakers from several different scientific communities, and environmental groups, and from the Mexican government itself. The crowd had thickened to over 10,000 people.

Only Tom, Jack, Peter and I were at the protest. Samantha wasn't feeling well and Jerry said he didn't like crowds. Jorge was laying out at the pool with a massive headache. Tom and I ran into him at breakfast and he surprised me by apologizing to us both for his behavior the night before. He was practically begging for Tom's forgiveness and I was shocked at the change in his attitude in just twelve hours.

"Just goes to show you what a good whack in the head can do," I said to Tom as we walked away. "Maybe I should have let Jorge give you a whack then, Jake. Maybe then you wouldn't be such a wise ass."

"I was just kidding,." I said, surprised at his angry remark.

Jorge's ear was swollen and it looked like a head of red cabbage was attached to the side of his head.

"What was that all about last night?" I asked Tom.

"I'm sorry I snapped at you.

"I'm upset about having to strike a friend of mine even if it was to protect another friend. Jorge's really not a bad guy. Believe it or not, he has a good heart. He has a bad temper, and when he drinks he loses control. If I had been paying attention I would have cut him off earlier.

"I had to hit him because I recognized that he was in one of his most dangerous moods and I didn't want things to get out of control. As it is, the manager of the hotel told Jerry we wouldn't be welcomed back to play again."

"It was a pretty bizarre scene, you have to admit, Tom. First they see you sitting there on stage singing Harry Chapin songs and playing Cat Stevens' "Peace Train" like a couple of folksingers from Woodstock, then you're knocking a man unconscious at poolside. You can't really fault the hotel."

Tom laughed and I was glad to see we were okay again. By mid afternoon the protest had deteriorated and total pandemonium had broken out on the dock. People on the dock began to pelt the Mexican authorities with eggs. They were dragging people away in handcuffs. Eggs were flying everywhere and I noticed a couple of clever young Mexican entrepreneurs had set up a stand and were selling them for five American dollars a dozen.

Jack and Peter had just come back from looking around the dock and I laughed when I saw that Jack was covered with egg from head to toe. "I got caught in a free for all at the end of the pier," Jack said. "I barely made it out of there when the fireboat arrived and started spraying people. People were falling everywhere and some flew right past me off the dock and into the water."

"Let's get the hell out of here," Tom said.

"You see what I mean, Jake, a total fucking circus. When it plays tonight on CNN the CEOs of Mardi Gras Cruise Lines and Consorcio H will probably wet their pants laughing."

When we returned to the hotel, Tom and I sat by the pool and discussed the day's events.

"Listen to me, Jake. I'm going to give you a quick lesson on environmental politics.

"Over a year ago, a complaint was filed by three Mexican environmental groups opposed to the building of the 848 foot pier over one of Cozumel's most popular shallow dive sites. The Commission for Environmental Cooperation, or CEC, a panel created by the North American Free Trade Agreement to monitor how well the U.S., Mexico, and Canada enforce environmental law, began an investigation.

"Rachel Vinson a spokesperson for the CEC said, that although the CEC has no power to halt the project or to impose sanctions if it finds violations, our recommendations will have the weight of the public shame factor. Can you believe that load of political horseshit? The Mexican government violated its own environmental law by allowing development group Consorcio H to build the pier. According to the Mexican Center for Environmental Law, the government failed to consider Cozumel's marine sanctuary designation and local laws, and didn't evaluate the environmental impact of the developers entire plan, which includes passenger terminals and an eighteen hole golf course.

"Gustavo Alanis-Ortega, president of the Mexican Center for Environmental Law, said, and I quote, 'This is the first issue the NAFTA commission has deemed worthy to follow up, so in a way we've had a certain victory.'"

Tom was quiet for a moment and then said, "That man thinks because NAFTA looked this way for a moment that his group accomplished something. The CEC thinks that they accomplished something because of the thirty-second sound bite that today's protest will receive on television, that they will now have the power of public opinion on their side. They see that as a victory."

I was impressed by Tom's wealth of knowledge and his strong conviction and passion for the subject. He was right, of course, despite the circle jerk of the politicians in the press, the pier was undoubtedly going to be built and hundreds of thousands of tourists would flood into Cozumel, turning it into another Cancun or Acapulco and I told him so.

"I've chartered a boat and tomorrow we are going to dive Paradise Reef so you can see first hand what is being destroyed, not an abstract idea or a political platform but an ancient living organism, a thing of rare beauty that we will never see again.

"I want you to take as many pictures as possible tomorrow, and I will forward them on to several magazine editors that I know and your work will be published alongside a letter to the editor which I will write. You and me, working together as a team to save a little peace of heaven, how does that sound, Jake?"

I was excited about the idea of working with Tom and in doing something of significance and my adrenaline was flowing. I jumped up and grabbed Tom's hand and said, "That sounds great, Tom, I'm in."

We awoke at 6 the next morning and chartered a boat called *The Cross*, captained by a grossly overweight and scraggly old Mexican named Chucho. There were six of us on board. I had learned that Jerry had already flown home and would not be traveling with us. Jack and Samantha were sparring around on the back of the boat, practicing what looked to me like a cross between tai chi and karate. Samantha was wearing a blue skin-tight nylon dive skin and Jack was wearing a pair of black swim trunks. He looked like the actor Carl Weathers from the movie *Rocky*, and his skin was shiny and wet with sweat.

He was taunting Samantha while he easily deflected her blows, which were thrown with lightning quickness. Samantha threw kick after kick. She was spinning and jumping in the air and seemed like an insect that Jack kept swatting away.

"Give her a break, you big bully," I yelled.

"My hero," Jack responded. "Maybe you would like to be her champion and defend her honor like a knight in King Arthur's court, Jake."

"That's okay," I said. "Please continue, she was doing just fine."

Tom came down from the flying bridge and I said, "Tom would you act as my second and give my lady a hand against the Black Knight. That's not a reference to your color, Jack, just your demeanor."

"Don't do me any favors, Jake," Jack said.

"I have no desire to mix it up with Big Tom. You may not know it but when Tom wasn't in the field as a SEAL team leader he was the senior weapons and martial arts instructor at San Diego. He taught self-defense and worked out with some of America's biggest bad asses from units that included Special Operations insertion teams."

"That was a million years ago, before I got old," Tom said. "Besides I'm too busy to play games."

"I think he's afraid of you Jack," Peter yelled down from the bridge, where he was drinking beer with Chucho. "Fifty bucks says Jack throws Tom overboard. Any takers?" Peter yelled out.

"I'll take that action," I said. "No offense, Jack."

"I got five dollars on the big black man," the captain chimed in, which made everyone on board, including Tom, laugh.

"What about you Jorge? You want to make a wager?" Peter asked.

"I'd be the last one to bet against Tom in a fight," Jorge responded and he rubbed his head to accentuate his point.

Tom was a big powerful man and I knew he was a tough son of a bitch but Jack was built like a redwood tree. His legs were twice the size of mine and he looked like you could hit him with a baseball bat on any part of his body and he would barely feel it.

"Okay," Tom said, "enough. It's not happening," and he sat down next to Jorge and leaned back against the rack of scuba tanks.

"Chicken shit," Peter yelled from above, then he sprayed beer down on Tom's head, hitting me and Jorge as well.

"Okay," Tom said. "One five minute round if you're up for it Jack."

We all cheered as Tom pulled off the Syracuse Orangemen sweatshirt he was wearing and stood in the sunlight opposite Jack. In the strong light his body looked deeply tanned and was lean and heavily muscled. His abdomen looked carved from granite and even his ribs were covered in thick hard muscle and stood out in strong definition. His chest and arms were also muscular, not bulky like a wieghtlifters, but were lean and ropy. Every sinewy muscle in his triceps and chest rippled when he moved. He looked like Michaelangelo's David come to life.

He took a fighter's stance but he kept moving his arms in the air. First up and then he would sweep them sideways in what resembled the movements I used to do in karate class when I was twelve.

Jack moved more like George Foreman or Joe Frazier. He was lumbering in slow motion and with no wasted movement.

"No hitting in the face or below the waist," Tom said.

Chucho stopped the boat and we all watched the battle of these titans, "The Flex-ico in Mexico" or "The Rumble in the Yucatan" is how Don King probably would have promoted it.

"Start your watch, Jake," Tom called out.

As soon as I said "GO!" Jack rushed at Tom with surprising speed and he swung his huge arms at his chest. Tom ducked underneath Jack's first swing and while he was crouched down low to the ground he threw a lightning combination of punches into Jack's stomach.

Jack took a step back and yelled, "That's it! That's all you got. Shit I've been hit harder by some of my ex-wives."

Tom jumped in the air and spun a backward roundhouse kick at Jack's face missing his nose by no more than an inch and it backed Jack up. In an instant, Tom followed it up with a sidekick to Jacks chest which would have cracked a smaller man's sternum.

Jack fell back against the tanks as we leapt out of the way and he sat for an instant rubbing his enormous chest.

"No head shots you said," Jack complained.

"I didn't hit you in the face, did I?" Tom responded.

"Two minutes left," I called out.

Jack jumped to his feet and slammed into Tom, knocking him backward, and started throwing combination after combination at Tom's chest and stomach. The attack was steady and powerful and Tom blocked the punches with his arms as fast as Jack could throw them. But the force of the blows was taking their toll and he was beating Tom back against the side wall of the boat below the flying bridge.

Jack used his size and weight to his advantage and pinned Tom against the wall. While Tom wrestled with him, Jack managed to turn him around and get him in a bear hug. Jack lifted Tom off his feet and stumbled to the center of the deck and he began to squeeze the life out of him. Tom's face was red and the veins in his head were bulging. Jack was yelling like a madman for Tom to cry mercy and Samantha was screaming for Jack to let Tom go. Suddenly, Tom went limp. We all thought he was unconscious. Then he threw his weight forward and in the blink of an eye he scissored his legs backward in between Jack's. With all of his strength he pulled Jack's legs out from under him as he snapped his neck and back and threw his body weight backward. Jack stumbled backward holding Tom in his arms and he fell. There was an earsplitting crash as both of them smashed through the teak door to the cabin below and tumbled out of sight. We heard a loud crash below and Jack scream out in pain and then we heard nothing.

Chucho jumped from the bridge in a panic when he heard the hardwood boards shatter. Tom rolled off of Jack, who was laying stunned, wedged tightly into the small space in the cabin below. Tom climbed out, visibly shaken, and Jorge handed him a beer, which he gratefully accepted.

"Help that son of a bitch up," Tom coughed out to me and Peter.

"My boat! Hijo de Puta!" Chucho screamed.

"We'll pay for any damages, Capitan," Tom said and he reached in his pocket and pulled out a roll of hundred dollar bills that were secured by a rubber band. He peeled off 10 and handed them to Captain Chucho.

Jack was standing, with the assistance of Jorge and Peter, as Samantha pulled several large splinters from his bloody back.

"When are you guys going to grow up?" Sam asked. "Someone always gets hurt." She sounded like a frustrated mother that was scolding her children.

Jack walked up to Tom and they hugged. "There isn't another man on earth that could do that to me, you tricky bastard," Jack said lovingly.

"Another minute and I would have passed out," Tom answered. "You didn't leave me too many options."

It was obvious that the two men had been friends for many years and that, although neither of them would ever admit it, they shared a deep love and respect for each other. We drove the boat another fifteen minutes to Paradise reef and then we tied off to a mooring site near one of the new pilings for the pier. After equipment checks and after I tested my camera equipment, we entered the water. When we descended to around twenty feet, Tom led us to the base of one of the pilings and we could see where extensive damage had been done to the reef.

Whole sections of coral had been obliterated and the reef was dying for fifty feet around each section. You could see where high explosives had been set and Tom signaled to me to take pictures of the area, especially around the pilings. We swam all along the reef and saw sea fans that had been three feet across that were now dead and torn and were laying on the sandy bottom. Giant brain corals and barrel sponges were cracked and torn and were either already dead or dying. We heard banging ahead and swam to where Samantha was calling to us and when we swam up to her she pointed to a large sea turtle that was laying dead in the sand, its shell split in half and with one of its flippers torn away. She was crying in her mask. My head was pounding with anger and I wanted to strike out at someone or something. Tom told me to photograph the turtle while Jack held it up and I shot over half a roll, bracketing to make sure I exposed the film properly. We dove for another thirty minutes and I remembered the last time I had dove this reef only a year ago. It was one of the most beautiful reefs in the Caribbean and it was known for its vast, diverse marine life.

The reef was known to be a great place for spotting sea turtles and was home to thousands of grouper, parrotfish, and an extensive variety of macro life, from shrimps to anemones. The reef was still mostly intact and it wasn't too late too save it if construction could be stopped. The reef systems can rejuvenate over time if left undisturbed, but if more pilings were driven into the sea and if cruise ships the size of skyscrapers frequented the area the reef would be completely dead in less than a year.

We all got back on board and everyone was quiet. Samantha sat beside me and I held her while the boat headed back to port. Tom told me and Samantha that we would be leaving early tomorrow and that Jack, Peter and Jorge would be coming with us.

He came and sat beside me and Sam and said, "How did it feel, Jake, to see man's greed and indifference to nature up close and personal? It's not the same when you read about it in a magazine, or you watch it on TV, or when you gloss over it in a flyer that arrives in your mail with a free World Wildlife Foundation sticker for your window?"

"It made me sick, Tom."

"What else? What else did it make you feel?" He was looking into my eyes with an intense stare.

"It made me angry. It made me so fucking angry that I wanted to break something or hit someone."

"Good, Jake. That's how it makes me feel. Now imagine seeing what you just saw occurring every day in every part of the world on such a colossal scale that it would horrify you if you knew the full magnitude of it.

"Imagine how angry you would feel then and what lengths you might go to in order stop it. I want you to think about that on the way home, then we'll talk again."

There were a lot of questions to be answered when I returned to Honduras. So many strange and thought provoking things had occurred in the past week that my mind was reeling. There was something very odd about Tom and his friends and this entire trip here this week. I've been on a lot of vacations but this trip didn't resemble any sort of vacation I had ever taken and I needed to think and sort through all the things I'd seen and heard to try to make some sense of them. I'd been in sales long enough to know when someone was building up to something, and I sensed that Tom was taking the long way around in asking me something important.

There was something strangely familiar about Tom and his friends but I couldn't put my finger on it. I had a strong instinctual feeling that all was not as it appeared to be and I had begun to feel anxious and uncomfortable over the past few days.

What I saw today appalled me and I wanted to do something to stop it. I felt frustrated and I didn't know how to begin. When we returned to Arrecife, I would work with Tom to get my photos and his description of the destruction published. For the first time in my life I felt that I might be able to do something significant and that I might actually be in a position to make a contribution to a worthwhile cause.

I really felt that I might be able to make a difference. I was excited about the prospect and I knew that destiny or fate or maybe even God had finally set my feet on the right path and as I held Samantha in my arms I thought about my mother and how proud she would have been of me today. I made a promise that I would do whatever it took to save that reef.

CHAPTER 22

"Breathe through your nose," Tom yelled back to me as he sprinted the last quarter mile to our destination. We were headed to the 200 foot rocky arch that hung over North Beach like an ivy-covered trellis. In the past three weeks since we had returned from Cozumel, my speed and my endurance had increased to the point where I could finally keep up with Samantha. I was in the best shape of my life. I weighed 172 pounds, only three pounds more than when I was a nineteen-year-old summer camp counselor.

In the last two weeks, Tom had begun to join us on our runs and to my great dismay I found that I now had someone new to chase after. Tom ran less than a seven and a half minute mile for the entire five mile round trip run to North Beach and even Sam who was in phenomenal condition had trouble keeping up with him. Occasionally, Tom would slow down so that we could talk and he never appeared to be out of breath. I cursed him as I struggled to find a rhythm and to control my labored breathing.

"Look on the bright side," Sam said as I pulled up alongside her. "After a month of running after Tom you'll be in good enough condition to run a marathon." We began to quicken our pace toward the finish line that Tom had just drawn in the sand ahead.

"Come on, Jake! Don't let her beat you! Stretch it out!" Tom yelled.

I lengthened my stride and I ran as fast as I could. My legs were numb and seemed to be moving on autopilot. The thick sand was pulling at my feet and made me feel as if I were pulling a train behind me. My chest was pounding as I tried desperately to hold it together for the last thirty feet. Samantha and I were neck and neck but when we were fifteen feet away I grabbed the back of her shirt and pulled her backward as I shot across the finish line and collapsed in the sand.

"You asshole!" Samantha screamed at me as she walked up to where I was lying on my back choking for oxygen.

"Jake," Tom said shaking his head, "you cheating bastard."

"For the first time you almost had her, fair and square, and you ruined it. I'm very disappointed in you."

"You wimp," Sam added. "I took it easy on you. I was going to let you win by a nose anyway and you had to fuck it up."

I couldn't believe my ears. Sam was really mad about a stupid little race I never wanted any part of, a competition that Tom forced on us. I stood up slowly, feeling pain in every joint. "I can't believe you two. I had no intention of racing at all. That was Tom's idea of fun. I would have been happy just to finish without an embolism or a massive MI.

"Jesus, I thought I was competitive. I know you're faster than me, Sam, and I also know that you're in better shape. Does that make you happy? Or do you want to humiliate me some more in front of Tom?"

"All right everyone, calm down," Tom said. "We're all friends, and Jake's right. This run wasn't meant to be a contest, just exercise. Kiss and make up now, that's an order from the man who signs both your paychecks."

"I'm sorry Sam," I said. "I knew you had me at the end. I had nothing left and I became desperate."

"Three weeks ago you wouldn't have made it to the finish at all," Sam replied graciously. "You've come a long way and I'm proud of you."

"That's better," Tom said.

We walked under the arch and when I looked up I could see that hundreds of birds had made their nests in the rocks above. There were flowering vines that covered the sides and were hanging down hundreds of feet from the rocks above. The arch sat above the northernmost part of the island and during low tide we could walk out to a little island that sat off of the end like an appendage. The water was high now and waves were gently breaking at our feet, just below the arch. The little island was separated from us by over fifty yards of water.

"Let's swim out," Tom said.

"I don't think so, Tom," I replied. "I'm dead tired and we still have to run all the way back to the hotel, besides I'm not a very good swimmer."

"Come on Jake, it's not that far and there isn't any current," Sam said with that look in her eyes that could talk me into almost anything.

"If you start to sink, I'll tow you to shore," Tom said.

For an instant, I thought about saying okay. The peer pressure reminded me of the first time I went out drinking with my friends in high school. I hated the bitter taste of the beer they kept handing me and when they weren't looking I poured my beer on the ground and then pretended that I was drunk for the rest of the night. The humiliation of them teasing me about it when I was finally discovered made my face flush at the memory.

"No way," I said. "You two go without me. I need to sit and rest and catch my breath."

"You're sure?" Samantha asked.

I wanted to ask her to sit with me but I told her to go ahead and the two of them ran to the edge of the arch, dove into the water at the same time, and began swimming in strong powerful strokes toward the little island. I felt a little jealous and a little insecure and inadequate but I reminded myself that they were two superbly well-conditioned athletes and that up until a couple of months ago the only thing I exercised were my options.

The last two weeks, Tom had begun to teach me some basic self-defense and we would spar with Jack and Jorge at sunset on the beach when most of the guests had left. Tom told me that Peter had to go to Australia to follow up on a story for the magazine that he worked for.

Jorge and I had become friends despite our rough introduction, and he always spoke of Tom with something akin to hero worship. Jorge was a high school and college wrestling star and he taught me some throws and holds. He was very powerful for his size and one day he even managed to tie Tom up in a scissors hold until he broke it with sustained brute force. Jack was a big teddy bear with a heart as big as his body and I liked him immensely. He showed me some pressure points and some key zones on a person's body to strike that would quickly immobilize anyone. Jack wrote blue grass songs and played the harmonica and a little guitar, and one evening he joined Tom & Jerry at one of their performances. Jerry was still tied up in the lab most of the time but on the few occasions that he joined us he was cheerful and friendly. One night, we were having a cookout for the guests on the beach with a clam bake and an enormous bon fire when Jerry showed up with two vintage bottles of Dom Perignon, announcing jubilantly that he had achieved a major breakthrough in his laboratory.

I had no idea what Jerry actually did all day holed up in the shack up on the hill. Tom had told me that the shed was strictly off limits, even to me, and Jerry would never answer any specific questions about his work. I would see him occasionally down by the water, returning from a shore dive with a plastic baggy filled with various marine animals, from jellyfish to sea urchins, and once he even had a juvenile moray eel. Samantha and I had grown closer the past two weeks and she slept in my room almost every night. I was happier than I could ever remember and at various times when I was certain that Samantha was also in love with me I was tempted to repeat the words I spoke to her that excruciating night on the dock.

I was startled out of my daydreaming when I heard a loud crack like the report of a rifle and jumped to my feet. I ran to the edge of the water under the arch and I saw a small fishing boat with four men aboard disappear behind the other side of the tiny island. I heard Samantha scream.

My heart was pounding and I dove into the water and swam as fast and as hard as I could toward the island. My body was flooded with adrenaline and my only thought was that I had to protect Samantha. I was halfway there when I heard another shot and my right leg began to cramp. I tried to stretch out my ham string as I floated on my back and the pain in my thigh as the muscle contracted into a ball felt like a stab wound from a red hot dagger. I rolled onto my back and with my leg extended I back stroked, using only my arms until I reached the beach.

My mind was racing and I had a horrible image of finding Sam and Tom shot dead on the beach. I washed ashore after what felt like an hour and I limped and hopped toward the other side of the beach. When I came around a large rock I saw that Tom and Samantha were surrounded by four large men. One of the men was the same one that Samantha and I had encountered in the jungle. He was cursing in Spanish at Samantha and the others held Tom in abeyance with their rifles.

I yelled to Sam and asked if she were all right as I limped over to where they were standing.

"You should have waited on the beach, Jake," Sam said.

The fat man came over to me and spoke into my face, just inches away. His breath reeked of a combination of cheap cigars and even cheaper whiskey. I couldn't understand a word he said even after months of learning Spanish from Carmen and Samantha and I asked Samantha to translate.

"He said more or less, that this is his lucky day finding the little man who snuck up on him in the woods and that now he will kick your ass face to face."

Tom stepped up and pushed the man in front of him backward and spoke in Spanish in a calm measured tone that sounded full of contempt. I asked Sam again for a translation.

"Tom told them that he is bored with them and their little game. He told them that if they leave right now he will forget they were ever here, but that if they continue to annoy him he will load their broken bodies back into their boat, then set it on fire."

"Big words for man with a gun on him," the fat man finally spoke in English.

"First, I have a little fun with your girlfriend, big man." After he said that he reached up and grabbed Samantha's breasts. I reacted without thinking. I felt a jolt of white hot anger course through my body. I grabbed the man by the hair and I pulled him back away from Sam. Suddenly, I felt my legs go limp and I dropped to the sand, feeling dizzy and lightheaded.

I realized as pain shot down my spine that one of the men had slammed his rifle butt into my back between my shoulder blades. I looked up to see through a sea of white spots that at least I had given Tom the diversion he needed to leap into action. He kicked the man that had struck me in the throat and then he spun around and slammed his heel into another man's groin.

Samantha was also on the move and she was throwing a combination of punches at the face of one of her assailants and she knocked him to the ground. I rose slowly to my feet and I saw the fat man stand up and raise his rifle at Tom. It seemed like I was watching a slow motion video as I watched his finger pull back slowly on the trigger. I leapt the two feet between us and slammed my shoulder into his back. The shot went wide and the rifle thundered in my ear and deafened me with the blast.

The man spun around and faced me with a look of pure animal hatred. He rushed toward me and swung his fist toward my face. I ducked under the punch and, remembering what Jack had taught me, slammed my fist into his throat with all my might. I heard his larynx and the small bones in his windpipe break with a small cracking sound.

The man dropped to his knees clutching his throat and his face turned red. The veins in his neck and forehead were bulging. The other men were laying about in various stages of destruction. They were rolling in the sand and moaned softly in their barely conscious states. Tom walked over to me and grabbed me around the shoulders as Samantha threw her arms around me. The fat man collapsed on his face in the sand and did not appear to be breathing, which alarmed me greatly, but didn't seem to bother Samantha or Tom in the least.

"You were amazing, Jake," Samantha said. "I can't believe you swam out here and risked your life to save us. That man could have just as easily shot you." She covered my face with kisses.

"You saved my life, Jake," Tom said. "I'll never forget that. Never."

"Excuse me, guys, but I think I just killed a man and the thought of rotting in a Honduran dungeon doesn't exactly fill me with joy."

Tom knelt down next to the man and rolled him over and touched his carotid artery with his fingers and felt for a pulse. Then he leaned over and listened to his breathing.

"He'll live, but he won't be swallowing anything solid for awhile. No, it will be strictly juice through a straw. Nothing else is going to fit through his swollen windpipe for at least two weeks."

"You learn fast, Jake," Tom said with pride. "I'll have to commend Jack on his instruction when we get back."

Samantha was glued to my side and she was beaming at me with pride as I turned to ask Tom how we were going to get back to the main island. There was no way I could make the swim with a pulled ham string and with my shoulder feeling the way it did. I could barely move my right arm now.

"Our ride is right over there Jake," Tom said pointing to the men's boat. "I'll phone the authorities to pick up this crew when we get back to the hotel. I don't think they'll be going anywhere for awhile."

We boarded the boat and sped off toward the hotel. It had taken us nearly half an hour to run to the end of the island but it only took seven minutes to return by sea. I was in a great deal of pain and my back and shoulder blade had become almost paralyzed. I could barely lift my right arm and was afraid something might be broken. Samantha was fawning all over me and I felt overcome with affection for her. While Tom was driving the boat he kept turning around to check on my condition, and he smiled at me and looked at me with genuine concern and caring. I felt closer to the two of them at that moment than I ever had to anyone, including my own family, and I hoped we would always be together. When we got to the dock, Tom barked out orders to two young workers who were sitting on the edge. They were dangling their feet over the side and were smoking American cigarettes. Tom lifted me in his arms like I weighed an ounce and he carried me up the stairs and to my bungalow. Normally I would have been embarrassed and I did entertain the idea of walking by myself but when I tried to stand up I almost fell over. I was dizzy and felt nauseous.

Samantha returned with a syringe which she told me was filled with Demoral and she injected it into my rear end. She pulled the covers up around me, nestled beside me and stroked my head until I fell asleep. I was exhausted and later Sam said that I was in a mild state of shock. The Demoral began to work its magic almost immediately. I felt like I had left my body and was floating above the bed. When I woke up, I could hear Tom and Samantha talking about me as if I had left the room. Their voices sounded like they were in another room or in a tunnel and I couldn't understand most of what they were saying. I thought I might have been dreaming when I thought I heard the voices of Jack, Jorge, and Jerry suddenly blend in with their voices. All the words overlapped and their sentences began to run together.

"Sons of Bitches." "How bad?" "He's not ready." "No, Tom." "Saved my life." "Tough little guy, surprised me."

"LIONFISH"?

"Don't worry. He's asleep."

Samantha crying.

"Leave him out of it. He's not like us." Then blackness.

I had dark haunted dreams filled with danger and fear but throughout the long night I had a comforting feeling that there was some protective presence that kept watch over me.

CHAPTER 23

It had been two full weeks of light duty and rest since our encounter with the locals at North Beach. When we returned to the hotel that day, Tom had them picked up by the local authorities. He went to visit them in the small makeshift jail they had set up on Roatan. Tom had learned that in addition to being pouchers on his land, a land they had hunted on for many years before his purchase of it, they were also hired laborers at the new resort on Roatan that Tom had actively opposed. Tom spoke with the men privately for over half an hour and when he left the island no charges had been filed.

I was the only one who seemed upset by this news and neither Samantha, Jack, Jorge, or Jerry questioned Tom about his motives or objected to his decision. Tom explained to me that the men would never return to his island, of that he was certain. He told me that they were poor and that he had no interest in ruining their lives or in endangering their livelihoods. It would only aggravate their relationship with the local Honduran people and it would make them more unwelcome in the islands. I was working in the office, doing paperwork, guest greetings, and correspondence. I also handled check-ins until my shoulder was completely healed. Three days after the attack I had a large purplish and black bruise on my back and I could not lift my arm or rotate my shoulder for over a week.

The best part was the hero treatment I was receiving from the entire staff, including Carmen, who hugged me every time I entered the bar area. I was getting a lot of sympathy from Samantha who would not let me do anything for myself. I was writing the story of the encounter in my journal. I was laying on a hammock under a tree near the beach when Tom and Jerry walked up to me and told me that they had something important to talk to me about. Their tone was serious, and Jerry looked upset and distracted. I thought that either something bad had happened or that they were upset with me about something I had done.

"Is everything okay?" I asked. "Manelo hasn't died has he?"

Manelo I learned was the name of the man who's throat I had crushed.

"No Jake. Everything's fine," Tom replied. "We have something to show you and it involves a great deal of risk on our part," Jerry said. "There has been some lively discussion surrounding you and what we are about to tell you. I want you to know up front that I was against it, but I was out voted by the rest of the group."

"You guys have really got my interest piqued. What's going on? This is all very mysterious and a bit dramatic. Am I being fired?"

"Follow us, Jake. Then we will answer all the questions you want to ask, and I'm sure there will be plenty," Tom said.

I followed them to the stairs at the south end of the beach, which led up to the hiking trails to the north end of the island.

"We are going to the shed at the top of the island, the one you've been asking about for the past two months," Tom said as we came to the top of the hill near the uppermost bungalow.

"Samantha is already there waiting for us, so are Jorge and Jack," Jerry added.

"I thought the tool shed or workshop or whatever it is was strictly off limits," I said.

"It is Jake, to the guests and to most of the staff, and until today, to you as well," Tom said. "After today, depending upon your reaction to our discussion, you will be able to come and go from the shed as you please," Jerry said.

We came around the bend in the trail where the shed became visible and I could see the outside floodlights had been turned on as the sun began to set behind us. We walked up to the heavy steel door and Tom removed a plastic card, which looked like a credit card, from his pocket. He slid it down through a black metal card scanner that was attached to the outside wall near the door, then he punched in a series of numbers on the keypad that was beside it. There was the sound of gears turning and locks being electronically released.

Tom turned to me when the door was halfway opened and with the most serious foreboding expression I had ever seen on his face he said. "Jake, you saved my life two weeks ago and I made a promise to you after you had fallen asleep that I would never let any harm come to you, that I would always protect you. I told you that from that day forward we would always be brothers and I meant it.

"Do you trust me?" He looked me in the eyes and held me by the shoulders. "Of course I trust you. I trust you with my life."

"That's exactly what you're about to do Jake," Jerry said. "And we're about to trust you with our lives and the lives of perhaps a hundred other people."

Tom looked at Jerry for an instant and said, "It's time. Lets do it."

We stepped through the door and a bright aqua light began to flood the room. My heart was steadily pounding from fear, apprehension, and profound curiosity, and I felt a little dizzy and light-headed. I stepped into the dimly lit room and my eyes were immediately drawn to a large Plexiglas tank that stood in the middle of the room. It was filled with jellyfish of a variety I had never seen.

On the shelves and workbenches around the room were all sorts of laboratory equipment, including chemistry analyzers and sterilizing equipment. There were several different sizes and shapes of beakers that were filled with different colored chemicals. The lab was very modern and was impressive considering the surroundings. I finally got to see where Jerry spent the majority of his time.

The floor was covered with white linoleum and the walls and counters looked to be covered in some type of a solid surface material similar to Dupont Corian. There were no visible seams or grout anywhere. There was also an enormous amount of stainless steel in the room. It was everywhere, from the sinks to the commercial freezers that lined the walls. The walls above the laboratory work areas were concrete block and the ceiling was built with heavy steel braces and concrete shingles. The place looked like it could survive a category 5 hurricane.

There was no sign of Samantha or the others anywhere and I turned to Tom and said "This is very impressive Tom, but I don't understand the need for all the secrecy. Where is Samantha? I don't see her."

"Follow us Jake. We'll take you to her," Jerry replied.

They led me to a large, white painted wooden door on the back left wall. There was a blue ladies room sign on it. Were they taking me to see Samantha in the bathroom? When they opened the door I saw to my surprise that there was a large polished stainless steel wall behind it. There was no door handle or opening in sight. I turned to Tom with a puzzled look on my face and he smiled and told me to wait a moment.

He opened a red metal fire alarm box on the wall nearby and hidden inside was another scan system for his card. He quickly slid his card through. In seconds there was a loud whirring sound, which I recognized from living in New York City most of my life was an elevator. The stainless steel wall slid back and did in fact reveal the inside of a small elevator. We stepped inside and Tom pressed the only button on the otherwise completely sterile interior and the door closed. I felt my stomach drop as we began to descend very rapidly to what felt like several stories before we came to an abrupt stop.

My head was spinning. I was trying to make some deduction from what I was seeing and I combined it with what I had known about Tom and Jerry and the other curious observances that I had made in the past several months, including the trip to Cozumel, and my hands began to shake. This installation had to have cost a fortune to build and I could not imagine what awaited me on the other side of that door.

My only comfort was in knowing that Samantha was involved, and if what they told me was true she was waiting for me on the other side. The door opened and to my great relief Samantha ran up and hugged me.

"Whatever you see or hear, Jake, you must be careful to control your reactions and to think before you speak," she whispered to me.

My eyes scanned the room quickly as we stepped all the way in and I could see immediately that it was at least four times the size of the upstairs laboratory. There were weapons everywhere. They were hanging on the walls or were standing in the middle of the floor. In the center of the room appeared to be several large computer mainframes and workstations and there appeared to be a very sophisticated communications center.

There were undersea maps and charts on several walls, and I saw diagrams and drawings on large wooden easels that were standing near the back walls. Off to the right was a small classroom with twenty or more chairs and I saw a blackboard attached to the wall in front that had the words "Operation Corona" written on it in large letters.

On several walls were enlargements of the photographs I had taken in Cozumel. There were pictures of the pier and the protesters and the pilings that had been driven into the reef. There were also photographs of several people I didn't recognize and some large blueprints and photographs of several cruise ships tacked to the corkboard easels around the room.

I stood there looking around for over five minutes and no one said a word. It seemed to me that I was being allowed to discover in part, on my own, what was going on here. My eyes kept coming back to the enormous amount of munitions and armament in the room. There were rifles and machine pistols and rockets everywhere, and in the back of the room were two full-size zodiac boats and a disassembled helicopter gunship. The light was very weak and only half the room was lit so I had a hard time making out a drawing or a logo on the side of one of the boats.

I thought I recognized it and I squinted to see it better. "What is that symbol on that boat, Sam?" I asked her quietly. I was in a mild state of disbelief and shock. I felt frozen for the moment in time not knowing if I wanted answers to the multitude of questions I had.

"Turn on the lights, so that Jake can see better," Tom said.

All of a sudden, the room became brightly lit and I could see Jack and Jorge, who had been standing in the shadows come into full view. I turned to look back at the boat and gasped out loud when I saw what had been crudely painted on its side in dark red paint.

It was a red rectangular box with a red trident inside and I spun around with a look of terror and confusion in my eyes to face Tom. I tried to speak but for a moment the words would not leave my throat as he stared back at me with a look of complete understanding.

"My God, you're RedTide, all of you," I screamed surprising myself and startling Jerry.

"What about you," I said to Samantha as I backed away from her and bumped into the edge of a table that held some strange looking scuba gear on top of it. "Are you part of this?"

"Calm down," Tom said as he walked up to me.

"Who are you?" I said to him as I felt for the edge of the table and looked madly around the room. I backed away and knocked my leg against a chair.

"Within this organization and among my men I am known as Lionfish," Tom said and his words slammed into me with the force of a tornado, knocking me into the chair beside me.

"I told you he couldn't handle it," Jerry said. "He's a civilian and although he may have some good intentions this is way beyond his ability to comprehend."

"Don't talk about him like he isn't even here, Stingray," Samantha said. "This would be alot for anyone to absorb. I remember when Tom approached me about joining the organization five years ago. I was just as blown away."

Joining the organization? Is that what this was all about? I thought.

Samantha had called Jerry Stingray, "Lionfish & Stingray, Tom & Jerry," I thought, putting it all together.

My mind was racing. This felt so unreal. I had seen or read about these people for over ten years but never in my wildest imaginings could I have predicted this moment. I was frightened, but I remembered what Samantha had told me about being calm and choosing my words carefully. I couldn't let them think I was weak, or worse yet, a threat to them. I was looking at Tom like I had never seen him before and I could not reconcile the man I knew with the ruthless terrorist the world knew as Lionfish.

Tom came over to me and pulled up a chair as the others including Sam gathered around. "I know this is a shock for you, Jake, and I don't expect you to say anything sensible tonight," Tom said. "I just want you to listen to what we have to say for awhile and I want you to just go about your life as normally as possible for the next few days. In a few days we can continue this conversation and discuss our future together.

"I will tell you that we want you to join us and I will ask for your promise that everything we tell you tonight will be held in the strictest confidence. You cannot talk with anyone about this, not your sister, not your friends, not even to any of us while any guests are around. We have taken an enormous risk by exposing ourselves to you and in letting you know our main base of operations. There are over 250 members of RedTide worldwide and only 10-15 people know of this location. I trust you Jake, and even though good judgment tells me that I'm making a mistake in telling you who we are, my heart tells me that I'm doing the right thing. We want you to join us. We want you to become an integral part of our organization.

"I will always tell you the truth Jake. Our work is very dangerous and most of what we do is illegal. We are fugitives from all the law enforcement agencies of the world and if you join us your life will never be the same. We will try to keep you functioning in a civilian capacity most of the time and you can continue to work here. But I also have to tell you that you will constantly be monitored by our own security personnel in order to contain leaks and you will never have a private conversation with a friend or family member again.

"You will never return to the life you once knew, and RedTide will have to review any future alliances, either personal or professional, that you might make. Any major life choices as to where you live or where you go will also have to meet with our approval.

"That's the down side and I don't want you to underestimate it. It involves a great deal of sacrifice. On the up side is the fact that for the first time in your life you will be doing something useful and for the first time you will really be able to make a difference in the future of this planet. You will be a soldier in the war to save the environment.

"You will go to bed proud of who you are and what you do and you will wake up each morning with the knowledge that you are doing something to right the numerous wrongs in the world.

"Do you remember during the Gulf War, all of the news coverage of the strategic bombings and the ticker tape parade that came afterward. There were alot of unsung heroes in that war, Jake, and there are several of them in this room tonight. Relatively speaking, there was only minor coverage of the damage to the environment during Saddam Hussien's rampage through the oil fields as his men set them ablaze. His men were also ordered to open the valves of hundreds of oil wells in the gulf. They flooded the Persian Gulf with millions of gallons of oil.

"It was a minor media event compared with the triumphant return of the US troops after a quick and decisive victory."

"We restored democracy to the Kuwaiti people," Jack said with distinct sarcasm.

"That war was strictly about oil," Jack continued. "I returned recently to Kuwait City on a reconnaissance mission for RedTide and I saw for myself the Kuwaiti idea of democracy and I was disgusted.

"I'll tell you, Jake, what I was proudest of during that war was my men and the bravery and commitment they showed on the battlefield. I was a Marine gunnery sergeant during the war, and one day some of my men came to me and told me that they had heard that Iraqi soldiers had broken into the Kuwaiti Zoo and were shooting the animals in their cages.

"They were eating some but mostly they were just killing them for sport. Without orders or proper support, six of my men and I, some just privates straight out of advanced infantry training, snuck away from our regiment and decided to close the zoo. We worked our way through enemy lines and we were heavily outnumbered. We arrived at the zoo after killing nearly 150 Iraqi soldiers. On the way we blew up their main command and communications center and we arrived at the zoo just in time to see over twenty Iraqi soldiers taking target practice on a cage full of chimpanzees. The chimps were screaming and running around in their cages to avoid the shooting. Several animals were wounded and several more were already dead.

"My men and I killed as many soldiers as we could until our ammo ran out and then we killed the rest with our bare hands and with the rifles we took off of the Iraqi soldier's dead bodies. We had to return to camp under cover of darkness.

"When we returned we were arrested for desertion and were threatened with court martials, but we were proud of ourselves and what we had done. The news of our trip and the destruction of the command center as well as our intelligence and reconnaissance information was reported to the top brass and instead of being court martialed we were all awarded Silver Stars.

"Jorge was one of those soldiers, and we both met Tom toward the end of the war when he approached us about a mission he was putting together to stop Saddam from dumping more oil into the Gulf."

"No one really knew how bad it was over there from an environmental standpoint," Tom said.

"No one knows or will ever really know exactly how much oil Saddam released into the sea. Our best estimate is between four to six million barrels. It was as if a fleet of monster oil tankers had run aground. Iraqi artillery ruptured oil tanks during the battle for Al Khafji and oil flowed into the gulf.

"The Iraqis released oil at the Sea Island loading area off Kuwait. It was one of the world's biggest spills, and to top it off the bastards brought in loaded tankers, seven we think and dumped their cargoes."

"If it wasn't for RedTide and two of the men in this room," Tom said pointing to Jack and Jorge, things would have been three to four times worse. RedTide worked by night because the Iraqi's had countless spies. One night we snuck into the Kuwaiti oil refinery at Mina Al Ahmadi where there was a large pipe that carried oil from storage tanks down to Sea Island. Those tanks held millions of barrels of oil that the Iraqis intended to release into the sea. We secretly closed a valve the Iraqis didn't know about and to fool them we changed the valve indicator to open.

"When they dynamited Sea Island to release the main spill, our valve held back the barrels in the storage tanks."

"The oil that was released caused irreparable damage to that area, Jake," Jerry said. "It killed thousands of dolphins, birds, and other marine animals including the dugong, or the manatee as you know them.

"I stood on the beach at Ar Ruways and saw hundreds of manatees that were lying dead or were slowly dying on the shores of the gulf. Imagine if that happened in the Gulf of Mexico in Florida. Imagine if a tanker ran aground and on the news people witnessed the slaughter of hundreds of manatees in their backyards. Imagine the outrage, the public outcry.

"It never even made the evening news during the war. The media was too busy making media darlings and television stars out of Generals Schwarzkoff and Powell.

"RedTide was fighting an environmental war in the Gulf long before Desert Storm began," Jerry said. "The Persian Gulf was one of the most polluted bodies of water in the world even before Saddam added his own special touch to the problem, and in a demonstration of Arab pride for his homeland decided to decimate his own people's environment further.

"A quarter million barrels of oil pollute it each year and it takes the gulf more than five years to flush out the contaminants through the Straits of Hormuz. The gulf was a prime fishery for millennia even before Jesus walked the earth and it fed countless civilizations. If Peter were a fisherman in the area today he wouldn't be able to eat the fish he caught.

"Now it is dying and it has forced countless species to the brink of extinction and no one cares. No one in this country will lift a finger to protect their own children's drinking water let alone lose a night's sleep over the possible extinction of the cormorant in Bahrain."

"Abdullah Toukan, the science advisor to King Hussien of Jordan, speaking of Saddam's burning of the oil wells, said, 'Strategically it was senseless, the only casualty was the environment'" Tom said.

"I was flying over the Burgan oil fields and the afternoon sky was black as night from the smoke plumes which rose as high as twenty-two-thousand feet above the desert sky. The fires released tons of pollutants daily. Even eighty miles downwind air was found to contain ozone, nitrous oxide, and sulfur dioxide higher than government standards. It was said to cover 10,000 square miles and soldiers today who fought in the Gulf, including Jack, are still suffering from symptoms caused by inhaling the toxins."

"That's right," Jack said. "I have friends who have had children with birth defects and some who have developed lung cancer as a result of their service in the gulf. The Veterans Administration and the United States government has turned their backs, for the most part, and refused to even acknowledge their responsibility to the brave veterans and war heroes who sacrificed everything for their country."

"Things change when the cameras stop rolling," Jorge chimed in.

"That's enough," Samantha said, sounding tired and annoyed.

"If you join us, Jake, you can look forward to one lengthy speech after another about how polluted the earth is and how corrupt the government is."

"Wait upstairs, Angelfish," Tom said in a forceful tone of authority I didn't recognize. "We're almost done for tonight and you look tired."

Angelfish, I thought. "The tattoo, of course."

Little by little, things were starting to come together. All the Navy SEALs, the trip to Cozumel, Samantha telling me in so many words that Tom had checked me out before I got here, and the fighting and scuba skills of almost the entire staff.

Not to mention the militant environmental guidelines of the hotel and Tom's story about his mother and his military background.

"I'm tired, Tom," I said. "Can we pick this up tomorrow. My brain is fried and I think I'm suffering from sensory overload."

"Like I said, take your time. We're not going anywhere and I promise that you are not in any danger. Go on ahead with Angelfish, Sam, I meant to say, and we'll continue this conversation in the morning. Remember Jake, you're among friends, family really, and we trust you. I think we've demonstrated that, so trust us."

I went up in the elevator with Samantha and we didn't speak a word. She wouldn't even look at me all the way down the trail to my cabin. The tension was palpable.

"I'm sorry," she finally said turning toward me and looking at me with tear-filled eyes. "I couldn't say anything and I wanted to protect you from this life, from the danger and the paranoia.

"I'm afraid of what you must think of me now. Now that you know that you've been sleeping with some kind of a terrorist."

I took her in my arms and kissed her. "I'm crazy about you, Samantha. You don't have to worry about my feelings. I know you were looking out for me, and I respect you too much to jump to conclusions about what you do or to judge you for your involvement in an organization I know so little about.

"Before I came here, I saw RedTide on the news and I cheered when I saw what they had done in Japan to save those dolphins. I remembered thinking at the time how much I admired their courage and their commitment. Most people complain endlessly about the problems in the world and they never lift a finger to make any real changes. So many Americans don't even vote, not even in the presidential elections, and then they sit at home and they criticize the government for making policies they don't approve of.

"I have to admit that I'm in shock at tonight's revelations and I am afraid of the risk and the danger involved in joining the organization, but I am also intrigued by the thought of the adventure and the pride that comes from doing something substantial with my life.

"I have tremendous affection and respect for Tom and I believe that he is sincere and that he is a man who has the highest sense of honor and integrity. I don't believe in coincidence, and something brought me to this island. I believe in fate and I seem to be following a predestined path that has led me to you and to RedTide.

"I'm going to talk to Tom a lot over the next few days and I'll be certain to think things through very carefully. If I decide to leave, I'll give Tom my word that his secret would be safe with me and I would want you to come back to the States with me."

Samantha took my arm and kissed my neck and told me that her place was here with the group. She told me that she had very strong feelings for me, but that Tom had saved her life on numerous occasions and that she had finally found a home. She told me that she wanted me to stay but that she did not want to influence my decision in any way. We didn't make love that night. We finally fell asleep after another hour of conversation about the group and its past. Meanwhile, downstairs in the basement headquarters of RedTide a lively discussion was taking place.

"I told you he'd freak out," Stingray said. "Did you see the expression on his face? I thought he was going to faint."

"Chill out Jerry," Tom said. "Every new member of this organization reacted that way when we first approached them, including Jack over there. Isn't that right, Jack?"

Jack nodded in the affirmative and Tom continued. "Jake trusts me and he's madly in love with Samantha. If for no other reason than that he's going to stay. I'm going to work with him over the next two weeks on his indoctrination and we will all take turns working with him on his weapons training. Jake is loyal and he's honest and I know he can be trusted."

"I think Lionfish is right," Jorge said. "Jake is all right. He's never going to be a killing machine like big Jack or like you Lionfish, but he's smart and he has a good heart. There are plenty of ways he can contribute. Man, he surprised the hell out of me by taking out that big motherfucker on the beach when he saved Tom's ass, and I think we owe him."

"I agree," Jack said. "Jake's come a long way and I have a good feeling about him. Besides like Jorge said, he saved the boss's life and that should count for something," Jack finished with a sarcastic grin.

"That's what you said about Blowfish when you first brought him aboard, Grunt," Jerry said, using Jack's codename. "He ended up floating in my jellyfish tank with two bullets in his head, after he stuck a knife in my brother's back of course."

"Son of a bitch," Jack said jumping to his feet. "When are you gonna let me off the hook for that. I brought him in five years ago and he was one of our best men. He even made lieutenant in the Marine Iguanas. How could I know someone would get to him and that he would turn. Who knows how many more men in this organization might be turned for a million dollars in reward money."

"There's a comforting thought," Stingray responded.

"Enough," Tom yelled. "Jake's in, if he wants in, because I say so. Does anyone have a problem with that? I'll take the responsibility if anything goes wrong."

"We all suffer if anything goes wrong, Tom," Jerry said. "And what if he decides to leave and go home? Then what? He knows where we are and who we are. He could destroy the entire organization in one fell swoop."

"As long as Sam stays, Jake stays, and Sam's not going anywhere," Lionfish responded. "If he leaves we will monitor him closely for as long as it takes to make sure he won't give us up. He won't be able to pee at a public rest room without us knowing what he had for breakfast. We'll wire tap his house, his car, and his family's lines. We'll follow him twenty-four hours a day if that's what it takes to make sure you sleep at night, Jerry."

"And if he makes a move to hurt us Tom, what then?" Jerry asked.

"If that day comes and I pray that it never will, then I'll kill him myself. And then I'll quit this business for good," Tom said.

CHAPTER 24

As I walked down the beach and approached the stairs to the dock I heard music coming from the end and I squinted to see Tom & Jack sitting on the edge with a couple of beers, strumming on their acoustic guitars. I walked slowly toward them. I could hear them playing together in perfect harmony, with Tom playing an acoustical lead and Jack backing him up. I recognized the song they were playing. It was "The losing end" by Neil Young from the album, "Everybody knows this is nowhere."

"It's so hard for me now but I'll make it, somehow, though I know I'll never be the same, won't you ever change your ways, it's so hard to make love pay, when you're on the losing ee..eend, and I feel that way agaa...aa...in."

They sang the chorus in perfect harmony with Jack's deeper baritone quietly backing up Tom's softer, sweeter soprano. Then Jack sang out "Tommy Pick it" and Tom played a beautiful acoustic solo on his vintage Martin guitar. Jack joined in again and they finished together, laughing from the sheer joy of playing the music they loved together. When they stopped playing, Tom looked up at me through his Ray Bans and said, "Good afternoon, Jake. Have a beer?"

"In a few minutes we're going for a shore dive," Jack said. "Feel like joining us?"

It was as if last night had been a dream. Neither of them mentioned a word about it and they looked like a couple of Key West street musicians that were performing for spare change down at the town's Sunset Festival on the pier. Tom was wearing a straw Panama hat with a faded green camouflage bandanna tied around the brim and a pair of faded and frayed Levi denim shorts. He wasn't wearing a shirt or shoes. Jack was wearing a pair of loud Hawaiian shorts and a tank top from Gold's Gym in Venice Beach.

I took a seat beside them and said, "I'm still thinking about what you all told me last night, Tom. I want to take some time and I'd like to talk some more about joining up with your group, but I'm nervous and a little scared about the consequences. If you don't mind, I'd like a little more time to think about it."

Tom leaned over to me and whispered in my ear, "Jake, let's not discuss this here, right now. We have plenty of time and I respect the fact that you're giving things the proper consideration that they deserve. We have a mission coming up in three weeks and we need time to prepare you for it. If you don't mind, we would like to discuss things with you while we put you through some basic training over the next couple of weeks. It will be good for you no matter what you decide to do."

"I don't mind," I said. "I could use the additional exercise."

"Don't worry, Jake," Jack said. "It won't be nearly as hard as Marine boot camp was."

I was about to ask Jack how he knew about my short stint in The Marine Corps when I caught myself and realized that they probably knew everything about me.

"If you know that I was in the Marine Corps, then you probably also know that I didn't exactly make a very good showing of myself during that time and you probably know all about my time in the brig at Camp Pendleton," I said, feeling vulnerable and self-conscious in front of two combat veterans, both of whom had distinguished themselves in the service.

"It would be hard for us to sit in judgment of you considering who we are and what we do," Tom said. "You were barely seventeen when you got in trouble and although I don't know all the details I do know enough to recognize that you weren't treated fairly by the men your family entrusted you to."

I thought about what Tom had said and I thought back to the day I came home from my father's house where I had been living at the time and told my mother that I had decided to join the Marine Corps. I hadn't talked to my father in almost five years since he walked out on us. I swore that I never would again, but the situation at home with my mother had become so intolerable that I decided I needed a change, and so I reconciled with my father and moved in with him for a short time while I was in my junior year in high school.

Toward the end of that year, I had destroyed two of my father's cars within a two week period of time and he had thrown me out of the house. I was sixteen and had just gotten my license to drive. My father made the mistake of allowing me to borrow his BMW 320i for a date, who wound up canceling on me at the last minute. So instead, I picked up three of my friends and a case of Carlings Black Label beer and we went cruising.

We drove around all night drinking and throwing our empties from the moving car at speed limit signs as we blew by them. It was foggy that night and the roads were slick. I was speeding around Schoolies Mountain Road and took a hairpin turn a little too quickly and lost control of the car. The car fishtailed and flew into a tree at over forty miles an hour. I slammed my chest into the steering wheel and my friend Sean's face smashed into the windshield. I only cracked a few ribs, but Sean wound up breaking his jaw and received over 170 stitches in his face.

One week later, my friend Russell Barnes and I borrowed my dad's

Ford Ranger 150 pickup truck and decided to go to a new housing development that was under construction around the corner from where I lived. Russ and I worked there on weekends as laborers for his brother, who was a mason and owned his own company. We had seen a Charles Bronson movie called *Mister Majestyk* the day before.

There was a chase scene in the movie in which Charles Bronson kept jumping his truck over six feet into the air. He would land without a problem and we mistakenly assumed that any four-wheel drive truck was capable of such rugged performance. We flew over one dirt pile after another and slowly as we gained confidence the dirt piles we jumped increased in height. Everything was going fine and we were having the time of our life. We spotted a hill of dirt near a newly-laid foundation and took off toward it, increasing speed until we were doing over fifty miles an hour by the time we hit it. The truck flew through the air with all four wheels coming off the ground and I could feel my stomach drop as the truck's rear end started to come around.

The truck landed on something and there was a horrible cracking sound before the truck bounced in the air again from the impact and finally came to rest over twenty feet from the hill. I tried to drive it but the four wheel drive made a ghastly gnashing and grinding sound and the truck wouldn't move. I turned to Russ and we stared at each other in sheer terror.

Russell leapt from the car and looked underneath and stood up and said, "You're fucked, Jake."

We walked back to town and got a tow truck to drag the wreckage to the corner Shell station. The mechanic told me that the axle, the steering and the four-wheel drive were destroyed. He also told me that my dad had recently found a buyer for the truck who was supposed to be coming to pick it up that very evening. My face turned white at the surprise news and I went home with Russell and hid out at his house for four days. I figured it would take that amount of time for my father to either find me or for the anger to pass so that he could see me without committing murder.

One day, the phone rang and Russell's mother told me it was my father. I walked to the phone slowly, afraid to even touch it and I held it inches from my ear as I said hello.

"Come home now, Jake," was all my father said and he said it in a calm even tone that filled me with terror. He didn't scream or threaten me as I had expected. When I walked into the kitchen, my soccer bag was lying in the middle of the floor filled with my clothes and my father was sitting quietly at the kitchen table waiting for me. He told me that I had to leave his house. He told me that I had made him suffer enough for abandoning us and that he now considered us even.

He said he didn't care where I went. I could go back to my mother or I could go to hell. He really didn't give a fuck. He said he was through with me forever. He stood up, handed me two fifty dollar bills, and said, "Get out" and then he turned his back on me and left the room.

My friend Russell had a brother named Tim who was a lance corporal in the Marine Corps and we both thought that he was very cool with his blue uniform and his stories about being stationed around the world at places like Misawa, Japan.

He was only twenty-years-old but he had money and a motorcycle and a great stereo. He had already seen more of the world than I had ever dreamed of. He talked me into enlisting and I went home to my mother to get her to sign the parental consent form I needed because of my age. When I told her about it over lunch at Maxwell Plums restaurant in Manhattan, she cried.

She wanted me to be an artist and she implored me to reconsider. "Move back in with me and go to Cooper Union to study Graphic Arts," she begged.

She told me I would be the only Jewish boy in history to join the Marine Corps and she was almost right. I wished I had listened to her at the time but I had no respect for anything my promiscuous, pot smoking mother had to say, so I told her that if she didn't sign the papers I would never speak to her again. Finally I was able to make her feel guilty enough to comply, but she had one condition. My mother wanted a guarantee from the Marine Corps that I would be stationed in the United States for my first year of duty and that I would have first choice of an MOS or Military Occupational Specialty, although she had no idea it was called that at the time.

I chose computer technology as my first choice and the military police as my second choice and went to Brooklyn for my final physical exam. I lived with my mother for a month and then I went down to Brooklyn again to be processed and sent on my way to the Marine Corps Recruit Depot in San Diego, California.

I requested as part of my guarantee that I go to boot camp on the west coast because I had been told that Marines who went through boot camp on the west coast were usually stationed on the west coast. I was also told that Parris Island in the summer was like Devil's Island. It was supposed to be filled with swamps and with mosquitoes the size of Volkswagens.

On the day I went to be processed I was taken into a room and after seven and one half hours of processing I was told by a Marine colonel that both my MOS selections were currently full and that I would have to sign a waiver to forego my guarantee if I wanted to leave that day.

I felt intimidated by such a high ranking officer in an organization that I believed represented the highest standards of honor and integrity and so when he told me that it was a technicality and that if I held out it would mean a delay in entering the service of over six months, I quickly signed the waiver.

The colonel told me that he could see that I was a very intelligent boy and that after the aptitude and IQ scores I would be taking in boot camp were reviewed I would have my choice of many highly skilled positions, including computer training and engineering.

After two months of torture and degradation at the hands of the Anti-Semitic Klansmen who called themselves my drill instructors, my MOS was announced to me in front of the rest of my platoon. On the day we all received our MOSs I was told that I was to be sent to Advanced Infantry Training where I would learn how to operate a radio.

2531 was my official MOS, Infantry Radio Operator, which meant that I got to hike around Camp Pendleton all day long in ninety degree heat humping a fifty-pound radio backpack.

My nights would be spent memorizing codes and thinking of ways to kill myself. When I finally landed at my assigned duty station at El Toro in Southern California I was already disenchanted and disillusioned with the Corps.

I appealed for a transfer to everyone from the chaplain to the commanding general. When my mother began to write letters threatening to sue the Marine Corps because of how she and I had been manipulated and lied to, things went from bad to worse.

There was a Second Lieutenant Walker who took an irrational dislike to me and through his agent, my direct superior, Staff Sergeant Brown, he assigned me every shit detail in the company. I planned on going AWOL or Absent Without Leave for over three months while I followed legitimate military channels to seek justice. When every appeal I made was turned down and every road I took led me nowhere, I packed up my things including some warm weather clothing I had purchased at the base PX in my seabag and I headed for the front gates.

Unfortunately, I had been very vocal about my plans to leave and I had spoken in my barracks with several people I thought were my friends. I waited until the weekend when I could leave the base without suspicion and I told people that I was going to LA to visit my sister.

I went to the workshop where we trained on the radio equipment and I opened my locker to clean out some things I wanted to take along. I also wanted to get the extra money I had been hiding in an empty container of shoe polish. It was Saturday morning and the place was practically deserted. When I slammed my locker and turned around, Lt. Walker was standing there in his chocolate chip, combat desert fatigues.

"Where do you think you're going, Marine?" He asked.

"I'm going to visit my sister in Los Angeles for the weekend," I replied in a nervous stammer. "I'm surprised to see you here today," I blurted out.

"Three months of fucking boot camp *Stein*," the lieutenant said with a contemptuous emphasis on my last name, "and you still don't address an officer as sir when you speak to him. And where the fuck is my salute?"

I felt my stomach acid boiling. This asshole had been riding me for months. He blocked every attempt I made to go above his head and he encouraged his NCOs to abuse me each and every chance they got.

"I'm sorry sir," I said. "It's the weekend and I'm off duty."

"A Marine is never off duty, Stein, even the ones who are trying to get out of being Marines. Who told you that you were off duty anyway? I have some extra work around here that needs to be done and I can't think of anyone else I would rather have do it. Now get back to your room and change into your desert cami's and report back here in one half hour prepared to clean every piece of equipment in this shed."

My face was bright red from anger and I felt like an animal that was trapped in a snare. I could see the lieutenant's pickup truck parked outside the door to the building and I knew what I had to do.

"Yes sir, Lieutenant," I said with a salute.

"I'll be back in less than twenty minutes," I replied, controlling my fury.

I saluted again and walked past the lieutenant, who looked puzzled at my calm response and the absence of my usual objectionable arguments at what had become his usual inappropriate behavior.

When I left the building, I jumped in the lieutenant's truck and to my great relief his keys were in it. I was just about to turn the ignition when the lieutenant reached through the window and grabbed me by the collar.

"Get out of that truck, Stein. Now!" He screamed. "This is going to lead directly to your arrest and court martial."

It was too late to turn back. Things had gotten way out of control and I knew I would wind up in the brig before the day ended. I turned the ignition and pried the lieutenant's fingers away from my collar. Suddenly I lost all control after three months of burying my anger and frustration and I screamed, "Fuck you, sir! Let go of me, you fucking prick."

I managed to pry his fingers away and I slammed on the gas pedal as I threw the shift lever on the column into drive. Unfortunately, the stubborn asshole hooked his arm inside the window and hung onto the vehicle. I dragged him over fifty feet and accelerated the truck quickly up to forty miles an hour. By the time I swung the truck around the outside of the shed we were doing fifty. The turn was very sharp and the lieutenant couldn't hang on.

In the driver's side mirror, I saw him roll head over heels on the asphalt. He rolled over twenty feet before he went off the road and landed in a mudpuddle. I had thrown my seabag in the back of the truck and I had my money and my plane ticket. I headed to the front gate and I returned the salute of the MP, who saluted the officers sticker on the lieutenant's car, before I headed for the airport. My heart was racing and I thought it would explode from the fear and exhilaration I felt.

For a second I wished I had killed the sadistic anti-semitic asshole, but the realization that I would be hung according to military law if he were dead made me hope that he had gotten up with only a few scratches. I went to LAX and hopped a flight to Lagaurdia airport in New York. I was watching for police and MPs the entire trip. I was surprised when I reached New York and stepped off of the plane that no one was waiting for me.

Over the next six months that I hid out, I lived in a constant heightened state of paranoia. I took the Long Island Railroad to Oceanside and hid out at the Blue Bay Motel, where I stayed for two weeks. I subsisted on cold cuts and macaroni and cheese that I purchased at the FoodTown supermarket across the street. I didn't call anyone, not even my mother and I was terrified to even leave the room.

I had no plans and I grew more and more depressed. After two weeks, when all of my money had just about run out, I decided to kill myself. I couldn't see any positive outcome to my current situation or any future for myself and I didn't want to return to face charges for desertion. I went to the FoodTown supermarket and purchased all the materials I would need to end my life. I was too much of a coward to cut my wrists or to hang myself. I wanted to go painlessly and quietly so I bought a small barbecue and a bag of coals and some lighter fluid.

I read somewhere that an entire family of illegal aliens had accidentally asphyxiated in their van from the fumes of the small barbecue they had used to fix their dinner. My plan was to light the coals outside and then when they were white and were burning well I would bring the barbecue into the bathroom and I would close the door. I would seal the bottom with a towel and I would climb into a hot bath and drift away.

I prepared everything, then I thought about my mother and I decided to call her. She became hysterical as soon as she heard my voice and yelled at me between heavy sobs that I was insane and that I had almost killed her with worry.

She told me that she had imagined that I was dead somewhere. I said I was in New York and she told me to shut up. She stopped me from making any other revelations when she told me that the FBI and the local police had been to her house and that I was wanted for desertion and for assault. She told me that my commanding officer was in the hospital with a fractured skull and a concussion as well as several other broken bones.

My heart sank when she spoke those words, but I also felt some relief for it only strengthened my resolve to take my life. My mother begged me to meet her somewhere and the grief in her voice and the knowledge of how much I had hurt her made me want to be with her and hold her. She told me that I should visit some old friends from West Pond, a bungalow colony we used to go to when we were kids. She told me that I should meet them tomorrow around noon and then she told me that she had to go and she hung up.

I didn't know what had just happened until I thought about it and I realized that my mother was afraid her phone might be tapped, or that someone might be tracing the call. She was trying to tell me something with her remark about visiting old friends from West Pond tomorrow and I racked my brain to think of who I still might know from those days. There were my cousins, but she couldn't mean them. Besides they lived all over the country, and none of them were in New York.

It took me two hours to figure it out. My mother's friend Pauline Berkowitz had a son named Donnie that my cousins and I used to pick on at West Pond when we were little. He now ran an auto body repair place in Baldwin. My mother went there several times and had become friendly with Donnie and his wife over the past several years. His wife had become a regular in my mother's salon and my mother had sent me to see Donnie when I damaged her Honda Civic a year before I moved in with my father.

Smart, Mom, I thought. *Very clever.*

I realized with some embarrassment how much I needed to see my mother. I felt like a frightened little boy who had just awakened from a terrible nightmare and wanted his mother to hold him and tell him everything was going to be okay. The next day I packed my stuff and counted the forty dollars I had left in my wallet and checked out of the hotel. I took the bus and had to make several connections before I made it to Grand Avenue in Baldwin.

It was 11:43A.M. and I stood outside at the curb and waited for I didn't know what. At 12:05, a black Toyota Corolla pulled up and a woman I didn't recognize rolled down her window and told me to get in. I jumped into the passenger seat and she sped away.

"So you're the asshole son," she said, taking me by surprise.

"Do you have any idea what you've put your mother through the past two weeks? Do you have any idea how worried she's been? She's had to take medication for the past week just so she could sleep. She was up for almost five days straight when you first disappeared."

"I haven't exactly been on vacation," I replied defensively to this perfect stranger. "I was afraid to call her, not that it's any of your business. Who are you anyway?"

My mother had so many friends that I could never keep track of them. I would occasionally be introduced to total strangers that she told me she had known for years. Some of these people were so fiercely loyal to her that they would kill for her.

"My name is Sheri and it looks like you and I are going to be roommates for a little while," she said.

I looked over at her. She was a woman of perhaps forty years of age. She had medium length blond hair, which was obviously colored and she had on black cat eye Ray Bans, so I couldn't really see her eyes. She had long legs and they were dynamite. She reminded me of my mom. She was a straight shooter and she had a mouth like a longshoreman. Despite her hostile greeting I liked her immediately and later we would become good friends.

"What do you mean we're going to be roommates?" I asked. "I don't even know you."

"You'll get to know me, Jake, and I already know all about you. Your mother talks about you all the time. You know it broke her heart when you joined the service. She told me that you were a very gifted artist."

I looked out the window and we drove in silence for awhile. We drove past the Oceanside Country Club, where I had once worked as a caddie for two summers. Ten minutes later, we pulled up to a small ranch style house under the largest oak tree I had ever seen.

"We're home," Sheri said. "And I've got a surprise for you inside."

I lifted my bag out of the back seat and followed this strange woman to the front door. When we got inside I smelled cigarette smoke. My mother emerged from the kitchen smoking a cigarette. She looked horrible and my heart sank when I saw her in the full light of the foyer. She had dark rings under her eyes and her face was deathly pale. She had red streaks on her face from crying and her face looked puffy and bloated. She walked over to me quickly and threw her arms around me and kissed me several times.

Then she stepped back and slapped me for the first time in my life.

"Miriam, don't," Sheri cried.

"You selfish little bastard," my mother screamed at me.

"You almost killed me with worry. I lay in bed crying for days thinking that you had killed yourself or that you had been in an accident somewhere in that stolen car."

I fell apart from a combination of the stress and the anxiety of my life the past three months. I began to cry and scream in pain and fear. "I was going to kill myself, Mom. I had it all set up last night but I got scared and like the coward I am I called for my mommy to save me. I'm a quitter at everything else, it should have been easy for me to quit my life, but I couldn't do it. I couldn't do it," I cried.

I fell into my mothers arms and she held me and rocked me. "Oh Jake, don't ever say that again. You're only seventeen years old. You've got your whole life ahead of you. Don't throw away the next sixty years of happiness because of something stupid you did when you were a boy. I love you so much it would have killed me and it would have killed your sister if you had gone through with it. I promise you we will work everything out. Don't worry, Jakey. Trust me. I've hired a lawyer and he assures me that we have a very strong case for your immediate honorable discharge from the Marine Corps. He says there may even be a few bucks in it for you, considering the circumstances surrounding your sign on guarantee and your age at the time of enlistment."

I had underestimated my mothers resourcefulness and her protective instincts where her children were concerned. I felt a great relief and I hugged my mother tight and apologized for frightening her the past two weeks. Sheri led us to the kitchen and we made some sandwiches and talked for hours, sitting on stools around the center island in the middle of the room. My mother told me that my lawyer's name was Michael Kuntsler. He was the brother of the famous or infamous attorney William Kuntsler, depending on who you spoke to.

William Kuntsler made a name for himself defending the Chicago Seven and was a colorful character who had long gray hair and a reputation as the defender of various radical left wing organizations. My mother naively believed that The United States Marine Corps would somehow be intimidated by the fact that Michael Kuntsler shared his brother's last name. What my mother and I didn't realize at the time was that there really isn't much in the world that intimidates the Marine Corps and that the mere mention of the Kuntsler name only infuriated and alienated the men who would ultimately be deciding my fate.

My mother also told me that I would be staying with Sheri until my case was decided, since it would not be safe to come home to her at this time. My attorney had told my mother that it would only take two months at the outside to resolve my case. It wound up taking over six months. Sheri had decided after only a couple of months that she wanted no part of housing a freeloader. She told me that she was sick of watching me lay about on her couch, and she forced me to go out and get a job.

I was terrified and so under an assumed name I went back to the Oceanside Country Club where I had worked as a boy and I caddied for tips off the books. I used the name Leighton Finch which seemed just pretentious enough for the country club crowd and just obscure and ridiculous enough that no one would think I had invented it. After six months, my mother and I met with my attorney in the city, at the 2nd Avenue Deli downtown. He told us that he had assurances from a Colonel McMurtry in the Judge Advocate Generals office at the Philadelphia Naval Yard that mine was an open and shut case. Colonel McMurtry told him that if I turned myself in I would be treated fairly and my paperwork for my discharge would be processed within two weeks.

He said the colonel told him that I would be given a private room in the enlisted mens barracks and that my case had pretty much already been decided. He also told us how all the brass had flinched at the mention of his famous last name and at his mention of his brother's possible involvement in the case.

The last thing he said was that he needed another two thousand dollars, which my mother paid him out of the remaining money she had left in her bank account. Two weeks later, my attorney called and told me that we would be leaving together in three days so I could surrender at the naval yard.

I was terrified at the prospect of being thrown back into the military grinder and didn't sleep for the next two nights. In only six months I had totally digressed back to my former civilian habits and dress. I had grown my hair out and had a short, scruffy incomplete beard. I wore nothing but jeans and T-shirts around the house, slept late and stopped exercising completely. I would get high with the other caddies while we were charging up the golf carts, and we would stay out late at night drinking.

My drill instructors would have had a stroke if they could have seen how quickly all their hard work and discipline had evaporated. I woke up at 6:15 on the day we left and Mr. Kuntsler picked me up at 7 sharp for the ride south. He kept reassuring me that I would be home very soon and that there was no way the Marine Corps wanted this thing to escalate.

I was led to believe that the same kind of men who had stormed the beaches at Iwo Jima and were our country's "first to fight" and first to die throughout our bloody history were deathly afraid of an seventeen-year-old boy and his lawyer.

I should have known better than to trust an attorney, but I was seventeen and I was innocent and impressionable when it came to people I perceived at the time as being successful or powerful. The funny thing was that as much as I resented authority, I was easily manipulated and seduced by some of the people who had it. That changed as I got older and I was consistently lied to and cheated by one person after another from the officers in the Marine Corps to just about every manager and employer I had. Inevitably I became the world's youngest cynic.

We arrived at the offices of the Judge Advocate General in the

Philadelphia Naval yard. As soon as we entered the room, two MPs jumped me, slammed me up against the wall and cuffed me. My attorney was led away and I was thrown into the naval brig at the base. I wasn't allowed to ask any questions and later that afternoon my head was shaved clean just like in boot camp, and I was issued a set of military clothing. I could not make heads or tails of what had happened. I was put into a small barracks with a locked gate for a door along with ten other deserters or anonymous criminals.

My bunkmate had been absent without leave for over five years and he had a heavy Texas accent. He told me that he was a real life cowboy, and that he had worked on a ranch in Montana herding cattle until he was arrested in a barfight and was picked up by the FBI. He told me that I could look forward to a year of hard labor, sixteen hours a day, then a dishonorable discharge.

He told me that the military code of justice was different from the civil courts and that the military could ignore the constitution and could do pretty much whatever they wanted with me. He told me that there was no such thing as a punishment that could be deemed cruel and unusual in the armed services.

They could make me finish out my entire term of four years in the prison at Leavenworth if they felt like it. I learned later on from my assigned attorney, a young butterbar or second lieutenant, that the brass was very unhappy about my choice of attorney and his constant threats and his general disrespectful handling of my case. He told me that they were being less cooperative than usual in regards to my case. I stayed in the naval brig in Philadelphia for six days and on the seventh day two FBI agents came to escort me back to El Toro, California. They both wore black suits and were the biggest men I had ever seen. I could see their guns in their shoulder holsters and for the first time I felt like a criminal. They took me to the airport and made me walk between them all the way to the gate in hand cuffs while children pointed me out to their parents and their parents made them look away. I felt humiliated and with my bald head and faded fatigues I probably looked like a serial killer. I wasn't allowed to talk at all or ask questions. The two FBI agents were rough and abusive in their handling of me. They were not allowed to keep me handcuffed on the plane because of FAA regulations, so they instructed me to sit quietly and not to move.

We landed at night in Chicago and then we got in a van and drove for what seemed like hours into the country. I felt terrorized and was I sweating profusely. My hands were trembling. I could not imagine where we were going and why we were not in California. I asked where we were going and they told me, "Shut the fuck up or we'll have to gag you."

My imagination was running wild and I thought for a second that they were going to take me out to a field and execute me. They would just make it look like I was trying to escape. We finally arrived at the Great Lakes Naval Base and I was delivered to the brig where I stayed for five days. I asked why I was there and when I would be returned to California and again no one would give me any answers. It had been over ten days since I had entered the system and I had not been allowed to call anyone, not even my mother. On the sixth day, the FBI men returned and we went to the airport again. This time we flew to Denver where I was deposited in the Denver County Jail. I could not believe I was in a civilian jail and my fear had reached a level at which my thoughts became so unreasonable and paranoid that I was sure I was going insane. I was placed in general lockup along with child molesters and wife beaters and one suspected murderer. I was eighteen-years-old and stood 5'8" tall and weighed 155 pounds. I tried to make myself invisible and I stood quietly in the corners away from other people, hoping not to be noticed.

When nighttime came and the lights went out I curled up in a ball on my cot and waited for what I thought would be the inevitable line of rapists who would each take his turn with me. I cried quietly into my pillow and tried to be brave. I could not control my shaking and I wished that I were dead. Suddenly, the man in the bunk above me jumped down from his bed and stood over me. He was a huge white man covered in tattoos and he had a long handlebar mustache and greasy hair. He told me that he couldn't sleep with only one pillow and he wanted mine.

I didn't know what to do. I thought if I acquiesced it would only open the flood gates of general abuse from the entire room and for one fleeting moment I had a thought, partly influenced from seeing too many prison films, that I should stand up to him. I handed my pillow to him quickly and said nothing and only hoped it would end there. He laughed quietly and climbed back into his bunk.

Two minutes later, a large black man with an incredibly deep voice came over to my bunk. He was the one I had been told had knifed a man in a bar over a woman and had ended up killing him. He walked right up to my bed and stood beside me. I lost control and peed in my pants and down my leg. The man told me that he wanted my mattress and I was so relieved that I jumped to my feet and without a word let him have it. I laid there the rest of the night wide wake without a pillow or a mattress on a bed of hard springs. I endured this hell for three days before the FBI agents came to get me.

I was quiet the entire trip to Los Angeles and when they turned me in at the brig at Camp Pendleton one of them had the audacity to compliment me on how quiet and cooperative I had been. I was in general lockup for three months at Camp Pendleton, doing twelve hours a day of hard labor. We would dig ditches and cut grass on the side of the road with swingblades in the blazing afternoon sun. Sometimes for fun, the guards would give us only buttermilk to drink when we told them that we were thirsty. They would stand around and laugh while we slurped down the warm, sour liquid. I saw my attorney only once and on my last visit he told me that it looked as if I would get three years hard labor and a dishonorable discharge.

I was desperately unhappy and stopped eating. I lost twelve pounds in ten days and was pale and sickly. I went to the chaplain and sat in one of the pews of the church and prayed for God's help. That's how desperate I was. I wrote my mother a letter and I told her that I had decided to take my own life as soon as an opportunity presented itself. One week later I was placed in solitary confinement on suicide watch. My mother had turned me in. I was in a 6x6 foot cell with a TV camera above me that watched me night and day and I was not allowed to leave except to shower under the watchful eye of a guard.

I could not read and I begged them to let me out. After two weeks in solitary I was released back into the general population and returned to work duty. One morning I was meeting with my attorney and our meeting ran late. I had to catch up with the work detail that had already left without me. The guard at the front gate made a mistake and without looking at my security level, which was on my badge, he let me walk out the front door so that I could catch up with the work detail that was already down the road at the tool shed. I was free and I couldn't believe my luck. I stood outside the prison and looked around and there was no one in sight. Two blocks away was the bus stop and the gates to the outside. All I had to do was take off my badge, cuff my pants and roll up my sleeves and I would blend in with the other 20,000 plus men on the base.

Instead, I walked down to the tool shed and into the officers room, which was next door. The captain in charge had a fit when he was told what had happened and he screamed and cursed and threatened to take everyone's stripes. My security clearance was downgraded two days later, and three days later my attorney told me that at the end of the week I would be returned to my duty post at El Toro where I would be confined to barracks. I was gladdened about being released but was aghast at the thought of facing the men I had escaped from six months earlier, especially Lt.Walker, who I knew would be waiting for me.

When I returned to the base, I was finally allowed to call my mother who cried and cried when she heard my voice. She told me that she had fired Mr. Kuntsler, or Mr. Cunt-sler as she told me Sheri referred to him. She told me that she was in touch with the general at my base and that she had written over a dozen letters to every officer involved with my case. She was on the phone daily and said that she had spoken with

Chaplain Boyer at the base as well. I thanked her but I also told her that I didn't hold out much hope that I would be released. She told me that she had a nice talk with General Cranston and that she explained to him the shenanigans involved around the day of my embarkation in Brooklyn. She also told the general that she could not understand in this day of a volunteer military why the Marine Corps would want someone who didn't want to be there. She couldn't understand why such a proud organization would want someone who didn't take any pride at all in being in the Corps, but wanted only to be released from his agreement, an agreement we were all tricked into making.

She told him in her usual charming and non-threateningly, yet subtly persuasive way, that she was reluctant to go to the papers to plead for her son's release. Two weeks later, there was a short hearing and I was told that I was to be offered the military equivalent of a plea bargain. I was told that if I agreed to sign an acceptance letter and a waiver indemnifying the Corps from any wrongdoing that I would serve only six months in prison and would then be released with a general discharge under less than honorable conditions. The Marine Corps would also pay me three thousand dollars in back wages for the time I spent in prison.

My military attorney wanted me to take my chances in court where I might win an honorable discharge, but I quickly agreed to their terms. The day before I was scheduled to return to jail, my door swung open with a bang and Lt. Walker came in. He grabbed me by the collar and threw me back on my bunk. He had a horrible scar on his forehead which ran back into his scalp and I noticed as he walked toward me that he had a slight limp in his right leg.

"Welcome back, asshole," he said. "I understand you cut yourself a deal. That's really too bad. I was looking forward to limping into court and testifying against you. I was looking forward to telling the court how I had to leave the Marine Corps on a medical discharge, and how, since you tried to kill me, I now suffer from migraine headaches on a daily basis."

His voice increased in volume as each hateful word rolled off his tongue. "My consolation is in knowing that you are a loser who will have a black mark beside his name every time you apply for a job or a bank loan. My comfort is in knowing that you've established a pattern of failure for yourself, Stein, which you will repeat time and time again as you continue to try to take shortcuts and cut corners," he said.

He leaned over my bunk and spit in my face just as the MP who stood guard outside my room burst in and respectfully asked the lieutenant to leave. I wiped my face and stood up and called after him as he was escorted down the hall.

"It was an accident. You wouldn't let go of the car."

He turned around and screamed at me. "Sir", he said. "You're still in the Corps, you son of a bitch and from this day forward until we unload your sorry ass you will continue to address an officer with the respect he deserves."

"I'm sorry, sir. I'm sorry about everything," I said, and I meant it with all my heart. I was sorry for what I had done to the lieutenant and for what I had done to myself and to my mother and to the Marine Corps. I wished with all my heart that I had gone to art school as my mother had begged me.

The lieutenant's words would haunt me from time to time. When I was turned down by the New York City Police Department because of my military record, that day came back to me in vivid detail.

I finished my story and Tom just smiled and said, "That was a long time ago, Jake, and you've been successful over the years. Your mother obviously loved you a great deal. I'm sure she was very proud of you. If you join with us over the next few years you will accomplish things that she would be even prouder of. But more importantly you will be proud of yourself."

"Let's go for a dive," Jack said. "You're both getting way too heavy for me on such a beautiful day."

We put our equipment together and when we were all dressed and ready to go, we took turns doing a giant stride entry off of the dock. Tom gave the OK sign and then the thumbs down and we all began to descend. When I was only five feet below the surface a small school of cuttlefish swam by and in the strong light from the surface their bodies looked iridescent, with shades of pink and purple. I wished I had my camera. It would have been a great closeup shot with so much available light. Tom led us down to about forty feet, according to my gauge, and as I crossed a thermoclime I felt a cool current of water run across my body.

I had begun to wear a wet suit the past few weeks since my body had become acclimated to eighty degree water, and now if I dove without a wetsuit on I felt a chill. Tom led us through a small barely discernible hole in the rock thirty yards north of the hotel toward Lovers Beach and we entered a small tunnel. After ten narrow feet it opened into a group of large tunnels and swim throughs. We swam in and out of tunnels varying in size from ten feet wide to over fifty feet wide. They were lined with black coral and sea fans and there were large schools of small colored fish everywhere. I was working hard to try to identify the varieties of marine life by name since it was a common question among the tourists who traveled to the island and dove with me.

I always found it funny how divers, especially new divers, will always return to the boat and try to impress everyone with the wealth of their knowledge.

They would say things like, "I saw a midnight parrot fish. I could tell by the dark blue coloring," and then they will pour over their fish and reef finder cards over lunch trying to identify every little thing they spotted during the dive. I think some of them even carried a variety of books that specialized in identifying invertebrates and plants and algae. It's almost as obnoxious as eating with them and listening to their endless stories about where they've been and the things they've seen. Older divers and couples are always trying to top the other in games of diving one-upsmanship.

It's the part of the job I despise the most, schmoozing with the guests. I know if Sam catches me even for a minute becoming impatient or sarcastic she will read me the riot act. As I looked around, I became more and more relaxed. The reef is like a muscle relaxer or a sedative for me and it never fails to calm me down and make me happy. I would have liked to borrow one of the rebreathing units I spotted in the "Hideout" last night so I could try staying down for a longer period of time, but Samantha told me, after she explained what they were to me, that Tom won't let them anywhere in sight of the hotel guests.

Jack was taking the lead with Tom behind him and I was following them through a very narrow shaft that was only six feet wide and went straight down. The shaft was getting more and more narrow and I was beginning to scratch my arms and bang my tank against the walls. I didn't know how Jack was fitting through and I started to get anxious as I did whenever I dove through a small narrow cave or tunnel. It was getting darker and I estimated that we had swam about thirty to forty feet down when it became a little wider and began to curve horizontally. Suddenly, we came out into the largest underwater cave I had ever seen. It was almost perfectly round and was at least 100 yards wide and perhaps sixty feet high. It was completely black except for a few holes in the ceiling which were shining light down into the cave in long narrow beams like the spotlights in a theater. I could see Jack in a perfect silhouette as he ascending in one of the shafts of light. It looked like he was being lifted into the air by some alien space ship's magnetic beam, or was ascending to heaven in the perfect white light so many people who experience near-death speak about.

Then I saw a school of large silver tarpon swimming in and out of the light. They would constantly disappear and reappear every few seconds as the light hit their bodies. The light bounced off of their silver skin and sent off little beams of light in all directions. It looked like a tiny spotlight hitting a disco ball that was suspended above a dance floor. It was a beautiful sight and I wondered why I had never been brought here before since it was so close to the hotel.

Tom came up behind me and startled me. He tapped me on the shoulder and motioned for me to follow him as I saw Jack descending again down the shaft of light. *Fallen from heaven*, I thought as he descended away from the light. Tom led me to a side cave and Jack fell in behind us. We swam twenty-five feet inside a long dark shaft led on by Tom's small but very bright flashlight. There were some small alcoves or caves on all sides and I gasped when I saw that there were large sharks that were swimming around or were resting on the bottom.

Tom kneeled down in the sand and wiped away an area with his hand and I saw a small black keypad lying embedded in the sand. Jack swam up close to me and looked me in the eye and nodded. Then he gave me the okay sign and signaled for me to tell him how much air I had left. I checked my gauges and reported to him that I had 1100 PSI remaining in my tank, enough for perhaps another fifteen minutes at this depth. Tom punched in some numbers and then the back wall began to slide sideways into the side wall.

I touched it as it passed and it was covered in a rubber material designed to simulate rock and coral. I looked at the side as it retracted and I saw that it was actually a half-inch thick stainless steel or aluminum door. We swam inside and Jack pulled out his large Underwater Kinetics halogen light, which illuminated the interior of the hidden cave. I could see that it was a rectangle twenty-five feet wide and fifty feet long. There were three large cases on each side layed end to end, totaling six in all, and in the middle were two underwater scooters. There was nothing else in the room. The cases were very large and looked custom-made. They resembled Zero Haliburton luggage.

They were silver in a brushed finish and I guessed correctly, I later learned, that they were made from stainless steel and aluminum. They were fabricated with a double sealing system of O-Rings so they wouldn't leak and looked strong enough to withstand a cave-in. Tom signaled for us to leave and we swam out after he looked the place over and he re-entered the numbers. The door closed and Tom covered the keypad again with sand. We swam out through an obstacle course of sharks and had to pause occasionally to let two or three of the large predators move aside. We swam toward one of the shafts of light in the side wall, which was throwing a beam of light sideways across the interior of the cave. It intersected with one of the vertical beams and made an X in the center of the cave.

Jack swam out first through the hole, which was only three feet wide, and I followed. When I looked back, Tom was emerging through the hole that hundreds of people probably swam by every day without noticing. He had an octopus in his hands, which was changing colors quickly to match Tom's blue gloves. Tom held it out to Jack and he grabbed it just as it squirmed out of Tom's hands and squirted a jet of black ink. As Jack held it in his hands it changed to jet black, the color of Jack's bare hands and we all laughed, blowing bubbles into the water.

Jack let it go near me and I touched it just before it swam rapidly to the reef and changed its color again to orange to blend in with the sponge it had landed on. We swam to the dock and Tom helped me out of the water. Tom's cooler was still full of ice and Coors beer and when we were out of our gear and had deposited it in the rinse tanks we sat on the dock and toasted our dive. We sat quietly for awhile and I hesitated to ask the questions Tom must have been waiting for me to ask. Why else would he have shown me his hiding place. I hoped he wasn't thinking that the more I knew the less inclined he would be to allow me to leave. I didn't think Tom was that calculating or manipulative.

I looked around and when I saw that we were completely alone I asked, "What was that place, Tom?"

"That is where we keep most of our money," Tom replied, "as well as some special weapons and explosives."

"You now know more than 98% of the people in our organization do," Jack said.

"Tom trusts you very much, Jake, and so do I."

"I don't have to tell you how important it is that you not tell anyone what you've seen today," Tom said.

"It's time we thought of a name for you Jake," Tom said with a smile.

"How about Sea Slug," Jack said with a sarcastic laugh and a punch in my arm.

"I don't know. I think it should be something that fits his personality," Tom said.

"Then how come you don't call Jack Hammerhead?" I asked with a laugh.

"I thought of you, Jake, when I first spotted that octopus," Tom said. "You're moody and you have a variety of attitudes and personalities. In your profession you have to be adaptive and chameleon-like, and you need to be able to assume the characteristics of your surroundings in order to blend in. You have to be flexible and you need to respond to ever-changing situations."

"He also moves his hands around so much when he talks," Jack said, "that it sometimes appears as if he has eight of them. When he gets really excited it's like a blur of movement."

"Octopus it is then," Tom said.

"What do you think, Jake?"

I felt so close to Tom and Jack at that moment and it felt so good to be wanted and to fit in with a group of men that I so greatly admired that I reacted to the emotion of the moment and told Tom that I liked the name just fine and that I would be honored to join the organization.

Tom asked me if I was sure, and when I said that I was certain, Jack picked me up and hugged me and spun me around the dock. We drank the rest of the beers and watched the sunset and then I hobbled back to my room. I felt relieved and I was also excited about the adventure that lay before me. That afternoon, while the sun sank into the Caribbean Sea, I looked up to see the prehistoric silhouette of a dozen pelicans as they passed between me and the darkening sky, and I realized that the old Jake Stein had died forever and that the Octopus was born.

CHAPTER 25

"Outstanding, Jake," Tom said when I placed my third shot in the heart of the paper target he had nailed to the tree. The rifle felt good in my hands and Tom's encouragement reminded me of the one time during Marine boot camp when I had gained the approval of my instructors. I was the best shot in our platoon and I had certified expert marksman on both the M16 and the 45 caliber handgun. Tom had fired five rounds first, to set the windage and elevation of the sights. He began to instruct me on its operation as we approached the target and I could see only two holes in the paper when we approached, that's how tight his grouping was.

I had placed five shots in the same area but my pattern was more spread out. We trained for over three hours and emptied over ten boxes of cartridges. We fired from several different positions and we even practiced firing on the run to simulate combat. The weapons both had silencers so that none of the guests on the other side of the island would hear us. Tom said he was very pleased with my sharpshooting and I tried to leverage his approval to get out of having to run all the way back to the shed with my rifle. It didn't work and I cursed under my breath as we ran up and down the trail until we reached the lower entrance of the headquarters, or Operations Center as Tom called it. Two days earlier, Tom had shown me the hidden entrance on the east side of the island, which sat just above the rocks at water level. There were no beaches on the east side of the island. There was just a rocky coral ridge. I had wondered when I first saw the larger pieces of equipment, including the Zodiacs, how they had gotten them downstairs in the elevator. There was a small cave at sea level which had two large doors that swung outward and revealed a ramp and the opening to the OPs center. It was very well camouflaged and again it could only be opened by a scan card and a numeric code that had to be entered on the keypad within ten seconds of using the card.

It could not be seen from the water and there was only a very narrow, well hidden trail to approach it by land, which we were now traversing. Inside the cave was a small metal walkway that was suspended above the water and I leaned against the wet cave wall as Tom punched in his security code. We entered the OPs center and the lights came on automatically. Tom led me to one of the easels in front of the classroom and asked me to have a seat.

"Operation Corona," Tom said as he flipped one of the pages on the easel and showed the next page, which displayed a blueprint drawing of a large cruise ship. Suddenly, there was a high pitched ringing on the overhead intercom system and Tom excused himself and told me that he had to take a stateside call on one of the secured lines.

While he was in the other room, I looked around and on one of the tables I saw a black leather briefcase. I picked it up, undid the clasp that sealed it and opened it. There was a report inside with the word "SweetTooth" typed on the cover. I only read one half of one page when I heard Tom coming back, and put the report back in the briefcase and sealed it. I dropped it back on the desk just as Tom walked up to me. I had only read half of one page but I read the date and the location of what must have been an operation that RedTide had obviously been planning for a long time. It was going to take place in the Florida Everglades at a sugar refinery on June 15. Tom looked at the desk and then at me but he didn't seem to notice that anything had been disturbed.

"Tomorrow the last of our guests will be checking out and tomorrow night ten more men who you have never met will be checking in as our new guests, only they will of course be RedTide soldiers.

"Friday night, you will attend your first strategy meeting and you will hear in great detail the plans for the mission we have organized for May 5."

Cinco de Mayo, I thought.

"I wanted to prepare you beforehand Jake, so that you would be more relaxed and receptive to it. On May 5, we will board a Mardi Gras cruise ship after it has unloaded the majority of its passengers in town. It is their newest and grandest ship, *The Royal Fiesta*, and we will intercept it while it is making its third stop on its maiden voyage at Cozumel, Mexico."

"After we offload the remaining passengers and its crew we are going to set it on fire. We are going to burn it and leave a hollowed-out skeleton floating on the surface. We have been planning this with our expert technicians, ordinance, and demolition personnel for over three months to make sure that the ship doesn't blow up, sink or spill any fuel or oil into the water.

"You will be on board, Jake, and will stay with me on this mission the entire time as my assistant. You will do whatever I tell you. For the most part you will be my runner and although we will all have radios, you will help to deliver important information to our officers so that they can facilitate the timely removal of the crew. I don't expect there to be any resistance and there should not be any casualties."

I could feel my pulse quicken as I realized that playtime was over and that I was about to become involved in a criminal act that could either get me killed or could land my ass in jail for twenty years.

"I don't want to talk out of turn, Tom, but what will this accomplish? The cruise line has over thirty ships in its fleet and they're not the ones who are building the dock."

Tom smiled patiently and sat beside me. "Jake, the politics and the economics of the situation are very complicated and I won't bore you with a long lecture. I will tell you that when we burn that ship and everything aboard it, including all the belongings of the passengers, that we will also issue a warning to the cruise ship line and to all the other cruise ship lines and their prospective passengers that Cozumel is not the place to take a cruise.

"Without the financial support and commitment from the cruise lines to send their fleets to the area the builders will have no choice but to close down the construction of the pier. It's either that or face certain bankruptcy. The cruise ship lines may decide to play hardball and they may at first issue a proclamation that their company policies are not set by terrorists, but without passengers it has no validity.

"Believe me, Jake, my plan will have the desired effect. The passengers will be standing on the town pier and they'll be watching the ship engulfed in flames one hundred feet high and they will realize that not only could they have been on board but that they have also just lost their jewelry and other valuables. They will never think of cruising Cozumel's waters again, and neither will their friends or relatives or anyone else who sees the fire on the evening news."

"I don't know how I feel about punishing the innocent people on board, Tom," I said. "Why should we be ruining their trip? Some of them could be honeymooners or retirees who are taking their first self-indulgent trip after a lifetime of hard work. They will lose their money as well as their irreplaceable mementos and photos, but they will also lose something else which is even more valuable. They will lose their hope and they will lose some small sense of security that we will replace with the feeling that even on a vacation in an idyllic location they're not safe. I'm sorry, Tom, but that really sucks. Those people haven't done anything wrong."

"Jake, I appreciate your feelings. I've wrestled with those same thoughts and feelings for years but I came to realize over time that what those people really stand to lose is greater than some trinkets and their two-week vacation. If, little by little, in all parts of the world we allow the natural world to be destroyed, over-utilized, and polluted they will lose their future and their children's and grandchildren's futures.

"In twenty, thirty or even fifty years no one will be able to visit places like Cozumel, or the rainforests of South America, or Antarctica, or Alaska, or the Galapagos, or any of the other unspoiled wilderness areas of the planet. The places we admire and long to visit because of their pristine conditions we are systematically destroying at an exponential rate.

"Don't feel sorry for the people on that boat, Jake. Believe me, the majority of them are selfish, self-indulgent and completely apathetic to what's going on around them. The wake up call they will get that day, although painful, will be the best thing that could have ever happened to them. They won't be able to avert their eyes and continue to pretend that they don't see. They won't be able to fool themselves by thinking that bad things only happen to other people. This whole mind set of 'not in my backyard' or 'let somebody else worry about it', will be destroyed forever.

"In the following weeks after the mission they will constantly be switching their TVs to the news with an interest they never had before, and they will be reading the papers with an appetite and an interest level they have never exhibited in their long catatonic existences. If for no other reason than to hear about their own experience. But at the same time they will hear about us and what we do and why we do it and maybe if just a handful of them become enlightened it will be worth it."

I had never seen Tom so fired up and I decided that he was probably right. It would take me awhile to get used to making painful decisions and to see the big picture, but I trusted Tom with all my heart.

"Tonight, Jake, you will meet some of the Marine Iguanas. They are my personal Praetorian Guard and they are some of my most trusted and experienced officers. They can be a little intimidating at first so just relax and I'll tell you a secret to level the field for you. You are a better shot than most of them and they will be impressed."

We left the OPs center after Tom showed me some of the weapons and equipment we would be using in Cozumel, including the Zodiacs and the large machine guns. Then I had to leave to meet Jack and Samantha on the beach to help bring the remaining guests to the airstrip on Guanaja. We were scheduled for additional martial arts training later that afternoon on the beach. It was a little uncomfortable for me having to spar with Samantha, especially since she would almost always win. We wore headgear and footgear and gloves, but I was still reluctant to strike her with any real force. I was having a hard time learning the kicks since I never really had much flexibility to begin with. Samantha was deadly with her feet and could even hold Jack at bay with her flying kicks.

Jack told me that I was a natural with my hands and that I had great speed and instincts when it came to blocking. I told him that it came from self preservation and an overwhelming fear of being hit in the face. One day I was sparring with Samantha and she was cursing me because she felt that I was holding back, which I was.

She kicked me in the side of the head and when I was down she kicked me in the ribs and I felt a rush of violent anger I had never felt before. I leapt to my feet, ignoring the pain, and I rushed at her, throwing a flurry of punches at her head and body. She was blocking me and I moved in close so she couldn't use her feet and I connected with a solid right cross to her cheek and nose that knocked her to the ground. I stood over her heaving in and out, the blood pounding in my temples and I felt disconnected to myself in that moment.

I loved her and the last thing I wanted to do was to hurt her, but for the last thirty seconds all I felt was deadly rage. Suddenly I felt sick to my stomach. She stood up slowly and Jack said, "Good, Jake" in the background, but I could barely hear him.

Sam took off her headgear and blood was pouring from her nose. "I'm so sorry, Sam," I said. "I lost control."

She looked up at me and wiped her nose. Then she lifted her head in a proud gesture and said something that broke my heart.

"I've been hit harder by men twice your size, Jake, just because I spilled their coffee or because they had too much to drink. You were defending yourself. Don't worry about it." Then she turned and walked off to her room.

Later in her room I kissed her and held her and put ice on her cheek where I had struck her. "I would rather cut off my hand than ever raise it to you," I told her. "I'm through training together. I'll work with Jorge or even Jack from now on."

"I meant what I said before Jake.

"You were defending yourself. That's what we're trying to teach you. The reason I was so rough on you was because I was trying to evoke the response I got. It's my fault, if there is any fault, which there is not. I was worried about you, Jake. You're gentle and sensitive and have no killer instinct. While I love that about you it will get you killed in this business. If you hesitate for even a moment because you have a crisis of conscience or because you decide to show mercy to your opponent, you will be dead just as quickly. It breaks my heart to have to see you change but I know that if you are determined to be "Octopus" instead of my Jake, then it is imperative to your survival."

We made love tenderly and with renewed affection and when she was asleep in my arms with her back to me I stroked her hair and whispered quietly to the back of her head.

"I love you Samantha. I wish I could tell you how much." I stood up and quietly left the room. I walked on the beach and thought about the mission in Cozumel. I reflected on our trip there and thought about all I had learned in the past two months and I remembered my pledge to protect the reef that day as we were returning on the boat. Like a Buddhist reciting mantras I repeated to myself the environmental facts until I felt a rejuvenation of my spirit and a strengthening in my resolve to become a part of the solution. As I walked back to Sam's room I thought about Jackie and John and all my friends back home who I would never see or talk to again. I prayed that night to my mother to help me to be strong and to walk beside me at my moment of truth. I had a new family now and they were counting on me. I would not let them down.

CHAPTER 26

It was 6:45 PM on May 5th. I was dressed in black from head to toe with black makeup covering my entire face. I was issued a small machine pistol and a combat knife and I was told to stay quiet and to wait for further orders. There were a total of thirty of us in Cozumel tonight. Some of us had flown in a week ago and some of us had arrived only yesterday. I had arrived yesterday with Angelfish on the Fiesta Cruise ship. We had been posing as passengers but now we were dressing in our cabin preparing to take over the ship. There were four other people from RedTide on the boat who were posing as passengers, including Lionfish and Dorado, also known as Peter, who had returned from his assignment in Australia. Peter was one of the team leaders who were sharing the cabin next door. According to the plan, we would leave our cabins and would work our way below decks to clear the ship. We were supposed to herd the remaining crew and passengers to the pool deck while the demolition teams rigged the ship with explosives and saturated the hallways and decks with the flammable gelatinous material they were bringing aboard.

I was initially supposed to follow Lionfish around, but after some persuasive arguing on my part, Lionfish allowed me to stay with Angelfish, assigning me to her team. Two weeks ago, at our first planning meeting, I was introduced to the rest of the team and I received an enthusiastic welcome to the organization. It was amazing to see Lionfish in action around his men. He was truly in his element, barking out orders and going over strategy and implementation. It was like seeing a completely different person and I was in awe of his organizational skills and his leadership abilities.

We went over tactics and planning every day and every night for two weeks, first as a group and then in individual teams. My team leader's name was Marlin, and I never knew him by any other name. He had been with RedTide for over nine years and he had risen quickly through the ranks to command a squad of Marine Iguanas. He was 6'3" tall and weighed about 190 pounds. He had a short blond crew cut and blue eyes and a very serious no-nonsense demeanor. I learned to like him and found him to be fair and patient although he scared the piss out of me whenever he yelled my name.

I also met Tarpon, the head of demolitions, who barely said two words to me upon our introduction. He and Stingray were in the shed and the laboratory day and night. Sometimes when we would leave the building we would hear them yelling and arguing from frustration. Lionfish told me one day that they had many concerns. One was that the ship would explode or spill fuel if it were lit on fire and that they were trying to find a way to contain the fire to the upper decks without allowing it to spread to the engine rooms.

Another major concern was air pollution from the burning plastic and oil and fuel on board and other toxic fumes that the burning ship would project into the air which would only fall back to earth again to pollute the water and surrounding area.

Eventually, they resolved one of the problems and designated one of the smaller teams, led by Jack and Jorge, to place small charges below deck to flood the ship and to flood the engine rooms and the fuel areas with salt water. They also had devised a way to seal the flooded areas and to keep the ship from sinking. In a brilliant display of resourcefulness, Lionfish had obtained a copy of the ship's schedule for refueling and he planned the attack at a time when the ship would be almost empty. One of our teams would offload the remaining fuel.

Stingray wanted to sink the ship at an 11,000 foot wall off the coast and argued vehemently for his plan. He thought it would be ironic and explained the poetic justice in replacing the reef the cruise line was helping to destroy with an artificial one made from their own 300 million dollar cruise ship. His plan was voted down in the end.

Lionfish and the other chief officers believed that the pressure at that depth would tear the ship apart and would scatter debris all over the bottom of the sea. They decided that the burning of the ship would be the lesser of two evils. The ship was supposed to be virtually deserted since it was the ship's last scheduled night in town and it was also Cinco de Mayo. Almost everyone on board was going to be in town, even the majority of the ship's employees. The ship's activity director had been advertising the festival for days and had distributed flyers and had made constant announcements about it. Lionfish had really done his homework.

There was only going to be a skeleton crew on board to run the engines and maintain operations. When I came aboard ship in the port in Hollywood, Florida and saw the size of it I couldn't imagine how only thirty of RedTide's men could clear a ship this size. The temptation to call my friends was overwhelming, standing at the port only twenty minutes from the LifeForce offices.

The ship was enormous. It resembled a floating city or a large metropolitan hotel. There was an atrium ten stories high in the lobby with ten elevators made of glass that were riding up and down within the ship. There were two pools and a bowling alley and a movie theater that was showing first run movies. There was a casino and a full gymnasium with basketball and racquetball courts and there were three dining rooms and ballrooms.

There was an enormous amount of food on board. They served enough at every meal to feed six starving nations for a year. I was surprised at how lax security seemed to be. What a noise RedTide would make when they totaled Mardi Gras' investment. I could see why they were hunted so tirelessly and had so many powerful enemies. The show was supposed to begin at 7 P.M. sharp and I checked my watch again. It was 6:50 exactly and I was afraid I might change my mind and decide to stay in the cabin until the end.

Samantha came out of the bathroom and I gasped in surprise. She was wearing a thin black nylon ski mask over her head and face. I couldn't see anything of her face except for her eyes. She had even put on black lipstick and had blended it in with the black face make up. Her hair was down inside her shirt and she was wearing the same black pants and light turtleneck shirt I was wearing. She was beginning to don her Kevlar vest and she told me to put mine on.

"I thought we weren't expecting any gunplay," I said.

"It's safer to always prepare for the unexpected, Octopus," she said hitting on my code name with a distinct trace of sarcasm.

"You look hot in that outfit, Sam," I said. "I think I should do some body painting on you with that black crayon just to make sure you're completely camouflaged."

"I'm surprised to see you joking at a time like this, Jake. The first time I went out on a mission I could barely talk. My teeth were chattering, and I had extensive military training."

"The truth is, Sam, that I'm scared shitless. I always joke around when I'm nervous. Please be careful. I'm more worried about you than I am about myself. I love you." I had finally summoned the courage to say it again. "You're one of the main reasons I'm here."

"This isn't the time," she said, ignoring my declaration of love for the second time. "You're here tonight because for whatever reason you felt it was right. It was your choice and I don't want the responsibility of your involvement on my head."

"Forget it. You're right," I replied with annoyance. "I wanted to be here today. It's totally my decision. I just don't want you to get hurt. Is that so hard to understand?"

She softened up and she pulled her ski mask off her face and kissed me on the lips, smearing black on my lower lip and teeth.

"No Jake, I understand completely. I'm worried about you as well. That's why I asked Lionfish to assign us together so that I could personally watch out for you. Don't worry, this is a cake walk compared with some of the things we've been involved in. No one is going to get hurt."

Samantha checked her watch. "Now, let's go. It's 2 minutes to kick-off."

I pulled on my knit cap, checked my makeup, and locked and loaded my weapon. Then I followed Sam to the door. We exited the room at exactly 7 and followed our outlined path to the stairwell. We descended to the Cortez Deck. So far we saw no one aboard, not even a bellman and Samantha reported in to Marlin, who also reported all clear to Lionfish. The demolition teams should have been on the upper decks by now after they pulled up alongside in their Zodiacs. By now they should have begun to spread the fuel mixture that Tarpon had manufactured.

We arrived on the Cortez Deck to find a commotion and my first contact with a live engagement. We found the rest of our team and the B team, which was led by Hammerhead. They were on their way below deck to begin the sealing and flooding stage and had run into a group of college football players from LSU who were drinking in their cabins. The students were startled when they came out of their rooms and ran right into a group of armed men in ski masks. After ten years of Bruce Willis's *Die Hard* sequels they immediately recognized the situation and were inspired to be heroic. Team B led by Hammerhead was in the process of immobilizing them when Samantha and I joined up with them. To my distinct displeasure, RedTide soldiers were kicking and striking them repeatedly. They had knocked some of them unconscious and had poured great amounts of their blood onto the blue carpet in the hallway.

"Help me tie these men up so that Team B can get below," Sam ordered.

I began to tie the men's hands and feet behind their backs with the pull ties that we were carrying for just this purpose, although I naively believed that I wouldn't be using them. Team B headed below decks to begin their work and Samantha and I were told by Marlin that we should sweep the area for any other passengers. Three of our men came into view at the end of the hallway. They had a large plastic barrel and they began to spread the liquid gel they were carrying along the carpet while we knocked on doors and looked for passengers. We were yelling FIRE! and ABANDON SHIP! and we could hear our teammates doing the same.

I found a young couple who were having sex in one of the cabins below and with my weapon pointed at them I ordered them out of their room. They joined the other thirty passengers that we had found. I looked into the faces of the passengers we had rounded up and I felt horrified at the combination of terror and hatred I saw there.

These were normal people, like my family or my friends, and I felt myself losing control of my senses. I wanted to run away and disappear until I looked up at Samantha and she nodded at me and asked me if I was okay. I was sweating profusely and the makeup was itching my face. We herded the passengers and crew to the pool deck and I checked my watch. Five men were sent below to carry out the bodies of LSU's offensive line. Only fifteen minutes had passed since we began. I felt adrenaline flowing like Niagara Falls through my veins and the feeling of exhilaration was intoxicating. When we arrived on deck I saw Lionfish for the first time.

Even in black clothing and black paint he was unmistakable. His bearing was regal and he exuded tremendous confidence and authority as he issued directives to his men. All the passengers and crew members were loaded into lifeboats, then were lowered into the water by the electric powered hydraulic cranes on the ship. Every detail and contingency had been planned for, even the operation of every part of the ship. I was confident that if needed Lionfish's men could probably have run the engines and navigated the ship out to sea.

When the last of the passengers were unloaded and the entire team was on deck, Lionfish looked at his watch and nodded to Hammerhead. He lifted a small black box in his hand and pressed a button. There was a loud rumble and a muffled boom from below decks and the floor began to shake like a small tremor from an earthquake. I knew from our briefing that the smaller charges that were designed to flood the engine rooms and lower compartments had been detonated. After five minutes, Lionfish signaled to Marlin to detonate the incendiaries.

Marlin raised the small black box and Lionfish ordered all of us into the Zodiacs. As Marlin moved his thumb toward the button a shot rang out and I saw his throat blow apart. He was thrown backward and landed writhing on the deck. I stood still in shock as total pandemonium broke loose on the deck. I looked up as shots sounded out and bullets ricocheted around me.

Our men began to fire back and as I leapt for cover I looked desperately for Angelfish. I couldn't find her. She and the rest of our men had begun to spread out and were firing back at the security men above who had obviously been hiding out while they waited for the passengers to get out of harm's way. The black box was against the railing where it had flown from Marlin's hand and I could see that Lionfish was trying to get to it. He was being held back from the continued gun fire that was being laid down in his direction.

I made a break for it since the path for me was almost completely well protected by equipment and metal barricades. I summoned up a reserve of courage and I ran toward the black box. I crouched behind a low metal wall and cringed as bullets slammed against the quarter inch metal that was directly behind my head. I reached for the box and picked it up.

I hesitated for a moment at the realization of what I was about to do and the number of laws I was about to break, then I heard Lionfish yell to me, *"Do it Jake."* I snapped out of it and I pressed the button. This time there was a thunderous explosion that shook the entire ship and made it sway slightly despite its size. In seconds, this was followed by the rolling sound of thunder, which was the fire ball consuming the ship from the inside, igniting the gel as it passed from deck to deck. Lionfish ran past me firing above and was momentarily hidden by a dark cloud of black smoke that was beginning to engulf the ship.

"We need to get off this ship, right now, Jake!" he yelled as he passed me. "The smoke will kill us and the guards in a matter of minutes."

"Let's go. Forget the guards," he yelled out to his men and into the microphone attached to his shirt. "The mission is accomplished. The smoke will take care of the guards."

We were working our way toward the stern of the ship, firing above as we retreated, and regrouped with the other teams. I looked around to see several men who were hurt and I saw that Peter was mortally wounded. Jorge tended his wounds and applied a pressure bandage. I became frantic and I looked for Samantha. I was overjoyed when I finally saw her among another group of men and I could see that she was unharmed. The smoke had momentarily taken care of the guards above and had temporarily blinded them but they were being driven below deck toward our level.

Thankfully the wind was blowing the smoke away from us. The deck was getting very hot and an orange glow already lit the sky and blended in with the colors of sunset. Some guards had already worked their way down and began to fire at us. I heard the sound of rounds whizzing past us and was terrified of being hit at any moment. I had not yet fired my weapon and I finally turned and fired at the area only sixty yards away where the guards were pinned down by Jack and his men. I was surprised at how heavily armed a security detachment upon a luxury liner was. They must have been preparing for some trouble, what with the recent protest by Greenpeace and the threats they were receiving from various organizations. Lionfish had told me that RedTide had issued no warnings and had sent no ultimatums.

Jorge came over to where I was standing and with tears in his eyes told me that Peter had died. Jorge joined Jack and they led several men to circle around behind the guards while a few men and I returned fire from our position. I could see Samantha on the other side of the ship with Lionfish and three other men. We were separated by thirty feet of deck and by a continuous barrage of high velocity bullets. The guards were keeping us from leaving the ship.

I heard Lionfish scream "NO" and I turned around to see that Samantha had been hit. I ran over to her and suddenly there was no more shooting and the ship became quiet. I could see she was hit three times by a spray of automatic fire. Two bullets had hit her in her chest and been absorbed by her Kevlar vest but one bullet had hit her in her neck only an inch above her vest The remaining guards had been rounded up by Jorge and Jack, including the one who had shot Sam, and they were herded to the back of the ship where we were standing.

I knelt down next to Samantha who was lying in Lionfish's arms and I screamed her name as the tears burst forth in a torrent from my eyes. I put my hand over her carotid artery to stop the flow of blood and as I applied pressure to the area I begged Tom for his help. I felt her life pump out between my fingers and I knew that she was almost gone.

"Jake," she whispered. I knelt down and put my ear next to her mouth and I felt her warm breath on my face. "I'm sorry, Jake. I'm sorry I hurt you. I should have told you that first night on the dock but I was so afraid. I do love you Jake. I have from the first day we met. Please forgive me."

I didn't think after my mother had passed away that I could ever experience that kind of searing pain again, but what I felt at that moment tore me apart from the inside out and drove me to the edge of madness.

I kissed her cheek and held her as she spoke her last words.

"Please Jake," she said, "get out. Go home while you still can."

Then she arched her back in pain and let out her last breath which I swallowed as I kissed her on her mouth for the last time. I looked up at Tom and his eyes were red, glistening in the glow of the fire.

"I'm sorry, Jake," he said. "We have to get off this boat. We can't wait and we have to leave Samantha."

"What should we do with them?" Jack said with tears in his eyes as he pushed two of the guards he had helped capture toward us.

Jorge yelled out, "*KILL THEM*" as he raised his rifle at the guards. I heard the words "*KILL THEM*" echo in my ears.

I went insane with grief and with hatred and I jumped to my feet and ran toward the guards. I began to beat them with my fists. I threw my weapon at the Marine Iguanas who moved in to stop me and I removed the combat knife I was carrying from its sheath. I raised it in the air and started to swing it at the security guard nearest to me when I felt a crack to the back of my head and I realized that I had been struck from behind by one of my own men. I collapsed to my knees and I hit the deck. The blow had made be involuntarily release my bladder and as I passed into unconsciousness I imagined that I heard laughter from the men around me. Laughter! How could that be, while my love was lying dead only a few feet away? I fought to remain conscious then I felt a hand brush the hair away from my face and I heard Tom's voice say, "I'm sorry Jake. You gave me no choice." I knew in that final instant of consciousness that it was Tom that had struck me from behind and then the world turned black around me.

CHAPTER 27

I HAD BEEN SLEEPING ON AND OFF for over a week since we had returned from Cozumel. It was 11:30 in the morning before I opened my eyes and rolled over and put my face in the pillow next to me. I breathed deeply and I smelled Samantha on my pillow and I wept for the first time since that night. I noticed the first morning that I woke up back in my cabin in Arrecife that Samantha's smell was still in the room. Thankfully I had left the "Do Not Disturb" sign on my door before we left for Mexico and none of the maids had entered the room. Now I wouldn't let them in at all and the room smelled dank and musty from the humidity and from my own body odor.

I had not showered or eaten in almost a week and I got out of bed only to go to the bathroom or to get a drink of water. I tried to will myself to die but knew it would take me over a month to starve to death. I also knew that I lacked the courage to see it through to the end. My head still hurt from where Tom had struck me and I had several bad nights where the headaches kept me awake. Tom came to my room with a doctor three times in the last week. Each time he came he asked me to forgive him and to try and understand why he had to stop me from assaulting the security guard on the boat. The doctor administered a sedative that only hastened my journey back into oblivion.

I wouldn't speak to anyone at all the first few days we were back. I would only stare off into space and daydream about Samantha and I would reminisce about our short time together. I kept replaying her last words to me over and over again in my head. I was trying to evoke or trigger some happy memories for myself. I was surprised that I felt so little. I actually felt nothing but emptiness and a dull ache. I intellectualized about my loss and I tried to evoke some feeling as I layed in bed hour after hour. I never cried or screamed or felt anything like what I felt when I lost my mother.

I cried almost continuously then and I felt such a deep burning physical pain that I would sometimes gulp down large glasses of straight vodka just to stop it.

"I love you," Sam had said, "I love you, Jake." She finally said the words I had so desperately wanted to hear but the words had come too late for us to celebrate our love together. Tom sat at the foot of my bed three days ago and pleaded with me to eat something. The insensitive asshole started to tell me what a success the raid had been in Cozumel until I looked up at him with incredulity and he stopped. There was a knock at the door and I ignored it. Suddenly Jorge entered the room and he pulled up a chair. He told me that I needed to get up and that Samantha wouldn't have wanted me to lay around feeling sorry for myself.

He told me about a time when Sam had lost a close friend and mentor on a raid and how she had bounced back from her grief. Then he said something that finally got my attention. He told me that RedTide had also taken some high level businessmen from Consorcio H as hostages as well as some Mexican officials on the same day of the raid and that one of them had been killed by an overzealous guard while he was trying to escape.

I finally turned and looked at him and I noticed that Jorge also looked as if he hadn't eaten or slept in a week. He noticed my appraisal of his appearance and with tears in his eyes he told me that I wasn't the only one who was grieving and that he had also loved

Samantha. I reached out my hand to him and he took it and we held on to each other like two drowning men who were clinging to one life preserver. When Jorge left I took a shower and I decided to confront Tom about what I had learned. I dressed and my legs and arms felt stiff from the lack of movement over the past week. I still felt hollow inside and I still felt a little like the walking dead but now at least for the first time I felt something: anger.

As I approached Tom's office I could hear Jack's voice and I walked through the half-opened door without knocking. "Welcome back, Jake," Jack said, and Tom looked up from his desk and smiled sadly in my direction.

"Thanks, Jack. I don't know if I'm back yet or I'm just visiting temporarily. I feel as if I'm functioning mostly on autopilot, kind of just going through the motions of being alive."

"That's not uncommon, Jake," Tom said as he came around his desk and extended his hand, "we've all been through it.

"We missed you around here and I was just telling Jack that I'm going to need someone to run the dive operation and the hotel for me. I was hoping it could be you, once you feel up to it."

"I'm leaving, Tom. First thing tomorrow. That's why I stopped by. I need to get back home to my family and to my friends. Besides, I've discovered that I'm not cut out for this lifestyle. I realized that on the boat even before.....Sam was hurt. She was the main reason I stuck around in the first place and agreed to join RedTide."

Jack stood up and walked to the door, "I'll leave you guys alone to talk," he said.

"I loved Sam, we all did and I know she loved you. You were good for her, anyone could see that. I hope you decide to stay," he said just before he left the room.

"Look," Tom said. "If you want off of active duty for a while I'll understand. That doesn't mean you have to leave altogether. You could stay here strictly in a civilian capacity and you could run the hotel for us. You don't ever have to participate in an operation again. Just supporting our cover would be a tremendous contribution. We travel 6-8 months a year and for all intents and purposes you would be the manager of this place. You've said it yourself. That's a dream job."

"I can't stay. There are too many memories of Sam here. Everywhere I go I run into reminders of her. For me this place is Sam and it's just too hard for me to be here without her. I could never be happy here. Everything's changed. My initial naiveté and infatuation about this idyllic place and the people here, including yourself, isn't what it was a month ago."

I decided to bring up the subject of the hostages. I wasn't angry any more after seeing Tom face to face but I was still completely disillusioned and I needed to confront Tom to see his reaction. Standing here in front of him I realized how much I had grown to love him and the realization of what or who he might actually be broke my heart almost as much as Sam's death.

"I know about the hostages and the murder, Tom."

"Why didn't you tell me?"

"I can't reconcile that knowledge with what I thought I knew about you and the goals of your organization. My own participation in the raid hasn't made me feel proud or fulfilled like I thought it would, it's made me feel sick and ashamed. I don't belong here and I know that now."

Tom looked sad and then his visage changed to one of anger and I felt a cold chill run up my spine as he walked slowly toward me. He stopped when his face was only a few inches from my own.

"So you're quitting.... Is that it, Jake? How many times does that make now? When I studied your file I lost count. You quit every hobby or sport you started when you were growing up, from wrestling to playing the guitar. You quit high school to join the Marine Corps, then quit the Marine Corps. Then you started college and quit after a few years. You've quit so many jobs I would need a Cray computer to tally the count. You've walked out on countless relationships, even an engagement once. You went to Israel, ostensibly to become a citizen, and then you came crying home after only three months because it wasn't comfortable there.

"You even walked out on your mother after your dad left her at a time when she needed you the most. I think I see a pattern emerging here, Jake," he said with extreme sarcasm.

"You get all fired up about something and then you can't wait to join. You're all full of piss and vinegar, then when the going gets tough, you get going somewhere else."

Tom was firing words at me and his voice was rising in timbre. I kept stepping backward as he spit his words in my face and he kept advancing until I was up against the wall.

"This isn't high school or karate class, Jake, and you're not fifteen-years-old anymore. Do you think you can just walk in here and tell me you don't feel like playing any more? This isn't a game. I've put the lives of over 200 people, including mine and my brother's, in your hands. Do you think RedTide is just going to let you get in a boat and sail away tomorrow?" He said waving his hand in the air behind him.

I was beginning to tremble as I realized the implication of what he was saying to me and his words began to choke me. I squirmed away from him and stepped into the center of the room.

"Obviously Tom you've done your homework and you're right about me, I am a quitter. I could blame my father for telling me my whole life that I was a worthless piece of shit and that I could never do anything and that I would never be anybody. I could spew some psychobabble about fear of success but I'm an adult now and it's time I accepted responsibility for my own choices.

"I don't have to explain myself to you, Tom."

I lost my fear and I became angry.

"Another thing, Tom. Please don't ever mention my mother again. My mother always believed in me and she suffered greatly at the hands of my father when she tried to run interference to protect me. You don't know a goddamn thing about my mother or our relationship.

"Who are you to judge me anyway? You're a murderer and a criminal. I don't even know your real name. The only two people that ever really loved me are dead and I don't really care what you or RedTide do to me. I'm leaving here tomorrow."

I headed toward the door. I was surprised at my own anger but I was still terrified at the sudden overwhelming realization of what I had gotten myself into. Tom stepped in my way and blocked my path and I felt my heart skip a beat when I looked up at him and again I saw what an enormously powerful man he was.

"You're right."

He was less angry and more conciliatory. "I'm in no position to judge you and I was out of line in taking a cheap shot and in commenting about you and your mom's relationship. I just want you to recognize what a serious breach of security your leaving would represent to the organization. I've gambled everything by trusting you and the depth of your commitment to our organization. You're talking about quitting already after only one mission and in less than six weeks as a member. You would be leaving here with enough information to force us to evacuate this island. It would force us to destroy millions of dollars that we've invested here, not to mention the time and the logistics involved.

"I like you, Jake, but we could never allow you to leave now without at least a week of debriefing and extensive preparation. It's not personal, it's a matter of survival. You need to take at least a couple of weeks to think about things and to allow yourself to get through the shock and grief of losing someone you loved. I think that's only fair.

"Forget work for a while. Go diving or sleep in. I don't care what you do just as long as you do it here. You need to get through this period of mourning without any distractions. I loved Sam also. I brought her into this organization after I broke the arm of a staff sergeant she had been dating. He was twisting her arm at a bar in Houston. That's how we met. I saved her life on several occasions and I alone carry the burden of responsibility for her death.

"You're not the only one who has conflicts about what we do and you're not the only one here with a conscience. You loved Samantha. Do you think she was a heartless killer? Don't you trust her choices? She was one of RedTide's most enthusiastic members and she participated in over twenty missions. I didn't tell you about the hostages because you didn't need to know. You had your assignment for the mission and the rest of our plans were highly confidential and were known only to the highest ranking members of the organization.

"If another soldier came in here demanding to know why he wasn't informed I would take his head off. I've already been accused of going soft and in showing you special consideration. If I've shown you more latitude it's because I feel a connection with you, Jake, that I can't explain, and I want you to stay.

"Promise me you'll think things over for awhile and that you won't force my hand. I don't want to have to do anything that I would regret."

Tom held out his hand and I took it in my own. I tried to look him in the eyes but I was afraid I might reveal my true feelings and so I looked down at the ground. I told him I would think things over and I promised him that if I left I would never do anything to hurt him or anyone here. I walked back to my cabin and I made plans for my escape. I knew I could never stay here and I also knew that if I left it up to RedTide they would never let me go. I decided to stay a week or more and I knew I needed to regain their trust. I knew they would be watching me every minute now. I hoped that they wouldn't just decide one day to eliminate me and bury me in the jungle.

My sister knew I was here so they had to know that if I disappeared the first place they would look would be here. I knew they were too smart to let the trail lead back to Arrecife and I knew that they would never let the authorities focus attention on the property. I would have to be extra careful if I went scuba diving since an accident would be an acceptable explanation for my death.

I returned to my room and could not believe how my feelings had changed in only a matter of hours. Fear could be a very motivating stimulant. I was surprised and disappointed at how easily self preservation could brush aside sadness and depression. The survival instinct really is amazing. I thought about Samantha and then I thought about Tom's words to me about her choices and her loyalties.

He might have been right about Sam's feelings of loyalty and her perceived debt to him, but he was wrong about how she felt about my involvement, but I knew I could never tell him that. I couldn't tell him what Sam had whispered to me just before she passed away.

I rolled over on my side and I closed my eyes and imagined that she was in the room and that she was lying beside me. I pretended I was holding her and we were laughing. I kissed her and stroked her hair while she gently scratched my back. I knew it would be harder and harder over time to recreate our time together but at that moment it seemed so real. I could almost taste her in my mouth and I cried and I ached for her. There was nothing for me here anymore and within two weeks I would be thousands of miles away from Arrecife and from RedTide.

Hopefully over time, my silence would prove that I could be trusted and I would never see or hear from RedTide again. I couldn't be that wrong about what I'd felt for Tom. He might have had to do many ugly things in his life to protect his beliefs and to promote his cause but I couldn't and I wouldn't believe that he would hurt me or that he would allow anyone else to hurt me. I told myself that over and over again as I daydreamed about Samantha, and I finally fell asleep.

I dreamed about my mother and my dreams were full of danger and warnings. In my dreams my mother seemed worried, and in one dream we were caught in a house and it was on fire. I was only six-years-old and I was stuck in my room. I was choking from black smoke and when I went to touch the door handle it burned my hand. I fell to the floor and I cried for my mother. Suddenly, I felt a pair of strong hands lift me from the floor and carry me from the room. A voice told me not to worry. I tried to look up to see who was carrying me but my eyes were burning from the acrid smoke of burning carpet and plastic. Finally the smoke cleared and I saw that it was Tom and that he was carrying me to safety.

I felt safe but as we approached the front door I heard my mother's voice in one of the back rooms and she was crying out for help. I screamed for Tom to put me down and to help me get her out of the house as her screams intensified. Tom pulled my hair and turned my head toward him and he said in a sinister voice, "Forget her, Jake. You don't need her anymore." He continued on toward the front door while I kicked and squirmed in his arms. I was screaming for my mother. Her screams from the back of the house sounded tortured and agonized.

"Jake! Jake!" She screamed. "Help me!"

I begged Tom to let me go to her and he began to laugh as he strengthened his grip on me. I woke up in a cold sweat, screaming for my mother, and I realized where I was. I shivered under my blanket and I strengthened my resolve to go home and to leave Arrecife behind forever.

"What do you mean, he's gone?" Lionfish bellowed as he grabbed Jorge around the neck and flung him into a nearby table.

"He was your responsibility and you were ordered to be his shadow twenty-four hours a day. I specifically ordered you to report to me every hour on the hour and now you tell me three hours after he first disappeared that you have no idea where he's gone."

Lionfish was in a rage and the men nearest to him began to maneuver away from the path of his infamous temper. Lionfish spun around and smashed his arm down on the heavy wooden table he was standing near and then he kicked a stool across the room of the OPs Center where he had convened this emergency meeting. Jack (Grunt), Tom (Lionfish), Jorge (Redfish) and Jerry (Stingray) had gathered there fifteen minutes after Jorge had burst into Lionfish's office and announced in a panic that Jake had disappeared.

Jorge and Jake had been leading a dive at San Francisco reef. Jorge had six people in his group and Jake had three, all beginners. Jorge's group entered the water last. When they came upon Jake's small group they were all ascending to the surface without Jake. Jorge quickly gave the thumbs up sign to his group and when they surfaced, Jake's entourage excitedly told Jorge that Jake had disappeared into Neptune's Throat.

Neptune's Throat was a long 150 foot vertical tunnel bored into the reef. It is 160 feet deep at the bottom where a small hole opens over the top of a 2000 foot wall. There is only one way out of the tunnel and it is through the very narrow opening at the bottom that shoots out over the wall. Most people swim down and turn around and swim back out the top. Then they circle around to get to the wall instead of taking the shortcut because it is necessary to remove your BC in order to fit through the small opening at the bottom of the tunnel. Jake's divers waited as he had instructed for over fifteen minutes for him to return. After twenty minutes they decided to surface and get help.

Jorge dove to the bottom of the tunnel to search for Jake after he loaded the guests back onto the boat. He searched the surrounding area for an hour and then he checked every dive boat that he came in contact with for another hour before he returned to the hotel to report Jake missing.

"He must have drowned and sank off the wall," Jorge said. "That's the only explanation."

"He's safe and sound and on his way back to Miami with the death sentence for this organization on his lips," Stingray said quietly from his seat near the elevator door.

"Stingray's right," Lionfish said more calmly after his explosive display a few minutes earlier. "Jake has gone home."

"What was the point of sneaking away?" Jack asked. "He had to know how easily we could locate him back in the States."

"Jake ran off because he knew we wouldn't let him leave and he's hoping that we won't follow him," Lionfish answered. "I'm sure he figured that he had no choice but to escape and now he'll take his chances on home turf. He's betting that we won't go so far as to assassinate him. He's probably assuming that we know that our secret is safe with him. He's probably also assuming that we know he would never betray us. He's hoping that our better natures will direct us to let him get back to his old life."

"That's quite alot of guesswork on your part, Tom," Jerry said. "It's amazing how perceptive you are where Jake is concerned. It's too bad you weren't that perceptive when you first decided to invite Jake to join our organization. If you remember correctly I pleaded with you at the time to reconsider. We all knew that Jake's decision to stay was more about being with Samantha than in doing anything worthwhile."

"Jake's a die hard spoiled civilian who's never been able to commit to anything. We all studied his profile and his biography before we voted on his membership. What's happened to you, Tom? Your instincts and your intelligence and security expertise have been absent without leave for the past six months."

Jorge and Jack had never heard Stingray publicly criticize Lionfish and they remained silent during the exchange, but they both felt the impact of his words on their morale.

"There have been more leaks and breaches of security in the last year than in the past ten years combined and now you've allowed a salesman to return to Florida with the fate of our entire organization in his control. What's even more frightening to me is his lack of control and his overwhelming instinct for self preservation."

Lionfish walked over to Stingray and whispered something in his ear and then walked back to the table he had kicked and sat down.

"We need to control this situation immediately. In less than five weeks we will begin the most important mission of the year against Florida's largest sugar producers in an attempt to save The Everglades. This is one of the world's most critical ecosytems and nothing can alter or interfere with our plans."

The three men in the room knew from long experience that every year on June 15 Lionfish scheduled RedTide's most significant operation and that no matter what happened they would proceed on that day. Only Jerry knew that it was the anniversary of their mother's death.

"Let's hear some ideas on how to contain this security threat," Lionfish announced.

"I hate to say this," Jack began, "but there really isn't anything to discuss. Jake has to be eliminated immediately. The instant that he's located."

"Jack's right," Jorge said. "I like Jake as much as anyone here and I don't think he would voluntarily give us up but we can't afford to take that chance. There's too much riding on trusting that he won't slip up or that he won't tell a friend or a family member."

"Aside from the obvious," Stingray added, "we all know that our enemies and the authorities are extremely resourceful. They've proven that beyond a shadow of a doubt recently by breaking down our security defenses on three separate occasions. I don't have to remind anyone about what just transpired in the desert. If Yamaguchi and Macgregor get their hands on Jake they won't be as gentle with him as the FBI. They'll have him talking in seconds. Jake could never hold out against torture or even a chemical interrogation.

"Jake has to be killed. It's the only way," Stingray finished. He looked up at the pained expression on his brother's face. Jerry couldn't understand Tom's feelings for Jake and he had to admit that he felt a little resentful, maybe even jealous about their relationship the past few months. Was it the connection between Jake and the recent death of his mother that struck a chord with Tom or was it the absence of a father? Tom was never that sentimental and he certainly was never the type to adopt a lost animal or an orphan. Nonetheless, Jerry could see that he was struggling with a decision he never would have hesitated to make in the past and he suddenly recognized with wonder that Tom loved Jake.

"What you're all saying makes sense, although I have to say that I'm surprised to hear Stingray, the pacifist of the organization speaking so matter of factly about assassinating Jake," Lionfish said with a harsh look in his brother's direction.

Lionfish paced back and forth for awhile with his hand to his chin. He was locked in deep thought.

"Look, Tom. No one here wants to hurt Jake," Jack said. "I've really taken to him myself and like everyone in this room I know he would never intentionally hurt us. But like Stingray said, there are too many other factors beyond Jake's control. There are elements that Jake hasn't considered in his naive assumption that if he decides to keep a secret that's all there is to it."

"There's nothing more to discuss," Stingray said. "Jake's got to be taken out. The future of the entire organization depends on it."

Lionfish turned quickly on Stingray with an angry look. " I'll decide what needs to be discussed and I alone will make the final decision. Were you all under the impression that because I asked for your opinion that this represented a democratic process in the final outcome."

"Take it easy," Jack said, standing on his feet.

"You take it easy and sit down," Lionfish commanded. "No one here is going to harm a hair on Jake's head until I, and I alone give the order."

Lionfish was heated up again and the men in the room became quiet and waited for his temper to abate.

"This is what we are going to do," Lionfish continued. "First, we have to find Jake. I'm sure he will be back in his own apartment soon. Since he knows he could never outrun us I doubt he would even try. Where would he go anyway? He's not going to leave his friends and family behind forever and he doesn't have that much money. I'm sure right now he's desperate to return to his old life and forget that he was ever here.

"Second, we make contact with Jake and let him know that we will be monitoring him for an indefinite period of time, both to contain him and to protect him from our numerous enemies. We also let him know how narrowly he escaped a death sentence today but that the execution of that sentence is always possible. It will hang over his head like the Sword of Damocles and it will be carried out should we perceive a threat to this organization.

"Third, we set up twenty-four hour a day surveillance on his house, his phone, his family, his friends, and his automobile. I want to be able to listen to every word he speaks, even if he talks in his sleep. I know how you all feel about this but my decision is final. I'm not prepared to murder an innocent civilian, especially a friend so easily, without first taking other measures and exhausting every other possibility. That's final. Now get to work and find Jake. This meeting is ended."

Jorge looked stunned and Jack just shook his head woefully as they headed to the elevator. When Tom & Jerry were alone, Jerry spoke.

"Tom, what are you doing? You know how I feel about violence, especially cold-blooded executions, but you also know that this is a mistake. What if Jake doesn't surface for awhile, let's say a couple of weeks. That's plenty of time for him to give us up."

"If we don't locate Jake for two weeks and the damage is already done as you fear, then what difference will killing him make at that point, except for retribution. The word will already be out at that point," Lionfish responded.

"The ideals and the integrity of this organization have been compromised enough over the past few years. I've done things I never would have imagined and I've had to kill people that I thought were my friends. I'm in no hurry to kill someone I know is my friend. I've also killed countless innocent civilians that we've written off as collateral damage in our war to save the planet.

"I've rationalized my actions as being necessary to the survival of the organization and I've told myself that if some sacrifices had to be made that it was for the greater good of the environment and the human race, even if it was sometimes hard to see a method beyond the madness.

"I'm tired Jerry," Tom said as he slumped in a chair. "I know that killing Jake is really my only choice but I can't make that choice. I can't."

Jerry studied his brother and for the first time he saw what no one else in the organization believed existed in him, mercy. Others might have interpreted it as weakness or confusion and uncertainty. Jerry loved his brother more than anyone in the world and he knew that he was a good man, an incredibly strong man, physically, mentally, and emotionally. Even though intellectually Jerry knew that Tom was wrong he was gladdened to see that his brother was capable of mercy and compassion.

"We seem to be experiencing some sort of a role reversal here," Jerry said with a smile.

"I'm usually the one who's pleading for amnesty at these meetings. Eventually you throw me out and you and the rest of your heartless thugs ultimately decide against me."

Tom stood up and the two brothers embraced.

Jerry squeezed his brother around his immensely powerful shoulders. He was barely able to make his hands meet around Tom's broad back. "I'm proud of you. I'll back you up no matter what happens. You know that, don't you?"

Lionfish smiled sadly as he pulled away. "You're the one constant in my life, brother, and the one thing I'm always sure of. That's why you're staying here during Operation SweetTooth in Florida," Lionfish said, bringing up a controversial subject. "I'm not taking any chances with your safety again. Too many things are happening at once and if we stick to our timetable the risks will increase significantly."

"Oh, Tom, not that again. Just when we were bonding," Jerry replied sarcastically.

"I'm going and that's final. Besides I'm the one who wrote the plan and you need me to implement strategy and to facilitate the deployment of the special tactical weapons that Tarpon and I have designed."

"I'm too tired to argue with you now. We'll talk about this some more tomorrow."

On the ride up in the elevator Tom turned to Jerry and said, "There's an important step to dealing with Jake that I didn't want to mention yet in front of the others. I want you to handle it personally since you're going to like it the least. I'll give you all the details in the morning and I'm warning you that it's going to occupy most of your time while I prepare for Florida."

"I hope this isn't an attempt to distract me from the mission and keep me away."

"Don't worry, Jerry. It's an integral part of enabling us to meet our June 15 date. You will find out soon enough just how important your assignment is to our success in Florida."

On the walk back to his cabin, alone in the moonlight, Lionfish thought about Jake and how pathetic his attempt at escape was and how frightened he must have been. He also thought about how alone and sad Jake must have been feeling, having lost his mother and Samantha so close together. Lionfish thought of his own mother every day and her memory gave him the strength to continue his work at difficult times such as these. He also remembered Samantha and how vulnerable and lonely she was when they had first met. Even though Sam had been through rigorous combat training she still behaved like a victim even though she tried desperately to break the patterns that were imbedded in her by an abusive childhood and adolescence. Lionfish remembered how happy she had become and how different she had appeared while her and Jake's relationship had blossomed. He remembered how enabling and empowering Jake's love for Sam had been. Jake reminded Lionfish so much of his mother Hannah. She was sensitive and she had Jake's oddball sense of humor. When Lionfish was with Jake he felt closer to her and to a part of himself that he had buried so many years ago, a part of himself that he kept even from his brother.

He missed Jake and no matter what common sense told him to do he knew he could no more kill Jake than he could kill Jerry, even if it meant saving his own life. But Lionfish was troubled. He knew that he had more than his own life to consider. He had to think of all the loyal men and women who had entrusted him with their safety and who had sacrificed everything to the cause. *Please Jake*, he thought to himself. *Please don't do anything stupid.*

CHAPTER 28

iro-ny /n, pl -nies
a: a usu. humorous or sardonic literary style or form characterized by irony **b:** incongruity between the actual result of a sequence of events and the normal or expected result (2) an event or result marked by such incongruity.

THAT'S THE OFFICIAL Webster dictionary definition of irony. I looked it up the other day. I always assumed that irony was associated with humor. Like the double entendres and plot twists they utilize in sitcoms on television. I never associated it with the cruel twists of fate and the curve balls that life could throw your way. I thought that I had found the adventure and the opportunity for self-satisfaction that I had longed for on a tiny island in the Caribbean. I went there to find peace and to come to terms with the loss of my mother. I went there to avoid, if only for awhile, the pain of that loss.

My dreams of adventure and freedom became a living nightmare. I ended up creating a jail for myself that I was afraid I might never be free from and my loss became compounded by yet another great loss that I didn't think I could survive. Jorge and I had spoken about the subject of irony just a few days before I slipped away and he told me a story that was stranger than fiction but brutally illustrated the expression, "Man makes plans and God laughs."

Jorge told me that his father had been killed in Vietnam. But not during the war where he had served two successful tours unharmed, but almost twenty years later when he and five friends, also Vietnam veterans, returned to take a motorcycle trip through the country.

Jorge's father and friends thought it would be a cathartic experience and under the advice of his therapist, his father organized it. They spent three weeks driving their Harley Davidson motorcycles throughout the countryside and they even visited Hanoi and Saigon, renamed Ho Chi Minh City. They received a warm reception from the people they met and they were having a wonderful time until one day fate reached out its hand and tapped Jorge's father on the shoulder.

Jorge told me that his father drove his bike off road through a field to pick some fruit that he saw hanging from a nearby tree. He was laughing out loud and was riding with his feet over the handlebars. His bike hit a twenty-five-year-old land mine and he and his motorcycle were blown to pieces. His friends stood by in shock and then they rushed to his side, ignoring the danger from the possibility of additional mines. When they reached him he was laughing. Jorge thought that he was probably laughing at the cruel joke that God had played on him. He never spoke a word, just took one last breath and passed away.

I was sitting in Miami airport waiting for John to pick me up as I wrote this story in my journal. I had just returned from Belize where I had spent two weeks on *The Aggressor*, a live aboard dive boat that traveled throughout Belize and Honduras. I needed to kill some time before I returned to the States and I thought the diving would be therapeutic. I had escaped from Arrecife and from RedTide but I knew that I would be hearing from them again soon. I had arranged for a Honduran fisherman to pick me up a mile from Neptune's Throat where I had disappeared and then I flew to Belize where I signed up for the cruise on *The Aggressor*.

I wanted to return to my old life again and I was hoping that RedTide would allow me to do that after they realized that I wasn't a threat to their organization. I had no where else to go and I refused to live my life in hiding. I also knew that wherever I went or whoever I pretended to be RedTide would eventually track me down. I might as well go home. I reasoned that if I went about my life normally it would make it obvious to Tom and the others that there was a clear reason I felt that I didn't have to hide. I had no intention of doing anything that would harm Tom and the others and therefore I felt there was no reason to hide or to play games. My return to my old life should demonstrate that unequivocally.

I had kept to myself on the live aboard and I dove almost continuously, as much as my computer would allow, sometimes five to six times a day. Below the waves was the only place I felt consoled and the silent beauty of a coral reef was the only thing that could relieve the agony that I felt almost constantly. One day, while I was diving I swam off by myself and I thought that I saw Samantha. I knew this was impossible but I imagined it might be her spirit or her ghost and so I swam off in the direction of the apparition. I kept descending deeper and deeper and the vision kept moving ahead of me. It stayed thirty to forty yards away. I screamed Samantha with tears flowing from my eyes until they flooded my mask. I could see her long blond hair flowing behind her as she swam away and I knew for certain that it was her. She was gliding effortlessly through the water like a mermaid. She was nude and she was diving without a tank or a regulator. I felt pressure behind my eyes and I equalized my ears and my mask and I continued to dive deeper and deeper. I was startled by the alarm on my Orca computer and I glanced at it. It read 185 feet. I checked my air and it was at 700 PSI. I knew I could not continue diving and I stopped at the edge of a large gray coral head. The reef was absolutely colorless at that depth.

Samantha stopped and then she turned around. We looked each other directly in the eyes. She looked up at me with a sad expression. She held her arms open and called to me. I felt so lost and so desperately unhappy. All I wanted to do was follow her and hold her and drift away with her to the bottomless eternity that waited for me in her arms. I began to swim toward her when I heard a loud noise above me. It was the banging of a dive knife against a tank and I looked up to see one of the divemasters over sixty feet above me.

He was waving frantically for me to ascend. I looked back toward Samantha and she was gone. I hesitated for a moment. I was dreading the return to the surface and the pain and the suffering that would envelope me like a death shroud as soon as I climbed back up the dive ladder. The banging continued and I reluctantly swam toward the surface.

When I reached the divemaster he was cursing and mouthing epithets at me silently underwater and then he wrote on his white plastic blackboard that we would need to do a safety decompression stop at thirty feet. He wrote that they would bring another tank below the surface for me. When I returned to the boat the captain gave me a stern lecture. He told me that if I wanted to kill myself I would have to do it somewhere else and then he politely asked me to leave his boat as soon as possible. They monitored me throughout the day for any signs of decompression sickness but aside from a headache I felt fine.

I called ship to shore the next day and made arrangements to fly home. I also called my friend John and in the privacy of the captain's cabin, which he was gracious enough to offer me I poured out my heart to him and told him all about Samantha. I swore him to secrecy and explained to him that it would mean my life if he repeated what I told him. When he swore to keep our conversation confidential I told him about RedTide. He urged me to come home and was sympathetic. He told me that I was at great risk not only from the people he called terrorists but from the law. He explained to me that I was an accomplice to what transpired in Cozumel and to the murder of the hostages as well.

I reminded him about the importance of keeping his mouth shut and I begged him not to discuss it with anyone. After I made my travel arrangements I packed my things and prepared for my return home. When I was in the airport in Belize I called John again and told him that I was on my way home. He told me that Al talked about me constantly and that he had cited me as an example one day when he was giving a lecture to a new hire about establishing timetables in order to close business. John told me that Danny had gotten engaged and, believe it or not, Danny had also been Salesman of the Month for the past consecutive two months. Apparently his fiancee was a tough as nails sales manager who worked for a large copier company and she was driving Danny pretty hard at home. The more we talked the more I felt like the past few months had all been nothing but a dream.

He told me that he was sure I could get my old job back. We cut the conversation short because of the costs involved with a credit card call and he volunteered to pick me up at the airport. He had been keeping an eye on my apartment for me. Since I had already paid the rent for six months in advance the apartment would be ready for me when I got home and I would have some time to decide my next move. I looked up from my journal when I heard John's voice calling to me across a sea of people who were waiting outside the customs baggage claim area. I stood up and rushed over to him and we embraced. John helped me carry my camera cases and we started toward the underground short term parking garage. We were near the elevator when three men in blue suits approached us.

"Is your name Jake Stein?" A tall man with gray sideburns asked me rather abruptly.

"My name is Special Agent Rhodes of the FBI," he said. As he introduced himself he produced an ID from his wallet. I felt my pulse quicken with fear and I almost passed out from the sudden rush of blood to my brain. Strangely, I felt an odd sense of relief as well.

"I'm afraid you will have to come with us, Mr. Stein," the short, dark man standing beside him said.

John looked defensively at the men. "Is he under arrest?" John asked Special Agent Rhodes.

"We have some questions for Mr. Stein and for his own protection we would like to take him somewhere safe to ask them. Mr. Stein knows why we're here and I'm sure he wants to cooperate."

"If he's not under arrest then he doesn't have to go anywhere with you," John continued. "Jake, you should go home first and call your sister. If these guys want to talk to you they can talk to you at home after you've spoken to your lawyer. You really don't want to be saying anything without the advice of council. Trust me, Jake. My brother is a State Trooper"

I was confused and I knew what John said made sense, but I would only be forestalling the inevitable, and maybe the FBI knew something that I didn't about the risks involved in staying out in the open.

"Your friend has already helped you enough by contacting his brother. How do you think we found you. The FBI is good but we're not Psychic."

I was stunned by his words."John, what the fuck is he talking about?"

"Jake, I'm sorry. I was worried about you so I called Bill for advice. He swore he wouldn't tell anyone."

"Mr. Stein, if you like we can stand around here and argue until someone takes a shot at you or we can return to your apartment later today with a warrant for your arrest. We can do this the easy way with your full cooperation or we can do it the hard way. If you prefer we can come back later and drag you from your house in handcuffs in front of your neighbors. The choice is yours.

"We know all about your involvement in recent terrorist activities in Cozumel and we have enough information right now to hold you over indefinitely without bail. I suggest we get you somewhere safe and give you a chance to save your life and maybe you can save yourself from a lengthy jail sentence as well by cooperating."

My head was spinning. If they knew about Cozumel then they had probably already tracked my whereabouts for the past few months and they were probably already aware of Arrecife. By talking to John I had inadvertently led them directly to RedTide and to Tom and Jerry. I had betrayed them all simply by mentioning them to my friend on the phone. I had probably gotten them all killed by speaking no more than a few sentences.

"It's all right John," I said. "I'll be okay. Thanks for looking out for me but you better get going."

"Are you sure, Jake, I think you're making a mistake!" John replied with great concern.

"I'm sure. I'll call you later when I get home."

"Right this way, Mr. Stein. We have a car waiting outside."

The third agent was a tall Nordic looking fellow who never said a word. He had a look on his face that could freeze molten lava. They led me to the curb where two gray Lincoln Town Cars were parked. Special Agent Rhodes opened the rear door of the second car and asked me to please get in. I entered the car and I gasped when I came face to face with a horribly disfigured man who was sitting in the back. His face was severely scarred from what must have been a fire.

"Please get in, Mr.Stein, and make yourself comfortable," he said in a thick Scottish brogue. He sounded like Sean Connery but he sure as hell didn't look like him. As the door slammed shut, the two of us were left alone with the driver. We quickly pulled away from the curb and entered traffic.

"There is no need to be afraid, Jake," he said. "It's not you we're interested in. As a matter of fact we're really your only chance of coming out of this alive. My name is John Wallace and I have been on the trail of your friends from RedTide for a very long time. As a matter of fact I received this fine makeover at the hands of the man you probably know as Lionfish," he said pointing to his face.

"I appreciate the fact that you have not once looked away when we are speaking, Jake. That shows good breeding and manners on your part."

I sat quietly for fifteen minutes while Special Agent Wallace explained to me his brief history with RedTide. When he finished he began to ask me questions.

"Where are they now Jake? How can I find them?"

"I really don't know what you're talking about, Mr. Wallace. I've been on vacation for the past two months and I don't know anything about RedTide except for what I've seen on TV, I assure you."

Mr. Wallace leaned over and smiled. His face contorted grotesquely making the flaps and rolls of scar tissue assume a frightful visage and he spoke quietly but with a threatening tone. "Do you think the FBI is a club for incompetents, Jake? That it's full of pencil pushing bureaucrats, Ivy League attorneys, and accountants with guns? Why do you insult my intelligence by spewing this bullshit at me? How do you think we found you? We already know all about Arrecife and the hotel," he said, and my heart skipped a beat with concern for Tom & Jerry's safety.

"The place is deserted and the outbuildings were destroyed by a combination of fire and explosives," he continued.

"There isn't a trace of Tom & Jerry left anywhere in the Caribbean."

"Yes Jake," he said when he saw his words register surprise on my face. "We know everything now thanks to you and I can assure you that you're life expectancy has decreased significantly."

"How did you find me?" I asked.

I had to ask to know for sure if John had betrayed me.

"Networking," he blurted out, startling me.

"Isn't that one of the things they teach you in sales, Jake? Your friend confided in his brother who in turn contacted a friend at the FBI about a hypothetical situation and the inquiry found its way to me. One of the things they teach you at Quantico is that there is no such thing as a hypothetical situation and everything that is related to RedTide eventually comes across my desk.

"It was simple to connect you to the State Trooper's brother since you work together and then to trace you to Arrecife. Do you still want to sit there and tell me that you've never heard of RedTide, Jake?"

"If you already know about RedTide's hideout and their cover then what do you want from me?" I asked. "I have no idea where they would be now and obviously I'm out of the loop on any future plans they might have."

"That's a good question, Jake," he said.

To my relief I saw through the window of the car that we had pulled into my apartment complex.

"It's a question I want you to think about, Jake. While you're thinking about how you can help us I want you to realize that your old friends at RedTide are thinking about the same thing. They're wondering how and when you will release information that will lead to their arrest, while they also think about ways to eliminate you."

He reached over and opened the door and said, "Don't take too long, Jake. You're a nice kid who got in the middle of something he didn't belong in. I'd hate to see you get hurt."

"Agents Rhodes and Jorgensonn will be outside your apartment twenty-four hours a day for your protection, and I will be back tomorrow to finish our conversation. If you decide to cooperate I promise you full witness protection including a new identity and relocation anywhere you want in the world. Maybe we could set you up as a dive instructor in Hawaii or the South Pacific. How does that sound, Jake?"

"It sounds like I would be looking over my shoulder for the rest of my life," I said as I shook his hand. I tried not to flinch when I felt the two missing fingers that had been burned away.

"I don't believe I'm in any danger, Mr. Wallace, unless I talk to you. I believe my silence is the only guarantee I have that I won't be seen as a threat. The men I know would find me no matter where you hid me, but I thank you for your concern and for the protection you've offered me."

He laughed and he said, "I like you, Jake. Your innocence is very refreshing. I'll see you soon." He closed the door and his car pulled away. I went to my apartment and looked down from the balcony in time to see my two body guards had parked their car and were taking their positions for the night.

Before I even looked around my apartment I went to the phone to call my sister, but when I picked it up it was dead. I forgot that I had paid the final bill when I left and that I had put in a request to have it disconnected. I would need to take care of that in the morning. I went into the bedroom and turned on the light. Luckily, the apartment complex had insisted that I leave a three-month deposit with them for FP&L before I left and they had been taking care of the electric bill while I was away. I was exhausted and despite the day's travels and travails I fell asleep as soon as my head hit the pillow.

I dreamed that I was back at The Aquarium in Honduras and I was swimming with a large group of sea turtles. I thought it was remarkable to see over twenty sea turtles swimming in a school and their sweeping movements as they formed a tight group and then spread out were identical to the way small schools of fish form a large shape to deter predators. The water was very clear and very warm and I could see for over 200 feet. I held onto the back of one of the larger turtles and I rode along with the group toward the opening in The Aquarium which leads to the open sea.

Suddenly I looked up and noticed Samantha. She was floating weightless a few feet outside the exit. I gasped when I realized for the first time that I wasn't wearing a tank or a regulator and that I was breathing the salty tasting sea water into my lungs. I became anxious and then I realized that I wasn't drowning. I was actually absorbing oxygen from the water like a fish using its gills. I stared at Samantha and I saw that a group of turtles was passing around her. She was stroking them as they passed over and around her. She was very pale, almost bone white and her beautiful hair was everywhere. It was falling around her face and it was floating above her.

She looked very sad as she held her arms open to me and I swam toward her as quickly as I could. Suddenly the water turned crimson and the turtles began to panic and swam away frantically in all directions. I looked for Samantha but my view was obstructed by three large turtles. I could only see her legs from the calves down and as I scanned around the area I could see that the ocean was turning red. The color was spreading out in all directions for hundreds and hundreds of feet. I swam toward Samantha and as I pushed a large green turtle away I suddenly tasted blood in my mouth. I looked up and saw Samantha's face and she was screaming.

Her throat was torn open and blood was pouring out at a frightening rate from the wound. It looked like the rush of water from a garden hose and it was spreading out from her as far as the eye could see. I screamed her name as loudly as I could underwater and made almost no sound. I screamed again and I woke myself up. I was in a cold sweat and I was screaming Samantha's name at the top of my lungs. Suddenly, I heard my front door being kicked in. Tears were running down my face and I was drenched in a cold sweat when Agent Jorgensonn entered my room.

"What the fuck are you doing?" I yelled at the behemoth who was standing beside my bed holding a very large automatic weapon.

"I could hear you screaming bloody murder all the way downstairs," he replied in a thick Nordic accent, which surprised me.

Did the FBI hire agents who were not born in the United States? I wondered.

I was more than a little embarrassed to be sitting in my bed in such a state of upset with a 250 pound FBI agent hulking over me and I told him that I was okay. Then I asked him to leave. When I composed myself I walked down to the office of the apartment complex and I borrowed their telephone in order to call my sister.

"Jacqueline Stein-Dougherty's office," her secretary said after the phone rang ten or more times.

"I was beginning to think the office was closed for a holiday, but I couldn't think of what it could be?" I said in a sarcastic tone.

"Can I help you?" She replied with obvious annoyance.

"This is Jacob Stein. I'm calling to speak to my sister."

Jackie always hated it when I announced our relationship to the office personnel. She didn't want anyone to know that she might be wasting valuable billing time on a personal call. I always wondered what a paranoid work environment my poor sister had to endure. She worked 80 hour weeks for over 7 years and even though she rose so quickly within the firm she still had to be nervous about her secretary's perception of her work ethic.

"What," my sister said when she finally picked up the receiver in her large corner office.

My sister always answered the phone in the same unpleasant manner. It was always "What" or "What do you want." I'm sure that if it had been a client or a colleague who was calling, her greeting would have been more obsequious.

"Hello to you too. I'm just fine thank you," I replied.

"I'm very busy, Jake. What do you need?"

I lost my temper and hung up.

I had called for legal advice but decided I had already told one person too many about my involvement with RedTide, and witness protection didn't sound too appealing. I would have to spend the remainder of my life under an assumed name. I would have to move from city to city and I would be lucky if I could keep one step ahead of a group of zealous, professionally trained killers who would make it their mission in life to kill me. I would never see my sister or the baby again. I thought I knew RedTide and its leader. He wasn't a bloodthirsty, cold-hearted person who killed indiscriminately. He wasn't going to let anyone else harm me unless he felt threatened, but at this point with the FBI giving me a ride home and circling my apartment, I tell you what, I wouldn't blame him if he did.

Before I left the office I called Southern Bell to have my phone service reactivated and they told me it would be on by tomorrow afternoon. Then I went to the Jacuzzi and I tried to calm down while I watched the sun set. The coconut palms that bordered the property were a silhouette against the red sky. I saw the red glow of a cigarette outside the fence and I realized that my bodyguards were still around. They had done a brilliant job of remaining inconspicuous. All the time I was in the office and on my walk to the pool I had looked for them and I could not see them anywhere.

I thought about Tom and I tried to convince myself that he would not hurt me. I also believed that he would protect me from others who would argue for my termination. The last few weeks before I had left the island we had become as close as brothers and he had bent over backward in every way to make sure that my training was effective. He saw to it personally that my transition from civilian to eco-soldier and my induction into the organization had been thorough and comprehensive. I decided to go for a run and I told Agent Rhodes of my intentions as I left the pool. He said that it was out of the question and I told him that I didn't need his permission. He was upset and he tried to explain to me that I would be too exposed out on the road. It would be almost impossible for them to protect me.

"Look," I said, "like I told your boss, if I were in any real danger I would already be dead. I didn't try to hide or cover my trail from Honduras. Look how easily you found me. If I were perceived as a threat by RedTide they would never have allowed me to have lived this long. Besides, now that they've left the island I don't know any more than you do about where they are or where they're going. I couldn't help you find them if I wanted to."

I knew this was only partly true. I remembered reading about "Operation SweetTooth," which was scheduled for only twelve days from today. I went upstairs and I changed into my running shoes and my sweat pants. I started my run slowly and then I headed south down Powerline Road and quickened my pace. I hadn't ran in almost two weeks and I had expected to be weak and breathless, but I felt stronger than ever. Running in Honduras had been up and down hills and through jungle. It had also been over sand and rough trails. Running here in Florida was flat and the asphalt felt almost springy beneath my feet. I ran as hard as I could to exorcise or exercise the demons of fear and grief that had tortured me day and night.

I looked behind me and the gray Lincoln was following. It had its hazard lights blinking and it was forcing other traffic to go around it. Not a very unusual sight in Boca Raton, I thought, an incredibly slow moving American luxury automobile. If it had been a Cadillac it would have fit right in. I was about two miles into my run and I was passing by a chain link fence that encircled a new construction sight.

The sign the builder had erected showed a large illustration of a pink building. The name painted below it in script said "Golden Palms." It didn't say what Golden Palms was but I knew it was a nursing home. I had called on a few nursing homes while at LifeForce and it always depressed me. They ran the gamut from completely disgusting and filthy to the private high-end institutions that were complete with fine furnishings and regularly scheduled entertainment.

The publicly-run organizations were so poorly run and were so filthy that the smell was assaulting immediately upon entering the facility. The one common denominator among the homes were the people inside and the overwhelming sadness and helplessness on their faces. They would have their wheelchairs parked at every available exit door or window and would sit staring out into space. I always imagined that they were dreaming of a pardon from their life sentences, or that they were waiting for the next visit from a grandchild.

I used to always tell myself after I would leave that I would never have allowed that to happen to my mother and I reflected that sadly I would never have that worry. I was lost in thought when I heard the frantic blaring of a car's horn and I turned just in time to see a pickup truck that was driving directly at me.

I turned to run as the truck jumped the curb and I realized that I had no hope of outrunning it. The truck was only yards away and I jumped onto the chain link fence and quickly climbed to the top. I had just put my right foot on the top bar of the ten foot high fence and I looked back to see the grill of the truck was only five feet away. I leapt into the air as the truck crashed into the fence and tore it apart. It dragged great lengths of fence along with it as it barreled on another fifty feet before it stopped. I flew through the air and crashed to the ground twisting my ankle.

I looked back to see Agents Rhodes and Jorgensonn had stopped their car and were running after my assailant. They were chasing him into the woods. I lay there in shock until the agents returned. Agent Rhodes knelt down beside me and asked if I were all right. I couldn't answer him as the surreal realization of what my life had become came crashing in around me. I was deafened by the thunderous roar in my head of an internal alarm that warned of danger.

On the ride back to my apartment Agent Rhodes chided me for disobeying his warning. He asked me if I was still convinced of my own safety. When we got upstairs, Agent Jorgensonn stayed outside and stood quietly by my door. Agent Rhodes removed a vial from his pocket and brought me some water from the kitchen.

"Take two of these," he said, surprising me with the offer of narcotics.

"They're only muscle relaxers," he continued. "I take them for a bad back. They'll help you sleep."

I gladly accepted his kind offer and layed back on my bed. I noticed for the first time how dusty it was. I closed my eyes as Agent Rhodes headed for the door.

"Don't worry, Jake," he said. "We'll be right outside the door for the rest of the night and in the morning we'll be moving you to a safe house. I wanted to take you there right this minute but those were my orders. Sleep tight," he said and he closed the new door behind him. The handyman had replaced it while I was running. Whatever he gave me was very powerful and I was asleep in minutes, despite the pounding of blood in my head when I layed it upon the pillow.

RING! RING! RING!

I was suddenly awakened by a phone that wasn't supposed to be working and looked around me in the darkened room. I was disoriented by the drugs and by the surprising sound of the telephone.

"Quite a day, Jake," the voice on the telephone said in a heavy Scottish accent. "I'm sorry to wake you, but it is rather important. Life and death you might say."

"How were you able to call me?" I asked in a hoarse voice, almost slurring my words. "The phone is dead."

"In point of fact, the phone works quite well, as I have so aptly demonstrated. I had it fixed this afternoon, although we will no longer be needing it. You'll be leaving your apartment in three hours, never to return."

"Hold on a minute." I turned on the light and after waiting for my eyes to dilate I checked my watch. It was 4:30 A.M.

"You're a very presumptuous person, Agent Wallace. Unless I'm under arrest I believe that I'm the one who needs to decide when and where I go."

He laughed and said, "You've got a lot more guts than I originally gave you credit for, Jake, but you're also being extremely foolish. I'm offering you the protection of The Federal Bureau of Investigation and after yesterday's run in with RedTide's assassins I would think you would be begging for my protection. Instead, you continue to resist me."

"I have no way of knowing for sure that the driver in that truck wasn't some drunk or that it wasn't some kid in a stolen vehicle who went out of control. Your men didn't stay around long enough to wait for the police, and if it were RedTide then your men sure as hell didn't do a very good job of protecting me."

"Jake, don't be a fool. You know that it was no drunk driver and that coincidences like that are as rare as the appearance of a comet. My men warned you not to go running and you decided to be stubborn like you're being right now. It was the warning from my agent's car horn that allowed you to escape. You were about to be squeezed through that fence like cheese through a grater and if they hadn't been following you, we wouldn't be having this conversation. I'm not going to argue with you anymore. If you choose to stay you do so at your own risk. Unfortunately, I don't have enough evidence to arrest you. I can't force you to cooperate, so despite my good intentions I will have to walk away."

I felt relieved at his admission that I was at least safe from prosecution but I was terrified at the thought of another encounter with Lionfish's agents. I was crushed at the thought of Tom and his obvious decision to have me eliminated. I couldn't make myself believe it, despite the overwhelming evidence the throbbing in my ankle and my near death experience provided me with.

I still wanted to believe that my refusal to cooperate and the fact that Tom had no way of knowing that I knew anything about SweetTooth would ultimately save me. Would Tom take revenge or retribution on me for forcing them to move their hideout or because I spoke to John and it had reached the FBI?

I was aware of Tom's intelligence network and I knew that he had to have been aware that I was refusing to cooperate. Why hadn't he called me or contacted me in some way. I was still not willing to intentionally betray them and to tell the FBI about Operation SweetTooth. Confiding in John was a mistake and I would be more careful in the future. I would rather take my chances with Tom than with the FBI.

"I'm sorry, Mr. Wallace, but I still believe that associating with the FBI would be a mistake and I'm not ready to run away and leave my life behind forever. I'm not so sure that would be a better choice than staying put and taking my chances. I believe that what happened yesterday was a warning. The men I knew don't miss and they don't make mistakes. If they wanted me dead I would already be dead and it would be just as easy for them to hit a moving target."

"As you wish, Jake," he replied. "I think you're making a grave mistake, but it's your life and it's your choice to make. I will continue to leave Agents Rhodes and Jorgensonn assigned to your protection for a little while longer, and if you need me they will know how to reach me. Good luck," he said and then hung up.

I decided I would visit the offices of LifeForce Technology today and I would have breakfast again with the old gang. It would be great to get together like old times and tease Danny unmercifully about his upcoming nuptials. I closed my eyes and fell back to sleep and I awakened with the sun. I looked outside and there was no sign of my guard dogs anywhere. I even looked for their car but it was gone. I was a little nervous and I wondered for a second if they had been removed by Wallace, or by Lionfish. I dressed in a hurry and headed out the door. I went to the garage where I kept my baby blue and white 1959 Corvette convertible and started the engine.

It turned right over after months without being driven and I patted the steering wheel and thanked my baby for her loyalty. I loved my car as if it were an animate warm-blooded creature. Only I knew the blood, sweat, and tears that went into earning the cash to purchase a car that I had dreamed of owning since I was thirteen.

I allowed the engine to warm up for a few minutes. I pulled away from the garage and I sped out onto the road. I always loved stopping at traffic lights and seeing how people stared at my car and at me. It was in mint condition and I had done an extensive restoration on her. I had even reconditioned the chrome and the leather. The seats were also baby blue and white two tone. She was the most beautiful car on the road.

I never considered myself a spiritual person but it was funny how the whole time I was in Honduras with Samantha, I thought sadly, I never once thought about my car. I marveled at how when a person is truly happy he doesn't need cars or jewelry to distract him or to occupy his lust for material things. It felt great being in my car again, driving off to see my old friends, but I was truly at the unhappiest point in my life. I had planned on going back to my old life, and even considered asking

Al for my old job back. As I turned on to I95 I realized that I had moved on already; I would never be happy choosing that direction again. I wondered if I had done the right thing in leaving Arrecife.

I decided to go to the breakfast place where we all used to meet and surprise my friends. I parked my car outside Bagel Twins. I took up two spots in order to protect her from the half-blind, aged drivers who frequented the place, and I walked through the door and scanned the room for my friends. It wasn't long before I heard Frank's loud voice echoing off the walls and I made my way over toward their booth.

"JAKE!" They all shouted when they saw me. My eyes began to tear up when I saw John, Frank, and Danny sitting together in our usual corner booth. They all stood up and hugged me at once, which drew a half a dozen stares from some octogenarians on both sides of the restaurant.

"Man, I missed you," Danny said.

"He didn't miss the competition though," Frank said. "He's been cleaning all our clocks ever since you ran away to find yourself."

"How are you feeling Jake?" John asked as we sat down. He had a guilty look on his face. "I tried to call you but I got no answer. Did you get everything worked out yesterday with your friends?"

I was grateful that John had not told the others about the FBI and said that I had heard today that my friends would be okay and that their legal issues were settled. He smiled and said how relieved he was to hear that. We all talked for almost two hours about my trip and the diving and Al and the business and we laughed and reminisced. I realized how much I loved them all.

I ordered the house special, matzo brie, and ate it all in minutes. I realized that I hadn't eaten in a day and was famished. Finally we got around to the subject of Danny's fiancée and he blushed when Frank began to tease him about how beautiful she was and how much he adored her. Frank told me how Danny's cubicle was literally a shrine to his fiancée and was covered with pictures and greeting cards she had given him. John explained how driven Danny had become to be number one in sales in the office.

Danny explained what a great influence his fiancée had become. He told me that she was so motivating and so positive that it was like living with a female Anthony Robbins.

"Well, once Jake comes back you're really gonna have you're work cut out for you, Danny," Frank teased.

"I won't be coming back, Frank," I said and they all got quiet. "I'm through with selling. I just don't have the heart for it anymore."

"You're the best I've ever seen, Jake," Frank said, "and I've seen them all. A little lazy, yes, but so fucking talented it makes me hate you just a little."

"I'm through," I said again. "I don't know what I'll do. Maybe I'll travel some more or maybe I'll write a book. I always wanted to write. Maybe I'll teach scuba for a while. Whatever I decide to do, one thing is certain. I'm going to simplify my life, sell my car, and reduce my overhead."

They all laughed. "Sell your car," Frank said skeptically.

"That's the funniest thing I've ever heard," Danny said, and they all agreed. Except for John, who understood. He smiled at what he would have interpreted as my spiritual awakening.

"You need that car," Frank said. "It's as much a part of you as your curly hair or your sarcastic sense of humor."

"My needs have changed. I need to be happy and the car isn't going to make me happy. It never did."

We finished breakfast and I said I would follow them back to the office to see Al and the rest of the office personnel. My hair had gotten very long. It was almost to my shoulders and I hadn't shaved in three days. Frank said he would kill to see the expression on Al's face when he saw me looking like a rock star. We stepped out onto the curb and I hugged them one by one. I was standing facing the parking lot. My chest and my head were open to the street. Danny stepped in front of me and he opened his arms to hug me good-bye. A shot rang out and he flew into my arms. Tissue from his chest mixed with blood splattered onto my chest and arms. I dropped to the sidewalk and I held him. I rolled him over and he was dead. There were no last words, no good-byes, just an open-eyed expression of disbelief on his face.

I screamed "NO," as Frank and John stood by. They were both as pale as sheets and in obvious shock. People came out of the restaurant and were crowding around us. I heard a woman scream and someone yelled "call 911" but it all sounded far away. Suddenly Agents Jorgensson and Rhodes burst through the crowd. They tried to roll Danny off of me while they lifted me off the ground.

I screamed and fought them until Agent Rhodes said, "That shot was meant for you, Jake. Now let's go before you endanger someone else. There are kids here."

They practically had to carry my heartless, deadened body to the Lincoln. When they put me in the back seat, Wallace was waiting.

"I'm sorry, Jake," he said. "I've called the local police and they will handle things here while I get you to a safe house in Miami."

I began to cry and to pull at my hair. I was wrenching bloody pieces of it from my scalp. He moved quickly and sat beside me and he grabbed my hands.

"Stop that, Jake," he said, and he held me tight while I continued to scream and cry out my grief. It was more than just grief. There was also an overwhelming sense of guilt.

"Drink this." He handed me a sterling silver flask that he withdrew from his jacket. I swallowed a large gulp of burning hot liquid and almost coughed it up all over his shirt.

He smiled sadly, "That's thirty-year old Scotch. It's supposed to be as smooth as silk."

"I killed him as surely as if I had pulled the trigger myself," I cried. "You warned me. I just didn't want to believe it, and now I've killed my best friend, three weeks before his wedding day."

I swallowed another large gulp from the bottle and this time it felt smoother and it was easier to keep down. I swallowed again, feeling the numbing power of the liquid enter my bloodstream.

"You didn't kill anyone, Jake," he said. "It was an accident that your friend happened to move in front of you at the last second. If he hadn't you would be lying dead back at that restaurant."

"Those sons of bitches," I screamed. I felt my anger swell up and grow like an avenging angel as it rose up and opened its arms. Danny was the sweetest guy in the world. He would never hurt anyone. They call themselves environmentalists and soldiers. They're nothing but butchers and murderers."

"I know you won't understand this, Jake, but it's not personal with them. It's business and you are a threat to the future of their entire organization. They have no choice but to eliminate you and believe me they won't rest until that's accomplished. This is only the beginning. They will do anything to accomplish their goal. They will try anything to draw you out, even threaten your sister or your niece. They are cold and hard and merciless. That's how they have managed to survive for as long as they have."

Yesterday the idea that Lionfish would harm my family would have seemed absurd and I would have seen Wallace's statements as manipulative, but now I knew he was right. I trusted him right now more than anyone else in the world.

"I'm going to hide you down south and you will not be allowed to leave the house," he said. "I don't want you talking to anyone until this is settled, not in person, not even on the phone. I'm bringing in more men to guard you. They will be here today. I need you to trust me, Jake. I need your help to end this and to clean up this organization once and for all. We need to bring them to justice. Will you help me?"

I sat quietly for a moment feeling the alcohol settle my pulse and calm my heart. I suddenly realized what I had to do. I felt all my emotions and all my feelings of grief for my mother, for Samantha, and now for Danny coalesce and transform into hatred.

"Yes, I will help you," I said calmly, staring into his eyes. "I know exactly where they will be in less than two weeks. They're coming to

Miami," I said with a sick laugh. "How's that for irony? And I know the exact time and date they will be here. But before I give them to you I want something in return."

"What?"

"I want to be there when you arrest him. I want him to know that it was me who ruined him and his group of murdering trash and I want him to see my face when you slap on the cuffs."

MacGregor leaned back in his seat and put his arm around Jake's shoulder. He turned his face out of sight and he smiled. Finally after two years of close calls followed by failure after failure he had him. He finally had Lionfish and this time he would see him die by his own hand. He would give Jake what he wanted and somewhat more than he wanted. He would allow Jake to see Lionfish die. Then he would shoot Jake in the back of his head and he would throw his body on top of his fallen hero. *Yes*, MacGregor thought as he smiled again, *it was finally coming to an end.*

CHAPTER 30

THERE ONCE WAS A TIME not very long ago, relative to this planet's age, when the aquifer below The Florida Everglades flowed with such force that it created freshwater springs fifteen to twenty miles off of the Florida coast. Sailors on galleons would dip their buckets overboard into these bubbling springs without even making landfall as recently as the early part of this century. There are still people in Miami who remember those springs from their childhood. But that was long ago when Miami was young, before hundreds of thousands of settlers began to make use of what was considered a useless swamp. Since then one of the world's most valuable ecological systems and its over 1,400 miles of canals and levees has been systematically ditched, diked, drained, and diverted to clear the way for condominiums, farms, and golf courses.

More than half of the grassy web which filters most of south Florida's drinking water has been lost forever along with ninety-three percent of the egrets, herons, and other birds who made their homes there. Scientists worried that the recent reductions in the numbers of birds who nest in The Everglades indicated that something was very wrong and that the wetland's ability to clean and store water had decreased significantly.

Lionfish was standing at the front of the airboat feeling the wind in his face and he looked out over the picturesque landscape. He breathed deeply the humid air and thought how beautiful the view was. He was thinking about Hannah as he always did on this day. There were six airboats following behind him in a tight formation as they cut their way through a remote area of The Everglades, which was restricted to park personnel. Lionfish heard a thrashing in the water off to his right and saw a seven-foot alligator that was devouring a large snook. The sky was blue and was filled with large white clouds. This was truly big sky country, because of the flat expanse of the region one could see for miles and miles.

The horizon was broken by the tall leaning bodies of large palm trees and vast blankets of saw grass dappled with bayheads (tree islands that grow in depressions in the park's limestone bed). Everywhere Lionfish looked he saw herons and large egrets. He hoped they would see a Florida panther on this trip but Stingray said that it was highly unlikely. Stingray was riding behind in one of the airboats and Lionfish fumed over his presence. He had assigned him to clear out the island hideaway in Honduras and to destroy any vestige of RedTide ever having been there. He was sure the distraction would have interfered with his plans to join them on this mission. He was wrong.

Stingray wanted to gather samples in The Everglades and he had insisted on coming along, despite very heated discussions and Lionfish's stoic arguments. Lionfish had also been thinking about Jake. His senior advisors had pleaded with him to allow them to remove him.

Remove him, Lionfish thought, *like a small growth*.

They had said it in a way that made him cringe. Not that Lionfish was squeamish about such things. He had personally killed over twenty-five men, some with his bare hands. Lionfish's men had tracked Jake to Belize and to the *Aggressor* and they were prepared to kill him or to capture him as soon as he got off the boat. Lionfish had ordered them to leave him alone and to allow him to travel back to Miami. He told his men to keep an eye on him and to report his movements. He had listened quietly to the tapes of the conversation between Jake and his friend John that Jake had made from the boat.

Although he was angry at Jake's carelessness, he understood why he felt the need to pour out his heart to his best friend. Stingray and his other senior officers, however, saw Jake's immediate breach of confidence as a threat and as confirmation of their earlier doubts about his ability to keep a secret. They lobbied for his elimination and they presented some very strong arguments. In the end, Lionfish told them that Jake knew nothing that hadn't already been revealed and that he no longer represented a threat. They had evacuated the island and the covers which they had invented at such great cost had been blown. Lionfish told them that Jake had no way of knowing about today's mission. Lionfish was more concerned for Jake's safety than in any additional harm he might cause RedTide and he instructed two of his best men to follow him to Miami airport and to keep an eye on him.

His men had not reported in for over thirty-six hours. Jake had disappeared and soon after Lionfish's men were found by the police. They were floating in Biscayne Bay with their throats cut. Lionfish found out about the murder of Jake's friend Danny from an informant at the Miami Herald. He was afraid that MacGregor now had Jake. His stomach boiled with acid as he thought about the torture Jake would have to endure and his inevitable death at the hands of the Scottish mercenary.

When this mission was over, Lionfish would settle the score once and for all. He planned to put everything else on hold until he killed the man who had relentlessly pursued him for the past two years.

CHAPTER 30

JOHN MARKS PULLED HIS SILVER, Porsche 911 Carrera 4 into his reserved parking space beside the long corrugated metal Quonset hut that housed the 200 Haitian workers he had brought in to cut his cane. He was on his way to his office when he heard his name being called by his foreman David Hernandez. He walked toward the back of the red Ford pickup truck and heard a young man crying out in pain.

"What the fuck is going on here, Davey?" he asked the man who had worked for his father for over twenty years. In the back of the pickup was a fifteen or sixteen-year-old Haitian boy who was crying in pain. He was holding his bleeding foot in both hands. John almost laughed when he saw the deep cut on the boy's foot. He couldn't believe that David had bothered him with this. John knew from experience that the boy had cut it with a machete while he was cutting the cane. This type of accident happened at least twice a week.

"So he cut his fucking foot. What are you calling me for? Take care of it."

When John Marks said take care of it he meant that David should throw a few stitches in it and bandage it up. Then in a few days when the boy could walk he was supposed to send him back to Haiti since he could no longer work. The workers on his farm were little more than indentured slaves and they worked for less than two dollars an hour. They had no medical benefits and had absolutely no rights, especially the right to complain. John Marks had complete control over their destinies. The only way a worker could stay in the country and could continue to send their meager earnings back home was if he allowed it.

He housed over 200 men in little more than a large community barracks and the toilet facilities and washrooms were constantly in a state of disrepair. His family had farmed first tomatoes and then sugar in Florida for over 100 years and his father had made several fortunes in land development, banking, and tourism. He had died a little over a year ago and had left John everything, including his banks and hotels.

At thirty-five, John Marks' personal fortune was estimated at over 300 million dollars and it was said of him that he could account for every penny of it. He owned eleven automobiles, including a Lamborghini and a customized Hummer that had real twenty-four karat gold trim, but he fed his workers stale bread and beans.

The working conditions were appalling, but no one dared complain. John Marks was what is known as a sugar baron in South Florida and he ruled his enterprises and his farms like a feudal lord.

"I'm sorry to bother you, Mr. Marks, but we have a problem."

David Hernandez was a proud sixty-five-year-old Cuban immigrant, but he kept his head down when he spoke to the man almost half his age. "The boy's father insists that we send his son to a proper hospital."

John Marks laughed out loud and then his smile contorted and changed to a scowl. His temper took control. "He does, does he? Well let's see the man and hear all his demands. Maybe he would like us to stop on the way back from the hospital so we can get his son an ice cream cone."

David Hernadez felt his stomach turn and he could taste bile in his mouth. With his own eyes he had once seen the boss kick a worker to death out in the fields because he complained about the working conditions. David could now smell trouble brewing. The father stepped up to John Marks and he held his head high despite the fear he must have been feeling. He spoke in painfully slow broken English. John thought that he recognized the man. David had pointed him out last week and had explained at the time that he was somewhat of a trouble maker, but John had been too busy too listen to him.

"I'm sorry bother you, boss. My son need good doctor, not field boss fix his leg."

"You should be happy that your foreman can handle a needle and thread or your son would really be in trouble," John Marks said to the man in a menacing tone.

"David sews up three to four men a week and this is little more than a scratch, besides the hospital is over sixty miles away and I don't have the men or the time to spare. Now get your ass back to work while you still have a job. We'll take care of the boy."

The man reached his hand out and grabbed John's shirt as he began to walk away. He said, "Please, boss, me don't want no trouble but this my only son. I call Mrs.Tate if you no help."

John spun around and slapped the man across the face with a savage backhand. There were over a dozen Haitian men who were watching the exchange. They were armed with machetes and they were standing outside the barracks. They yelled in anger and began to advance toward the pickup truck.

Suddenly, there was the crack of a gun shot and a voice yelled out in a thick Scottish accent, "You men get back to work and mind your own business. Move it. NOW!"

John Marks turned and looked at the man who had interceded on his behalf. He knew he was the man he had been scheduled to meet in his office over fifteen minutes ago. He nodded in MacGregor's direction and signaled his thanks. John was momentarily taken aback by the man's appearance. He thought to himself that MacGregor's face alone would have been enough to frighten the workers he had disbanded with his pistol. He turned back toward the man who was lying on the ground. He was wiping his blood from his mouth and John Marks said, "I know you've become sort of an unofficial leader among the men lately. David warned me about you last week but I was too busy to deal with you. Now you have the audacity to stand on my property and threaten me. You think I'm going to allow you to sick that bitch reporter from the *Miami Herald* on me.

"David, I want this piece of shit and his idiot son off my property and on a slow boat to Haiti by this afternoon. Do you understand?"

David Hernandez nodded his understanding and he thanked the Lord that the boss hadn't killed the man and his son on the spot. John Marks walked over to the tall stranger who had called and requested a meeting with him two days earlier.

"I owe you one, Mr. MacGregor."

"You'll owe me a lot more than that when the day is over Mr. Marks."

They settled down into the thick leather chairs in John's office and John poured them some well-aged Tennessee bourbon. MacGregor asked him what the altercation had been about.

"We had a reporter from the Herald out here a month ago. She told me that she was going to write a story about family farming in south Florida. She was snooping around here for weeks. She wrote an extremely biased and inflammatory piece on the working conditions on three to five sugar farms in South Florida, including Gro-Sun Sugar and American Sugar.

"After her article appeared some state agencies and even the Fed's started sniffing around. I got slapped with over 300,000 dollars in fines. Everything began to blow over after me and the head of the Sugar Cane Growers Alliance began to flex our muscle in Washington. We deployed our lobbyists and things got back to normal.

"There are quite alot of senators and congressman with sweet tooths in D.C. Since the Fed's showed up, the workers have started to become more assertive and we've even heard talk that union organizers have been infiltrating their ranks. Unions, can you imagine? Those black bastards aren't even fucking citizens. Back home if they even opened their mouths to complain, they'd be dragged out of their clapboard shacks and shot dead in the street.

"Goddamn country is being taken over by the fucking bleeding heart democratic liberals. If it isn't the workers rights it's the goddamn fairy ass environmentalists crying about The Everglades and the plight of the snail kite."

MacGregor listened patiently to the incessant whining of the spoiled American millionaire, then he smiled at the opportunity that fate had presented to him. He would be able to make a little side money while in Mr. Yamaguchi's employ. He turned toward Marks and said, "That brings us to the reason for my visit, Mr. Marks. I am not only going to save you many millions of dollars but I am quite possibly going to save your life."

"Keep talking," John Marks said, obviously intrigued.

"I am going to host a little surprise party for some uninvited guests of yours tomorrow and I will need your full cooperation. I am also going to require a lot of money as well for my services, which you will be more than happy to pay. John, I would like to start by telling you a little story and like most great stories this one will have a tragic ending."

CHAPTER 31

LIONFISH HEARD THE BLAST of the air horn, which signaled them to stop the boat. They formed a lazy circle by a bayhead which was covered with trees and mangroves. Stingray jumped from his boat onto dry land. He was clutching something in his hand.

"This is the original version of Marjory Stoneman Douglas's classic book, *The Everglades, River of Grass*, he said, holding it aloft. In the final chapter titled "The eleventh hour" she warns about the environmental doom which is upon us.

"The year was 1947," he shouted as he reached over and grasped a spectacular cowhorn orchid from a nearby tree. It had yellow, cigar shaped stems and it was so beautiful it looked unreal. "This national treasure," he said, pointing toward the glades, "has been under attack for over fifty years and no one has really taken notice."

"This is as much a national park as Yellowstone or Yosemite, but it pales by comparison in its attempt to capture the imagination of the public. Is it because there is no 500 foot Bridal Veil falls to marvel at or because it lacks the majesty of 12,000 foot granite peaks to inspire wonder and amazement?

"If what is being done here were being done at The Grand Canyon or in Sequoia National Park there would be a deafening outcry from the public such as the world has never known. It's easy to fall in love with the redwoods or with the prop-scarred manatee, whose image Floridians put on license plates and hang from their car bumpers. Unfortunately it is not so easy to get the public to love a swamp.

"What is The Everglades anyway?" he asked, prepared to answer his own question. "Is it a swamp to be drained? A mosquito infested wilderness to be avoided? A watershed to tap? Or is it an ecosystem to cherish and preserve?

"Literally the word glade means a clearing in a forest. Did someone once view this great expanse of prairie grass and water as a forest? A long time ago this was a river flowing fifty miles wide and six inches deep. It flowed unimpeded over a huge porous bed of limestone. It flowed down the Florida Peninsula from Orlando south through broad marshes that once bordered the Kissimee River to Lake Okeechobee, the source of The Everglades.

"It fed great aquifers beneath the coastal ridge and flowed freely to Florida Bay and the Gulf of Mexico. Now Florida Bay, which constitutes one third of the park, is dying.

"Florida Bay which stretches from the southern tip of the mainland across to the Florida Keys shows signs of sickness and the once sparkling blue bay has recently turned a sickly shade of green. The bay has been deprived of freshwater from the mainland and the result is hypersalinity. Salinity levels in the bay have climbed to seventy parts per thousand, more than twice the normal level, contributing to a massive sea grass die off that has denuded the bottom. Then there's the domino effect. The sea grass serves as a nursery for pink shrimps that later migrate to the Dry Tortugas.

"Without the nursery the shrimp population has dwindled, leaving Tortugas fishermen with lower catches. Nor is there enough sea grass to absorb the nutrients stored in the bay's sediments. Algae, which thrives off of these nutrients, has spread like an oil spill across most of the bay. Three hundred miles south of here is the Florida Keys. It is the number one dive destination in the world and it suffers from myriad water quality problems related to farming in The Everglades which is only 100 miles to the north. Animals whose ranges extend beyond the park have lost critical habitat. All of which only compounds the problems faced by over fourteen species of wildlife in the park that are either endangered or threatened, like the American crocodile, the southern bald eagle, and the loggerhead turtle. I would like to introduce a friend of mine and our guide for today, Kenny Tiger."

Kenny Tiger was an environmentalist and a Miccosukee Indian who lived in Everglades City and ran air boat rides through The Everglades for the tourists. A long time ago when he was in the Navy SEALs he was under Lionfish's command and the two had kept in touch for many years. Kenny was arrested for smuggling marijuana and Lionfish had provided the money for proper legal representation. Lionfish had also given him the down payment to start his own business. He had grown up fishing in The Everglades and knew every canal and waterway. In the last five years he had become very involved in the environmental movement and had established a name for himself in South Florida. He was a thorn in the side of big sugar and he had received more than his share of death threats.

"Good afternoon," Kenny began.

"Many people don't know this but there are over 600 different types of animals in this park and over 900 plant species, including the mangrove forests and the dry pineland ridge, one of the highest points in south Florida at seven feet," he laughed. "There are also several types of tree islands like the one I am standing on, including bayheads and tropical hardwood hammocks. Because of the diversity and variety of life here this park has been designated an International Biosphere Reserve and a United Nations World Heritage Site. There are buttonwoods, poisonwoods, rat snakes, and even pygmy rattlers here.

"There are black-whiskered viroes, and red-shouldered hawks. There was a time when I would come here as a boy and the skies would blacken with the flight of millions of birds of a hundred different varieties. I saw my first bald eagle here as a boy but today they are an endangered species. Over the years, eagles who ate fish laced with DDT laid eggs with abnormally thin shells that collapsed before the embryos matured. A later ban on DDT has helped a little, but other pollutants from upstream have countered that progress.

"Among the other endangered species in the park are the snail kite whose main source of food, the apple snail was decimated by overdraining of The Everglades. There are now less than 900 left. The American crocodile is disappearing quickly as well as the wood stork and the red-cockaded woodpecker, whose nesting sites in the old growth pine forests were cut down by loggers."

Kenny pointed to his right and said, "Over there is a barred owl, and over here is a palm warbler, and right over there you can see a yellow-bellied sapsucker."

Lionfish was glad now that they had stopped. Even though the mosquitoes were a nuisance, he felt an even greater appreciation for The Everglades and its subtle beauty.

"In the 1840s, Florida's first state legislature called The Everglades wholly valueless and appealed to congress for help in draining the swamp. The dredging and digging began in earnest in 1905 when newly appointed Governor Napoleon Bonaparte Broward began fulfilling his campaign promise to 'build an empire of the Everglades.'

"Since the 1940s, politicians have pushed the transformation of The Everglades into high gear. They instructed the Army Corps of Engineers to dredge, dike, and divert to provide flood control, create and irrigate farmland, dry out land for new homes and businesses, and to supply drinking water to millions of new Florida residents.

"The pulpwood industry brought in Melaleuca and planted them all over the park to soak up water and it worked all too well. The trees adapted to our environment and eventually overran native species. You see all that," Kenny said pointing around behind the airboats, "that's all Melaleuca. It can invade over 50 acres a day throughout Florida and has no natural enemies."

Kenny walked over to a nearby tree where something had caught his eye and he picked up a small colored shell. "This is a Florida Tree Snail," he said.

"Stingray could probably tell you the scientific name."

"*Liguus Fasciatus*," Stingray called out without hesitation.

"When I was a boy and it was still legal to collect these, I had six or seven different kinds I kept in a fish tank by my window. This one I believe is called a dryas. You can see the yellow banded shell and the pink tip. I'd say this one is about two years old. There used to be thousands of them in all different colors in the tree hammocks around the park and now they're not so easy to spot.

"They are now just one more endangered species that no one will miss. I suppose most of the people living in south Florida aren't even aware that they exist. I grew up in Everglades City, and growing up next to a national park used to be idyllic. Everglades City used to be a busy commercial fishing village where fishermen like my dad used to run their boats out to the ten thousand islands to catch mullet and pompano, stone crabs and oysters. Not any more.

"There has been some talk lately about fixing The Everglades, a huge overhaul that would remove some of the area's plumbing, canals and levees, locks, and spillways. The project could possibly restore the natural flow of water in parts of The Everglades and could give the ecosystem another chance. It's not too late.

"But the obstacles are formidable. The overhaul would cost billions of dollars and no one can agree on what Everglades restoration means exactly. There are also powerful forces at work to stop the project. Several years ago, for example, the federal government sued the state of Florida for failure to enforce regulations that would stop the sugar farmers south of Lake Okeechobee from polluting The Everglades. Although state and federal authorities finally reached a settlement, the farmers could keep the case tied up in the courts for years."

"Which brings us to the reason why we are here today, gentleman," Lionfish interrupted. "Thank you, Kenny," Lionfish said as he steeped off of his airboat. He walked over and shook Kenny's hand.

"There is a light at the end of the tunnel, gentleman, but is it the light of hope for the restoration of this endangered eco-system, or is it the lights from a locomotive called BIG SUGAR that is barreling down the tracks and is heading straight for this park? Today we are going to stand on the tracks and we are going to step in front of that locomotive and hopefully we will derail it. The sugar barons are lobbying as we speak to halt the restoration of one of the world's most important eco-systems and they want to saddle the Florida taxpayers with the majority of the costs associated with the cleanup of their pollution.

"It's time we all said enough is enough, and said it in a way that only RedTide can."

CHAPTER 32

It was an unreasonably hot day even for south Florida and the mass of people protesting outside the Fort Lauderdale offices of the American Cane Growers Co-op were sweltering in the waves of heat that were rising from the asphalt beneath their feet.

It was a cool seventy degrees inside the conference room where John Marks and nine of the largest Sugar farmers in the state were meeting. Both sides of the sugar tax issue had amassed huge warchests over the past year and were funding advertising campaigns that stretched the limits of credibility. On the pro-tax side, one man had made the campaign possible. His name was John Henry Drake II.

Of the 10.5 million dollars that were raised to fight big sugar, 9.7 had come from the New York commodities broker. Many suspected his motives as being driven by greed rather than any environmental concerns. Many of his critics accused him of trying to manipulate the price of sugar for his own gain, but it had never been proven that he had any financial investment in the commodity.

Among the smaller contributors to the Save The Everglades Fund were Dave Barry, Carl Haissen, and the Miccosukee Indian tribe. But financially they were no match for the combined power and political reach of Gro-Sun Sugar, The American Sugar Corp. and the nine men who convened in the black glass office building on Federal Highway in Fort Lauderdale. They were meeting to discuss the issue while the protesters chanted their disapproval outside.

"We're dealing with a religious movement," John Marks said to the other eight men who were listening attentively as they sipped their coffee from expensive china that was poured to them from silver pots.

"Look at them out there," he said as he pointed out through the smoke glass floor to ceiling window he was standing in front of. "The National Parks and their constituency. The environmental movement. We are basically dealing with a religious movement. Don't they understand how many jobs are threatened by what they are proposing? Not just the jobs of the people who work the farms but the jobs of all the people in the support industries. From the people who sell us our conveyor belts to the heavy equipment manufacturers we buy from. Not to mention all the shipping, packing, and delivery people whose lives depend on us."

"You might even have to sell one of your Ferraris, John," Douglas Van Owen said to the general amusement of the group. Van Owen was the senior man in the room and he had been life long friends with John's father.

"Very funny Douglas. They also refuse to recognize that the future of restoration is inextricably linked to the sugar farmers. The restoration depends on a healthy sugar industry. But they want to close down my family's farm. A farm my great grandfather, my grandfather, my father, and now myself have worked for over one hundred years. After over a century of farming, they are telling me that farming land that forms the border of The Everglades is no longer acceptable. My farm employs over 500 people in this state and several small businesses depend on me to make a living. I tell you gentlemen, we need to increase the pressure on our appointed officials in Tallahassee and in D.C. The only way I'm leaving my farm is if I'm carried out."

"The sugar industry would like us to believe that this tax will mean fewer jobs," Dennis Bennett said to the crowd. Bennett was an environmentalist and a columnist with the *Sun Sentinal* and he was one of the organizers of the rally.

"They say that over 40,000 jobs will directly or indirectly be effected if they are forced to pay the penny tax. Well, for now we will set aside the sugar alliances propaganda and I will tell you all the truth. If The Everglades continues to be polluted, drained, and destroyed at its current rate, hundreds of thousands of jobs will be lost. Eventually, if this crucial eco-system is lost it will cause an environmental chain reaction that will be felt around the world, and it will effect the lives of countless millions. The National Audubon Society says that The Everglades serves as the foundation for over thirteen billion dollars in annual tourism that employs over 365,000 workers. More than one and a half billion visitors from around the world flock to the two national parks, the four national wildlife refuges, and the national marine sanctuary that are part of the famed river of grass. But of all the national parks and preserves in America, The Everglades is the closest to extinction, according to park superintendents. The protected lands are not protected from the elements that are choking the life from it, cattails! Yes I said cattails, the unmistakable calling card of the agricultural fertilizers used by big sugar. Cattails, which are non-existent in a natural saw grass marsh, have become prolific weeds that are growing like mad in The Everglades because they thrive on the fertilizers that are flowing from the cane fields. They are choking out native species and are destroying the habitat that sustains some of the rarest wildlife on earth. Biologists call cattails, 'the markers on the gravestone of The Everglades.'

"Vast expanses of marsh have been consumed by the thick reeds in their relentless march south from the cane fields. The US department of the interior estimates the cattails are eating up The Everglades at a rate of three to five acres a day. And for every acre of cattails there are probably ten acres with killer sawgrass, sawgrass with explosive growth fueled by fertilizers, like sawgrass on steroids. Fed by phosphorous from nearby farms, the marshes' knee high blades grow to gargantuan proportions. These tall sharp-edged, deadly killer grasses form tall dense thickets in which wading birds and other residents cannot feed. Phosphorous escaping downstream from sugar farms found its way into Lake Okeechobee and has caused an explosive rate of growth of algae. Sawgrass and cattails that are choking the life from The Everglades and are causing drastic increases in the salinity rate. In Florida Bay there are dead zones in which algae thrives and the seagrass beds have virtually disappeared along with the marine life it sustains. I would now like to introduce Congresswoman Nancy Pletcher of Florida who makes her home right here in Aventura."

A tall, blond, smartly dressed woman climbed the stairs of the makeshift stage and strode to the podium. "Good morning and thank you for coming here today," she began.

"I know it's hot and I thank you for your patience and for your commitment. I want to talk a little about the power of your vote in this, the greatest democratic society on earth. We live in cynical times and voter turnout for even our presidential elections is at an all time low. People say that they feel powerless to change things and see their one small vote as inconsequential. I am here to tell you that as individuals and collectively as a community you can make a difference. On November 5th, you will have an opportunity to protect one of the world's most important environmental areas. It will be an opportunity to send the message that enough is enough to big sugar who are armed with their powerful lobbyists, and their billions of dollars in resources. In 1988, a lawsuit filed by U.S. Attorney Dexter Lehtinen of Miami accused the water district and the state environmental agency of allowing polluted water from farms into The Everglades. The 1994 Everglades Forever Act, which calls for the marshes' restoration, was enacted to settle the lawsuit. This very important piece of legislation:,provided for creation of 40,000 acres of filter marshes that will clean the water entering The Everglades. It will require farmers to implement farm pollution controls to reduce phosphorous from runoff. It will provide for increased flow of water to The Everglades. The price tag for this cleanup of farm polluted water is estimated at one and a half billion dollars, according to the water management district. Through real estate taxes, property owners in sixteen counties will pay the lions share of removing fertilizer from The Everglades which will amount to 730 million dollars over the next twenty-five years. The sugar industry is only slated to pay 237 million dollars of the cleanup. The majority of the cost will fall on the shoulders of the taxpayer. IS THAT FAIR?"

"NO!!!!" The crowd answered.

"A portion of toll revenues from Alligator Alley, the main road through the glades will also go toward the restoration but the state is still 800 million dollars short of the funds needed to complete the project. On November 5, you and your fellow voters in the state will decide whether sugar growers should pick up the rest of the tab for the fertilizer cleanup by paying a penny a pound impact fee on raw sugar. I don't have to tell you that this is an initiative that is vigorously opposed by the industry. All we are asking them to do is to clean up their own mess. They are responsible for at least half of the phosphorous in The Everglades and they have reaped enormous profits while they have shown a contemptuous disregard for the environment. They have left a terrible legacy for our children and our children's children, a future without clean water. Environmental impact fees are not uncommon. Most of the state's businesses and industries pay to mitigate damage they may have caused. The phosphate industry pays a tax on every ton of the mineral mined. By refusing to acknowledge their responsibility and by their continuous opposition and intense lobbying the sugar industry has managed to cap its liability and has forced us to put the fate of The Everglades in the hands of the voters, allowing you to levee this tax. Preserving and restoring what is left of this fragile and complex eco-system that serves as a biological lifeline to over 1,500 species including five million people in the region is vital to the healthy future of south Florida and its residents. I ask you on November 5th to vote YES! to the penny a pound tax and to stand together as a community to fight for this beautiful land that we call home. Thank you!"

There was thunderous applause as John Marks pushed the power button on the remote control in his hand and turned off the television that was hanging in the far corner of the room.

"We're going to lose this fight, gentlemen," he said as he rose from his chair. "The momentum is moving away from us."

He walked to the door and before he left he said, "I have to return to my farm immediately to deal with another problem. It seems that a group of environmental fanatics had planned to abduct or kill most of us at my house today and then they were going to burn my farm to the ground."

There was a collective gasp in the room but before anyone could ask questions John Marks raised his hand palm up.

"That is the reason why I called you all yesterday and rescheduled the time and place of this meeting."

John Marks had a sinister smile on his face and said, "Don't worry, gentlemen, I have things under control, and ironically this could turn out to be just the media opportunity we've been looking for. With recent events in this country, from Waco to Oklahoma City, even the mention of domestic terrorism could have a way of swinging public opinion 180 degrees in our favor. It's not often that we have the opportunity to be seen as victims." He laughed incongruously and then turned and left the room.

He had a helicopter waiting for him on the roof that was costing him over 500 dollars an hour and he didn't want to keep it waiting. He needed to return to his farm in time to catch the show. He had insisted, despite MacGregor's warnings to the contrary, on being present at the ambush and the slaughter of the men who had planned to destroy his property. He smiled as the chopper lifted from the pad and he held his prized possession in his hand and polished it with a silk handkerchief. It was a polished stainless steel Colt Python, a .357 Magnum with a six-inch barrel. It had been given to him by his father upon his graduation from high school. When the terrorists plans were foiled and RedTide's men were eliminated, John Marks would call 911. Then he would call several local television stations and report the incident. By the time the spin doctors that the sugar industry employed were finished he would be seen as an American folk hero and the environmentalists would receive a body blow they would not recover from before the vote on the 5th.

Yes, he thought to himself, the gods had again smiled on him and before the day was over he would be one step closer to realizing his dream of controlling all the sugar in the state.

CHAPTER 33

MACGREGOR HAD HIS MEN DEPLOYED in various strategic locations around the equipment sheds, the offices, the refinery, and the storage areas. They were ready and he was waiting to strike the decisive blow that would end his long frustrating pursuit of Lionfish and his men. MacGregor was almost drooling at the thought of Lionfish unknowingly walking right into the trap that he had set. Lionfish and his men were quickly approaching John Marks' sugar plantation, "Sunshine Farms."

MacGregor had seven men dressed in suits who were posing as the Sugar Co-op executives. They were seated around the mahogany table in John Marks' office conference room. He even filled the parking lot with limousines in order to complete the illusion that the meeting had gone ahead as planned. All the men in the conference room were armed with

Uzi machine guns. He had a sniper set up in the 100 foot fire observation tower on the main farm road near the waterline to spot RedTide and to give the alert when they were nearby.

He had ten men in three airboats that were hiding in the Glades waiting to circle behind RedTide's boats when they arrived. They would block their escape by water and he had two SeaDoo Bombardier jet skis that were tied to the dock near the refinery to chase down any possible escapees. He also had two in reserve on a trailer in the tool shed.

He had thought of everything. He and John Marks would be in Marks' office. It adjoined the conference room. They would spring his trap the moment Lionfish entered the room. MacGregor had argued furiously with Marks to vacate the premises, but he had relented the moment that the man arrogantly reminded him of who would be signing his bonus check. Marks went on to remind MacGregor that he was working for him.

MacGregor just smiled and said, "You're the boss, John." What did he care if the man wanted to risk his life. He secretly hoped that he would catch a stray bullet before the day was ended and MacGregor insisted on being paid half his fee in advance, 250,000 dollars.

MacGregor instructed his men not to be overly confident and he made his point with the strong visual reminder of his hideously scarred face. He told his men that Lionfish and his men had successfully escaped his traps before on several occasions. MacGregor had every possible escape route covered and he indulged his optimistic attitude about the day with the acknowledgment that once Lionfish entered the offices he would be trapped within two sets of walls by an overwhelming force of men. It was MacGregor's hope that he could take Lionfish alive so that he could earn his million dollar bonus from Yamaguchi. He would have the drop on Lionfish and his men and he hoped that few shots if any would have to be fired. He checked his watch.

According to the information that Jake, his perpetually drunken captive in Miami had given him, Lionfish and his men should be arriving within fifteen minutes. MacGregor had refused to allow Jake to accompany him today. MacGregor indulged Jake's self-pity and he encouraged him to drink. He supplied his attempts to drown his pain with an endless supply of bourbon. He hoped to keep Jake in an alcohol-induced fog until Lionfish was captured. He promised Jake that he would be present at Lionfish's capture and in a way he was telling the truth. When Lionfish was brought back to the safe house and Mr. Yamaguchi arrived, he would allow Jake to confront Lionfish and then Jake would be forced to watch as Mr. Yamaguchi dismembered Lionfish with his family heirloom, a 600-year-old Samurai sword.

Then he would explain to Jake how his betrayal had led to the deaths of Lionfish, Stingray, and the other members of RedTide. MacGregor would watch for awhile as Jake came apart and when Jake's inevitable sobbing and cries of self-loathing began to bore him he would put a hollow point behind his ear at the back of his head.

David Hernandez was already nervous about the day's activities in the fields, but when he returned to the shed his agitation increased. He saw that the farm had become an armed camp. He had been told by Mr. Marks to keep the workers in the fields as long as possible today and to work them an extra four hours. The heat had reached an unexpected 95 degrees with an equal degree of humidity and the workers were dropping from fatigue in record numbers. Some of them had to be carried back to the barracks. The workers were highly agitated and almost a dozen had walked off the job, heading toward the direction of the barracks.

There were rumblings throughout the cafeteria and in the bunkhouse and in the fields all week long about the mysterious disappearance of James Brutus. James Brutus and his son Peter had vanished after their confrontation with the boss on Tuesday. The workers were convinced that they had been killed and, despite David's protestations to the contrary, the men's morale was at an all time low. The worker's morale was never really good to begin with on this slave camp and it had declined steadily. Lately, the men had become short tempered and disobedient.

David had tried to warn the boss, but he had waved him off. He told David that he was busy with more important matters and that he should handle it. Now there were men with guns in the camp and David wondered as he heard another large group of workers heading for the bunkhouse if he should slip away and remove himself from the property.

In addition to the obvious outward signs of trouble, he also had an instinctual feeling that the day would end in bloodshed and he decided to radio his three assistants from his Jeep as he drove out of the garage attached to his private residence. He instructed them that he needed some supplies in town and that in accordance with the boss's wishes they should continue to work the men until well after sunset. He told them to keep the workers as far from the outbuildings and the workcamp as possible. As he drove down the farm road he spotted a man with a large rifle slung under his arm in the observation tower. The man was looking directly at him with binoculars.

It looked like the boss was ready for a war and he wondered if it had anything to do with the protesters that had been showing up at the farm every weekend for the past two months. For one moment of misplaced loyalty, he thought about turning around and he felt like a coward for abandoning his post.

That feeling was quickly replaced with the usual contempt that he felt for the man who had corrupted everything his father had built. David remembered the degradation and the disrespect that he was subjected to on a daily basis. He had worked at Sunshine Farms for over twenty years and had become a U.S. citizen, but John Marks still treated him with the same contempt that he treated the rest of his workers. He would often direct snide racist comments at him. John Marks was a greedy, violent, evil man. Whatever trouble he was expecting today, David couldn't help but hope that some small measure of justice would be meted out and that for just once Marks wouldn't be able to tip the scales of justice with his gold.

Jake awoke in a haze, reeling from a three-day drunk and an excruciating hangover which beat a rhythm in his head as it tightened the knot in his stomach. Since he had been brought to this safehouse somewhere in Miami Beach he had began to drink and he had continued to drink as MacGregor's men restocked his room with an endless supply of Scotch and bourbon. He had been haunted by images of his mother, Samantha, and Danny and no matter how much he tried to block the thoughts or to dull his senses with alcohol he couldn't escape the guilt he felt and he couldn't seem to wash Danny's blood from his hands. There were guards outside his room and at every doorway of the house that Agent Wallace said were for his protection. There were no phones and no televisions in the house and Jake got the distinct feeling, although his instincts and his senses were not at their sharpest, that he was being held prisoner, that he couldn't leave if he wanted to.

Not that he had anywhere to go. He had no interest in speaking to anyone, especially his friends or family and he already thought of himself as dead. He was only living for the day that Lionfish would be brought to trial and he would be brought to the stand as a federal witness to testify against him.

He would pass by Lionfish at the defense table and he would whisper to him, "This is for Danny."

Then he would spill his guts and "Sing like a canary," as they said in the old gangster movies. After the trial, he would continue to drink himself blind and when the alcohol had sufficiently bolstered his courage, he would finally do something worthwhile with his life, he thought with a sickly smile. He would end it.

CHAPTER 34

REDTIDE'S AIRBOATS were within sight of John Mark's farm and Lionfish quickly drilled his men on their assignments and the timeline for engagement. His men were to fan out around the four buildings that made up the compound and Lionfish and five men would enter the offices. They would interrupt the meeting by bursting into the conference room and he would get their attention by spraying the ceiling with a burst of gun fire. Lionfish was carrying an automatic rifle equipped with a grenade launcher, a combat knife, a 9MM beretta, and a machine pistol.

He was also carrying ten magazines of ammo and ten grenades and his combat vest weighed close to thirty pounds. The plan was to kidnap six of the top CEOs from the largest sugar growers and cooperatives in the state, then to burn the farm and every building on the property to the ground. The men would be held indefinitely on 800 million dollars ransom that was to be paid directly to a Cayman Island account.

Lionfish would then contribute in over 10,000 separate, individual, and anonymous donations to The Everglades Restoration Fund. As the boats drew nearer to the farm, Lionfish signaled to Stingray to come over to his boat. He instructed him and Kenny Tiger to stay on the boat and he assigned Eagle Ray, one of his Marine Iguanas, to protect them. MacGregor had all the Haitian workers that had returned to the camp under guard in the barracks and he would not let them leave the building. Lionfish had three of the air boats that were each holding five men, including Jorge and Jack, drive to the north end of the property a half mile from the buildings. He instructed the men that at exactly 4:35 P.M. They were to double-time it back on foot. Meanwhile, he and the other two boats would break away and head straight for the main buildings.

JOHN MARKS FARM: EVERGLADES

Lionfish stepped off of the airboat, holding his grenade launcher waist high, and scanned the area. He thought it seemed unusually quiet even though he knew from his intelligence reports that the workers would not be returning from the fields for another two hours. He silently signaled to his men that he would take the point and he proceeded ahead. According to the plan, Jack and Jorge and their men should be working their way through the cane fields to the north and would soon be approaching the refinery, where they would set the plastic explosives. The timers would be set for thirty minutes and would be placed around the highly explosive tanks of fertilizers and chemicals that were used to grow and refine the sugar. Several bombs would be placed on the gas generators that were kept for emergency backup of the entire compound.

Lionfish spotted the barracks and noticed that no one was milling around outside and that no one was coming in or out of the building. His highly developed senses and his combat survival instinct tripped an early warning device in his head and he removed his radio and made contact with Jack. Jack told him that it was all clear on his end. He told Lionfish that they had been delayed because they had to circle around some workers that were cutting cane in the area near the water. It only delayed them by a few minutes, but otherwise he had no problems to report. He told Lionfish that they could now see the observation tower and it seemed to be empty, "another lucky break," Jack had said. MacGregor's man in the tower had sounded the alarm and he was crouched down. He was holding his high-powered sniper rifle with the telescopic sight in one hand and his radio in the other. He was communicating with MacGregor on his radio. "I just saw nine men dressed in combat fatigues and heavily armed coming out of the cane fields at the north end of the compound. They haven't spotted me and I could probably take out four or five of them before they could find cover. What should I do?"

"Do nothing for now," MacGregor replied. "I don't want any shooting until Lionfish is too far within our trap to escape. Stay out of sight and wait for my command. When and if I need you I will give you the word to use the Mauser to pick off any strays or escapees."

Lionfish signaled for his men to fan out. He sent three men to the tool sheds and two to the cane fields to circle around the offices from behind. The remaining three men he took with him as they came around the cafeteria building. From his current position he could observe the office building and the main road. Lionfish lifted his small field glasses to his eyes and from the concealment of the cafeteria building he observed the area. There were six limousines parked out in front of the office building and he could see the drivers as well as three other men. They were probably bodyguards. The men were milling about. They were talking among themselves and they were smoking cigarettes. He knew that they would all be armed and he instructed his men to be extra careful.

He waved to Stonefish to hand him the weapon that Stingray had designed over the course of the prior six months. He checked the magazine to make sure it was full and he tightened the silencer that was mounted on the barrel. It was a high-powered automatic rifle that could fire over 200 tranquilizer rounds per minute. The rounds were lead-tipped darts and they would inflict a painful bloody wound but it would not be deadly. The tranquilizer that Stingray had concocted from the venom of the Australian Blue-Ringed Octopus could knock a 250 pound man unconscious virtually upon impact.

Lionfish checked his watch, a Brietling chronograph that Stingray had bought him for Christmas, and when the second hand hit :30 he raised the rifle to his eye and fired twenty to thirty rounds in a matter of seconds. He sprayed the men with what would have been deadly accuracy had the ammunition been ball or explosive rounds. The first few men who were hit barely had time to open their mouths in warning as the entire group collapsed in the dirt. Lionfish and his men were moving before the last round was fired and with great stealth they covered half the compound before the last man standing hit the dirt face down.

MacGregor's man in the tower carefully peeked over the top and saw Jack and Jorge's group enter the refinery, where he knew MacGregor's men were waiting. He turned back toward the office just in time to see seven of his colleagues collapse in the dirt. They were clutching their arms and chests where bloody wounds appeared. "They're coming up the front stairs right now," he called into the radio, "and from what I can see they're carrying a lot of firepower."

MacGregor smiled incongruously at the news that his men outside had been taken out. He had to fight to control his excitement at the anticipation of finally meeting his adversary face to face.

"Keep your weapons under the table until I enter the room," he ordered his men. Then he went into the adjoining office to await Lionfish and to make his grand entrance. *The expression of surprise and stark realization on Lionfish's face when he recognized and comprehended the futility of the situation would be worth everything, even his gross disfigurement,* MacGregor thought.

Jack, Jorge, and the seven men they commanded had just entered the refinery and Jack was surprised to see that it was dark and empty. According to intelligence reports, they should have just finished a shift change and although the late afternoon/night shift had only a third the personnel of the day shift he was still expecting to find between ten and fifteen workers in the facility.

All the doors were closed and the windows were shaded. At what should have been the height of afternoon production, there were no workers in sight. Jack lifted his radio to his mouth to call Lionfish when suddenly the lights came on with blinding intensity and over twenty heavily armed men came out from behind crates and called out from the catwalks above them.

They were surrounded on all sides and were covered from above as well. Jack squeezed slowly on the trigger of his weapon and then he froze, realizing the futility of the situation.

"Drop your weapons, ... to resist would be suicide," a voice in the shadows above called down.

Jack glanced at Jorge and checked his watch. Lionfish would just be approaching the offices and there were only a few moments left to warn him of the trap. Jorge saw the look in Jack's eyes and the fierce loyalty in his resolute expression and he understood what they had to do.

Jack fired his weapon at the catwalk above him in a furious blast of automatic weapon fire as Jorge and his men fired simultaneously at the men behind the crates. They blasted hundreds of splintered hunks of wood in all directions. Lionfish was halfway up the steps when he heard gunfire. He and his men turned to make a run toward the Glades and the airboats.

Lionfish realized he would never reach the water so he broke into a serpentine run, accompanied by Puffer and another soldier, and they headed toward the east side of the refinery. They were fifty feet from the building when the man on his right was blown out of his boots by a shot from the sniper in the tower. Lionfish continued to hear the firefight in the refinery and his heart nearly exploded with worry when he thought about Stingray alone in the Glades with only one guard.

Puffer went down from a shot to the head and Lionfish quickly surmised that the source of the sniper shots must have been coming from the tower. It was the highest, most secure spot in the compound and as Lionfish gauged the distance he realized that it was still out of range. MacGregor burst from the adjoining room, screaming bloody murder and ordered the men who were already on their feet to chase after them.

What could possibly have gone wrong? MacGregor wondered. He knew the gunfire had erupted from the refinery. He had told his men not to come out of hiding until Lionfish was inside the conference room, no matter what. He made a mental note to kill the man responsible with his own hands when the day was over.

"What the fuck is going on?" John Marks demanded. "You told me there wouldn't be any shooting. There's a fucking war going on out there on my property, probably destroying the place. The equipment in that refinery alone cost me millions and the place is a tinderbox full of explosive chemicals and gasoline."

MacGregor ignored the man as they left the building together to survey the situation. MacGregor tried to make radio contact with his men at the refinery but to his great discomfort he received no answer. The sniper in the tower reported that MacGregor's airboats had just circled RedTide's airboats to the north and that they had taken two prisoners. He also reported two kills in the area outside the offices. He told MacGregor with pride that he had taken them out with his rifle.

Inside the barracks, the Haitian workers were highly agitated by the gunfire and were convinced that the boss had hired killers to exterminate the majority of his workers. It made little sense to the few men who tried to reason with them but, considering the geo-political climate of their native homeland and the volatile and unpredictable temper of their employer, their arguments were falling on deaf ears. The men were also very angry about the recent disappearance of Brutus and his son and they had reached their breaking point. After months and months of deprivation, abuse, and exploitation they rebelled. Without warning, a riot broke out within the barracks and men produced swingblades and machetes and crowbars from under their mattresses. They rushed at MacGregor's men and unleashed a fury of pent-up frustration and hostility.

MacGregor radioed his men in the barracks and received no answer. He turned to look at the building, when suddenly the door burst open and one of his men ran out the door screaming. He was spurting blood from a severed arm as he burst forth into the yard and then collapsed in the dirt.

In seconds, over thirty men armed with crude weapons of death were running in his and John Marks' direction. MacGregor turned to see the ashen look on Marks' face and he smiled at the cowardice of the arrogant bully. MacGregor raised his automatic weapon, fired at the front line of men as they approached, and ten of them dropped to the dirt. MacGregor expected that to stop them, but they kept coming in wave after wave. Marks had his enormous pistol out and he fired all six rounds. His hands were jerking so violently from fear that he missed all six shots. MacGregor realized in that instant as he emptied his magazine what he would need to do to save his life. He turned to Marks and struck him with the butt of his rifle in the small of the back. When Marks collapsed to his knees MacGregor said, "Pleasure doing business with you, Johnny."

He ran for the refinery, where his strongest contingent of men were busy slaughtering RedTide's men. MacGregor's plan worked. He looked back over his shoulder from a dead run and he saw a sight that made him grimace with revulsion. Over ten men armed with machetes and crowbars were slashing away at Marks' neck, head, and torso. They severed his limbs as he tried in vain to defend himself.

Lionfish ran to the cover of the refinery building and as he approached he noticed that the firing inside had stopped. He hoped that it was his men that were left standing. As he turned the corner to check the sniper's position in the tower he almost got his head blown off. He pulled back just in time as a bullet tore through the corrugated metal of the large Quonset hut and impacted just inches from his head. He was too far away to make a clean shot with the rifle and the sniper was protected by the wood and metal structure of the tower.

Lionfish readied the grenade launcher, then he dove out from behind the cover of the building and rolled to his knees. He immediately fired a round high into the air toward the tower. The round exploded two feet from the top of the tower. It disintegrated the watchtower and its sole occupant in a shower of blood, steel and wood.

Lionfish circled around the north end of the refinery. He was looking for an opening to peer within. He crouched down behind two large metal barrels and he listened for the enemy. He heard the sound of an airboat approaching from the north, where Stingray was positioned, and he hoped it was his brother making his escape. Lionfish picked up his radio and tried to contact Jack.

"Can you read me?"

"I read you loud and clear, Lionfish," MacGregor responded.

Lionfish instantly recognized the voice and was not surprised to learn that it was MacGregor that had sprung this trap today. Lionfish's heart sank at the realization that his men inside were probably dead.

Jake, Lionfish thought to himself. *But how could he have known? He must have spied out the documents in the OPs center when I wasn't looking.*

It was careless not to have locked them up, but Lionfish never felt the need to since every single person who had access to the OPs center also had a secured clearance to read those documents and was proven trustworthy beyond reproach. Besides, anyone who had access to the OPs center would have been here today. Except Jake!

"Where are my men?" Lionfish demanded in a surprisingly calm tone of voice.

"I'm afraid your men foolishly tried to fight their way out of a crossfire against overwhelming odds," MacGregor replied. "I suggest you learn a lesson from their mistake and turn yourself in. Your men at the tool shed are dead. Your men in the refinery are dead. And we have captured your brother. Unfortunately we had to kill his bodyguard and the Indian. I'm afraid you are the only one left and I have you surrounded on all sides."

Lionfish froze, unable to think for a moment at the news that Stingray had been captured. Jake had probably given MacGregor a complete description so he would know who the leaders were. MacGregor would never kill Stingray while Lionfish was still on the loose. If he turned himself in they would both be killed, of that Lionfish had no doubt, but he also knew that there was no way he could leave here without him.

Lionfish had to move quickly. He knew he would soon be discovered, so he told MacGregor that he would see him again soon and when he did that he would gut him like a fish. Then he smashed the radio and ran to the cane fields. He was thirty yards from the edge of the crop when bullets tore up the ground around him. He dove the last five feet and rolled into the field. He stood up and fired two grenades behind him, lobbing them blindly from the field toward the refinery. When they exploded he heard screams, and then he tore off toward the water in a northwesterly direction. His head was pounding as he thought about Jack and Jorge and the other twenty men he had led to their deaths. He blamed himself for his error in judgment. He should never have allowed Jake to leave the island alive. The one time he had allowed sentimentality to cloud his judgment and look at the cost. On the most important day of the year for Lionfish, the day he planned for his greatest success, he realized his final, greatest failure.

Lionfish headed for the riverbank and he peered out through the cane to survey the situation. His heart skipped a beat when he saw MacGregor's airboats only fifty yards downstream. They were riding up and down the banks looking for Lionfish and on the last boat closest to him he saw his brother, tied to the pilots chair but unharmed.

Lionfish slipped into the water and began to intentionally hyperventilate. He did his breathing exercises to prepare for a long breath hold and he slipped beneath the water.

"DogPack 2, come in," MacGregor said over the radio to the team leaders aboard the airboats.

They responded that they had seen no sign of Lionfish. The men searching the cane fields reported negative as well. MacGregor ordered them to keep looking, all with the exception of the boat that Stingray was aboard. He ordered that boat to report back to the refinery as soon as possible. He left the refinery to return to John Marks' offices and he took ten men with him to disband the rabble that had turned Marks into chopmeat back at the compound. He told his men at the refinery to bring Stingray to him as quickly as possible. He wanted to ensure his safety so he could use him to barter for Lionfish's surrender. He was so close and he had killed all of Lionfish's forces and yet the man miraculously still eluded him.

Lionfish swam through the murky green water for over one and a half minutes as he listened for the sounds of the airboats above to guide him. When he was only thirty feet away, a ten-foot alligator slipped from the embankment into the water nearby and approached stealthily to within a few feet of him.

Just as the alligator opened his mouth and prepared to make his final lunge, Lionfish was able to see the bottom of one of the boats in the three-foot visibility. He quickly surfaced and he boarded the airboat as he removed his large double-edged combat knife from its sheath. He slipped aboard quietly, his movements covered by the roar of the propeller. He was able to sink his blade deep into the spine of the pilot before the other three men aboard even noticed his arrival. The men quickly turned on him and he kicked one man in the neck as he lowered his weapon and blew the other two men into the water where the grateful alligator was waiting to finish them.

Lionfish now had control of the boat, but was disappointed to find that his brother was not aboard. He saw a second boat approaching him. It was firing from a distance of fifty yards downstream and he could see off in the distance the boat that was holding Stingray was pulling up to the dock.

"Damn it," he swore as he turned the boat and accelerated to full speed. He churned the water as he headed directly toward the enemy boat in a high stakes game of chicken. The two boats were heading straight at each other and when Lionfish guessed that they had reached the maximum range for their weapons he stopped the boat. He fired a grenade at the water in front of them which created an enormous wake and a curtain of water over twelve feet high. The boat hit the wake and pointed straight up in the air before it fell upside down in the water. The four men in the water were suffering from minor injuries and they were floating on the surface treading water. They were only a few feet apart from each other when Lionfish accelerated his airboat and ran them over.

He could hear a thud and the boat jumped slightly as it slammed across the tops of their heads. When Lionfish looked back they were floating lifeless in the water. Blood spread out in a widening arc from their bodies and the water filled with alligators. Lionfish had only one thing on his mind as he clenched his jaw in a vengeful rage.

I will get my brother back even if I have to kill every living thing in the compound or I will be killed in the attempt, he thought.

He approached the dock as MacGregor's men ran out to meet him. He fired a grenade at the dock and blew it to bits along with five men who had run out to its end. The jet skis had come untied from the dock in the explosion. MacGregor's men had voiced some reluctance to riding the vehicles in the alligator-infested waters. MacGregor had told them they would be used only in an emergency and that they would probably not be required. He explained that they were faster than the airboats and would be effective at hunting down any escapees.

Lionfish fired his automatic weapons from both hands now as he climbed onto what was left of the burning dock. He forced MacGregor's men to retreat back into the refinery. When they had retreated inside, Lionfish remembered what Stingray had told him about the combustibility of the place and he fired three grenades in rapid succession deep within the building. He dropped the Uzi in his left hand since its ammo was spent, and ran to the splintered end of the dock and dove into the water. He didn't know what to expect from the blast. When his hands broke the surface of the water the refinery went up in a series of explosions, which finally ignited the combustible highly explosive materials inside. The final explosion detonated the entire building, sending up a fireball 100 feet high and spread a curtain of fire across the water over Lionfish's head that was over fifty yards wide. The blast broke all the windows on the property, including the ones in the office MacGregor was currently in, and blew a thirty-foot high and a fifty-foot-wide dent in the metal Quonset hut nearby. It looked like an empty soda can that had been stepped on.

MacGregor stood up from the floor and brushed slivers of broken glass from his hair and shoulders. He cut his hand and he shook his head to try to clear the ringing in his ears.

"Your brother puts on quite a show," he said to Stingray, who was being held between two of the ten men that MacGregor had left alive. MacGregor quickly figured his losses at over thirty-five men, most at the hands of one man.

"Wait until you see what he does for an encore," Stingray replied defiantly. "He's just getting warmed up."

MacGregor laughed out loud even though he felt enormously frustrated. He was near his breaking point and he was trying desperately to control his anger.

"I see you are looking at my scars. Rather ghastly I suppose, even to a man of science."

"Maybe you should try a sunscreen with a higher SPF rating," Stingray said.

"A sense of humor seems to run in your family," MacGregor responded in an ominous tone. "Tell me if you find this amusing," he said as he swung his rifle butt into Stingray's chest, breaking two ribs.

Stingray collapsed to his knees, his breath gone. The pain was excruciating and his eyes filled with tears.

"Hold him up," MacGregor ordered his men.

"I need you alive in order to bring your brother to me, but how alive and in what condition I suppose is irrelevant."

MacGregor drove his fist into Stingray's face, breaking his nose. Blood ran down Stingray's face and his labored breathing whistled through the smashed bone. He passed out and MacGregor ordered his men to throw him on the leather sofa in John Marks' office. MacGregor chided himself for losing his temper. He sat down and he took a Cuban cigar from the humidor on John Marks' desk. He told his men to get some ice and to tend to Stingray's wounds. There were ten men left in MacGregor's party out of an original forty-five and they were all encircled around the office in a tight cordon of protection. They had killed over thirty Haitian cane workers before the rest of them disbanded and took off through the cane fields to escape the farm forever. MacGregor couldn't remember seeing this much carnage since he had worked for the South African police in the 80s. He had worked with the South African government for two years and had helped to assassinate over 100 members of the ANC.

Lionfish emerged from the water and swam toward the shore. One of the jet skis had exploded from the flames and pieces of it were floating around the water, along with wood and other debris from the explosion. Lionfish was covered in black soot and oil.

He had only two grenades left and one rifle with two remaining banana clips. As he reached the shore he saw the other jet ski, which was badly burned and blackened. It was resting on the shore on its side. It appeared to be in operating condition and Lionfish stood it upright and hit the starter. It started up and Lionfish quickly turned it off to stop the noise. He pushed it downstream and hid it in a thicket.

He was now south of the barracks and the offices and he began to make his way back toward the office. Twenty minutes earlier, MacGregor ordered his men to unload the jet skis from the toolshed, since all of the airboats except one had been destroyed in the melee. He called Yamaguchi to arrange for a helicopter to remove him and his hostage from the battle zone. Only Yamaguchi would have the juice to get a helicopter on such short notice and a pilot who wouldn't ask any questions when he touched down in the middle of what looked like Armageddon.

He was told the helicopter would be there in twenty-five minutes, and MacGregor told Yamaguchi only what he needed to know. He told him that he had killed every member of the organization that had killed his son and that he had captured Stingray. MacGregor was stunned and Yamaguchi was furious to have learned weeks earlier from Jake that Stingray was still alive and that the man who had leapt to his death in the desert was an imposter. He could now tell Yamaguchi that Lionfish's capture was imminent. Yamaguchi was pleased but he was also disappointed that the head of the organization was still free. He questioned MacGregor's earlier assurances that this time he would bring Lionfish to final justice. MacGregor's plan was to leave the area and remove any possibility that Lionfish might pull off another miracle and rescue his brother.

He would then negotiate under more hospitable conditions from a safe and secure location for the surrender of Lionfish in exchange for his brother. He really had no interest in harming the scientist and neither did his employer, but he yearned with every fiber of his being to see the man known as Lionfish, first suffer and then die. The longer he remained here the greater the chances were that something else could go wrong. He would leave his men here to wait for Lionfish to return. His instructions would be to hunt down Lionfish until daylight and then his men could escape in the limousines.

Lionfish crept up from the banks, as MacGregor's men lowered the two spare jet skis into the water alongside the one remaining airboat that they had located. They were about to begin searching for Lionfish along the waterways and canals. They were sure that he had escaped on one of the airboats. The men looked up when they heard the helicopter that showed up right on schedule.

Lionfish heard the rotors as the chopper approached and settled down outside the offices. He ran as fast as he could toward the building. MacGregor left the building with the still unconscious body of Stingray. Stingray was being supported by two of MacGregor's men and MacGregor had his men form a circle around him and Stingray as they escorted him to the helicopter. MacGregor wasn't taking any chances and he made sure to remove any possible shot that Lionfish could take without hitting his brother.

Lionfish shot the men by the water first, dropping all three with a small burst of automatic fire. He ran screaming toward the helicopter and MacGregor's men immediately opened fire on him. He dove and rolled to the ground as a bullet tore into his left shoulder. He ignored the pain and he fired at the men as the helicopter lifted off. He fired a burst of gunfire at the helicopter. He was hoping to force it to the ground while it was still at a height from which Stingray could survive the crash. He watched the helicopter fly safely away as he ran toward the water with bullets whistling past his ears and ricocheting around him.

He knew it was too late to save his brother at this moment, that his only hope of ever getting him back was to escape alive so that he could track him down. Lionfish knew that MacGregor's only motivation for keeping Stingray alive was to capture him, and if he were killed MacGregor would dispense with Stingray immediately. Lionfish needed to get back to Miami and tap every intelligence contact he had in order to find his brother. He would spend every dime of the considerable fortune they had accumulated over the years on bribes and payoffs until he found the answers he needed, but first he had to escape.

The pain in his shoulder was excruciating and he could feel blood running down his back. He jumped aboard the jet ski and took off at full throttle through the reeds and marshes. MacGregor's men were in quick pursuit. They followed behind on the two Bombardiers and the airboat. The sun was setting and Lionfish figured he would have a few minutes of light to make it to Alligator Alley to commandeer a vehicle.

MacGregor wanted to pursue Lionfish in the helicopter, but Stingray's condition had taken a turn for the worse. Stingray was blowing blood bubbles from his mouth. One of his broken ribs had probably punctured a lung and MacGregor needed to get him immediate medical attention. Lionfish would never believe that Stingray was alive without speaking to him. MacGregor could not lose the bait he needed to reel Lionfish in.

Lionfish was doing over fifty miles an hour on the jet ski. He was flying over the water and skipping over thick grasses, being careful to avoid the killer sawgrass and the bayheads. He had only a vague idea of where he was going, but he knew if he headed southeast he would slam right into the highway only a few miles away. The jet skis were slaloming and banking into sharp turns almost throwing the riders. The bottom could disappear in this area in just a few yards. The going was treacherous and Lionfish blasted past a crocodile who lashed out at him as he flew by. Lionfish roared through a large group of birds and with his vision obstructed he hit a small bayhead. The jet ski flew five feet into the air and landed with a crash, almost dislodging him.

Lionfish turned around and saw the jet skis behind him in single file and they were narrowing the gap. When he was in a clear straight area of water he jammed the accelerator in place and removed his hands. He spun 180 degrees in his seat and began to fire at the skis behind him as his jet ski got faster and faster and finally topped out at almost sixty miles an hour.

He was bouncing backward in the seat and he fired the last few rounds in his clip. One round found its mark and hit one of the men directly in the chest. It blew him backward off his jet ski. It flew onto a bayhead and smashed into a tree with a loud crash. Only one jet ski and the airboat remained in pursuit, and as Lionfish turned around in his seat, he spotted a small tunnel up ahead that ran below a narrow park road built by the state to allow rangers and workers access to the park.

The tunnel was only a few feet high and Lionfish headed straight for it, not knowing when he got to it if he would fit through or not. When he approached the opening he realized it would be a very tight fit and he removed his left hand from the steering wheel. He held the accelerator lightly in his right hand and he steered with only two fingers and his thumb. He hung his body way over on the right side of the jet ski below the height of the handlebars and hugged the body of the jet ski tightly. Lionfish flew through the tunnel with barely six inches of clearance on either side and scraped the skin on his right hand and knuckles almost down to the bone as he flew out the other side.

The jet ski followed Lionfish into the tunnel, copying his technique, but the airboat was forced to stop. The sky above was a deep red and orange and the clouds were gray and violet above the still, reflective water of The Everglades. Under other circumstances it would have appeared beautiful to Lionfish but right now it was a prelude to a darkness that would rob him of all available navigable light. He was followed out of the tunnel by one determined rider who was hell-bent on collecting the 200,000 dollar reward MacGregor had offered the men just before he left the compound.

Lionfish could see Alligator Alley ahead. It bisected the Glades and the state like a long, narrow scar. He headed straight for the road and as he gunned the accelerator he wondered how he would get over the fence that lined the road. He heard shots and a round whistled past his ear.

He had one grenade left that he had been saving for the end. He held the rifle behind him with his left hand and fired at the jet ski. He missed the jet ski but the grenade landed close enough to send up a wake and the jet ski flew in the air, dislodging its passenger.

He skipped across the water like a stone before he was stopped by a dense clump of sawgrass that shredded him like a hunk of sirloin dropped into a meat grinder.

Lionfish accelerated as quickly as he could toward the embankment and aimed for a small elevated earth ramp near the fence. The jet ski hit the natural ramp at sixty and it flew over twenty feet into the air, clearing the fence. Lionfish let go of the jet ski in mid-air and he flew through the air before he landed on the soft grassy shoulder of the road and tumbled head over heels. The jet ski landed with a crash in the back of a pickup truck heading west down the middle of Alligator Alley. The truck swerved wildly and caused a five-car pile up in the westbound lane a few miles east of Everglades City.

Lionfish rose to his feet and forced his broken and battered body to walk toward the road. He raised his machine gun at a man in a Toyota 4Runner who was just ahead of the tangle of cars. Lionfish walked up to the man covered in ash and blood and oil. His clothing was torn from head to toe. He asked the man if he could borrow his car. The man almost fainted as he handed over his keys. Lionfish sped away toward Everglades City, where he knew friends and relatives of Kenny Tiger's who would smuggle him to Miami.

Three days later, he had settled in at the Delano hotel on Miami Beach. He called Doctor Tanabe, a local ER Doctor who was friendly to the cause and liked RedTide's money. He paid Doctor Tanabe 20,000 dollars for the illegal medical attention he recieved. With the use of a portable X-ray machine, Doctor Tanabe assessed that Lionfish had several small fractures. He removed the bullet in his shoulder and sewed him up. Doctor Tanabe dressed the wound and administered antibiotics and painkillers intravenously. Lionfish rested for a few days while he planned his next move and waited for a message from MacGregor. First, he would find his brother, then he would kill MacGregor. Then he would find Jake and he would settle all his debts.

CHAPTER 35

Jake had already consumed over a fifth of bourbon in just the few hours since he had awakened. Daylight had broken through his window and had hit him full on with a blast of sunshine and he reached for his bottle and pulled the shades. He remembered being awakened last night to the sounds of cars in the driveway and he had listened to the shuffle of men outside. It sounded as if they were moving something into the house. He stumbled to his window and he caught a glimpse of Wallace and his men as they entered the house. They were wheeling someone on a cart through the front door. He distinctly remembered going to the door of his room and finding that it was locked from the outside. He banged once or twice for his guards to open the door and then he gave up and collapsed in a drunken stupor back onto his bed. Now he heard voices downstairs and he recognized Wallace's Scottish accent, although it was barely audible as it came through the vent on the floor beneath his bed.

Stingray woke up with an enormous headache and there was a stabbing pain in his chest every time he breathed. He was being kept heavily sedated and would awaken only when the pain of his injuries exceeded the dosage of the tranquilizers. He fought the sedatives and he shook his head to fight for consciousness.

"Good Morning."

He heard a voice, although it sounded as if it were ten miles away in a heavy fog. He recognized the accent and an immediate feeling of dread and anger generated a flow of adrenaline which helped bring him the rest of the way back to consciousness.

"I hope you slept well," MacGregor said. "I would hate it if a houseguest of mine were uncomfortable."

"Go fuck yourself," Stingray managed to spit out at the man standing beside his bed.

Stingray tried to raise his arms and he found that they were unable to move. MacGregor laughed, "For your own protection we have you in restraints, both chemical and physical.

"We wouldn't want you to aggravate your condition and we don't want you to try something stupid like escaping. That might force one of the trigger-happy Neanderthals who work for me to shoot you. I deeply regret my uncontrolled display of emotion yesterday. I want to apologize for allowing you to provoke such uncivilized behavior back at the farm. I have allowed you to awaken from your long nap because I want you to help me get a message to your brother. I realize that I could just place an ad in the paper or in the Sunday classifieds or personals. Maybe under "Man Seeking Man." But I was hoping to be more discreet and I know that your organization uses the Internet to send and receive messages. My employer has given me implicit instructions that no harm is to come to you. Neither my employer nor myself have any interest in harming you. You will be released the moment that we have your brother in custody. Mr. Yamaguchi is flying here as we speak and he is a man of honor. He knows that you are a scientist and that you were not directly involved in the murder of his son. He has asked me to give you his word that you will be treated fairly."

"What about Lionfish?" Stingray responded, already knowing the answer.

"Your brother is a murderer and a terrorist and needs to be brought to justice," MacGregor answered with an impatient and slightly angry tone in his voice. "Your brother will be tried in a Japanese court of law for his crimes in that country and for the murder of Nobuaki Yamaguchi and the other people he killed at Mr. Yamaguchi's factory. After he is found guilty, he will more than likely be extradited to a number of other countries including the United States who will want to try him in their respective nations for his various crimes against humanity. There may even be a single trial in the world court, if that can be arranged. Mr. Yamaguchi wants there to be a public trial so that the entire world can witness the list of crimes for which your brother and his organization are responsible. It is not respect for the criminal justice system, or sympathy, but rather political necessity that motivates his decision. Mr. Yamaguchi wants to discredit RedTide in a public trial and it would also be good for his business. I have had carte blanche to run my operation any way I chose; I was instructed to use any means necessary to capture Lionfish. Mr. Yamaguchi is not a violent man and he has not been privy to my methods thus far. My contract only calls for the capture of your brother and my work is done. When my mission is completed, Mr. Yamaguchi and his lawyers will take over and the violence will end. What ever happens to your brother after that is for the courts to decide. I won't lie to you, though. Chances are that Lionfish will be convicted and that he will be sentenced to death. But a trial will provide a forum for him to promote his views and his environmental stance and he may be able to swing enough public opinion to save his life. If he should decide to cooperate with the world's governments and to confess to his crimes, he may buy some additional leniency. We both know that eventually Lionfish will find you. When he does, we will be waiting for him. I promise you that if he comes to me first, you will all die, including Jake, who is passed out upstairs. I need time to arrange a meeting place, and I need to inform Lionfish of its location only minutes before he arrives. I can't allow him to arrive with reinforcements or to have time to prepare. When he shows up I will turn you and Jake loose and Lionfish will be flown to Japan to stand trial. I give you my word. Think about it for a little while." MacGregor removed a syringe from his pocket and he injected something into Stingray's arm. "Sleep tight," he said softly. "Soon it will all be over."

Stingray fought to stay awake but he could feel the sedative beginning to work and he knew he would only have a few seconds before he blacked out. With great effort, he inhaled as much air as his lungs could hold. The expansion of his broken ribs sent thunderbolts of pain up his spine. He let the air out in a long yell, shouting as loudly as he could, **"JAKE!!!!!"**

Jake backed away from the duct on the floor where he had been listening as if he had stuck his hand in a pot of boiling water. That was Jerry's voice he heard. Were they both victims of this man who called himself Wallace? Were they both pawns in a plot to kill Lionfish? Jake tried desperately to piece together the clues to a puzzle that had destroyed his life and had killed his friends and loved ones.

Suddenly Jake heard MacGregor coming up the stairs and he ran to his bathroom and turned the water on. He pretended as if he had been tidying up. MacGregor burst into the room just as Jake came out of the bathroom.

"Up early today," MacGregor said, even though it was already 11:00 A.M.

"What was that noise?" Jake asked with a slight slur to his speech. "I thought I heard someone yelling."

"One of the men just found out that his wife had delivered his son and he was celebrating."

"Don't you let your men off when their wives are in labor?"

"Government agencies Jake, especially the FBI, aren't known for their sentimentality. How are you feeling today? Do you want some breakfast? I had Agent Garcia run out and pick up some bagels. I know they're your favorite. Come downstairs with me and get some coffee. You look like shit."

When Jake reached the living room downstairs he glanced quickly to his right and saw a man standing guard outside the room where they must have been holding Jerry. MacGregor steered Jake to the dining room table. The dining room was surrounded by windows that overlooked the intercoastal waterway. Jake sat down in front of a large platter of bagels and a pot of hot coffee. Jake had to force himself to look the man in the eyes. Jake knew he would have to play along with MacGregor's cover as an FBI agent. Hearing Jerry's voice and being under guard in a locked room had convinced Jake that he was being used. His hands were shaking violently and his mouth was as dry as a desert.

Jake smiled at the image of a hired Scottish killer serving bagels and lox to his captive.

"What's so funny, Jake?" MacGregor asked. He looked slightly annoyed.

"Nothing," Jake said as he poured a shot of Baileys into his coffee. "I was just thinking about my mother. I would have this same breakfast every Sunday at her apartment and when I looked up and saw you I thought, there's the last person I would ever expect to see serving smoked salmon."

"I know you like it, Jake, and I do want you to be comfortable. I have some good news and some bad news. I have a problem and I need your help. Thanks to you, we have successfully thwarted RedTide's attempt to kidnap and murder the executives of the Florida Sugar Growers Alliance, but Lionfish has escaped."

Jake felt his stomach roll over at the realization that MacGregor had set him up and that more than likely he was the one who had killed Danny. Jake suddenly realized that his betrayal had probably cost the lives of his friends, including Jack and Jorge. He had to dig his fingernails into his palms to retain his composure. His only relief came from the knowledge that Lionfish had escaped, and that there was still some hope remaining. Jake didn't really care what happened to him. If Lionfish wanted to kill him he couldn't blame him, but he wanted desperately to reunite the brothers, so he needed to find a way to save Jerry.

"You told me that your plan was foolproof and that you would have them surrounded over ten to one by your men," Jake said angrily. "Not to mention in your own words that, the element of surprise was on your side."

"I'm as disappointed as you are, Jake," MacGregor said honestly. "My men sprung the trap a moment too early and Lionfish is an experienced combat veteran who is trained to exploit such opportunities. I lost over forty men, Jake, and now the bureau is launching an investigation into my leadership. They are questioning my execution and implementation of departmental policy and guidelines at the farm. Needless to say, Lionfish now knows that you set him up and your life is in even more danger than it was before. We need to apprehend him quickly before he begins to draw on his considerable intelligence network in order to track you down and kill you."

Jake removed the small silver flask that MacGregor had given to him as a present and took a gulp of liquid. Jake had emptied the original contents into the toilet upstairs and he had filled it with tap water just before MacGregor had entered his room.

"You should slow down on the drinking, Jake," MacGregor said in a false show of concern. "You're killing yourself with that shit."

"If you're so concerned, then why do you allow your men to keep supplying me with it?"

"I told my men to give you anything you asked for," MacGregor responded.

"I've asked for a TV and I've asked for a phone. I've asked for a newspaper and I've asked to get a message to my sister and your men have said no to every request. Why should I be worried?" Jake asked. "I've got you and the entire United States government to protect me. Besides, If Lionfish wants to kill me, let him come. He'd be doing me a favor."

"Jake, we need to get a message to Lionfish so we can arrange a meeting. We are going to offer him a deal. Do you have any idea how we can contact him without publicly disclosing our intentions or the location of the meeting?"

"I don't know," Jake replied. "You're the expert. Why not send him a coded message in the papers or on the internet."

"We already thought of that. We need it to be more specific, since we have no way of knowing what he will be reading or where he is located. Since we will want our meeting to be in a secret location which only he will know about we need to keep it from public viewing or at least from public understanding. If we send a code we will need to know more private and relevant information about Lionfish. We need to send something which only he would understand, based on his history or his relationships. Jake, what more can you tell us about the man?"

Jake swallowed another large gulp from the flask and he clumsily got to his feet. "I wish I could help you," he said with a more pronounced slur. He staggered toward the stairs.

"They never told me all that much." He climbed the stairs and then he belched loudly. "I'm going back to bed," Jake said as he climbed the stairs to his room. "Call me when the bogeyman arrives."

Son of a bitch, MacGregor thought to himself. *I've created an alcoholic monster. I told my men to keep Jake well supplied and I encouraged Jake to drink and now he's become a useless drunk.*

For a moment, MacGregor let his anger get the better of him and he contemplated following Jake upstairs and putting him out of his misery, but he wouldn't deny himself the pleasure of following his plan to the end. He wanted to see Jake's expression when he saw Lionfish die and he realized that MacGregor had set him up. He also needed to increase his odds of finding Lionfish and two hostages were better than one, especially when one of them was badly injured. MacGregor grimaced at the reminder of his unprofessional conduct back at the farm.

He was a fool to have allowed Stingray to get to him. He was a fool to have roughed him up like some teenage gang member.

Unfortunately, he still needed Jake and there was still no way of knowing how he might serve them. He would never again allow his anger to rule his mind. He would not make the same mistake twice.

On his way upstairs, Jake thought ironically that depression with all its many negative attributes was also liberating. There was a certain freedom in not caring anymore and for the first time in a long time he wasn't afraid. Without fear of the consequences, Jake could now take greater risks, and he knew if he were to be successful at helping to free Stingray he would need to risk his life. He went to the vent, sat down on the floor beside it, and leaned back against the wall. He had to think of a plan and he had to find some way to contact Lionfish. Jake had no idea where he was. He knew the house that he and Stingray were captive in was located somewhere in South Florida and that it was somewhere on the Intercoastal. That much he could see out the windows. From what he could see, the house was non-descript, looked like a thousand other houses from Miami to Boca Raton. There were no phones wired in the house. He had seen several of the guards talking on cellular phones and he had seen MacGregor once using his laptop and his modem with a handheld cell phone. Jake would need to find a way to make contact with Stingray and he would need to get hold of one of the guard's cellular phones. He knew time was running out and racked his brain to think of a way to warn Lionfish. Jake leaned over the vent and called, at first softly, then in increasing volume to Stingray below. He was being careful to listen for the guards. He tried for over thirty-five minutes to make contact without a response and then gave up. He was leaning over the bed for support to lift himself up when he thought he heard a sound.

Over the next two days, Jake studied the movements of the five men who were assigned to stand guard over Stingray and him. He began to act more drunk than usual and to douse his clothing with bourbon. He also began to gargle with it. He pretended to fall asleep on the living room couch and at the kitchen table. He carefully studied the guard's every movement and the location of their cellular phones. The guards began to become more and more relaxed around Jake, especially when MacGregor wasn't around.

He noticed on several occasions that they would leave him alone and that they would gather on the back deck to smoke cigarettes and to watch the bikinis that floated past the house on the decks of recreational boats. Jake noticed that the guards often left their cellular phones on the kitchen counter close to the stove. He also noticed on more than one occasion that the guard outside Stingray's room would leave his post to go to the bathroom or to join his friends on the pool deck.

Jake considered the security pretty lax, attributing it to the condition of the men being guarded. Both Jake and Stingray were obviously stoned most of the time, although Jake was sure that Stingray's condition wasn't voluntary. One day, Jake was seemingly passed out on the living room sofa and a boatload of girls on a Searay passed by the house. There were five girls in thong bikinis. Wallace's men, who had been holed up in the house for over two weeks, called out to them. When the girls teased them by baring their breasts and mooning them, Jake knew he had his chance. The guards inside the house practically ran to the backyard when they were told what was going on, and they congregated on the back deck, behaving like a pack of fraternity boys. Jake went to Stingray's door and tried to open it. It was locked. He expected this so he removed the instruments from his pocket that he had collected for this purpose and he began to jimmy the lock. It sprang open and Jake was surprised to see that Stingray was awake.

"JUDAS!!!, JUDAS!!!!," Stingray screamed.

Thankfully, his voice was weakened by the sedatives. Jake sprang to the bed and quickly covered Stingray's mouth. Jake told him to be quiet and in a few minutes explained what had happened to him. He told Stingray about the murder of his friend Danny and the sudden appearance of Wallace. He explained how Wallace began to manipulate him and how he had used RedTide as a threat and as a weapon against him. Jake wasn't looking for forgiveness, only cooperation so that they could escape. They would need to work together to find a way to warn Lionfish.

"We don't have much time," Jake said. "I'm going to remove my hand. If you scream they will kill us both and any chance we have of saving you and your brother is gone."

Jake slowly removed his hand.

"Jake, I understand," Stingray whispered. "We should have told you about MacGregor, who you've known as Wallace, so that you would be prepared when he inevitably appeared. It was just one more tragic error that we made."

"Like letting me leave the island alive," Jake said.

Stingray shook his head sadly in agreement. "It's an ugly fight we are involved in, Jake. We fight a sentimental cause, but it is our own sentimentality that is our greatest weakness. It will eventually undo us."

Jake heard the guards and the girls who had pulled up to the house out on the dock. They were laughing out back.

"Jerry, I need to know how to contact Tom and I need you to suggest a meeting place to MacGregor. We need to give MacGregor a way to arrange a meeting with Lionfish. When you have suggested to him the time and the place of the meeting, I will need you to let me know so that I can get a message to your brother."

"Why don't you untie me, Jake, and we can make a run for it right now?"

Jake had considered this option, but while he had studied the movements of the guards he observed that no matter how lax they might become the guards at the front and side doors never abandoned their posts. If Jake escaped MacGregor would skin them alive.

"You're in no condition to go anywhere, Jerry, and the exits are covered. Remember, it's vital that you suggest to MacGregor the date and the time of the meeting. Make sure that you suggest the important details, but lead him to it so that he thinks it's his idea. Think of some historic significance so that he feels compelled to follow your scheduling."

Jake grabbed Jerry's hand and they stared at each other for a moment.

"I'm sorry, Jerry, for everything I've done. You've got to believe me and trust me. I may not be much, but right now I'm your only chance."

"I'm the one who's sorry, Jake, for more than you can imagine. I know how you can contact my brother."

Just as Jake was about to leave, Stingray said "be careful" and Jake's eyes filled with tears. He slipped from the room just in time as the ringing of a cellular phone brought the party outside to a halt.

Jake could tell that MacGregor was on the line by the rapid apologizing of Agent Garcia as he made his way past the foot of the couch where Jake was pretending to be passed out.

Jake had four vital steps left in his plan and he was hoping that he would be able to pull them all off, especially the last step, which would call for tremendous courage on his part. Step one would be for Stingray to arrange the meeting place with MacGregor. Step two would be getting hold of one of the cellular phones. Jake was going to call in a classified ad in the *Village Voice* to warn Lionfish. Stingray had explained to Jake that if he, Stingray, were ever in trouble or if he and Lionfish were ever separated, that Stingray was to get a message to Lionfish in the classified section of the *Village Voice*. Lionfish would check the paper on a daily basis. Step three would be to make sure that Jake went to the meeting with MacGregor. Step four, the most dangerous part of Jake's plan, would have to wait until they arrived at the location.

When MacGregor arrived back at the house, his patience was exhausted and he was in a foul mood. Jake was upstairs and he maneuvered over to the air duct when he heard MacGregor enter Stingray's room.

"I'm tired, little man, and I warn you that my waiting has come to an end. I will ask you one more time. How can I get in touch with your brother?"

"You don't scare me, you Scottish sack of shit. If you kill me you've lost your bait, and if my brother doesn't hear my voice, confirming that I am still alive and well, he will never agree to meet you. Then he will hunt you down. When he finds you he will tear you limb from limb with his bare hands."

MacGregor laughed menacingly. "I've already thought of that and, as a matter of fact, I considered it as an alternate plan. It really was not a bad plan at that. I kill you and then let it be known by a few leaks here and there that you suffered greatly before I put you out of your misery. I also let it be known where I am. Then, when your brother is in an uncontrollable rage and he is hell bent on vengeance, he will most likely begin to act emotionally and will be more apt to make mistakes. I just sit here and wait for him to come to me. This time, I double the guard and surround myself with a cloak of invincibility, a force field, so to speak. When your brother enters my web I stamp him out like an insect."

"Then do it, you Scottish whore. Kill me, or is murder a service that you can only perform for a fee."

"Jake will also die, as will your brother. Hasn't there been enough violence already?" MacGregor said in a conciliatory tone which did not suit him and which sounded grossly insincere.

When Stingray flinched MacGregor knew he had him. "I'm counting to three and then I am ordering my men to drag Jake downstairs for a brief reunion before I blow his brains out all over your bed sheets. One...Two...Thr.."

"The Internet," Stingray said.

"There is an editorial section on the Neptune Home page where we receive urgent cryptic messages during times of heightened security, or in the case of an emergency. I'm sure by now my brother has called in every marker he has and he has probably touched base with every security contact and informant RedTide has ever known. He will be checking the web site daily for any information about my whereabouts."

"Very good. Very good indeed," MacGregor said. "I need to arrange a meeting, but I have no intention of allowing your brother phone contact with you. How else can we assure him of your safety?"

June 30 is the anniversary of our mother's death, or her murder as my brother believes. Our mother was a well known naturalist and it is a day of tremendous significance for us. If you write an editorial, telling people that on that day, which I believe is four days from now, a brass plaque will be hung at the Miami Seaquarium in her honor, Lionfish will know that I sent the message and he will know that is the time and date of your meeting.

If you post the time for the ceremony at 10:00 P.M. people will assume that it is a hoax since the aquarium is closed. Simply write: 'On June 30th at 10:00 P.M. a ceremony commemorating the work of Hannah

Peterson, which was not my mothers real name and will be another clue to Lionfish, will take place at the Miami Seaquarium. At that time a plaque will be hung in her honor. For information, call. Then, if I were you, I would leave a cell phone number for my brother to call. I assure you that unless he speaks to me he will never show up. You will have to deal with other callers and you will have to filter them out. There probably won't be too many since it is an obscure web site for environmentalists and diving enthusiasts. You will know Lionfish when he calls. He'll be the one threatening to kill you."

"You are a very smart man," MacGregor said. "I underestimated you and I assumed that a scientist would have very little understanding of warfare or of tactics, but you not only understand the situation, you have made a brilliant attempt to set me up. You're right, of course. Your brother will need confirmation of your well-being before he agrees to meet; this I already knew. I had no intention, as you proposed, of allowing your brother to know days in advance of our rendezvous so that he could prepare. I had planned instead to run him all over God's creation before I allowed him to arrive at his final destination. I want him to be alone and unarmed. My men will follow him from site to site so that they can make sure that he remains alone and that he doesn't pick up any reinforcements along the way. I do, however, like the idea of meeting at night at the Miami Seaquarium on the anniversary of your mother's death. That is, in fact, three days away, not four. There is an irony and a poetic justice that appeals to these old Scottish bones. You've done well, lad, and no one can fault you for trying to provide your brother with some early warning. I give you my word that no harm will come to you or your brother if he surrenders quietly."

Jake had turned down the air conditioner to quiet the unit. He stopped the rush of air through the ducts, increasing his ability to hear.

MacGregor sat at his laptop, on the internet. He brought up the home page for The Neptune Regulator Company Inc.'s bulletin board after using the AltaVista search engine to locate it. It was a very small web site, and it was also very slow to download. He went to the readers' editorial section and wrote:

> A Marine Biologist at the University of Edinburgh, Scotland has discovered a cure for Alzheimer's disease using the venom of several marine animals, including the stingray. Ciba-Giegy, the pharmaceutical company heading the project says FDA approval is imminent. For further information contact: Dr. Colin MacGregor at 1-305-436-8987.

CHAPTER 36

For an entire day the phone was inundated with a surprising number of calls from people all seeking a cure for a parent or grandparent who was suffering from the debilitating illness, but there were no calls from Lionfish. At 4:35 P.M., MacGregor received a call from the V.P. of Marketing for Neptune who had just spoken with the general council for Ciba-Giegy. That company had demanded an explanation, and they threatened a lawsuit if the section pertaining to their company on the Neptune web page was not pulled immediately. They also insisted that Neptune post a retraction, to be followed by a written explanation and a full apology.

MacGregor explained to the man that like Neptune he was also a victim of a practical joke and that he had been barraged by phone calls all day long. The page was immediately deleted and the phone had begun to ring less often. MacGregor received only a couple of calls an hour, but still there was no Lionfish.

At 9:45, when MacGregor had finished his third glass of Scotch and was on the verge of falling asleep on the couch, the phone rang just inches from his ear and it startled him awake. He knew even before he answered it that it was Lionfish and he let it ring several more times before he answered it.

"Hello, Suicide Hotline. Can I help you?"

"That's an appropriate greeting coming from a man who signed his own death sentence a few days ago," Lionfish said with icy calm. MacGregor was surprised when Lionfish's voice sent a chill up his spine.

"I'll keep this short," MacGregor said. "You want your brother and I want you. At 6:00 P.M. on Tuesday, two days from today, I want you to go to a pay phone in the lobby of the Shelbourne Hotel in Miami Beach and I want you to wait for further instructions."

"I want to talk to my brother or this conversation ends right now. Then you can start running and you can keep running until the day you draw your last breath through a tear in your throat. When you die, the last thing you'll see when you look up will be my smiling face staring back at you," Lionfish said.

"You'll have to wait a few minutes until I can stop my hands from shaking," MacGregor responded. "You know they still hurt from the beating I gave your brother the day you ran away and abandoned him."

Lionfish forced himself to remain calm. He could not allow the man to push his buttons or to give MacGregor any satisfaction whatsoever. MacGregor walked to Stingray's room and put the phone to his mouth.

"Say hello to your brother. He misses you."

"I'm fine," Stingray said, "and Jake's here also. This bastard set himmm......"

"That's enough. As you can see he's having the time of his life here at the Doral Spa. Later he's having a facial and a pedicure."

Lionfish almost stopped breathing when he heard his brother's voice and his eyes were tearing from the joy and the relief of finding out that Stingray was still alive.

"If I show up where you say, you'll kill us both. I'm not a fool, MacGregor," Lionfish said.

"I'll show up and walk in at your final meeting place the moment my brother talks to me on my cell phone from a public phone I've selected in Miami International Airport. After he passes through the security scanners of course. I don't have anything you want except myself and I know that your men would be following me closely all night. What's to stop them from taking me out any time they have a clear shot and you give the order. The only thing keeping me and my brother alive is my freedom and the fact that you don't know my whereabouts. Forget the run around. I will call this number one hour before our meeting and you will tell me where to go. Five minutes before I present myself to you I will call a number that I will give you in the airport. If I don't hear my brother's healthy voice telling me that he's okay, I walk."

"You are being very demanding considering that I hold all the cards. I'm tempted to put a bullet in your brother's eye right now just for spite."

"Your employer wants me and he's paying for me. Besides, I'm the kind of trophy that a hunter like you loves to hang on his wall, MacGregor. I'll call you two days from today at 8:00 P.M." CLICK...

MacGregor was frustrated. He had no intention of turning Stingray loose and didn't trust Lionfish not to pull off another miracle once his brother was released. He understood Lionfish and what he said made perfect sense. If MacGregor were in his position he would never have agreed to less. He needed an alternate plan and went to the study of the house to think quietly and to plan his next move.

It was just before sunrise and Jake had crept downstairs. He explained to the guard outside his door that he wanted to get some orange juice from the kitchen. It was dark downstairs and Jake opened the refrigerator. He used the door to block his movements and he used the light from inside to find his way to the stove. The cell phone was not there. He opened the top left drawer and BINGO, there it was, a small Motorola Flip phone. He hid the phone in his underwear and closed his robe. He took a bowl of Cheerios and a glass of orange juice upstairs. He went into the bathroom where he ran the water and he dialed the *Village Voice* in New York City. They were closed. A computerized voice mail attendant gave him a list of options, including the classified section, where to his relief another computer attendant was standing by to take his order. He had his wallet and his American Express card ready and when the computerized voice gave him his cue he read his ad. He prayed that his ad would be picked up and that it would be printed.

Memorial Service for Hannah Peterson
Tuesday, June 30th 10:00 P.M.
Miami Seaquarium
A plaque will be presented to the family,
which will be hung at the dolphin exhibit.
In memory of an environmental hero
and a true pioneer in the field of cetacean studies.

CHAPTER 37

Tuesday, June 30, 8:30 A.M.

Jake was up all night. He was so tired that he could barely see straight but the anxiety and trepidation he was feeling about today's events gave him a surge of nervous energy. The dark rings and the bags under his eyes would only add to the illusion that he was badly hung over and when he saw MacGregor and his men this morning he would make sure to be conspicuous about sipping water from his flask.

MacGregor was also tired from an all night strategy meeting he had held with his men in the library of the house in Lauderdale. Earlier he had phoned Yamaguchi to ask for assistance in solving the problem that Lionfish had presented in turning over Stingray. Yamaguchi had referred him to his best technicians at a small electronics research and development facility he owned in Misawa, Japan, who in turn referred him to a computerized communications hardware company that Yamaguchi owned in San Luis Obispo, California. In only twelve hours, he had his answer and he smiled at how everything had fallen into place. Finally, after two long years things were finally beginning to go his way. He felt absolutely certain that the time had finally arrived when destiny would allow him to capture and destroy RedTide once and for all. Like Jake, despite his physical exhaustion, he was exhilarated by the anticipation of tonight's meeting.

Tuesday, June 30, 3:30 P.M.

Jake was sitting on the couch playing Super Mario Brothers on the hand-held Gameboy that he had asked for last week. MacGregor walked into the room and sat down beside him on the couch. He had just come from the Federal Express office on Las Olas Boulevard and his next stop was Stingray's room where he would begin to interrogate him about Lionfish. He was going to conduct the interview with the help of a number of strong chemicals including a mixture containing sodium pentathol. Once the drugs began to wear down Stingray's resistance, MacGregor would engage him in a long conversation about his past and about tonight's schedule of events.

"Jake, put down that toy. I have some very important news for you."

Jake looked up through bloodshot eyes. He made sure to breathe the fumes in MacGregor's direction from the Scotch he had gargled with moments earlier. "You're being deported?"

"That's very funny," MacGregor said. "Drinking seems to have made you even more sarcastic. We've located Lionfish and he will be turning himself in tonight. It's almost over and very soon we can begin to make arrangements for your new life."

Jake feigned surprise, he sat up straight, and looked MacGregor in the eyes.

"He's voluntarily turning himself in. It's not that I'm not happy, but I find that hard to believe. How'd you pull off that miracle?"

"Pulling off miracles is my specialty, Jake. That's why I get the big bucks. Despite strong protests from my superiors I've decided to honor my promise to you. I recognize that none of this would have been possible if it hadn't been for you and I want you to be there tonight when Lionfish surrenders."

Jake reflected that sadly what MacGregor had said was true. None of this would have happened if it were not for him and he clenched his fists and told himself that he had to be brave enough to see his plan through to the end. "I'm looking forward to that," Jake said. "I'm looking forward to walking up to him and spitting in his face, for Danny and for forcing me to live the rest of my life in hiding," Jake said with a sincere combination of anger and sadness.

"It's very possible, Jake, that we will be able to arrange for you to visit your family once or twice a year around the holidays and I will personally see to it that you are relocated anywhere you choose and work in whatever field you desire."

Jake could not believe how skilled the man was at deception and how sincere he could appear. He was the coldest, most calculating and manipulative person Jake had ever met. The hairs on Jake's arms stood up as a chill ran up his spine. Al would have killed to have had him on his salesforce, Jake thought with a smile. MacGregor took the smile as a positive response to his offer. He stood up and he asked Jake to go to his room. He told Jake that he wanted him to rest up and prepare for tonight. When Jake got upstairs MacGregor went to Stingray's room carrying the box he had received from California only an hour before.

Tuesday, June 30, 6:30 P.M.

Jake came downstairs reeking of alcohol and he stumbled into the living room where MacGregor and two of his men, Jorgensson and Garcia, were waiting.

"Jake, I told you that I wanted you to be sober this evening," MacGregor said with anger.

"I'm fine, believe me. I just needed to take the edge off my nerves so I could face Lionfish tonight."

"You will be leaving here in a few minutes with Agents Garcia and Jorgesonn," MacGregor said. "They will take you to dinner and they will try to sober you up a little. At exactly 9 o'clock, you will meet up with us in Miami."

Jake left the house, breathing deeply the fresh sea air he had not tasted in what felt like months. He sat in the back seat of the Town Car as it sped away from the curb and he prayed for the second time in as many days that he would have the strength to do what he had to do at the Seaquarium. He squeezed his hands together to stop them from shaking and stared out the window.

Tuesday, June 30, 7:35 P.M.

MacGregor gave Stingray an injection containing half the usual amount of tranquilizer. MacGregor's men helped Stingray to his feet and escorted him to one of the cars. When he was seated in the back between two agents, they headed off toward the airport. He was awake and his injuries had healed well enough so that he was able to move but the tranquilizer he received would slow him down. MacGregor was insistent that he remain conscious throughout the evening.

Tuesday, June 30, 8:10 P.M.

MacGregor's cell phone rang as his car sped down the on ramp of I 95.

"Finnegan's Pub, where the ladies drink free all night long."

"Where's my brother?," the voice on the phone asked in a steady monotone. Lionfish was exercising great control.

"I'm sorry, but this morning he tried to squeeze through a small window in the upstairs bathroom and my men were forced to shoot him in the ass," MacGregor said with a smile.

MacGregor was determined to enjoy every moment of tonight's rendezvous to the last. There was a long pause and Lionfish said quietly and with calm, "I will be calling the second pay phone from the left opposite the Starbucks coffee shop near gate C11 at exactly 9:30. If I don't hear his voice the deal is off and then I come after you, and trust me with the money I have at my disposal, I will find you."

"Slow down, cowboy. I will meet your demand to turn your brother loose at the airport but I have to make sure that you are nowhere near there to attempt a rescue. From this point forward you will do as I say. I want you at the pay phone outside The Waffle House on Citrus Blvd in Miami at exactly 9:35. Ten minutes later at 9:45 I want you to call me, prepared to meet me in fifteen minutes at 10:00 P.M. My men will escort your brother up until the time we meet and I assure you that they are extremely capable of ending his life on the spot, undetected."

"I also have two men at the airport, MacGregor," Lionfish said, "who will be waiting at gate C12 to receive my brother. One of them will be watching him receive my call so don't try any tricks. And as far as receiving a call at The Waffle House, that is out of the question. I will call you five minutes after I speak to my brother and you can tell me where to go at that time."

MacGregor had expected Lionfish to place men at the airport and he had planned for it. He hungered for this type of adventure and confrontation. He was confident that he had covered every contingency in his plan to capture the elusive devil who was now playing cat and mouse with him on his cell phone.

"I want your men at the airport to leave immediately or our deal is off," MacGregor said.

"I know that your men are highly skilled and I don't want them to attempt to rescue your brother before we have the opportunity to be formally introduced. I am a flexible if not an understanding person so I will agree to throw out my request for a call from The Waffle House, but I don't trust you and I will not allow you access to your brother until you are well within my reach. I want you to call me at 9:00, just before you talk to your brother, and I will tell you which direction to head. I want you to call me again at 9:20, and I will give you further instructions and more specific directions. At exactly 9:35, after a short conversation with your brother, which I will limit to one minute, I want you to call me again for final instructions. My men will stand in the center of a busy crowd at the airport. They will be holding your brother by the arms. They are prepared to kill him if your men do not leave the airport or if they try anything.

"After your final call, you will have ten minutes to meet me. If we do not meet face to face within seven minutes or less, my men will kill your brother with the hardened plastic shivs they have smuggled into the airport. They will be holding them against his ribs. We do not trust each other for obvious reasons, but I have made my last concession and this is the only deal you're getting. I'm losing patience with the entire affair and I am prepared to take out the one brother I have rather than risk losing you both, so don't push me. I will be waiting for your call," MacGregor said, then he hung up.

Tuesday, June 30, 9:28 P.M.

Lionfish had just gotten off the phone with MacGregor and had received his second set of instructions. He was parked outside a bodega at the exact corner where his mother had been killed. It was just three blocks from the Miami Seaquarium. The bodega used to be an auto body shop and Lionfish stared at the wall where his mother had been thrown after the car had hit her. Lionfish was transfixed as he traveled back in time to that awful day. He snapped out of it when the portable alarm clock he had put in the car went off. It was 9:30. He picked up his phone to dial the airport, anxious to hear his brother's voice again.

"Hello Topper," Lionfish said using the nickname his mother had given Jerry as a boy.

Lionfish waited for him to respond using his nickname.

"Hello Dusty," Stingray responded, and Lionfish relaxed. "I'm fine, Stingray continued, aside from some sore ribs."

"Jerry, I want you to move away from the men that are guarding you as soon as you have the chance and I want you to make a commotion," Lionfish said. "I can rescue you from the authorities a lot easier than I can from MacGregor and you will be a lot safer."

"If he moves an inch, I will shove six inches of hardened plastic between his ribs," MacGregor's man interrupted. He had been listening in to the conversation through an earpiece on a customized device that he had attached to the phone. He instructed Stingray, "Say good-bye now."

"Don't do it, Tom," Stingray said, "don't meet them, they will kill you on sight. They wouldn't dare harm me at the airport in public."

MacGregor's man pulled the phone away and said, " I think we both know better, don't we?" Then he hung up.

At 9:35, Lionfish dialed MacGregor. "So I've kept up my end of the bargain as you can see, MacGregor said, now it is your turn. I want you to come to The Seaquarium within the next seven minutes or your brother dies. I assume you know where it is. I have timed it and you should be walking through the front doors in five minutes. I will be waiting."

CLICK.

Tuesday, June 30, 9:30 P.M.

Jake was full from his steak dinner at The Outback Steakhouse and he was continuously burping up 'Bloomin Onion' to the dismay and disgust of his chaperones. He drank a pint of Samuel Adams beer as well. His guards tried to stop him, but they were not prepared to make a scene over one beer. When they pulled into the parking lot of the Miami Seaquarium, Jake was feeling sick to his stomach from the food and from a strong case of nerves. On the way into the stadium, he asked Agent Jorgensonn if he could stop to use the restroom. It was obvious that he was going to be ill and Jorgensonn didn't want it to be all over his suit so he agreed. He told Garcia to go on ahead without him and he led Jake to the men's room. Jake noticed that there were already three other cars in the lot and that five men were walking the perimeter on guard duty. He also noticed that there were no security people from the Seaquarium and he wondered if they had been killed or paid off.

Jake walked up the stairs, leaning heavily on Agent Jorgensonn for support. He made gagging noises, which made Jorgensonn pull him along faster. Jake looked up at the man and he appraised his size and build. He wondered if he would have both the courage and the strength to implement Step 4 of his plan. The man was well over six feet tall and was built like a linebacker. When they had reached the men's room, Jake fumbled to find the light switch, and while Jorgensonn waited outside the stall, he leaned over the toilet and forced his finger down his throat. He threw up the entire contents of his dinner. The smell making him wretch again and he wondered how people with eating disorders purged themselves on a regular basis. He wiped some of his vomit on the front of his shirt and with tears flowing from his eyes and snot running from his nose he opened the door and stumbled into the arms of Agent Jorgensonn.

At the same time he shoved the eight-inch carving knife he had stolen from the house between Jorgensonn's ribs and while he thought of Danny and Jorge and Jack, he twisted the blade and wrenched it up as Jack had once taught him to do.

The man wrapped his enormous hands around Jake's throat, but before he could apply any real pressure he was dead, collapsing at Jake's feet. Jake moved quickly. First, he checked to make sure that he had no blood on him, then he pulled out the knife and wiped it clean. He removed Jorgenson's weapon from his shoulder holster, shut the light, and moved down the hallway toward the stadium floor. Luckily, Garcia had been carrying the small walkie talkie, so no one would be checking in with Jorgenson any time soon. When Jake was almost at the end of the hall, he saw Garcia returning to check on them. Jake gasped almost loud enough to be heard and then he began to stagger ahead. Jake stopped five feet from Garcia and he doubled over against the wall. He positioned himself at a sideways angle with his back to the man and began to make wretching noises. "I knew I shouldn't of had that fucking monstrous fried onion."

"I'd say it's the pint of beer you could have lived without," Garcia said with a smile and a short laugh. "Where's Jorgensonn?" he asked.

"Taking a dump."

Jake turned from the wall and fired two shots point blank into Garcia's chest. The silencer muffled the shot but in the tunnel it made enough noise to concern Jake. Garcia had a look of total surprise on his face as he fell against the wall and slipped to the ground.

Lionfish had just arrived at the Seaquarium. The moment his car stopped, two men armed with MAC-10s pulled him from the vehicle. Back at the airport, MacGregor's men had gone back to the pay phone to check in. They were standing with Stingray between them. He was disguised in a long black trench coat, a black hat, sunglasses and a beard.

On the right side of Stingray and his guard was an attractive businesswoman in a light pink suit. She was speaking on the phone to her boss while she rifled through the pages of her organizer trying to locate a phone number. On the left side of them was a short heavyset black woman who was talking in what MacGregor's man thought was either Creole or Haitian.

MacGregor's man had just dialed the last number of MacGregor's cell phone when the businesswoman beside him dropped her Franklin Planner on the ground. Pages flew everywhere. As he bent over to help her, MacGregor's phone began to ring. The woman leaned over to thank him and she touched her hand to his face just below his jawline. All he felt was a small pin prick.

The black woman on the left side was frustrated by the amount of space MacGregor's man was occupying despite her enormous bulk and she pushed him and made a commotion. While she cursed him for elbowing her aside she pushed him. She placed her hands on his chest and he also felt nothing but a small pin prick.

Both men were unconscious in milliseconds and they collapsed to the floor. The businesswoman grabbed Stingray by the lapel and hustled him away while the black woman made her escape. A woman at the pay phone began to scream at the sight of the two men who were crumpled on top of each other. Security was alerted.

The businesswoman told Stingray that there was a car waiting for them outside and that they needed to hurry before security shut the place down. She told him that she liked the disguise he was wearing and that it would help to conceal his true identity until they were away from the airport. She saw five security men heading toward them through the crowd and she turned sharply and led him to a four-stall circular pay phone in the far corner of gate C15. They hid at the phone stall, which faced the back corner. The gate was empty since the next flight wasn't scheduled for another two hours.

She picked up the receiver to fake a call and she turned to Stingray. He had not yet spoken a word and the woman said, "That was a close call. When Lionfish briefed me on this assignment he said that it would be very risky and that there was a good chance that I wouldn't get out of the airport alive."

The man impersonating Stingray leaned in close and said, "He was right" as he shoved a large plastic shiv into the woman's chest. He stabbed her five times and then he sat her down in the seat that was attached to the small phone stall. He removed his beard and his coat and hat. He piled them on top of her, then went to the USAir Club and found a phone to call MacGregor.

Tuesday, June 30, 9:45 P.M.

Jake came out of the tunnel leading to the dolphin pool and saw MacGregor and four men. They were standing in front of the tank, watching the dolphins surface and descend.

"Where the hell are Garcia and Jorgensonn?" he asked as Jake drew closer.

"I got sick," Jake said feigning embarrassment.

"We were on our way here when we heard a noise coming from the storage area. They told me to go on ahead while they checked it out."

Jake had Jorgensonn's weapon tucked into the small of his back. He had pulled out his Polo shirt to cover it up. When he walked he could feel the large semi-automatic weapon pushing against the back of his shirt. He made sure that he moved slowly toward MacGregor, keeping his back away from his men.

"Get over here, Jake," MacGregor said as he pulled out a small radio from his coat pocket.

"Let's see what the fuck is going on with your detail."

Jake held his breath as MacGregor squeezed the transmit button on his radio. Suddenly MacGregor was interrupted by the appearance of Lionfish. He was being roughly escorted down the stairs in between the bleachers.

"At last," MacGregor said, savoring his victory.

Jake looked up and his breathing stopped when he saw Lionfish and the condition he was in. He was limping slightly and his left arm looked dead at his side. His face was badly bruised and it was swollen on his left side as well. He looked as if he hadn't slept in weeks. He also looked as if he had lost some weight since they had last been together.

"I guess I have you to thank for choosing this venue," Lionfish said to Jake as he drew closer.

He stopped five feet from where Jake and MacGregor were standing. Lionfish looked quickly around the Seaquarium and saw six men at the top of the bleachers and three men standing beside MacGregor. Including the five men he saw outside that made a total of at least fourteen including MacGregor. Jake noticed Lionfish's survey of the situation and he thought, *Not great odds even for Lionfish.*

Jake considered that Lionfish was alone and unarmed.

"I guess I have a lot to thank you for Jake," Lionfish said menacingly. Lionfish's attitude told Jake that he had not received his warning and that they were all doomed.

"Have you checked him for weapons?" MacGregor asked the two men who were standing on either side of Lionfish.

They responded in the affirmative and MacGregor smiled.

"Don't blame Jake," MacGregor said to Lionfish. "He was just trying to protect himself from your assassins. We both know you would not have allowed him to run around free for much longer."

"I don't know what this murdering swine has told you, Jake, but his real name is Colin MacGregor and he is a hired mercenary trying to collect a bounty. He killed your friend in order to frame RedTide and to manipulate you into giving us up. From our meeting here today it would seem that his plan has worked perfectly."

MacGregor allowed Lionfish to talk for another five minutes. Lionfish recounted their long history together and while he spoke MacGregor studied Jake's face. He was thoroughly enjoying Jake's reactions and he interrupted only once to confirm Lionfish's story.

Jake didn't have to pretend that the words Lionfish spoke were painful to him, and as he listened he remembered his friends. Jake realized that his betrayal and his lack of trust in the people he had known had led to their deaths. His only consolation was in knowing that he had killed two of MacGregor's men and that in the end he had tried to save the men he had helped to trap.

He knew he had only a few more minutes to live and that as soon as MacGregor became bored he would kill Lionfish and himself. Jake looked at Lionfish and spoke slowly and softly. "I'm sorry, Tom. I had no way of knowing. Everything Special Agent Wallace represented to me made perfect sense and they had proper identification. When I thought that you were responsible for Danny's death all I could think of was revenge. I was blind with rage and hate. I felt the same way you would feel if you wanted to avenge someone you had loved.

"I'm not making excuses. For helping to kill Jack and Jorge and the rest of the team I deserve to die. In the last few weeks I've wished I were dead."

"Well, Jake, Lionfish responded, "you're about to get your wish. Isn't he?" Lionfish said, looking at MacGregor.

"I'm sorry, Jake," MacGregor said, confirming Lionfish's insinuation. "I've actually grown quite fond of you in the past few weeks and as I said before, I have you to thank for bringing us together. I do need to tie up all the loose ends and you do know more than you should. It's just business Jake, not personal."

How many times had Jake heard that line used in business just before someone was about to get a royal screwing. Jake could see MacGregor adopting the American colloquialism and using it just before he put a bullet in his victim's head with the same detachment as a CEO who closed a plant and dumped 10,000 workers out into the street.

"Enough talk," MacGregor said as his radio beeped. One of his men informed him that their final guest had arrived.

"We have a special guest here with us today. Someone who has been waiting a long time to meet you," MacGregor said to Lionfish.

All eyes turned to the bleachers where a small Japanese man escorted by two large Japanese bodyguards had entered the stadium. Lionfish knew who it was even before he was halfway down the stairs and he clenched his hands into fists and steadied his breathing to prepare himself for what he knew would be their final confrontation. Lionfish heard a splash in the tank and he was momentarily distracted by the dolphins who were leaping out of the water. They were obviously curious about what was going on outside their home at this time of day. When the small Japanese man and his guards reached the group, MacGregor spoke. "Allow me to introduce my employer, Akiro Yamaguchi."

Jake had heard the name for the first time in Stingray's room in Lauderdale when Stingray had given him a history lesson on their captor. He studied the man's face. He must have been around seventy-years-old but he appeared fit and his face was not heavily lined with signs of age.

"I have waited a very long time for this day," Yamaguchi said. "You have done well," he said to MacGregor.

He walked up to Lionfish, and as he looked up into the taller man's face, he said, "You do not look as I had imagined."

"What did you expect? Lionfish asked. "A monster? I'm a man just like you, Mr. Yamaguchi."

"We are nothing alike!" Yamaguchi screamed. "You are a terrorist and a murderer of innocent men and women."

Lionfish stood silently for a moment, then faced Yamaguchi. He surprised Jake with what he said.

"I am glad that I have been given the opportunity to do something that I never get to do face to face in my line of work. It seems appropriate since it is probably the last thing I will do before I die. I am deeply sorry, Mr. Yamaguchi, for the unfortunate accident that led to your son's death and if I could undo it I would. I will not apologize for our intentions on that fateful day nor will I apologize for our overall goals as an organization. If I did that I would be a hypocrite and it would cheapen your son's death and do dishonor to his memory. We are at war, Mr. Yamaguchi, and your company is one of the environment's greatest enemies. My organization tried for months to warn you and educate you to the environmental holocaust your chemical plants and industrial factories had wrought on this planet and its inhabitants and you chose to ignore us. In war there are casualties on both sides, and sometimes there is collateral damage that involves civilians. It is one of the worst by products of war but we cannot falter in our commitment or countless millions will die. I know you loved your son, Mr. Yamaguchi, and I know that you seek vengeance for his death, for that I cannot blame you. I can prove to you that the ways in which your company practices business endangers the lives of tens of thousands of sons and daughters who are equally loved by their parents. I have lost countless friends and loved ones in the last ten years, including my own mother. She was murdered not ten blocks from here, trying to protect what she held dear. I hope that your son's death has not hardened your heart so much that its only significance would be to fuel feelings of hate and vengeance that will continue to destroy us all."

"Do not speak of my son!" Yamaguchi screamed in fury, seemingly hearing nothing that Lionfish had said. "My son was a man of honor who struggled to do what was right for his family and for his country, and you are a miscreant who tries to cover his heinous acts with ridiculous platitudes and rationalizations. You know nothing of my loss, but today that will change and you will learn the true meaning of sacrifice."

The lights came on suddenly in the dolphin tank and Lionfish froze when he followed MacGregor's eyes and looked up. He saw Stingray standing on the edge of the elevated board that the dolphin handlers used to feed the dolphins. It is a board that they stand on as they hold the fish out for the dolphins to jump up and catch them. Stingray had a guard behind him and he had a gun at his back. MacGregor laughed, and Jake trembled as he tried to remain calm.

"Take off his gag so that he can say hello to his brother," MacGregor bellowed to the man above them. "Maybe you should leave now, Yamaguchi San," MacGregor said. "We will bring Lionfish to you when we are done here."

Yamaguchi was only interested in Lionfish and did not want to be party to what ever else MacGregor insisted had to be handled. He was not a murderer, and he had argued and then ordered MacGregor to turn the scientist and the other man loose. MacGregor had told Yamaguchi that he was being paid to deliver Lionfish and that he had done that. The rest was his business and for his own protection he needed to eliminate Jake and Stingray. If Yamaguchi wanted to be protected from the remainder of the dirty work that was fine, but MacGregor would do what was necessary to cover his trail and to remove the remaining witnesses, whether Yamaguchi approved or not.

Yamaguchi went to his limousine to wait for Lionfish to be delivered to him and he prayed while he polished the ancient sword that had been in his family for generations. It was the only thing that his father had managed to save for him. He would kill Lionfish himself in ritual fashion, according to Samurai tradition. He prayed for the strength to carry out the task and he thought of his son to give him the courage to perform the grisly act.

When Lionfish turned back to look at MacGregor he saw that he was holding a black box the size of a small tape deck.

"In answer to your obvious question Dusty, I used a combination of extremely powerful truth serums to elicit the information I needed. I knew that you would test my impostor at the airport and so I used the latest digital voice recording and recognition technology and turned it inside out to suit my purposes. Your brother spilled his guts as if he were telling his life history to his therapist, and I recorded the entire conversation. Then I asked him some questions I knew would elicit the words I would need to reconstruct the conversational responses required to fool you at the airport. Nothing to it really. The Japanese are wizards with electronics. Now you and your brother will get to leave this world side by side.

"First, I have staged a little show for your entertainment in honor of your mother's work and the anniversary of her death."

MacGregor signaled to the man above who was guarding Stingray. He lowered his automatic rifle with silencer toward the water and fired at the dolphins in the tank. Lionfish moved forward but he received a hit in the small of his back with a rifle butt for his troubles. Two dolphins that were close to the surface were hit before the rest of the group dove deep to escape the rifle fire. The water turned red as the blood swirled in circles around the pool. Jake clenched his jaw and he gasped at the horror as he saw the lifeless bodies of the two dolphins sink to the bottom of the tank. MacGregor howled with laughter and Jake glared at him.

Suddenly, a dolphin flew from the water and slammed his body against the aluminum railing above where Stingray and the guard were standing. The dolphin slammed into the rail, striking Stingray and the guard and knocking them back. The guard regained his balance and aimed his rifle again while he waited for the dolphin to break the surface. The dolphin came up again, but when the guard was about to pull the trigger Stingray slammed his head into his chest and knocked him off of his feet. Stingray's arms were bound behind his back and he stood defenseless as the guard came at him.

"Enough!" MacGregor shouted. "Kill him!!!"

Lionfish knew he had to move quickly. There was a man on his left, one on his right, and there was only one man standing beside MacGregor. The guard above leveled his rifle at Stingray and there was a shot.

Stingray's guard grabbed his chest where he had been hit. He toppled over the rail and landed in the pool. MacGregor turned toward Jake, who was standing with a gun in his hand. Jake was aiming it at the guard to the right of Lionfish and he fired another round. He knocked the man off of his feet as Lionfish drove his elbow into the throat of the man on his left side, crushing his windpipe. MacGregor pulled out his weapon and aimed it at Jake. Lionfish had a five-inch throwing knife that he had concealed in his belt. He removed it and threw it just as MacGregor fired.

The blade struck MacGregor in the left shoulder and his shot missed Jake's heart by a few inches. Jake was struck in the chest at close range by a .45 caliber bullet and he landed with a crash in the bleachers. As MacGregor's men began to run from their positions in the bleachers shots rang out from above and they began to drop.

MacGregor looked up but saw nothing. Lionfish crashed into him and drove him into the side of the tank, knocking the gun out of his hand. Lionfish's stitches came apart and the pain in his shoulder was excruciating but his anger was white hot. He pummeled MacGregor's face and head.

MacGregor was a combat veteran and a trained killer as well and knew he was in a fight for his life. He drove his foot into Lionfish's chest and pulled the blade from his shoulder to use as a weapon.

"I'm going to kill you very slowly by breaking you up a little at a time," Lionfish said as ten of his men dressed in all black, including their black parachutes, began to land in the bleachers around the Seaquarium.

MacGregor looked around, genuinely puzzled at the sudden reversal of the situation and he knew that he was finished. With nothing left to lose, his only thought was to kill Lionfish. If he could do that much before he died his mission would not be a total failure. Empowered with the knowledge that he was already dead, he rushed at Lionfish. He swung his blade in wide arcs toward Lionfish's face and throat.

Lionfish ducked one blow but caught another across his cheek. The blade opened a wide gash and blood flowed into his mouth from the wound. Lionfish threw two side kicks, missing both times and he blocked a roundhouse kick using his wounded arm and shoulder.

The blow totally finished the use of his left arm. "Stay away!" Lionfish screamed at two of his soldiers who rushed to his side and were brandishing their weapons at MacGregor. Stingray was kneeled down over Jake applying pressure to his wound.

"Ignore Lionfish's orders and kill that son of a bitch," Stingray ordered the man standing beside him.

The man politely refused, knowing it would be his ass if he complied. There was just too much history there and he knew Lionfish would want to finish MacGregor himself.

"Very sporting of you," MacGregor said. "You know I always admired your resourcefulness and I greatly respected you as an adversary. Nothing personal, Lionfish, although I have to admit I will enjoy killing you."

"You're wrong MacGregor. This is very personal," Lionfish said.

He charged MacGregor for the last time. MacGregor swung the blade toward his chest and Lionfish stepped aside as he threw a kick that landed hard across MacGregor's face. Lionfish grabbed the wrist that was holding the blade and he snapped it.

MacGregor fell to his knees and Lionfish kicked him again, sending him crashing into the glass wall behind him. MacGregor slowly rose to his feet. He could barely stand or raise his arms. With lightning speed, Lionfish slammed him against the wall and drove the blade into his eye down to the bottom of the handle. There was suddenly the loud sound of a helicopters rotor's and ripples appeared on the surface of the pool as Lionfish released MacGregor and he fell dead to the floor.

The large black helicopter from which RedTide's men had leapt minutes earlier landed gently on the surface of the pool just as Yamaguchi was being dragged down the stairs of the bleachers toward where Lionfish was standing.

"Load Jake aboard and get everyone else ready to go," Lionfish commanded.

Akiro Yamaguchi was brought before Lionfish.

"I suppose now you will kill me," Yamaguchi said.

"I told you before, Mr. Yamaguchi, that we are not murderers. The man you hired," Lionfish said, pointing to MacGregor, "was an indiscriminate killer who was going to murder Jake and my brother. He had already killed numerous innocent people, including a friend of Jake's who was killed for no other reason than to implement a plan of deception. I lost many men last week, including two lifelong friends. The killing has to stop and I am stopping with you. Teddy Roosevelt once said that if I had to choose between righteousness or peace I would choose righteousness. That has always been my choice but today I am choosing peace. Will you do the same?"

Yamaguchi said nothing but his eyes showed his painful remorse at the actions of his hired mercenary.

"Turn him loose outside the gates and hurry back here," Lionfish ordered.

"We will not see each other again, Yamaguchi San," Lionfish said. "You're free to go. Do honor to your son in ways he would be proud of. Tomorrow I will donate $250,000 dollars to the Save the Oceans Foundation in his name," Lionfish said. "In the future, I will abort any missions that put civilians at risk. You have my word. Will you give me your word that there will be peace between us?"

Yamaguchi paused for a moment and then he bowed slightly at the waist and said, "It will be peace. My heart is tired and my soul seeks salvation. I will return to my garden to finish the few remaining days I have in reflection. You will not hear from me again."

Yamaguchi was led away with his guards, passing into the tunnel and away from Lionfish's view forever.

When everyone was aboard the helicopter, Lionfish stepped up on the small stepladder they had placed against the glass wall and he looked down at the dolphins who were congregated around their fallen comrades. He thought of his mother and how disappointed she would be with him for bringing death and pain to the place she used to call her island of tranquillity in a rolling sea. The chopper lifted off and they headed out to sea. Lionfish knelt down over Jake who was hooked up to an IV, receiving saline and plasma.

"I'm sorry, Tom," Jake mumbled through the morphine.

"You already said that."

He had forgiven Jake the moment that he had received the warning in the *Village Voice* and knew that only Jake could have sent it. He also understood the situation now and he blamed himself for not having predicted it, and for not having prepared Jake for MacGregor's tricks.

"You saved our lives today Jake," Lionfish said as he brushed Jake's hair away from his forehead.

"I'm the one who put you in harm's way in the first place and I got Jack and Jorge killed," Jake said, his eyes filling with tears.

"That wasn't your fault, Jake. MacGregor was a master of manipulation, as you learned yourself. But when it came time to step up to the plate and to do the right thing you risked your life and you saved us all. Remember that."

"Do you think I'll see my mother? Jake asked. "I can hear her singing to me very softly like she did when I was boy."

"I hope someday you will. I'm counting on seeing mine when I go, but you're not dying, and if you hear your mom that's probably the morphine at work."

Lionfish confirmed with Nurse Shark, the medic, that Jake was going to live. As Jake was falling asleep in Lionfish's arms he looked up to meet his brother's eyes. Lionfish told him that he loved him without speaking a word. Lionfish leaned his head back and he thought about the past and about the future of the organization. He was so tired. Tired of the war and the constant deadly reminders of the dangers that were involved in his life's work. It had always been a dream of his to save the planet and to protect it from mankind. How incredibly arrogant that seemed to him now. One thing was clear: They could not continue as they had before and Lionfish knew that things had to change. He had thought about quitting before, walking away, but there was always so much work to be done. He was bombarded on a daily basis with the overwhelming number of crimes that were being perpetrated against the planet.

He thought about the dolphins they had left behind and about the millions of animals that they represented. He thought about his mother and he remembered a song that she used to sing to him when they were traveling together chasing dolphins around the world. He played it in his head as he tried to remember her voice.

It had been one of her favorite songs for awhile and she would sit him on her lap while she strummed the guitar. She would hold his hands over the strings to teach him to play. The song was called "Lay down your weary tune" by Bob Dylan, and Lionfish struggled to remember the words as the helicopter banked hard left and headed for the boat that would take them back to his beloved Caribbean.

> "The ocean wild like an organ played.
> The seaweed's wove its strands, they crash in waves like
>   symbols clashed, against the rocks and the sand.
> "Lay down your weary tune, lay down.
> Lay down this song you strum,
>   and rest yourself 'neath the strength of strings.
> No voice can hope to hum."

photo by Leslie Green

JEFFREY GREEN is an avid scuba diver, underwater photographer, and amateur environmentalist. A world traveler, he has scuba dived everywhere from the Red Sea to the Great Barrier Reef, and spent months on a kibbutz in Israel. He is married and has a young daughter.